PRAISE FOR M.J. SCOTT'S

The Shattered Court

Nominated for Best Paranormal Romance in the 2016 RITA® Awards.

"Scott (the Half-Light City series) opens her Four Arts fantasy series with the portrait of a young woman who's thrust into the center of dangerous political machinations… Romance fans will enjoy the growing relationship between Cameron and Sophie, but the story's real strength lies in the web of intrigue Scott creates around her characters."
—*Publishers Weekly*

"Fans of high fantasy and court politics will enjoy The Shattered Court. Sophie is such a great heroine…"
—*RT Book Reviews*

Fire Kin

"Entertaining…Scott's dramatic story will satisfy both fans and new readers."
—*Publishers Weekly*

"This is one urban fantasy series that I will continue to come back to…Fans of authors Christina Henry of the Madeline Black series and Keri Arthur of the Dark Angels series will love the Half-Light City series."
—*Seeing Night Book Reviews*

Iron Kin

"Strong and complex world building, emotionally layered relationships, and enough ac[...] I want to know what's going to happen next to the DuCaines and their chosen partners, and I want to know now."

—*Vampire Book Club*

"Iron Kin was jam-packed with action, juicy politics, and a lot of loose ends left over for the next book to resolve that it's still a good read for series fans."

—*All Things Urban Fantasy*

"Scott's writing is rather superb."

—*Bookworm Blues*

Blood Kin

"Not only was this book just as entertaining and immensely readable as Shadow Kin—it sang in harmony with it and spun its own story all the while continuing the grander symphony that is slowly becoming the Half-Light City story. . . . Smart, funny, dangerous, addictive, and seductive in its languorous sexuality, I can think of no better book to recommend to anyone to read this summer. I loved every single page except the last one, and that's only because it meant the story was done. For now, at least."

—*seattlepi.com*

"Blood Kin was one of those books that I really didn't want to put down, as it hit all of my buttons for an entertaining story. It had the intrigue and danger of a spy novel, intense action scenes, and a romance that evolved organically over the course of the story. . . . Whether this is your first visit to Half-Light City or you're already a fan, Blood Kin expertly weaves the events from Shadow Kin throughout this sequel in a way that entices new readers without boring old ones. I am really looking forward to continuing this enthralling ride."

—*All Things Urban Fantasy*

"Blood Kin had everything I love about urban fantasies: kick-butt action, fantastic characters, romance that makes the heart beat fast, and a plot that was fast-paced all the way through. Even more so the villains are meaner, stronger, and downright fantastic—I never knew what they were going to do next. You don't want to miss out on this series."

—*Seeing Night Book Reviews*

"An exciting thriller . . . fast-paced and well written."

—*Genre Go Round Reviews*

Shadow Kin

"M. J. Scott's Shadow Kin is a steampunky romantic fantasy with vampires that doesn't miss its mark."

—*#1 New York Times bestselling author Patricia Briggs*

"Shadow Kin is an entertaining novel. Lily and Simon are sympathetic characters who feel the weight of past actions and secrets as they respond to their attraction for each other."

—*New York Times bestselling author Anne Bishop*

"M. J. Scott weaves a fantastic tale of love, betrayal, hope, and sacrifice against a world broken by darkness and light, where the only chance for survival rests within the strength of a woman made of shadow and the faith of a man made of light."

—*National bestselling author Devon Monk*

"Had me hooked from the very first page."

—*New York Times bestselling author Keri Arthur*

"Exciting and rife with political intrigue and magic, Shadow Kin is hard to put down right from the start. Magic, faeries, vampires, werewolves, and Templar knights all come together to create an intriguing story with a unique take on all these fantasy tropes. . . . The lore and history of Scott's world is well fleshed out and the action scenes are exhilarating and fast."

—*Romantic Times*

ALSO BY M.J. SCOTT

The Wild Side series

The Day You Went Away (free e-only prequel short story)

The Dark Side (Book 2)

The Half-Light City series

Shadow Kin

Blood Kin

Iron Kin

Fire Kin

The Four Arts series

The Shattered Court

Find out more at www.mjscott.net

Copyright © 2016 by M.J. Scott

Visit M.J. at www.mjscott.net

All rights reserved.

All characters and events in this book are fictitious. Any resemblance to real people, alive or dead, is entirely coincidental.

No part of this book may be reproduced in any form or by any electronic or mechanical means, including information storage and retrieval systems, without written permission from the author, except for the use of brief quotations in a book review.

Cover design by Hang Le.

ISBN: 1537269976
ISBN-13: 978-1537269979

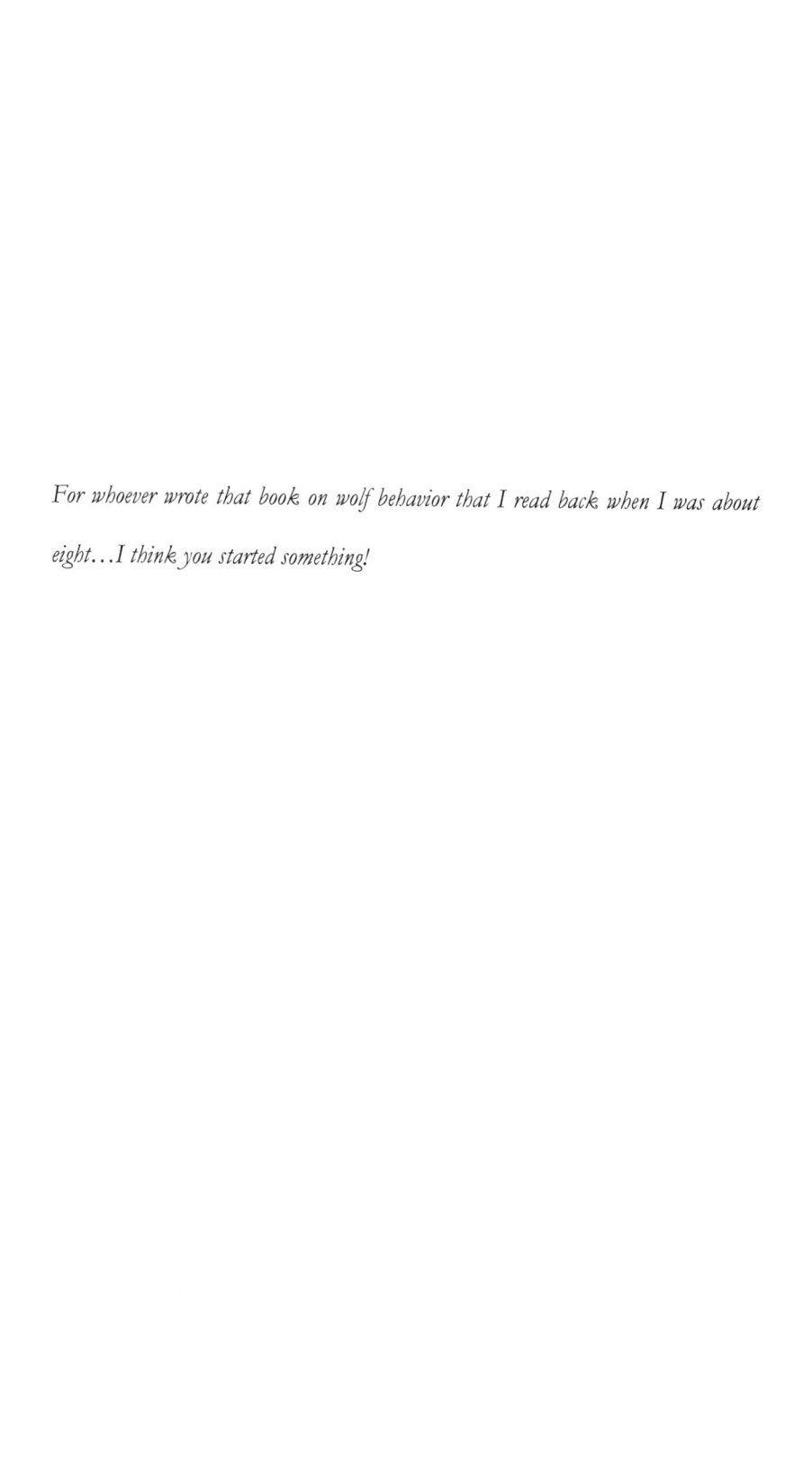

For whoever wrote that book on wolf behavior that I read back when I was about eight…I think you started something!

ACKNOWLEDGMENTS

Thanks to the usual suspects —the fabulous Agent M, the lovely Lulus and the all the awesome people who make my world better each day.

CHAPTER ONE

WHEN YOUR PAST FINALLY catches up to you, the smart thing to do is start running. Me? Apparently I'm not so smart. I just sat and stared at the man my PA was ushering into my office. The man I'd never wanted to see again. "What the he—"

"Ash," Jase interrupted, looking nervous, "this is Dan—"

"Daniel Gibson, I know." The question was why in hell he was here. I glared at Jase. If he hadn't already been dead, I would've strangled him. He did his best "I'm not here" impersonation. I turned my glare onto the man who most definitely *was* here.

"Ashley. How are you?" Dan asked, with a grin that could've melted the Titanic's iceberg.

I curled my fingers around my silver pen, hoping like hell I'd fallen asleep and this was a nightmare. But Dan didn't disappear in a poof of smoke or turn into a talking rabbit. He just stood there in a slightly rumpled dark blue suit, looking even better than I remembered.

I'd always liked him in blue.

He needed a shave and his dark hair was, just like it had been when I'd last seen him four years ago, too long.

He looked like Dan. Like memories I couldn't afford to think about. Not a dream. More like a nightmare. And I was wide awake. Maybe I should just stab myself through the heart with the pen. It would be less painful than letting Dan back into my life. Not that I was going to do that. As soon as I kicked him out he could be just a memory again.

I stood. "I have nothing to say to you." I had to fight to keep my voice steady. "Jason, please show Mr. Gibson out."

Jase stood his ground. He'd adopted that blank unreadable expression vamps are so good at. He wasn't giving me any clues what was going on. "He's with the FBI. I think you should hear him out."

"Yeah, Ash," Dan drawled as he dropped into my visitor's chair. "Hear me out."

The look I shot at Jase had him backing out of the office in a hurry, closing the door with a decisive click. Leaving me alone with the one person in the world I didn't want to be alone with. I got a waft of the familiar spicy smell of his aftershave and the tantalizing something that was pure Dan. I gripped the pen harder. "There's nothing you can say to me that I'd be interested in."

"Really?" he said. His eyes caught mine and I tried not to fall into the silvery gray depths.

"Really," I said, looking down at my desk. Avoiding his gaze felt stupid but stupid was better than sorry. His eyes had always been my weakness. But I was in no mood to be charmed.

"How about the name McCallister Tate?"

My eyes snapped back to his as my stomach lurched. "What are you saying?"

A slow smile rolled over his face. "So maybe there is something I can say that would interest you?"

"Daniel, I will hurt you, I swear." My heart kicked into overdrive. The mention of McCallister Tate's name had sent enough adrenalin shooting into my system that I figured I could take Dan if I had to. Or at least get in one good punch. "What about Tate? They said he was dead."

"No body was ever found. No staking. No burning."

"I know that. What's changed?" I lowered myself back into my chair, not breaking eye contact. The pen rolled through my fingers and clattered onto the desk, coming to a rest against the pile of spreadsheets I'd been working on.

"One of his accounts was accessed."

"How do you know?"

"I have my sources."

He was asking to be punched, truly. "What's it got to do with me?"

"I'm on the taskforce. We need some help tracing the transaction."

No way was that the whole truth. "The FBI doesn't have forensic accountants?"

"Yes, we do. But I told them I wanted the best."

The best? I narrowed my eyes at him. I knew gratuitous flattery when I heard it. I was good: good enough to break away from the big firm I'd started with, take eighty percent of my clients with me and keep growing from there. Ashley Keenan. Untangling the finances of vamps, weres and humans across Seattle. My own little niche. "You have the best." I worked with the top IT guys, investigators and the police—but the FBI had access to things I'd never dreamed of.

"Maybe." He shrugged, a particularly fluid Dan gesture so familiar it made my stomach hurt. "But it's not personal for them."

The ache in my stomach doubled. *Shit.* He had me. He'd had me from the moment he'd waltzed through my door. Like the past four years had never happened.

Because it *was* personal. McCallister Tate ripped a hole in my life twelve years ago and I'd never been able to fill it. Not completely. If I could help catch him...

"This isn't fair, Dan." Catching Tate was one thing. Helping Dan to do it might just come with another price. One too high for me to pay.

He shrugged again. "Life's a bitch, Ash. You know that. But this is a chance to make it less so."

No, it was only a chance to swap old, old pain for newer pain. One way or another. "This doesn't change anything."

The smile—that old familiar steal-my-heart-away smile—bloomed again. "I take it, that's a yes?"

"I charge eight hundred an hour." And where Dan was concerned, that wasn't nearly enough.

"Don't worry, we can pay." He folded his arms, straining the lines of his suit as his biceps flexed. "You look good, Ash."

I bared my teeth at him. "If you're going to flirt, it'll be double. Like I said, this doesn't *change* anything."

He nodded, one eyebrow lifting slightly. "Yes, you did."

It was hardly a promise to behave. My nerves were zinging like I'd just mainlined a triple espresso and every instinct I had told me this was a bad, bad idea. But he had me over a barrel. For anything else but Tate I could've kicked Dan out of my office and back out of my life. But a chance to take down Tate? That was the offer I couldn't refuse.

But first, I needed some time. "Are we done?"

"Ash, honey, we're only just getting started." His voice rumbled slightly and I couldn't stop the tiny flip of my pulse at the sound. I could, however, recognize the stupidity of the reaction.

I stood. I wasn't going to sit here and let him weave that voice around me. "Oh no, I think we're done. You can have your people call my assistant and set things up."

Dan just grinned at me, not going anywhere. I could tell he was enjoying this. Bastard.

"I think you're out of luck. I'm the official accounting liaison."

"You wouldn't know a balance sheet if it bit you on the ass."

"Yeah, but I'm the one who deals with the humans mostly. You are still human, aren't you Ash?"

I bared my teeth at him again as the implications sank in. He wasn't just on *a* taskforce. He was on *the* Taskforce. The FBI's Supernatural Crime Taskforce. The one staffed mainly by vamps and weres. Shit.

"Yes. You still a werewolf?" Stupid question. There's no going back once you changed. One little bite and everything's different. Whether you like it or not.

Don't get me wrong, I'm okay with supernaturals, mostly. I'd worked hard to be okay with them after Tate. After all, unless I wanted to live like a hermit, it was hard to avoid them. And I wasn't going to let Tate turn me into a recluse. So I did therapy and then did my best to fight the fear and treat them like everybody else. But my hard won live-and-let-live attitude didn't mean I wanted to become one. I get my shots—my Dad was an immunologist and *big* on vaccination—but we all know they're hardly perfect protection against either virus. Dan was proof of that.

"Furry and lovin' it." He laughed, a rumble that stroked across my skin. I told myself it was basic were energy that made him sound so good. Made me want to curl up in the sound until all the bad stuff went away. Which was a lie because he'd made me feel that way long before he'd become a werewolf.

It wasn't funny to me. It felt like getting my heart broken all over again. And stomped on. I looked down at my desk again and swallowed until I knew my voice would be steady. Then I looked back up. "Well, then," I said coolly. "Like I said. Nothing's changed."

One dark eyebrow arched up. "Is that so?"

"Yes." I hoped he'd believe me.

For a few long seconds he just looked at me, and then something that might have been pain shimmered through his eyes. Shimmered then disappeared, leaving cool silver glass behind. He nodded once. "If that's the way you want it."

I felt like screaming at him. *Nothing* was the way I wanted it when it came to me and Dan. Nothing could be that way ever again. And I'd worked a long time on convincing myself that was fine by me.

Why hadn't he just left me alone?

No snappy comeback rose to my lips. No pithy little phrase to casually let him know that he was less than nothing to me now. I was never that good a liar. I just dug deep for the poker face that let me regularly fleece my friends at our monthly card games and hoped he wouldn't push things any further.

He didn't. Instead he reached into his jacket pocket and tossed a business card down onto my desk. "Meet me at my office. Nine a.m. tomorrow."

Nine a.m.? Was he joking? My office hours are set to deal with my clientele. All species. Most of the vamps work around the sun but there are some who stick to tradition. I work midday to midnight. "Fat chance, I'll be asleep."

"This is important."

I shrugged. He was right but I wasn't going to let him push me around. Not even for Tate. I'd agree to help. I'd agree to spend more time with Dan than I wanted to. But I wasn't going to let him order me around. "And I need my beauty sleep. I have a business to run here, Daniel." My voice should've frozen him to the chair.

"I have *murders* to solve." His voice rose a little.

"Then get one of your little FBI accountants to help you. I can't just drop everything because you crook your finger."

His fingers dug into the arms of the chair, the leather denting. I was surprised the arms didn't crack. Weres are strong, even in human form. But most of them have pretty good self-control. Particularly the ones that work for the FBI. So it was interesting that Mr. Cool, Calm and Collected was showing the strain. I wondered whether it was the case or me. Then cursed myself for even thinking it.

"Fine," he gritted. "What time can you come?"

I took my time consulting my calendar. I still had a long night of trawling through balance sheets, asset listings and many, many pages full of tiny numbers trying to unravel the Anderson mess ahead of me. Divorce is ugly at the best of times. But being undead adds a whole new dimension. That of long, long, periods of time.

In the Andersons' case, both spouses had been squirreling away assets for over a century and now didn't want to share. I was meeting Mrs. Anderson—who prided herself on being the modern vamp—at one p.m. the following day. I'd planned a couple of free hours after that for a massage and a workout. I'd need both after dealing with Elena Anderson. Now it looked like I'd get neither. "I can do two thirty."

Dan nodded again. "Good. I'll see you then."

He stood and I did the same, fighting against the little pang inside that said, *"Don't go. Stay. Tell me what you've been up to. Do you miss me?"* That little pang was the voice of insanity. I locked it back up in the mental rubber room it deserved.

"I guess you will." Hardly a zingy goodbye but it was better than nothing. Dan sighed, sounding more irritated than upset, then he shrugged and walked out. Leaving me staring blankly at the door. For a whole thirty seconds until Jase opened it.

"Before you say anything," he said. "I brought you chocolate." He put a brownie in front of me and then plopped himself down in the chair Dan had just vacated, looking penitent.

"Chocolate doesn't come anywhere near close." But I took a bite anyway, figuring sugar might calm my pounding heart. I was too thrown from seeing Dan to yell at Jase for not being a mind reader and knowing not to let Dan in.

"So that's the guy, huh?"

I choked on my brownie. Then coughed and spluttered. "What do you mean?"

"The one who got away or whatever."

I took a mouthful of cold coffee to wash down the brownie crumbs and shook my head as I swallowed. "Dan is old news."

"You still have a picture of him in your house."

"I do?" I frowned, trying to remember.

Jase nodded. "Yep. There's a group photo on your mantel. He's the guy next to you. The one hugging you."

Oh, *that* picture. Stupid vampire eyes. And memory. Not much got past Jase. It made him a great PA but an annoying friend. It also explained why Jase had let Dan into my office. He was matchmaking. He thought I needed a life. Maybe he was right but I couldn't have one with Dan.

I'd tried that. It hadn't worked.

"Group pictures don't count." Or at least, that's what I told myself every time I attempted to throw that picture away. I never could. I'd pick it up, even get so far as the trash can but then I'd look at it and remember being happy. And carefully carry it back inside.

My answer earned me an eye roll from Jase. Jase was very good at eye rolls. Normally they made me laugh. Today not so much. Still, I summoned a smile to try and prove—probably to myself more than Jase—that I was okay. Jase was one of the few exceptions to my 'let's keep the supernaturals to business only' rule. We'd been friends before he'd been turned. And after? Well, I'd lost too many people to supernaturals in one way or another. I didn't want to lose another. Besides, vamps are safer than werewolves. They can't infect you with just one bite. Besides which, Jase wasn't likely to want to bite me—I needed a Y chromosome to be his type. He was safe. I needed safe.

"Uh huh. So what does Mr. Old News want?"

I pushed what was left of the brownie around the plate. "He needs some help with a case."

"Fraud?"

I shook my head. Fraud would be easy. But McCallister Tate was nothing as ordinary as fraud. "Murder. A rogue."

Jase frowned, looking suddenly less like a safe best friend and more like an overprotective vampire. "Why do they need an accountant?"

"Cold case. The guy vanished. They froze his assets and now someone's finally tried to tap one of the accounts."

Jase looked even less happy. "Cold? How cold...wait a minute, old flame. Cold case. Tell me it's not Tate?"

I looked down at my computer screen.

"Fuck, Ashley. Tell me you're not stupid enough to go after Tate. He's not a normal vamp. He's pure evil. I never would have let him in if I'd known it was about Tate."

He'd gone pale—hard for a vampire. In fact, he looked so horrified I figured he really hadn't known why Dan had wanted an appointment. That made me feel a little better. "What do you know about McCallister Tate?" It was hard to say the name without letting my mind summon the images. But I managed—just. I knew I wouldn't be so lucky once I was lying in bed alone in the dark.

"I read the newspapers the same as everybody." He tugged at his immaculate pale green silk tie, loosening it and pulling it off-center. Which meant he was *really* upset.

"Tate's old news," I said. I hoped. Hoped the FBI was wrong and Tate was dead.

"He might be old news but I remember. And vamps talk. There are some scary mothers who don't like to say Tate's name too loud."

I shivered. I couldn't help it. A rogue vampire was bad, bad trouble. And Tate was one of the most sadistic on record even though in vamp terms he was young—not even fifty. Supposedly he'd been a psychopath before he'd been turned. Some vamp had made a huge mistake in picking him as a good candidate to become a vampire. It was said that one of the first things he'd done after turning had been killing the vamp who'd made him. Which was pretty much unheard of in vamp society.

Tate was the real deal. The big bad. A bogeyman to all species. Or he had been until he'd disappeared twelve years ago after committing his worst atrocity. Thirty murders in one small town in one night. Including my parents, my little sister and my best friend.

I shivered again. It didn't matter how scary Tate was, or what going after him might do to my life, I couldn't pass up the chance to bring him down.

CHAPTER TWO

"THERE'S COFFEE ON YOUR DESK," Jase said as I walked into the office the next day around midday. I didn't bother to take off my sunglasses, despite the fact the UV screens made the lighting dim compared to the blaze of summer sun outside. Tate and bad memories had made sleep elusive, and I'd had about three too many glasses of red wine in an attempt to chase them away. So now I'd be dealing with Daniel and with a hangover. Not one of my finest plans.

"Thanks." Maybe caffeine would help. "Do we have aspirin?"

Jase reached into his drawer and tossed me a bottle. I managed to catch it, just. He'd obviously slowed down his throw in deference to my condition. Though how he knew what my condition was before I walked in the door was something I didn't want to think too hard about.

Jase was a mere baby vamp. He'd turned voluntarily three years earlier when he found out he had pancreatic cancer. He'd only been twenty. Not ready to die. Most people who've been vaccinated and then try deliberately to turn have limited success. Which is kind of the point of the vaccines in the first place, to make being turned, voluntarily or not, difficult. Some don't change, some die, some become vamps with lesser powers (but on the plus side they get higher tolerance of sun and reduced need for the red stuff), a few start off weaker and gradually strengthen as they age (if they survive that long).

Of course some people who get the vaccine are turned by it, which is why it's not terribly popular yet. Even the lycanthropy one—which is somewhat more reliable—occasionally changes someone.

One day they'll make both vaccines more effective and then the vamps will have some thinking to do. At the moment they do okay. The law-abiding ones drink the manufactured blood or have willing donors and humans generally leave them alone unless they're thrill seeking or looking to be turned.) What will happen when the vaccinations become more effective and the pool of potential new vamps starts to shrink is anyone's guess.

Werewolves don't have the same problem. They don't rely on humans for food. Plus wolves can be born as well as made.

But when it came to choosing to turn, Jase had won the lottery, at least from his perspective. He had the full suite of vamp powers. Including, as much as he tried to hide it from me, what I was starting to suspect was a pretty impressive psychic ability. It was kind of spooky to think my PA had the potential to become some sort of vamp leader if he chose. But that was something I didn't have the headspace to think about right now.

For now, I could just about manage to focus on the fact that he made great coffee. I gulped down the mug he'd left on my desk, willing the caffeine to kick my brain into gear. I took another swallow to take the aspirin and then drained the cup. After a few minutes my headache had receded a little. Not quite enough though. I wandered back out for a refill.

"Rough night?" Jase asked.

I pushed my sunglasses up onto my forehead. "Now why would you think that?"

"Ash, if you don't want to deal with Daniel or Tate then pull out of this. You don't need the money."

No, but I did need the chance at revenge. "It's not about money."

"I know," Jase said. "That's what worries me."

"I'm human but that doesn't mean I'm fragile," I pointed out. "And I'll be safe. It's not like accountants go out in the field."

"Just make sure you don't."

"I'll be surrounded by FBI agents. Taskforce agents, if you want to get picky. I'll be fine."

Jase muttered something that sounded like "you'll need more than a taskforce," but I ignored him and returned to my office with my coffee.

Two and a bit hours later my head was throbbing with renewed vigor and my stomach churning. But I couldn't blame it on the hangover or the painful hour I'd spent with Elena Anderson trying to pry info from her that would help me track down her soon-to-be ex's money. No, this time, the pain was all about the rest of my day and what I was about to do.

Revisit the past I'd run so hard from.

The Taskforce has its headquarters in one of the nondescript, don't-even-think-about-a-government-agency-being-here buildings that the FBI has around Seattle. It was gray and square and boring. As long as you didn't notice the high number of cameras pointing at you as soon as you walked in the door or the higher than usual number of guards manning the lobby.

I made it through the scanners, submitted my briefcase and purse for inspection and then walked to the reception desk.

"Ashley Keenan. I'm here to see Daniel Gibson," I said, not knowing if that was the right way to ask. Was it Agent Gibson? Or Special Agent Gibson?

"Yes, ma'am." The guy behind the desk had a crew cut and a suit stretched uncomfortably over a body built like a bulldozer. "I'll call you through."

He picked up a phone and a few minutes later an icy looking blonde emerged from one of the elevator banks and made her way over to me. "Ms. Keenan?"

I nodded.

"Come with me please." She pivoted neatly on her three-inch heels and, without looking to see if I was following, headed back to the elevators. She moved with the kind of innate grace that made me think she wasn't human. But as I hurried after her, I didn't quite get close enough to judge whether she was vamp or were. I wasn't sure if I wanted to know.

She was beautiful whatever species she was and I was busy telling the tiny part of my mind that was all "Daniel works with *her*?" to shut the fuck up. And thanking the stupid side of me which had tried on about five different outfits this morning before settling on my favorite don't-mess-with-me-I-do-designer suit. And the heels that brought the top of my head just about up to Amazon girl's chin. And I'm five nine in the heels.

But once we were in the elevator, heading down rather than up, it became perfectly obvious she was a were of some kind. She wasn't still enough to be a vamp and standing next to her made my skin tingle in the way I associated with shifters. Something to do with their aura or magic or whatever it is that lets them change or perhaps their revved up metabolisms means weres tend to give off energy. Some people feel it and I'm one of them.

If I'm not careful, it can result in a kind of contact high. Dealing with Dan with a buzz on wouldn't be the brightest thing I could do. I shifted half a step further away from her and her head turned.

"You can feel me?"

I nodded again.

She frowned. "But you're human?"

"Lots of humans can feel weres," I pointed out.

"Most don't feel me."

Probably because they were too busy gazing in lust—or envy if they were female—at the perfection of her face, all high cheekbones and large dark blue eyes. I squished down the little green monster. "Lucky me."

She looked annoyed. I have no idea why. I hoped she wasn't one of the weres who thought humans were inferior. It was going to be bad enough working with Daniel without adding a snippy alpha bitch to the bargain. Or maybe she was a feline. Werewolves are most common type of shifter in the US but there are a few groups of big cat weres. I'd never met one but if they were going to show up anywhere, the Taskforce seemed likely.

The elevator came to a smooth halt and the doors slid open. There was a brief flash of red that told me I'd just been subjected to a full body scan, then Ms. Blonde moved forward. "If you'll follow me, Ms. Keenan."

I stepped out, trying to scan my surroundings discreetly. I'd never had any actual involvement with the Taskforce before and my ideas of what a secret agency looked like relied heavily on old Bond movies and my collection of spy shows. I was disappointed when the room turned out to be a pretty normal looking reception area. White walls, the seal of the President on the reception desk, and one long low leather bench against the wall closest to the elevator doors. Smoked glass doors in the left hand wall had no signs to indicate where we were. Guess that meant that if you'd gotten this far, you were meant to know where you were.

There was a woman behind the desk. Unlike the valkyrie I'd ridden down with, she was short and dark. She looked sweet and harmless. But in this place she had to be fairly high level FBI. She could probably kill me with her pinky even if she was human.

"Ms. Keenan?" she asked. When I nodded she handed me a lanyard with an ID badge clipped to it. "Welcome to the Taskforce. Please wear this at all times."

I looked at the badge. It had a picture of me, but not me today. My hair was longer, well past my shoulders. I hadn't worn it that length for over a year. I frowned, trying to work out where they'd gotten the picture. Then I shrugged. The damn FBI could probably get any picture it wanted. I should be more worried about the 'welcome to the Taskforce' line.

I slipped the lanyard over my head as the blonde glided past me and pressed her palm to a small screen by the glass doors. They slid open with a soft hum and she turned back to me. "This way."

I followed her into a long, low-ceilinged room bright with harsh artificial light that in no way disguised the fact we were underground. Rows of cubicles formed two orderly lines marching down the length of the floor and the place hummed with familiar office noises. What wasn't so familiar was the fact that the cubicles were filled with vamps and weres.

I'd never been around so many non-humans in one space. My skin tingled even though I wasn't standing close enough to anyone to feel them under normal circumstances. I guess if you put enough weres in a room, the effect gets stronger. My heart started pounding—an instinctive reaction to being surrounded by people who potentially viewed me as a snack. And the fact that I knew the vamps—and probably some of the weres—could hear my racing heartbeat didn't make me feel any more relaxed. I spent a lot of time over the years trying to control the fear supernaturals caused me. I hadn't wanted to let Tate win, let him turn me into someone full of hate and fear. I thought I'd mostly succeeded. But apparently this many supers in one spot was pushing my limits.

The small smirk on the face of my escort told me she was enjoying my discomfort. It was tempting to accidentally let my silver charm bracelet rub against her and see how she enjoyed a bit of discomfort herself. But that would be small minded and petty. Plus she could probably throw me across the room if I pissed her off too much. I stuck my chin out instead and worked on calming my breathing.

After a seemingly endless walk past the cubicles, with the occupants watching us pass with unnervingly quiet scrutiny, we came to a row of offices, each with a neat nameplate. We stopped at the one that said Special Agent Daniel Gibson. So now I knew what to call him. If only I didn't have to call him anything at all.

"Come in," Dan's voice said in response to the blonde's knock. I didn't wait. I pushed open the door. Dan was on the phone but waved me in with one hand. The blonde hovered in the doorway. Dan finished his conversation and hung up. He smiled at blondie. "Thanks, Esme."

Esme? The blonde goddess was called Esme? Call me shallow but that cheered me up.

Dan's office was small and crowded. Files were piled on almost every flat surface. A stack of multi-colored folders teetered on the corner of his desk nearest me. I resisted the urge to push it to a safer position. If Dan wanted to lose his files, then so be it.

"Hey," he said with a smile that was just a little too friendly for my liking. This was so not about me and Dan getting cozy. It was about catching the thing that killed my family.

"I'm here," I said. "Let's get on with it. Tell me about Tate."

Daniel studied me for a moment. I thought he might be going to push his luck and try some small talk but he just passed me a folder. "This is everything we have about Tate's finances when he disappeared. The accounts were frozen and no one's been near them for twelve years. Two weeks ago, someone tried to tap the account on the top of the list on the first page."

"Two weeks?" So much for wanting the best. I figured Daniel had tried just about everything in his power before coming to me. "What makes you think I can find anything when the FBI has failed?"

He shrugged. "You always said you were the best. Prove it."

That earned him a glare but I still ran my eyes down the list of accounts. Most of them were US banks but there were a few in the usual tax havens. The total balance was well into the millions. And I doubted the list was complete. Either being a psychopath paid well or Tate had used his talents for mayhem and violence in a profitable way. I didn't want to think about how he might have done that. "If this list isn't complete, he's probably been living off other funds. Or accumulating new funds. Or he's dead and the attempt has nothing to do with him. Maybe it was a dumb hacker challenge." It wasn't unusual in my line of work to come across computer geeks deciding that trying to beat the Swiss banking system or something would be fun. It probably was fun. 'Til they got caught and copped some heavy jail time.

"It wasn't hackers. At least, no sensible hackers. It was a straight access attempt from a public terminal."

Damn. Public terminals were designed to be anonymous and untraceable. Though they weren't foolproof, they were a good place to start if you wanted to hide your tracks. "Surely Tate's not going to do something that obvious."

Dan shrugged. "Who knows? Maybe he's bored and wants to play games."

"I assume you checked out the terminal already?"

A nod. "Yep. Rented under a fake id. Not one of Tate's known aliases. And the proprietor doesn't remember any faces. It was a Saturday night, big gamers' night. The place was packed."

"Surveillance?"

"Nothing. The tape got fried somehow. And before you ask, yes, we pulled the guy's servers and the actual terminal. So far there's nothing worthwhile on them."

Double damn. Whoever did this knew what they were doing. The challenge was enough to raise my professional interest. I ran a finger down the list. "Well, I've got a few things I can try but there might not be anything to find. Give me the soft copy of this and anything else you've got and I'll see what I can do."

"You'll have to work from here."

I dropped the folder. Spend time here, in the bunker with Dan? No thanks. Not gonna happen. I knew lunacy when I heard it. "I have a business, remember? An office?"

"It's not secure."

I bristled. My security systems are state of the art. My clients depended on my discretion. I had firewalls on my firewalls and encryption systems a spook would be proud of. My office had alarms, back up alarms, body scanners and cameras. Plus pretty damn good security in the building before you could even get up to my floor. I wasn't up to the FBI's standard maybe but I figured I was covered. "Gee, Dan. You work for the FBI. Maybe they could secure my little ol' computer."

"It's not just your computer I'm worried about."

Tate? He was worried about Tate coming after me? Sheesh. Dan had always been the protective type but combine that with alpha wolf instincts and he'd gotten paranoid. "Tate doesn't even know who I am." The police in Caldwell had always told me the attacks were random. No pattern. No reason to choose the victims. "How would he know I'm working on this?"

Dan's face stayed stony. "I'm not taking chances."

"Why, Dan, that's so sweet." I laid on the sarcastic tone and his eyes narrowed. Score one for me. "But I'm not working here every day. I'm not stupid. I have security." And even if I didn't, I wouldn't agree to spend every day in the same building as Dan. I'd made my decision when it came to him. And it had cost me. I didn't need a daily reminder of just how much.

"Your PA? Tate's more than fifty years older than him. Stronger. He'd rip his head off."

I shuddered. "Thanks for the mental image. But no, my security system is not just Jase."

I'm not dumb. I deal with vamps and weres and I take precautions. I wear a cross. My accessories are all solid silver. I carry a big ass gun with silver bullets and I know how to hit what I aim it at. The vase of flowers on my desk is full of holy water. If any of my clients decide that

I look tasty, then they'll get a nasty surprise. They might still get me, but I make pretty sure I could hurt them in the process.

"This is not up for debate, Ashley."

I pushed the file back across the desk, a little harder than strictly necessary. "Then I won't take the job."

His face twisted. "You always have to do things the hard way, don't you?"

"You mean not the way you want me to? Yep. Sue me. It's my life."

"And you'd throw it away to spite me?" Dan snapped.

"Oh, get over yourself. I don't run my life around you—" I broke off as he pulled another folder out of his drawer and tossed it in front of me. "What's this?"

"I didn't want to show you these."

"Show me what?" I stared at the folder as if it were a box of tarantulas. It was white and the seal across it was black. The neat little label read 'Tate, McCallister. SF10536.' It gave me the willies.

"These are photos we found in one of Tate's properties. We tracked it back to him about six years ago."

Now I *really* didn't want to see the contents. The house where a psychopathic vampire serial killer lived? There was nothing inside *that* I wanted to see. "What's that got to do with me?"

"Just look."

I opened the folder reluctantly. The first photo was of a fairly average looking house. Well, a fairly average looking mansion. High walls, trees, big iron gates. Pretty standard. I felt my nerves ease. Then I turned to the next photo and my heart almost leapt out of my chest.

It was a picture of me. Standing by my parents' grave. For a moment I tasted bile but I fought it back.

I recognized the shot; it had run in all the big papers at the time. I hated it. Me in black, my face swollen from crying, watching them bury my life. I was sixteen in that photo. Sixteen going on three hundred. I'd never really felt young after Tate. The thought of Tate having *that* picture made me feel ill. But I wasn't going to let Dan see that.

"So he likes to read the paper."

"Keep going."

I turned to the next photo. Me again. But this time not so young. College graduation. Years after the Caldwell massacre and Tate's disappearance. I tasted bile again and dropped the photo as if it were red hot. "But these are—"

"Keep looking." Dan's tone didn't invite argument.

Swallowing hard, I leafed through the photos. Me at school. Me at college. The final picture was of a room in Tate's house. Pictures of me covered one whole wall, a sinister montage. Suddenly the room seemed awfully hot. I closed my eyes as everything started spinning, trying to breathe and not throw up.

"Ash?"

Dan was round the desk and by my side before I knew it.

"Shit, Ash. I didn't mean to scare you that much." He put a hand on my back. The warmth of his skin radiated through my suit. God. It was so tempting to lean into him. To let him chase the fear away. Except, when it came to Dan, the scariest thing was Dan himself. He was a werewolf. I couldn't afford to forget that.

"Yes, you did," I managed, forcing myself to shrug his hand off. The spinning started to slow down. It seemed that anger trumped panic, at least for the moment.

"Here, have some water."

He closed my hand around something cool. I cracked one eye open and lifted the glass to my mouth. The act of swallowing made the spinning recede even further. "I'm okay."

He didn't touch me again but he didn't move away. The tingle of his shifter energy flowed around me. "Take your time. If it makes you feel any better, he had walls with pictures of the families of all the Caldwell victims."

No. No, that didn't make me feel any better. All these years I told myself the Caldwell massacre was a random event. That Tate was a monster and that sometimes bad things just happen. The thought that there might be more to it than that – that the monster had a plan, a plan that might not yet be played out, sucked all the warmth from my body. I wrapped my arms around myself. "He has photos of my college graduation. That means he was still alive then. All the statements made about him say that he was believed dead?" All these years I'd told myself it was true. That Tate wasn't out there somewhere. I'd had to believe it in order to survive.

"We hoped he was. And we've never found anything else since that house that indicates he's still around."

"Excuse me if I don't find that comforting." My voice shook a little. I clenched my teeth. "Why didn't you tell me this before?"

"I wasn't part of the taskforce when they found these pictures. And by the time I joined, you'd made it quite clear that I wasn't allowed to contact you."

"You didn't think I'd make an exception for this?" It wasn't fair of me, I knew. He was right. I'd told him not to come near me.

"Honestly? No. Not when we had no idea where he might be or how long ago he'd abandoned that house," he said, sounding defensive.

"Besides which, we don't release information that might jeopardize an ongoing investigation."

"Even if it jeopardizes lives?"

"If I'd believed you were in danger, I would have done something," Dan said. "But we had no evidence. None of this is my fault, Ash."

"You know, you really need to work on your bedside manner," I snapped. Being mad at him was the one thing I could control. I made myself open both eyes to glare at him.

He grinned. "I don't get many complaints."

"The world is full of stupid women." I was determined not to be one of them.

The grin died. "I'm sorry for scaring you. But I didn't want you going into this blind."

"I appreciate that." I didn't really. I wanted to go back to my nice deluded safe place where the bad stuff was in the past, and hadn't happened for a reason, and there was a chance the rest of my life might be normal. I liked it there. But instead I was in a government agency office, surrounded by the supernatural and my ex-lover. And the vampire who killed my family knew who I was. "Now you've told me. I'm still not going to be able to work here every day. So you'd better get your boys onto securing my office. Otherwise I can't help you." I didn't want to help him as it was. I wanted to get on a plane and take up residence on an island somewhere with lots of sunshine and no facilities for vampires. Somewhere safe. But I couldn't run. Not this time. Not if there was a chance I could help catch Tate.

Dan's eyes were silver glass again. Angry. His eyes had always been beautiful but they were more than that since he'd changed. Shifting silver that revealed too much. Unless he did the stonewall cool thing like now. "Fine. We'll do it your way. For now. I'll get a team to your office and your house."

"My house?"

"It's the easiest place to get at you," he said.

"You wish," I said, but he was right. My house had alarms and good locks but it lacked the additional levels of security my office building offered. Until now I'd never felt vulnerable there. I don't know why: Tate had taught me safety is an illusion. Now Dan was reminding me.

"Better safe than sorry."

"You sure know how to show a girl a good time," I said. "Was there anything else?"

He obviously figured he'd pushed things far enough. "No, that's it."

I stood, so did Dan. I stepped towards his office was very small. "Then I'll be seeing you."

"Yes." He stroked a finger along my cheek and I flinched away as warmth bloomed over my skin. "Yes. You will."

There was nothing more to say. My head was pounding and so was my heart. Time for an exit. I turned on my heel and left. And tried to tell myself I only imagined the soft "I'm sorry, Ashley," that followed me into the hall.

CHAPTER THREE

I'D NO SOONER STEPPED through the FBI building's glass doors into the cool damp city, when my cell phone rang. I fumbled in my purse for it. "Hello?"

"Ashley?"

The sound of traffic made it hard to hear. I stuck my fingers in my free ear and moved back towards the building. "Aunt Bug? Is that you?"

"Yes, it's me. Who the hell else would I be?"

I grinned. Aunt Bug was exactly what I needed to improve my mood. "No one. But lots of people call me."

"Do they have as much trouble getting hold of you as I do?"

Rolling my eyes, I tried to remember if I'd missed returning any calls from her. "When did you call?"

"I'm calling now. I was just making a point."

My head started to hurt again. Aunt Bug is my favorite relative. Hell, she's my only close relative and she'd jumped in feet first as surrogate parent after Tate but her conversational style, at times, drove me round the bend.

"Aunty—" she hated being called Aunty— "I'm kind of busy. Do you need something?"

"New client?"

"Kind of." I wasn't going to mention Daniel. Aunt Bug and I had never agreed on Daniel. At least, not once he'd changed.

"And how is Daniel?" she asked.

God. I should've known. Aunt Bug had some sort of sixth sense coupled with a grapevine that would've made J. Edgar Hoover proud.

If she'd gone into law enforcement, they'd know exactly what had happened to Hoffa, who shot JFK and where the Lindbergh baby was buried. She generally knew what I was up to. Sometimes before I did. "It's just a job."

She snorted. "Sure, and I'm a ballerina."

The thought of Aunt Bug—who looked good for a sixty eight year old but was built on lines that tended to tall and solid rather than dainty—in a tutu made me smile again. "I'm buying you pointe shoes as we speak. Did you call for something other than Daniel? Because there's nothing to discuss on that topic."

"I just wanted to see if we're still on for dinner."

"Of course. I'm looking forward to it." Every couple of months, Aunt Bug came into town for the weekend. We went for dinner at a swanky restaurant and she drank more martinis than her doctor and maid would think sensible and stayed at her favorite hotel. It was always hilarious. And I'd been so busy lately that I hadn't made it back to Caldwell since her last trip here.

"Good," she said. "Then I'll see you Saturday. And you can tell me all about Daniel then." She hung up before I could say anything else leaving me glaring at nothing.

I must have looked really cranky because a woman walking past made a wide detour around me after we made eye contact.

Shoving the phone back in my purse, I wondered exactly what I'd done to deserve the day I was having. If I got lectured by Jase when I got back to the office then I'd be three for three. Of course, I'd rather be lectured by Jase than Aunt Bug. And that should tell you something about my aunt when she gets going.

I'd have to keep the martinis flowing on Saturday to avoid the sort of interrogation that would make a Green Beret spill their guts. Aunt Bug was a teacher before she'd retired. And she had that particular teacher skill of being able to convince you she knew all and make you feel guilty about it into the bargain. Being Bugged was never pleasant.

She was actually my great aunt. My Dad's mother's younger— much, much, younger as in late life surprise—sister. Gran had been the oldest. Aunt Bug was actually only seven years older than my Dad—or rather, than he would've been if he were still alive. Her real name was Matilda but her Dad had called her his little June Bug and the rest of the family had shortened it to Bug.

Only Reverend Flannery back in Caldwell ever called her Matilda. I always had to stop for a moment and work out who he was talking to when he did. Aunt Bug was a central fact of my life and a force of nature. And now she was going to be on my case about Daniel. If I wasn't careful, she was likely to wangle the news about Tate out of me and then I'd never hear the end of it. For the first time ever it was tempting to cancel dinner.

Only, if I did that, she'd probably turn up on my front door step and demand to know what was going on.

Between avoiding Dan and not giving anything away to Bug, I was in for a real fun packed week.

I looked at my watch and decided I couldn't face going straight back to work. Instead I did what any sensible girl would do after the day I'd had so far. I went shopping.

My shopping spree made me temporarily happy and I imagined the resulting bill would put a smile on the face of the good people at Visa as well. But it didn't change the fact that I had to go back to work eventually and face Jase. At least I could do it wearing a totally awesome pair of new boots.

Despite the boots, I hadn't spent as long melting my credit cards as I thought I would. It was hard not to examine the faces around me and wonder if any of them were there to watch me. Worrying about potential stalkers can throw even a dedicated shopper off her stride.

When the unease became definite prickles down my spine, I threw in the towel, loaded up on Godiva and headed back to work.

Jase took one look at my boots and the other bags weighing me down and wisely decided not to ask me about my experience with the Taskforce. Instead, he demanded a fashion parade. Did I mention Jase was gay? When he made me coffee to go with my candy and requested to see what I had bought, I knew he was trying to be particularly nice. Jase has good taste but he's far more interested in male fashion than female.

His enthusiasm distracted me for a while but my buzz ended when I was packing the last pair of shoes back into their box and turned around to find a grim looking guy in a bland gray suit carrying a clipboard standing at the door of the office. He flashed a Taskforce badge then he and two other agents proceeded to subject the place to the sort of security inspection I would've expected if the President and her retinue were dropping by.

"What's going on?" Jase asked as we watched the men put our office under the microscope, poking and prodding in all sorts of weird places and working IT geek voodoo on our computers. Jase hovered around them at first doing his grumpy vamp look but eventually he drifted back to me, parked his Hugo Boss-clad butt next to mine and glared from a distance.

"Let's just say Special Agent Gibson and I have a difference in of opinion over the adequacy of our security. He's checking us out."

"I could bite him if you want me to," Jase whispered, glancing in the direction of the security team.

I laughed, which eased the congealed knot of tension in my stomach. "Thanks. But Dan's a werewolf. He'll bite back." Vampires can feed from weres but they can't turn them. And a lone wolf against a lone vamp is a pretty even match most of the time. Depending on how strong the vamp is. Or the wolf.

As a result wolves and vamps generally have a kind of mutual respect, don't-bite-me-and-I-won't-bite-you thing going on.

"I still think you should turn this job down." Jase picked up a stack of mail from his desk and started flicking through it, irritation clear in his jerky motions.

I put my hand on his arm. "Too late. But I'm considering raising my rates." Not that any amount of money was going to be enough to make up for the fact Dan was back in my life. Or for the knowledge about Tate that was spinning around my head.

Jase looked a little mollified at the mention of more money. The security team finished with my computer and told me they'd be back the next day with some 'additions' and the Tate files. I shooed Jase back into the reception room and tried to settle down and do some work.

The fourth time I lost track of where I was in my spreadsheet I gave up. I leaned back in my chair, staring at nothing, trying unsuccessfully not to think of Dan or Tate.

How my life had gotten so complicated so quickly? Werewolf ex-lovers and vampires of the scary variety. I tried to avoid both. I live in the world. I accept that vampires and weres and possibly other things that go bump in the night are part of life but like I said, outside of business, I prefer, on the whole, to limit my interactions with them.

The only good thing about the day so far was that it was going to be over soon. And tomorrow was Friday.

Though on Saturday Aunt Bug was coming to town.

We'd go shopping, we'd do dinner and we'd probably argue about Daniel and whether Aunt Bug's shots were up to date. Which are pretty much the two things we always argue about. Daniel because Aunt Bug doesn't understand why I couldn't still date him after he changed and the shots because she believes fate is fate and why shouldn't she take her chances? She says the chances of something bad happening are higher from the vaccines than from a vamp or were attack. And she's gotten even more stubborn since that bad batch of vamp vaccine hit New York last year.

Maybe she's right but I can't stand the thought of losing someone else to them so I nag her just like my Dad used to. I take the shots.

shadows. One minute there, one minute not. Talk about freaky. But I did as I was told and stood in the semi-dark between the house and the drive whilst my pulse banged hard enough I figured every vamp or were in a ten block radius could hear me.

Seconds stretched and stretched. I felt a sitting duck, one who'd been sitting far too long. There was a sudden thump and snarl from the direction of the porch and I belatedly realized who my late night visitor probably was.

"Jase, wait." I started toward the house at a run. Too late. By the time I bounded up the stairs, Jase and Dan were grappling with each other.

"Stop that," I said. Loudly. They didn't even glance in my direction. Jase threw a punch and Dan ducked, another snarl—not human in the slightest—vibrating from his throat.

"Stop it!" I repeated. I had a silver cross in my purse. Maybe I should get it out. Silver would give Dan enough of a jolt to make him back off—the lycanthropy virus does something to were immune systems to make them react really badly to silver—and Jase isn't too fond of crosses. No one has ever figured out exactly why blessed objects hurt vampires but they do. So maybe there really is a God. Or Gods.

But I decided to try something less drastic first. I backed down the stairs and grabbed the hose from the front flowerbed. Twisting the handle and cursing male hormones as my heels sank into the dirt, I aimed the water squarely at them.

It worked. They sprang apart with a volley of curses.

I released the trigger on the hose but didn't turn off the water. Both men turned to glare at me as I stalked back up the stairs.

I glared back. "You don't like getting wet? Next time, pay attention."

"But he—"

"I was just—"

They spoke over each other. I held up a hand. "It's late. I'm tired. Both of you, go *home*."

"No way," Jase said, earning him another low rumble from Dan. "I'm seeing you inside."

My hero. Only problem was, Jase in hero mode was likely to push Dan into full-blown alpha wolf mode. My porch might not survive the experience—let alone my sanity.

"How about I see myself in?" I suggested. Surely if someone was lurking inside—and how had I gone from happy my-home-is-my-castle Ashley to someone-might-be-lying-in-wait Ashley in less than twelve hours—all the noise would've scared them off by now?

Both Dan and Jase turned their glares on me, the water dripping from their faces doing little to disguise the barely reined potential for violence. Even though I knew neither of them would hurt *me*, it was more than a little intimidating. I'm five foot six in my flats and both of them are over six foot. Dan beats Jase by an inch or so. Plus both of them are supernatural. They're scary when pissed. But I wasn't going to be pushed around on my own porch by my PA and my ex just because they were feeling the testosterone.

I crossed my arms and stood as straight as possible. "I said GO HOME."

"I need to talk to you." Dan jumped in before Jase could protest again.

"Now?" It was almost midnight. Even the FBI had to sleep. "Can't it wait until tomorrow?"

"Would I be sitting here waiting for you in the middle of the night if it could?" Dan said. There was still an underlying rumble to his voice that increased the intimidation factor.

The question hung in the air between us, heavy with all sorts of undertones. Once upon a time we'd both spent a lot of time waiting around to get a chance to get our hands on each other. He'd hung out in my dorm lobby until they'd practically made him an honorary resident and I'd known every detail of the lives of every doorman in every building he'd lived in. Both of us had been studying or working our way up in the world and putting in long hours.

But long hours were a price we were willing to pay for what we'd had. Which was a lot of mind blowing—really mind blowing—once in-a-lifetime sex. Or at least it had been once in a lifetime for me. I hardly been celibate since Dan changed but nobody had quite been the same. And more than that, a basic, indescribable sense of fit that meant we were happiest together. True love. The real thing. But I wasn't going to bring *that* up.

"Probably not," I admitted.

"Exactly." Dan folded his arms, looking like he was perfectly prepared to stand there all night if necessary. Dan can out-stubborn a glacier when he sets his mind to it. It would be quicker to let him say whatever he'd come to say, then send him packing.

Plus there was the annoying but true fact that part of me was happy to see him. And that part, my think-with-hormones-not-with-brain part, wasn't ready to let him leave just yet.

I would indulge that part a little. Just enough to shut it up so I could lock it back up and bury the key. Besides I was too tired to try and mediate a Mexican standoff between a vamp and a werewolf any other way.

But to deal with Dan, I had to get Jase to leave.

I turned to face Jase and put on my best I-pay-your-salary-don't-mess-with-me face. "Jase, it's fine. I'm fine. I'll see you tomorrow."

I didn't feel as confident as I sounded. Jase was putting out some big scary vamp vibes. I knew vamps could do this—exude a sense of danger, if not downright menace—but I'd never actually experienced it. In the moonlight, with his sandy red hair turned silvery gold and his pale skin almost glowing, he didn't seem like my nice guy PA. Didn't seem like my friend.

I'd never seen him like this before and I wasn't exactly sure how far I could push him. I just hoped that my staying calm and to the point would turn him back into just Jase before he and Dan got physical again. If any blood got spilled, the whole situation could get very nasty very fast.

"You heard her," Dan said.

"Don't help me," I snapped at him, keeping my eyes on Jase. "Jase, really. You can go. Dan won't be staying long." Just long enough for me to hear what he had to say and try to stop myself from kicking his butt for giving me a crappy end to what had already been a shitty day. I focused on my growing anger at the whole situation, hoping it would drown out my stupid nostalgia.

I wasn't so sure it would. The night was cool and a slight breeze carried the scent of Dan's aftershave straight to me, a smell that would be forever associated in my mind with lust and heartbreak and that had nothing to do with rationality or logic. And, even worse, tonight the familiar spice was under laid with something earthier and deeper. A wild tang that meant his anger was calling his wolf to the surface.

It made his smell even more enticing. It bypassed my brain and connected directly with my libido. Much to my horror I had to fight not to move closer to him.

This was a complication I hadn't counted on. After Dan's attack, after it was clear he was going to change, he'd been taken away by the local pack to learn how to control himself. He'd been gone for weeks. Weeks of me being in limbo, not knowing what was going to happen. I'd wanted to try. I hadn't wanted to lose him. I'd told myself I could cope. That I'd be safe. But then two nights after he'd returned home—the first night we'd spent time together because he'd wanted to be sure of his control before he saw me—everything I'd been denying had happened.

Driving home, we'd been rear ended. I hit my head. I bled. And Dan wolfed out in the car. By sheer instinct, I'd managed to fling open the door and get myself out before he got to me. But he smashed the window lunging at me before he had gotten himself under control. I wound up with his blood spattered across my shirt and I'd realized that if it had hit me higher, had gotten into the cut in my head then that could be all it would take.

I'd be a werewolf too. My children would be werewolves. I fought so hard to have a normal life after Tate. A normal human life. I couldn't risk losing everything I wanted. I loved Dan but I couldn't risk being infected. I couldn't date a wolf. Couldn't be with one. It was too risky. I broke up with him the next day. I didn't see any other option.

A serious relationship with a werewolf was a recipe for disaster for someone who didn't want to become one. Sex with a were is relatively low risk if you play safe. But low risk wasn't *no risk* and Dan and I weren't casual lovers. We were the real deal. We were headed for marriage and the white picket fence and the 2.4 kids. The only way for it to work was for me to change. Wolves mate for life when they settle down. And they live a long time. Not forever but longer than humans.

But I couldn't choose to become what he had. It felt like a betrayal of my family. For them I needed to live as a human.

There'd been no break-up sex, no chance of reconciliation, although he'd tried to change my mind. Once. I agreed to see him once but the resulting argument led to him going crazy and smashing up the room we were in. The pack member on new-wolf-sitting-duty stepped in and hustled him off before the damage count included me but not before I'd seen exactly what his being a werewolf meant. I'd seen his wild side and it was terrifying. After that I refused to see him.

Talk about ironic. My mind wouldn't let me love a werewolf but it seemed my body didn't share those qualms.

Or maybe I could chalk my wholly inappropriate reaction to stress and fatigue. God, I hoped so.

I glanced up at the sky and almost sighed with relief when I saw the moon was new. Which meant Dan should be in complete control and had no reason to change unless he chose to do so. Hopefully, if Jase left and Dan calmed down, he would go back to smelling like normal Dan—not super-pheromone catnip-for-Ashley Dan.

I made a mental note to invest in some stronger perfume and forced myself to turn back to Jase. I had to assume that, knowing how I felt about him being a werewolf, Dan wasn't about to change voluntarily around me, so Jase was the more dangerous of the two at this point. I had zero desire to move closer to Jase. But I figured talking him down might take just that.

I took a deep breath, pushed thought my very human instinct not to approach the vampire when he was in a snit and then stepped forward to put a hand on his arm. "I'll see you tomorrow."

The touch worked, thank God. Jase stared down at me for a moment, then blinked. Like a switch had been thrown, the swirling sense of danger emanating from him vanished.

"If that's what you want," he said in a tone that suggested he wasn't happy that I'd picked Dan over him and that my coffee would be cold and decaffeinated for the next few days. "I'll see you at work."

I made another mental note to hunt up a peace offering in the morning. "Thanks."

He nodded then disappeared in a split second. He *was* pissed. He rarely did anything that a human would consider overtly vampy around me. Sure, he couldn't hide his quick reflexes or graceful movements but he rarely did the superhuman speed and strength thing unless there was some sort of problem.

"Well," I said, fumbling for my keys as I walked past Dan. "That was fun. You should really come over more often, Special Agent Gibson."

CHAPTER FOUR

I DIDN'T WAIT TO SEE if Dan was following, I just stomped down the hall, flicking on every light switch I passed, until I reached the kitchen. Wishing I hadn't left my Godiva at the office, I reached for the next best thing—the bottle of Cuervo Reserva I keep in the pantry for days like these—and poured myself a glass.

"Can I have one of those?" Dan said, just as I took my first drink.

He stopped too close for my liking. His scent floated across to me so I moved to the other side of the island bench and took another mouthful hoping the warm slide of agave would temporarily distract my sinuses. "Aren't you on duty?"

He shook his head. "I finished an hour ago."

"Knock yourself out." I poured him a glass and pushed it across the bench.

"Thanks."

I let him take one mouthful. I wasn't completely heartless. After all, he was the one who first introduced me to the stuff. "Why are you here? What's so important?"

"I wanted to make sure you're okay. I didn't mean to scare you earlier."

I shrugged, trying to be casual. "You said that already. So if that's everything, you can go now." Go before I did anything stupid. I drained my glass and poured another. Anything, even the hangover I would certainly have if I kept downing tequila like this, was better than standing in my kitchen in the middle of the night with Dan, nothing between us but the past.

Dan held his glass out for a refill. I pushed the bottle across the bench.

"It's not the only reason I came," he said and my heart sank. Either he had more bad news or he was going to bring up us.

I couldn't really blame him. Our break-up was pretty much the definition of 'no closure'. I'd stonewalled every other attempt he'd made to see me or talk to me. He deserved better. But there is no good way to say, "I can't handle what you are now" to the man you love. Particularly when what he is isn't his fault.

Dan got bitten on the job. He and his partner got called to a bar fight one night. Problem was the caller didn't mention the fact that the combatants were weres. All I know is one of them changed, bit Dan, and suddenly I had a werewolf for a boyfriend.

One stupid moment in time and everything had changed.

"This had better be Taskforce related," I said.

He bristled. "For Chrissakes, Ashley, can't we have a conversation? Would it kill you to be nice to me?"

"Probably. We don't really have such a good track record. And I don't want to buy new furniture."

The look on his face told me he knew exactly what I was referring to. "I'm not a newbie werewolf anymore. I can control myself."

Maybe he could. Control wasn't the issue. Judgment was. Mine. I couldn't afford to be stupid about Dan. And I didn't trust him not to be stupid about me. "That doesn't matter. I made my decision. You have to respect it."

"And when do I get to make a decision?" he said quietly. "All my choices got taken away from me in that bar."

The pain in his voice made my fingers clench around my glass. After all this time, my first instinct was still to try and make him feel better. Knowing he was hurt made me hurt. Which was exactly why I couldn't let him back in my life. "I know. And I'm sorry. But that doesn't change where we are."

"It could. There are quite a few weres in the Taskforce who date humans." He reached for the bottle, poured more tequila. The muscles in his forearm stood out and I wondered how much control he was exerting right now not to shatter the glass.

"Date. Not marry. Not have kids with." I closed my eyes as he winced. Talking to him about this was just too damn painful. I'd wanted his children. Little dark haired boys with gray eyes and cute grins like their Dad. I still dreamed I had them sometimes.

Dan made a harsh sound in his throat. "Doesn't mean it can't happen."

"It's not going to happen. Not for us." Not in this lifetime. Not while I had any choice about it. And despite what Dan seemed to think, I doubted the local pack would be encouraging their members to marry humans.

"Damn it, Ash. I miss you. I've missed you every day for years. Tell me you haven't missed me." His voice dropped a notch, like he was struggling to sound calm.

"I won't lie to you." I owed him that much. Owed him honesty.

"Then can't we try something? Friendship?"

I laughed, not a good laugh. "You think you and I can be just friends?"

He shrugged. "Others do it. You're friends with Jase. He's a vampire."

"Jase doesn't want to date me," I pointed out. "He and I were always friends."

"So were we."

"Yeah, but we were more than that. You can't go back in time."

"Why not?"

I shook my head in frustration. He knew as well as I did why not. Even now, when I was angry and exhausted and confused, he pulled at me.

It took all my willpower not to go to him, not to give in to the heat rising in my body and press myself against him, let him chase away all the confusing stuff. I could see the same heat in the back of his eyes. The same hyperawareness in the way he tracked my movements, in the way his eyes kept flicking to my mouth. "You know why not."

"No, I really don't."

Energy rose from him, more than the general buzz of a were, an intensity that told me his wolf still prowled somewhere just below the surface. It felt good. In fact, between Dan and the Reservo, I was in danger of getting a little too buzzed. A little too reckless.

I slid my hand across the bench towards his, stopping with my fingertips maybe half an inch from his. At that distance I felt him even more strongly, like the pull of a magnet. I watched his face and knew from the way his eyes dropped to our hands that he felt the same pull.

"You really think you and I can just be friends?" I inched my hand forward slightly, saw him clench his jaw in the effort not to move, not to close the gap and touch me. "Pals? Buddies? Nothing more."

He nodded even as his fingers trembled. "I do."

"Really? You have no urge to touch me right now?"

"No."

"Liar." I knew beyond a doubt he wanted me. Still. Always. That's how it was between us. And why we couldn't be together.

Because, if we couldn't be lovers, being friends wasn't going to satisfy either of us. Even worse, being friends was going to put us in the sort of proximity that might just let our hormones forget exactly why we couldn't be lovers.

"Ashley..." It wasn't a denial. More a plea. His eyes weren't cool anymore. Now they were silver heat. Liquid lightning. The lightning that always flared between us.

I snatched my hand back. I'd pushed my luck far enough. "I'm sorry," I said. "I really am. But I told you when you came to my office. Nothing has changed."

"All work and no play make Ashley a dull girl," he mocked. His voice held a bitter edge.

"Yeah. But dull is better than dead."

"As a werewolf, you'd be harder to kill."

Pain seared down my throat to my gut. The truth is always an ugly thing. A werewolf. He still wanted me to change. So much for weres dating humans and we could try to make it work. But I was glad he'd said it. It made me remember why I had to keep things between us strictly professional. "As a werewolf, I wouldn't be me anymore."

He jerked back, knocking his glass with his hand. His reflexes stopped it flying off the bench onto the floor and only a few drops spilled. No human could've made that save. Just another reminder he was no longer my Dan.

"Is that what you believe? That I'm not who I used to be?" The heat in his eyes had changed again. To anger.

I'd learned the hard way staying calm is the best way to deal with an angry werewolf. I shrugged. "You're not the same. You can turn into a wolf."

"And what? You think that makes me less than human? An *animal?*" The wild scent rose from him, stronger than ever, and his voice had a vibrating edge. There was little that was human in the sound and I backed up a step. "Not lesser, just different. And I'm not you. I can't pretend losing my humanity is something I want."

That drew a true snarl from him. "You think I've lost something? I *gained* something. You're the one who's lost something. Like your heart. What happened to you, Ash? When did you turn to stone?"

He didn't let me answer, just snarled again and stalked from the kitchen. A few seconds later, my front door slammed so hard the windows rattled. All in all, it was the perfect ending to the worst day I'd had in quite some time.

I drained my glass and tipped what was left of Dan's tequila out. Alcohol probably killed the virus but I wasn't taking chances when my judgment felt so shaky. The glasses went in the dishwasher on the extra hot cycle.

As I switched off the lights and headed for bed, all I could think was Dan should've stuck around for an answer. Because I knew the exact moment I'd become the woman I was now. 2:08 a.m., August 17, four years ago. The moment I answered the phone and they told me Dan was hurt.

Turns out the Reservo wasn't such a good plan. By the time I staggered into work the next day, I was late and cranky. Jase took one look at me, raised his eyebrows and then focused back down on the screen in front of him.

The silence was deafening

I stomped past him and wished I hadn't. Esme sat in my visitor's chair.

"What are you doing here?" I dumped my briefcase by my desk. Gorgeous blonde supernaturals were the last thing I wanted to deal with this morning. "Jase," I yelled, cutting her off as she opened her mouth. "Coffee."

I didn't ask Amazonian were if she wanted any. She didn't complain, just smiled slightly—more smirk than smile really—at me as I sat down carefully, not wanting to add to the pain in my head that the yelling had caused. I suppressed the urge to give her the finger. She might bite it off. "You were saying?"

"Agent Gibson wanted me to do the final security check before we give you the Tate files." Despite the smirk, there was a good dose of not-happy-to-be-here in her tone.

But at least she wasn't Dan. I could handle Esme. After last night, I had no idea if the same was true about Dan.

And, judging by the fact he'd sent Esme instead of coming over to bug me himself, he wasn't sure either.

"I'm sure my assistant can show you everything you need," I said as Jase glided in with coffee for two.

I narrowed my eyes at him as I flicked on my computer and he glided straight back out after depositing the mugs in front of us.

"I'm sure he can." Esme didn't budge from her chair.

"Something else I can do for you, Agent Walsh?"

"You should turn this job down."

I almost choked on my coffee. First Dan wouldn't let me get out of the job; now one of his team members was trying to talk me out of it. "I assure you, I'm good at what I do."

Her mouth turned down. "We shouldn't be wasting time babysitting humans."

Ah. One of those. Or was she? Maybe she wanted Dan for herself. Well, she could have him.

No, she can't, a little voice inside my head protested.

I told it to shut the hell up. "Who says I need babysitting?"

"You're using up valuable resources, resources we could use to track Tate."

"You don't even know if Tate's alive."

"Exactly why we shouldn't be wasting time with you."

No beating around the bush there. Frustration oozed in her voice, I figured she'd been beating her head up against the dead end of Tate's trail for a while now. But her frustration wasn't my problem. And I was feeling crappy enough to take a little pleasure in adding to it. "Well, I guess you'll just have to trust Dan's judgment, won't you?" I said sweetly.

She frowned, started to say something, then stopped.

I wasn't in the mood for peeved werewolves. Or whatever she was. Time for this conversation to end. "I tried to turn the job down. But Dan wouldn't take no for an answer. You know how he gets when he wants something." I stared at her then raised one eyebrow as color crept across that perfect skin. "Or maybe you don't. Or you wouldn't be here trying to get me to quit behind his back."

Despite the blush, she didn't blink, which was kind of creepy actually. I wondered again just what kind of were she was.

"Special Agent Gibson is in charge of this case. I'm following orders."

"Great. In that case, why don't you go tell Jason what you need and get to work?"

If looks could kill, I'd be one dead little human. Weres are great at the killer stare—it's that whole predator thing. Luckily I'd had Jase practicing his vamp version of a killer stare on me for several years. He'd never tried the full on 'you are under my power' bit vamps can do but he could do intimidating when he tried. As could my supernatural clientele. And I'd perfected my calm under pressure act being grilled by lawyers in court. So I was able to act perfectly calm under the weight of Esme's glare despite the hairs quivering on the back of my neck.

I took another soothing sip of coffee as Esme stalked out of my office. If she'd been in animal form, her tail would've been twitching and her hackles raised. Her annoyance ramped up the tingle her were energy gave me and the hairs on my arms joined the ones on my neck.

As soon as she was safely gone, I reached for the ibuprofen in my drawer and turned to my overflowing inbox. Hopefully the rest of the day would be less eventful.

Peace and quiet reigned for a few hours. I returned calls and emails, calmed one frantic client who was wigging out because of an approaching court date, ran some extra data mining routines to try and make some progress on the Anderson case and generally distracted myself from whatever Jase and Esme were doing in the other rooms.

My stomach had just started to demand something greasy to counteract the lingering effects of tequila when Jase popped his head around the door.

"All set," he said.

"What's all set?" I was still half focused on the spreadsheet in front of me.

"Agent Valkyrie has left the building and our security's as good as it's going to get."

I laughed. "Don't let her hear you call her that."

He wrinkled his nose. "She's a pussycat."

"Literally?" Knowing would make my life easier. The different species had very different protocols and hot buttons. But I wasn't going to give her or Dan the satisfaction of asking for the lowdown.

"Didn't ask."

"Some assistant you are. You were probably too busy staring at her face." It came out snippier than I intended.

Jase shrugged. "She's pretty, if you like that thin blonde look. I've always preferred brunettes. Or I would if I liked girls." He grinned.

"Enough with the sucking up. What else did she say?"

"Something about the files being delivered later today."

"Good. Then we have time for lunch." I stood, trying to ease the kinks in my back and looked at my watch. It was nearly four. "Let's hit Wash's. I need a burger." Wash's sold synthetic blood and served it in frosted milk shake glasses so it didn't look like blood. Jase would drink and I'd stuff my face and Jase would steal some of my fries. Vamps can eat human food but they don't need to.

The information about Tate arrived about an hour after I got back from my red meat and grease fix. An unsmiling guy in a boring dark suit that practically screamed 'government agent' delivered a box of printouts and a small pile of gleaming data discs neatly labeled 'Tate'. The name alone was enough to make me wish I'd taken Esme's advice, an echo of the nausea I'd felt from the photos swirling in my stomach as I lined up the information neatly on my desk.

"Stop being a wimp, Keenan." I muttered to myself. I'd taken the job, so now I had to suck it up and try to help catch the bastard.

Something told me it wasn't going to be quite that simple.

An hour into it, I knew it for sure. The data was old and tangled and Tate's accounts were slickly set up. Expressly designed to baffle the sort of investigation I was attempting. Which was a good thing. The challenge made it easier to forget about the vampire and the werewolf and focus on the purity of numbers and the data trail.

I just finished wading through the first stack of printouts when my phone rang. I hit the speaker button while I started slotting the printouts in files. "Ashley Keenan."

"Is that any way to answer the phone? What happened to 'hello'?"

"Hello, Aunt Bug."

"Hello yourself," she said tartly.

"What's up?"

"Just letting you know I'm in town early. I got a ticket to the matinee of that play I was telling you about. Are you free for dinner tonight?"

Aunt Bug was a theatre nut. I tried to keep her away from Jase. Every time the two of them got together, the talk turned to musical numbers, composers and choreographers. It made me want to stab my eyes out and only encouraged Jase's obsession with writing the first great vampire musical.

Given his musical talent was limited to a pleasant but not spectacular singing voice, this mainly consisted of him inserting 'vampire' in the title of the show and the lyrics. So far I'd suffered through renditions of *Funny Vamp*, *My Fair Vampire* and *The Vampire of the Opera*. Which was way above the call of duty. I didn't want him getting inspired all over again.

Plus I was still full of burger. "Let me check."

Aunt Bug hardly ever tried to alter our plans. I wondered if something was wrong and tried to pull my brain away from Tate to think about my calendar. Between the FBI and my usual clients, it was looking a bit chaotic. "Not really, Aunty. Work is just crazy. But tomorrow I'm all yours."

She sniffed. "You work too hard."

"Someone's got to keep me in shoes."

"You should find yourself a man—"

"I'm sorry, Aunty." I wasn't ready to have this conversation for the umpty-thousandth time. "I've got to go. There's a client waiting." I crossed my fingers, hoping she wouldn't call me on my little white lie.

She made a disbelieving humph noise but said goodbye. Lucky escape. Any discussion about men I have with Bug always ends back at 'why I was an idiot to leave Dan'. Mules have nothing on her when she makes up her mind. She'd lost the man she'd loved to illness too young. Which left her with very pointed views on not wasting love. She'd never remarried, said she'd just never met another man who made her feel the same way as her husband. I think that's why she became a teacher—so she'd have more children than she could ever had herself to watch over and nurture. Of all those children, I was the one she cared most about. So I got the most grief.

I replaced the phone and tried to settle back down to Tate. I had an hour before my next appointment, so I might as well dig in. Who knew? Maybe I'd get lucky and stumble across something right away that the FBI had missed. But something told me that was about as likely as Jase turning straight and Aunt Bug never bringing up Dan again.

CHAPTER FIVE

BY THE TIME I LEFT work just after midnight, I was looking forward to spending my Saturday with Bug and not thinking about numbers at all. Tate's accounts were convoluted in a way only a sick mind could have devised. So far I hadn't found anything the FBI had missed.

No way was I going to Dan with *nothing*.

I hoped that a day of shopping, great food and good booze might give my subconscious time to work on things and shake something loose.

After a good night's sleep, of course.

I spotted the car as soon as I turned down my street. It stuck out. I live on Mercer Island—Mercedes Island as it's known. The residents are well off, to put it nicely. The moms drive expensive SUVs, the dads drive sports cars or even more expensive SUVs and the teens have whatever the cool car of the month is.

Nobody drives the sort of boring white sedan parked a few houses up from mine. The windows were tinted and I couldn't see who was inside but I guessed it was one of Daniel's agents. It should've made me feel safe. Instead, it pissed me off. Upgrading my security arrangements was one thing but I hadn't agreed to be kept under constant surveillance.

Jase had already spotted two guys with earpieces in our lobby during the day. That much I could live with but I didn't like the thought of Daniel knowing my every move. I almost pulled up next to the car then thought better of it. The agent was just doing his job.

Daniel, on the other hand, was being annoying.

I pulled into my drive in a worse mood than I'd started the day in. I needed a bath, some ice-cream and some sleep. By morning I'd be in the right frame of mind to yell at Dan before heading out to join Aunt Bug. I bumped my front door shut behind me, not bothering to turn on the hall light. Then I froze. Something about the house felt strange.

My heart bumping crazily, I held my breath and listened. Nothing. Silence. My ears picked out a vague hum of traffic, the louder gurgling of my refrigerator and the tick of the clock on the wall above my hall table. Nothing to cause the hairs on the back of my neck to stand up the way they were.

Not that I was likely to hear a vamp or were if they lay in wait. Jase or Dan would know in a second but I had to rely on human senses. I waited, straining to hear, trying to keep my breathing soft despite the panicked thumping of my heart. The house smelled normal, like the lilies on my hall table and a faint hint of coffee from breakfast. Nothing out of the ordinary. No subtle buzz in the air that might mean a were nearby.

"There's an agent right outside," I told myself firmly. I was just being jumpy. Dan had spooked me more than I'd known. I took a deep breath, reached out carefully and flicked the light switch.

The weird feeling vanished as warm yellow light flooded the hall, and I sighed with relief. Then froze as another sensation replaced the weirdness. One just as disquieting. *Loneliness*. My house felt empty. No warmth. No life. No other person to give me a hug and tell me I was okay. That I didn't have to do it all alone. I'd had that once but now there was just me and an empty house. Empty enough to make me do something stupid.

Like haul out my cell and dial Dan.

He answered before I had a chance to think better of it. "Hello?"

I'd expected a sleepy voice but he sounded wide awake. And there was noise in the background. Voices and laughter and music.

Was he out?

"It's Ashley. I—"

"Is everything okay?" His agent voice, all controlled and professional. Suddenly I felt foolish.

"Yes, I—" I stopped as more laughter bubbled up in the background. Female laughter. My hand curled tight around the phone. Now I *really* wanted to know where he was. "Sorry, I'm interrupting."

"It's fine. I'm—" he hesitated, just for a second. "I'm at a pack meeting."

A pack meeting. With the other werewolves. With female werewolves, presumably. Ones who probably didn't mind at all that *he* was a werewolf. For a moment I had an insane urge to cry. But, somehow, I kept it together. "Isn't it kind of late?"

"We had a couple of successful First Changes last week. We're still celebrating."

"Oh." First Change. That was a big deal. For the kids, it happened around puberty. For those who got bitten—voluntarily or not—the first full moon after they got infected. Not everyone survived, so successful transitions were cause for joy. And week long parties, it seemed.

"I should let you go."

"Ash, why did you call?"

I'd bite my tongue off before saying 'I'm lonely and I miss you'. Not when he was out partying with the very people who'd taken him from me. I focused on the anger in that thought. Anger was easy. I was used to it. And it helped keep the other stuff away. "I just wanted to tell you that if you don't want me to know I'm under surveillance, you'd better tell your boys to pick more appropriate vehicles for their location."

"Who says I didn't want you to know?"

"For Christ's sake, Daniel. I'm not a child."

"What's that got to do with anything? Tate might be out there. He won't care how mature you are when he rips your throat out."

I knew he was right. I was more than happy someone was watching out for me. I just hated the fact it was Daniel. And it was turning me into a four year old. A four year old thoroughly creeped-out by the image he'd just put in my mind. "And if he finds me then whose fault is that?" Which was completely unfair. If the pictures were anything to go by, Tate had no trouble keeping track of anyone he wanted to.

Dan swore. "You know, this is fun but if you're just calling to bitch at me, then perhaps it can wait until morning."

"Fine."

All I got in reply was silence. My cell showed he'd disconnected. Great. I slid down the wall till I was sitting then tipped my head back to bang it gently against the plaster a few times.

I had to stay away from Daniel. All the energy between us had to go somewhere and if it wasn't being used for sex then it would drive us both crazy as we took swipes at each other.

After I'd finished calling myself five kinds of idiot, I hauled myself to my feet and walked to my bedroom. Every light in the house was blazing by the time I'd finished the trip and I'd satisfied myself no monsters were hiding in the closets or under the bed.

But despite the evidence of my eyes, I couldn't shake the unease, probably due to Dan's latest charming image. I kept picturing Tate looming out of the darkness. Kept picturing someone finding me in the sort of dark clotted pool of blood I'd found my parents lying in.

I wasn't getting to sleep any time soon. And I didn't want to work. I wanted contact. *Any* kind of contact.

So I changed into my slinkiest jeans, spiked heels a dominatrix would be proud of and a silver halter top Jase had given me for my last birthday. It had about as much material in it as a handkerchief, so I'd never actually worn it in public until tonight. But tonight I was feeling defiant. I needed to do something alive. Needed to *feel* alive.

I slicked on eye shadow, a double coat of mascara and my favorite red lipstick then picked up the phone again to make another call. To someone I knew would be awake and up for whatever wildness it would take to soothe me.

Forty-five minutes later, the cab dropped me in front of Plasma and I smiled as Jase opened the door for me. "Remind me to give you a bonus this year."

Jase grinned, then whistled as he looked me up and down approvingly. "You give me a bonus every year. Looks like someone else might be getting one tonight. You look fab. I have great taste."

I grinned back, feeling some of my fears recede as we moved towards the club. Even from the sidewalk music pounded. "Sometimes." We bypassed the shorter than normal queue presided over by a vamp bouncer. Jase always got into the best clubs, straight or gay, living or dead.

"What are we drinking?" Jase yelled as the music swirled around us, a funky pop beat that was just what the doctor ordered.

I shrugged at him. "Surprise me."

He laughed and vanished into the crowd towards the bar. I made my way to a tiny table near the dance floor and watched the crowd flow to the beat. Plasma is a neutral club—sure it plays up the blood theme with black walls, neon red dance floor and gimmicky drinks served in blood packs but that's as dangerous as it got. Open to humans and non-humans as long as everyone behaved, it attracted the curious, the hip and the just-out-for-a-good-time. Vamps like Jase who had little interest in snacking on humans, the occasional were, and humans who were fine with supernaturals who weren't scary.

The no biting, no nonsense policy was strictly enforced by the club's owner and his crew of vamp bouncers. Anyone who didn't want to play nice, or was interested in playing the sorts of games that went on in the dark clubs, was quickly weeded out and sent on their way.

It was crazy and fun and full of beautiful people who knew how to shake their asses. And relatively quiet for a Friday. Normally a table by the dance floor would be prime real estate. I frowned slightly, scanning the crowd. Plenty of humans. A good sprinkling of weres, which made sense given the moon had been full last week. Not so many vamps.

Fine by me. Maybe there was a party on at one of the other clubs. Jase reappeared with two glasses brimming with bright green fluid.

I took a cautious sniff. "What's in that?"

He wrinkled his nose. "Don't ask."

Fair enough. I didn't really care. I drained half the glass and dragged Jase onto the dance floor as the music grew louder.

We danced for a while, shaking off the offers from the guys who flocked around both of us. After half an hour or so, I was getting thirsty. I made a drinking motion to Jase and headed to the bar.

"Water. And two of those green things."

The bartender nodded then looked past me and batted his eyelashes. I turned to find Jase at my shoulder.

"Sweetie, there are several gorgeous young men waiting for you to return." He reached past me for the glass beside mine.

I shrugged and sipped my drink.

Jase laughed and waggled the little paper skeleton hanging from his drink at me. "That's just mean. You can't go out dressed like that and spend all night dancing with me."

"Am I cramping your style?"

He shook his head. He wasn't dating anyone at the moment, having had his heart stomped on a few months earlier. "You're cramping yours. Why don't you take one of those guys home with you and work out the kinks?"

Tempting. A few hours of sweaty sex and I might sleep like a baby. I'm not a nun, I haven't been celibate for four years but somehow I knew whoever I took home, the only face I'd see above me tonight would be Dan's. And that wasn't going to relax me at all. "I'd rather just dance." I swiveled on my barstool, surveying the crowd, which had thinned out even more. "It's a little quiet here tonight. Is there something on somewhere else?"

Jase looked down at his drink and took a swig. It wouldn't do him any good, alcohol doesn't affect vampires, but Jase hadn't been a vamp long enough to shake all his human habits.

"Jase?"

He hitched a shoulder. "Maybe."

His tone made the booze in my stomach slosh uneasily. "What does maybe mean? Is something going on?"

"No."

Which either meant 'no' or 'I don't want to tell you'. The range of possibilities I didn't want to hear about in the vamp world was huge. But I didn't think Jase was avoiding telling me about something bloody going down at one of the dark clubs. "I don't believe you."

That earned me a sigh. "I thought you wanted to have fun?"

"I do. I also want to know what the hell is going on."

"Just rumors."

"Rumors?" My voice went higher than I'd intended and I gulped some more of the green stuff. It had a kick like a zombie and went a little way toward calming the sudden swirl of nerves in my stomach. "What sort of rumors?"

"Vague ones." Jase looked serious. "Not even rumors really. People are just...nervous."

By people he didn't mean humans. Nervous vamps. Wonderful. Not exactly a sign of good times ahead. "About what?" I started shredding the little paper skeleton. I kind of already knew what he was going to say.

"Tate. People are starting to say he's back."

Fuck. The FBI had a fucking leak. Or the vamp grapevine was even better than Aunt Bug's. I glanced around. I couldn't see any vamps close by and the pounding music would help stop anyone trying to listen in. Still, I dropped my voice to a whisper. "It's just one account. It might not be even *be* Tate."

Jase flashed a smile that was more fang than happiness. "Maybe. But like I said. People are nervous."

Nervous enough to stay out of the clubs. Tate was a non-discriminatory monster. He preyed on supernaturals as well as humans, if they were foolish enough to get in his way. So from their point of view, staying out of the human clubs would be sensible if Tate was about to resurface. And if the vamps were restless maybe it wasn't a cold case at all.

I scanned the crowd, all urge to party suddenly gone. Obviously the rumors hadn't gotten as far as the weres yet but it couldn't take long. They'd notice the lack of vamps in a couple of days and start to wonder why. Then the humans and, inevitably, the press would get wind of it.

Then Dan would have more than just me making his life miserable.

And people other than me would have a psycho vamp haunting their dreams. The entire population of my hometown for a start.

Great.

I scowled at my drink then drained it.

"Wanna keep dancing?" Jase asked.

I could tell his heart wasn't in it. "How about we go back to your place?" I didn't feel like going home to my empty house, agents or no agents. And my place wasn't set up for Jase. No blood. No windowless rooms if he did want to sleep. His place was better. For one thing, it meant any monsters coming after me would have to go through him.

Jase reached over and squeezed my hand. "It's going to be okay, sweetie."

I nodded, not believing it for a second. If Tate was really back then there'd be blood and pain before this was over. I just hoped it would be his, not mine or that of anyone I cared about.

CHAPTER SIX

"LATE NIGHT?" AUNT BUG DRAWLED as she opened her hotel door to me at half past too-goddamn-early the next morning.

I winced. Bug never spoke softly and the noise level made the nails currently spiking my brain spike harder. "Kind of." Next time I'd find out what was in the drinks. Letting a vamp determine the appropriate alcohol content was not such a good idea. I'd managed a couple of hours sleep at Jase's before I'd had to go home, change and get into town to meet Bug. Emphasis on the couple. Like two.

Her mouth quirked. "The good kind?"

I shook my head. "Not really."

"Hmmm."

She examined my face and I fought the urge to drop my gaze to the floor like a teenager caught crawling in after curfew.

"Well, come in. Room service just brought up some coffee."

Coffee sounded like heaven. I let my nose lead me into the living room of Bug's suite and practically inhaled the first cup.

"Better?" Bug asked, pouring a refill.

I nodded as the caffeine started to do its job and the nails retreated a little. "Much."

"I assume it wasn't Daniel keeping you up all hours?"

"Not in the way you think. And can we hold off on the Daniel talk until I'm awake?"

She arched one finely drawn eyebrow at me, head tilted to one side. Her gray hair was piled into its usual smooth bun, showing off her still great cheekbones and focusing attention on her nose. The Keenan nose, sharp like a blade. Luckily I'd escaped that little family legacy. Overall, her expression put me in mind of a grandmotherly eagle.

I gulped more coffee, trying not to feel like something small and furry waiting to be pounced on.

"As you wish." She picked up her own cup. Her movements were, as always, graceful and controlled.

In my current sleep-deprived, hung-over state, I felt like a slob in comparison and straightened on the sofa. "What did you want to do today?"

"I thought CoCA. Then shopping." Her mouth curved up. "But maybe we should start with a facial?"

Did I look that bad? Oh well. A facial sounded heavenly. Definitely better than contemporary art. The day spa attached to the hotel was wonderful and Aunt Bug couldn't grill me with a face covered in mud. Plus I might even be able to catch a nap. "Sounds great. I'll call the concierge."

Seven hours later I felt much better. After a facial, lunch and a coordinated blitz of the all the best downtown shops, everything was back to normal. I'd coaxed Aunt Bug into getting a makeover at Sephora then giggled as she earned a whistle from a couple of old guys hanging out at the deli near the hotel.

"See, Aunt B. You've still got it."

She rolled her eyes at me but she was blushing. "Don't be silly, Ashley. Those men should know better." She stopped in front of a jewelry store and peered in at the display, avoiding looking at me.

I laughed. "They're old, not dead."

"And you're young, not old. Do you want to start talking about *your* love life?"

I saw her eyebrows arch in her reflection in the window and shook my head hastily. "Nothing to talk about. How about you? Is the Reverend chasing you around the pews yet? Or that guy from bridge...what's his name?"

"Stanley. And he's just a friend."

"Men never want to be just a friend, Aunty."

She turned from the store window and pinned me with the eagle eye again. "That's a very cynical view of life. You and Jason are friends."

"Jase is gay. And a vampire."

"You and Dan were friends."

Yeah for about two weeks before we decided we'd better jump each other before we spontaneously combusted. "And look how well that ended."

"He loved you."

"He's a werewolf. And I really don't want to talk about him."

"So you keep telling me." The tone said she wasn't really ready to drop one of her favorite subjects but that she'd let me off for now. She looked at her watch. "It's time to go back to the hotel and get changed for dinner, anyway."

Three martinis, one rib-eye and a decadent chocolate mousse later, Bug finally returned to the topic of Dan.

"Are you going to tell me about this case you're working on?"

"I can't really."

"It must be serious for the FBI to be involved. You did say Daniel worked for the FBI now, didn't you?"

I hadn't but what did that matter? Bug's grapevine had provided her with the information anyway. "Yes, he does. And yes, it's serious. But there's nothing for you to worry about." I twisted in my seat, signaling for another round of drinks so she wouldn't see my face as I lied.

She'd never give up pushing and prodding at me if she got the faintest hint there was something to worry about. And she wouldn't stop worrying for a second if she had any inkling Tate might be back on the scene.

She'd given me my freedom as a kid. In fact, she'd practically forced me out the door and back into some semblance of a normal life. Still, it had definitely cost her at times. She stayed up 'til I got home and she very rarely slept before I was safely tucked up in bed, the doors were all locked, and the alarms switched on.

She worried about me. Worried I wouldn't ever get over losing my family and have a normal life. Worried more about what might happen to me if I did. She'd been overjoyed when I'd fallen so hard for Daniel straight out of college.

Maybe that's why she hadn't quite let go of him yet; she was looking for someone who'd protect me as fiercely as she had. Who loved me as much as she did. Someone to keep me safe when she couldn't any longer.

The waiter brought two more martinis, dirty, the way Bug liked them. I'd rather have a margarita any day but the martinis were our thing. Bug sipped hers slowly and just watched me.

"Daniel's fine," I said at last, more to get it over and done with than anything else. We had this conversation at least once every time we hung out. At least this time, I had some information other than "I have no idea". It might mollify Bug into letting me off the hook. "He's doing well at the FBI."

"Is he seeing anyone?"

"I don't know. I didn't ask."

"Why not? If you're over him, you wouldn't care if he was dating."

Ouch. That hit a little too close to home. I stabbed at the olives in the bottom of my glass with a toothpick. "I don't care. I just don't want to know. I'm helping him with a case. That's it. So don't go picking out wedding colors or anything crazy in your head."

She pursed her lips, shook her head a little. "I'm not." She wasn't? Why not? Just because I wasn't dating Dan any more didn't mean I'd never marry. I'd dated a couple of other guys since—granted, not for a long time, but I'd tried. I just hadn't hit the jackpot yet. "I'm only twenty-seven. There's plenty of time."

"Time goes faster than you think," she said owlishly then drained her martini.

I sighed. She was right, I knew that. Just like I knew she only pushed me because she loved me. I knew just how fast things could be taken away. But time, slow or fast, wasn't going to fix Dan and I. The only thing it might do was let us both let go of the pain.

I was getting closer. I could feel it. There's an element of luck to what I do. Or instinct, maybe. Sometimes there's nothing else to explain the feeling telling you to follow one trail and not another. To chase down one name in a list of company directors or try a certain account number when there are hundreds to choose from.

It doesn't happen often but when it does, I've learned to listen.

And today, after a lazy Saturday with Bug and a Sunday spent mostly running into brick walls at work, certainty that I was making progress had filled me. No Monday-itis for this little accountant. I hummed as I typed in the last six digits of a complicated account number and hit enter. But instead of the log-in screen I expected, my screen went black.

'I'm watching you'. The letters that flashed up next were huge and blood red. Then they changed to the photo of me at my parent's funeral. Startled, I squeaked and pushed my chair back. Jase was in the room before I could blink.

"What?"

"The screen." I sucked in a breath, trying to convince myself I was being stupid, and then laughed. But even to my ears it came out high and strange.

Jase looked at me, concern drawing his eyebrows together. Then he stepped between me and the desk, bending down to look at the monitor. "It looks normal."

I peered around him. He was right. Just my normal island wallpaper and my browser page. "O-kay."

Jase turned back to me, leaning against the desk with his arms crossed. "Ashley, what did it do?"

"It said..." I tried another laugh—surely this was someone's idea of a sick joke—but it came out more like a yelp. "It said 'I'm watching you'."

"I'm calling Agent Gibson."

"No." I grabbed for Jase's arm but he avoided me easily, twisting with unnatural speed to move around me. I turned to face him. "Don't do that. And don't panic. I've come across this sort of thing before."

I had. People hiding their tracks often set up booby traps to scare off anyone who tries to find them. This was just one of those.

Yeah, right, said my subconscious. *If it's a generic booby trap, then why was there a photo of you?* Something *not* to think about. I tried to shake off the vaguely queasy feeling in my stomach.

Jase took advantage of my distraction to get between me and the computer again, breezing past me in a waft of expensive aftershave. He started tapping at my keyboard.

I tried to see around his back. "What are you doing?"

"Esme said they'd be recording whatever you did on your computer."

"They what?" I gave up trying to look, sinking down into my chair instead.

They were recording? Oh God. My emails? Everything? I tried to remember if I'd bitched to anyone about Dan or the Taskforce via email over the last few days. I couldn't remember anything. I tended not to use my work computer for anything personal anyway. My private accounts were on my phone and my home laptop. "And you didn't think to tell me about it?" I scowled at Jase.

He shrugged one shoulder. "I assumed you knew."

Which was reasonable. After all, I was the one who'd made the agreement with Dan. Dan who hadn't mentioned this level of surveillance. Obviously we needed to have a discussion about full disclosure. First the agents watching my house, and now this. I should've doubled my hourly rate. I shuffled my chair closer to Jason, watching him in resignation as he worked some computer magic.

Jase kept tapping and then, as I watched, made a satisfied noise as the screen turned black and the letters flashed again. He growled, low in his throat. "Is this what you saw?"

I nodded, "I—" then the photo flashed up again. Crap. Now I was in for it.

"Fuck, Ashley. That's bad." He grabbed the phone, hit something on the speed dial. "Can I speak to Special Agent Daniel Gibson please? Tell him it's Jason Trent from Ashley Keenan's office."

"Give me the phone." And why the hell did I now have Daniel's number on my speed dial? I was rapidly tiring of 'let's keep Ashley in the dark'.

He avoided my grab for the phone, shook his head, nodded toward the computer. "You weren't going to tell me about the photo, were you?"

"I would've." I grabbed for the phone again.

Jase stood, holding it out of reach. "Sure, you would. You're playing with fire here. And it's dumb to do it just because you don't—" he brought the phone back down—"oh, hello, Agent Gibson."

I heard the vague rumble of Dan's voice on the other end of the line. I wanted to hit speaker-phone and listen in, but then Jase might get really peeved.

"We have a situation here. Ashley's triggered something on her computer. There was a message and a photo of her. Uh-huh. Okay." He yanked the network cable out of the back of my computer then hung up the phone. "They'll be here shortly. He said not to touch anything."

I sank back into my chair, scowling at the monitor. Hopefully Jase would think I was as annoyed as I looked. Truth was, I'd rather put my hands on a live snake than touch my keyboard right now. Not when the photo of me was still taking up the screen.

Jase scowled too, fangs bared. An indicator that he was very upset.

I bit my lip, wondering if *I'd* screwed something up, if I hadn't been careful enough?

What if it was Tate and I'd tipped him off?

Shit.

We both stared at the photo for a while, though I'm not sure what we were expecting to happen. With the network cable pulled out, my computer was cut off from the world. At worst, my firefighter of the month screensaver might pop-up and embarrass me a little, but that was about it.

"Coffee?" Jase asked eventually in an apologetic tone. His scowl had eased back to a vague frown of worry.

"No, thanks." I managed a smile. He'd done the right thing. When in doubt, yell for help. That was the smart thing to do. But I'd freaked out. When yelling for help meant yelling for Dan, my mental heels apparently dug in. I was going to have to get over that if I was going to make it through this case. Spank my inner two year old and act like an adult. An adult who wanted to stay alive.

"How was Aunt B?" Jase asked.

I appreciated the small talk. "She was fine. We—"

Dan appeared at my office door, two more agents behind him. He caught my gaze briefly, as if reassuring himself about something then looked at Jase. "Has the computer done anything else?"

"No," Jase said, then stopped and looked at me. "That was the first time, right?"

"Right."

Jase and Dan both looked as though they didn't believe me. I moved my chair out of the way of the desk and sat, not saying anything as Dan's agents converged on my computer. They were both weres, if the vague tingle in the air meant anything. Dan wasn't close enough to feel, which I was just fine with. So I had maybe three werewolves and a vampire in my office, all on edge. Not saying anything was the sensible plan.

Or at least not saying anything until they started firing questions at me. After I'd explained exactly what I'd been doing, what I hadn't been doing and answered every other obscure thing they asked, I subsided into silence again, gnawing a fingernail.

"You'll ruin your manicure," Jase said, coming over to perch on the arm of my chair. I jerked my finger out of my mouth. I could almost hear Aunt Bug saying 'Don't chew your nails, Ashley, it makes you look cheap.'

"Do you think it was Tate?" I said quietly.

Dan lifted his gaze from my monitor. "We don't know."

"I didn't ask what you knew, I asked what you thought."

"Speculating doesn't help. I like to work with facts." He turned back to the computer.

Me too. But the facts I had weren't comforting.

Fact. Someone knew I'd been after Tate's accounts.

Fact. That someone knew who I was.

Fact. Jase said the vamps were nervous.

Fact. I could smell Dan's wild scent again. Which meant, he wasn't as calm as he was pretending to be.

Fact. Neither were the other two wolves, if that's what they were. Their scents weren't as strong as Dan's or as enticing but I could still smell them, stronger than a man, or maybe just different. Nervous FBI werewolves.

That couldn't be a good thing.

And the biggest fact of all, the one I was trying not to think about, was that the last time Tate had taken an interest in my life, he'd killed a lot of people. My family. My—Panic bubbled up in my stomach. I wasn't the only potential target. "I need to call Aunt Bug." My voice shook a little.

Daniel didn't look up what he was doing. "Why?"

"She was here this weekend. If they were watching me, they were watching *her*." Jase put his hand on my arm. I shook him off. "Dan, I need to call Bug, *now*."

"I'm sure she's fine." But he tossed me his cell.

My fingers shook as I dialed the numbers. It took me three tries in the end. And I got her machine. I hung up. "She's not there. She should be home by now. She left the hotel this morning."

"Maybe she's out," Jase offered.

I shook my head. "She said she was going to have a quiet night at home." I pressed redial. Machine. Again. I left a message asking her to call me. Then tossed the phone back to Dan and picked up my purse. "I'm going to see if she's okay."

Dan moved around the desk, blocking my path. His scent rose around me, confusing my growing panic with an equally strong pull of attraction. I backed up a step, only to bump into Jase behind me.

"Hold on a second," Dan said as I headed sideways, trying to avoid both of them.

"No! She's my aunt. My *family*." All I had left.

He blocked me again. "Let me call the Caldwell PD, get them to send someone over." He gestured at one of the men, who pulled out another cell phone and started dialing as he walked out into the foyer so I couldn't hear what he said. Jase headed after him, going who knows where.

I glared at Dan. My hands kept balling into fists despite my efforts to relax them. My pulse pounded in my ears. "Fine, you do that. But I'm going anyway."

Jase appeared, holding my jacket. "I'll come with you."

"Nobody's going anywhere," Dan growled.

It was almost a shout and it jolted my attention from Jase to Dan. The agent by my computer raised his head too, looking at Dan with surprise. I took a deep breath. Which was a mistake. Dan's scent was stronger still. Which meant he was getting more agitated. Not reassuring on any level. I moved away from him, stopping when I hit the edge of the small conference table with a bump that sent the vase of flowers on it rattling.

Jase caught the vase before it could fall and I jumped at his too quick movement.

"The two of you need to calm down. Wait until we check things out." Dan said, lowering his voice a little. "If she's there you'll have driven all that way for nothing. And if she's not..." He paused and fear swept back like ice sweeping under my skin. "If she's not, then you could be walking into a trap."

Well, yes. I watched the movies too. Had shouted at the stupid heroines who went rushing into danger but now I understood the urge perfectly. Bug was my family. And the need to go to her —to know she was okay—was stronger than any concern for my own safety. I wanted to go. *Had* to go. If anything happened to Bug because of me...I gripped the table, nausea rising.

"Ash, sit down."

I wasn't sure who was talking. The fear buzzing in my ears made everything sound far away and echoey. "No." I tried to lift my head but the room swayed. All I could see was my baby sister. My parents. Lying dead. That couldn't happen to Bug.

Hands came around my arms, pushed me gently into a chair. When I opened my eyes, Dan was kneeling in front of me. "Don't try and stop me, I—"

"Agent Gibson?" The agent who'd been speaking to Caldwell PD, reappeared.

"Yes?" Dan said.

The agent shook his head. "I'm sorry, boss. They did a drive-by. There's a car in the drive but no lights."

CHAPTER SEVEN

"TELL THEM TO BREAK IN," Dan said as I surged to my feet. He rose with me, hands clamped around my arms. "Ashley, calm down. She could just be out."

"You wouldn't tell them to break in if you thought that," I snapped, trying to dislodge his fingers. Stupid. I couldn't break a werewolf's grip any more than I could blink my eyes and be transported instantly to Bug's house. All I was doing was earning myself a nice set of bruises in the shape of Dan's fingers on my upper arms. Didn't stop me trying. "I need to go. Let me *go*."

Jase murmured something soothing. Dan just held me, his grip relaxing enough to feel supportive rather than restrictive. "Ashley, you need to calm down. Get her something to drink," he added, looking over my shoulder at Jase. "I don't need her going into shock."

"I'm not going into shock." I jerked against his hands again and this time he let me go. I only just avoided falling backwards. "I'm *not* hysterical. I'm *not* a stupid female. I just want to get to Bug."

"I know that," Dan said. "But you have to wait until we find out what's going on."

"You find out. I'm going."

He made an exasperated sound. "Be reasonable, Ash. You can wait a few more minutes."

"Fuck reasonable. Fuck you." I stormed over to my desk, grabbed my purse out of my drawer, scrabbling for my car keys. "I'm going."

For a moment he looked plainly furious then his face became cool and controlled. He stalked towards me. I could practically see his hackles bristling. But I stood my ground, my fingers clenched around my key tag. He snatched the keys out of my hands anyway. "If you won't see sense then fine. But I'm driving."

"Not in my car, you're not."

"No," he agreed with an evil smirk. He tossed my keys to the agent behind me then pulled another set out his pocket. "We'll take mine."

"I'm coming too," Jase said.

"What makes you think my car is set up for vamps?"

"You're Taskforce," Jase replied smugly. "If it's not, then you're an idiot."

Dan's eyes narrowed but he didn't say anything. We headed down to the garage under the building. Dan's car turned out to be a very nice Jeep with very vamp-friendly UV screened windows. It would be dark soon so Jase would be fine at the other end too.

I sat in back with Jase, leaving Dan in lone splendor up front. As soon as we pulled into traffic, Jase pulled out his cell and started making calls, canceling my appointments for the rest of the evening. I could see Dan watching me in the rear-view mirror, checking how I was doing.

Terrible just about summed it up.

I folded my arms, staring out the window at the cars crawling along beside us battling rush hour. "Can't this thing go any faster? Don't you have a siren or something?"

"I do, but I don't have a jet engine. There's nowhere for me to go in this traffic. We'll be out of it soon."

Not soon enough. Minutes crawled by and with each second my fingers dug harder into my palms. What if Bug was—I fought the urge to scream. Jase finished his calls then silently offered a hand.

I took it, not caring what Dan might think about me holding hands with a vampire in his backseat. And contact, any contact at this point, was comforting even if the slightly cool temperature of Jase's skin only emphasized the fact he wasn't human.

"Have you heard anything?" I asked after another minute or so. I knew it was a stupid question but I couldn't help it.

"Have you heard my phone ring?" Dan steered the Jeep around an ancient looking truck and into a slightly faster-moving lane.

"No."

"Then I haven't heard anything." He shifted in his seat and his gaze met mine again in the rear view mirror.

"I thought maybe you might have…"

His eyebrows rose. "What? Psychic powers? I'm a werewolf not a vampire."

So what? Wolves did use a form of telepathy in wolf form, and some of them carried those powers into their human shapes. How was I supposed to know Dan wasn't one of them? "You must have vampires on the Taskforce who are."

"Yes, and we save those powers for when they're needed. Cell phones are more reliable."

Beside me, Jase started to laugh then turned it into a cough as I jerked my hand free of his. I didn't know whether Dan was being annoying to distract me or just because he couldn't help himself but I didn't want Jase joining in.

"Well, maybe you could use your phone and find out what's happening with my Aunt."

"Ashley. They will call me if there's any news. Let me concentrate on driving and we'll get there a lot sooner."

"Fine." I settled back into staring out the window, not really seeing the scenery, willing every mile to go by faster. The drive seemed endless. I was ready to explode when we finally reached Caldwell. Dan's phone had stayed silent the entire trip.

When we pulled onto Bug's street, I spotted flashing blue lights in the distance. I was out of the car almost before Dan pulled to a stop, Jase close behind me, heading for Bug's at a run. I came to a halt when a young-looking unfamiliar Caldwell cop blocked my path at the end of Bug's drive. I looked around, trying to see who was in charge. Dan appeared next to me and pulled his badge out of his wallet. He flashed it at the cop and we were waved through. Only Jase's hand on my arm stopped me sprinting for the house.

A knot of officers stood on Bug's porch. They looked up as we approached, watching with professionally detached expressions.

"She's not here." One of the cops—tall and competent looking—came over to Dan. He flicked a glance at me, but then focused back to Dan. "We're checking out some places where she usually goes but no one's seen her since early afternoon. The neighbors—" He waved a hand to the left and I swiveled around to see Mr. and Mrs. Peterson standing on their porch, looking worried– "said they saw her drive in around midday. And the maid told us she was given the afternoon off. Mrs. Brenner said she was going to have an early night."

"Someone's taken her," I said.

Dan, Jase and the cop all looked at me. I could see them deciding how to respond, how to calm the upset female. I tried to keep my voice even, so they'd take me seriously. "Bug doesn't just wander off. If she's gone, someone's taken her."

"It's too early for us to know that," Dan said. "Officer—" he looked down at the cop's name badge—"Carlson. Are you in charge here?"

"No, sir. That'd be the Sheriff. He's up at the house."

I broke into a run, heading for the house. Jase and Dan both cut me off before I could reach my destination.

"Hold on," Dan said, catching hold of my shoulders. He rubbed a thumb along my collarbone. It should've been comforting. It wasn't.

I shoved at his chest. "I want to know what's going on."

"I know. But running up there like a crazy woman isn't going to achieve that. Let me go and talk to them."

"She's *my* aunt."

"I know. And I'm sure they'll have questions for you. So you need to stay calm. Can you do that?"

Fury boiled inside me, feeding the urge to push past him and go and demand information from the police. But just enough sense remained to see his point. An irrational niece wasn't going to help the situation and if I charged in hysterically, the cops wouldn't do much more than pat me on the head and send me off to the corner with a nice deputy.

There was time enough for yelling if the calm approach didn't get me what I wanted.

The wary expressions on Jase and Dan's faces didn't make it any easier to control my temper, but I knew I had to for Bug. I had to treat this like I would talking down a difficult client. Stay cool. Stay detached. Keep the personal out of it until I had time for a breakdown. I closed my eyes briefly, breathing through my nose until the knotted mess of anger and fear in my stomach eased just slightly. "Okay," I said when I opened them again. "We'll do this your way. For now."

Dan nodded, and then walked away. I watched from a distance as he introduced himself to the knot of cops on the porch and had a brief conversation. It probably only took a minute or two but it felt like hours as I stood there, not knowing what was happening.

After far too long a time he turned back and gestured for us to join him.

Fear flared back to life. I sucked in a breath and Jase took my hand again as we headed towards Dan.

"What is it?" I said, taking the stairs two at a time. Dan put a hand on my arm and I shook him off. "Just tell me."

"No one's seen Bug," Dan admitted. "They're out looking but so far, nothing."

For a moment, the officer's faces seemed to swirl around me. Caldwell wasn't that big. It had a main street, the churches, the schools and a mall on the outskirts of town. There were a limited number of places for someone to go. And usually five other people knew exactly where you were the second you stepped outside your yard. If no one had seen Bug...oh God. Cold panic swept over me, my stomach churned and my heart raced. I bent over, sucking in air before I hyperventilated.

Sheriff Thompson, 'that new sheriff' as Bug had been calling him for close to six years, helped me stand. I tried to smile but my mouth wasn't co-operating. The whole thing felt unreal. I'd seen Bug just yesterday and now Kenny Thompson—who'd been the star quarterback the year I'd entered junior high—had men out searching for her.

"Ashley, why don't you come sit down?" Kenny said, his voice gruff but concerned. I let him lead me into the house, sat obediently in one of the velvet wing chairs in the front room, listening as the police outlined to Dan what they were doing.

Being here in Bug's house should have been comforting. But it felt all wrong. The smell of men—sweat, cotton, tobacco, and aftershave—filled the room instead of the normal rose scent of Bug's perfume. Male voices rumbled around me instead of soft music and the southern tones of Bug's maid. Plus, the front room was for company—I never sat there. It was weird and just made me feel even more panicky. I ended up pacing the room until Jase came and made me sit down again.

This time I chose the stairs, where at least I could see what was going on.

The house got more crowded as more police and agents arrived. I sat on the staircase, feeling helpless, watching the movement swirl around me and trying to fight down the panic rising with each breath.

I couldn't lose Aunt Bug.

Not on top of everything else.

Everyone has their breaking point—a limit to the pain they can take. I knew this would be mine.

I clenched my hands together, watching the knuckles turn whiter and whiter. Jase bustled around making coffee and tea but I shook my head when he offered me one of Bug's pretty china mugs, feeling sick.

Instead I retreated further upstairs to my old room, sitting on the bed and hugging the pillow to my chest. I tried not to breathe in the familiar smells of lavender, Bug's laundry powder and sunshine-fresh linen too deeply. That was Bug all over, keeping the linen fresh in my room even though I wasn't planning on visiting for weeks. The combination just reminded me what I might lose.

It was impossible to think of a world without Bug. Even though I told myself I was being crazy, that they would find her any minute and that I was freaking out for nothing, part of me couldn't help looking around the room and remembering. There was the row of my gymnastics trophies she kept polished and the line of photos on a shelf above my bed, one from each of our summer vacations. The wooden bed frame, desk and bookcases she'd let me paint bright purple when I turned seventeen, though I'd relented three years later and repainted them to a pale blue we could both live with.

Even the quilt I sat on had been made by Bug soon after I came to live with her, after endless arguments about colors and patterns and me protesting I didn't want anything as old fashioned as a hand-made quilt when my friends all had cool rooms.

But secretly I'd loved the quilt. I still did. I'd even gotten Bug to make me another for my bed at home. Though it wasn't the same as this one. I ran a trembling hand over the wash-softened cottons, feeling the ridges of the quilting. I'd watched Bug sew it, in those early months when I was still reeling from my losses. We sat quietly in the evenings, the classical music she loved playing in the background while she stitched and I watched. It almost felt like she was stitching my life back together.

And now it was threatening to come apart at the seams again.

I buried my head in the pillow, biting back the sob that rose in my throat. I couldn't cry. I *wouldn't* cry.

"Ash?" The voice was soft in the doorway. Daniel. The pressure of tears grew stronger.

"Go away," I said, not lifting my head. I was only just holding it together. I didn't think I could take Dan as well.

He didn't move. I could smell him over the other fragrances of the room, even over the comforting scent of the pillow against my face. I willed him to leave. "I said, go away."

Soft treads on the carpet came towards me, not away. The mattress dipped and I felt the heat of his body next to mine. I tensed but when he put his arm around me and drew me close, I couldn't resist any more. I dropped the pillow and buried my face against the comfortingly solid expanse of his chest, breathing in the Dan smell, trying to pretend, somehow, that I was back four years ago and nothing bad was happening.

"We'll find her," he said, one hand moving slowly up and down my back leaving a trail of warmth that made me press close to him. "I swear, Ash. I'll find her for you."

I knew he would, if it was at all possible. The question was; what would he find? My mind shied away from the thought, and I pressed harder against him, trying desperately not to cry. His lips brushed the top of my head so softly I wondered if I'd imagined it. But the tingle that passed through me told me I hadn't, which forced me back to reality.

Leaning on Dan was crazy. As tempting as it was to fall completely to pieces in his arms, I couldn't afford to. It would be too hard to let him go again. I drew a shaky breath, summoned my last few ounces of strength, and managed to sit up, inching away from Dan.

"Is there any news?" My voice sounded rough, as though I'd actually cried the tears I was holding back. I swallowed hard, trying to ease the burning sensation that came from fighting down fear.

He shook his head, his expression a mix of worry and frustration. "The sheriff's men are still canvassing the town."

Something in his tone made my stomach sink. "You don't think they'll find her, do you?" I looked into his eyes for the first time since he'd entered the room, seeking the truth in the gray depths. But he had his cop face on, his eyes slick mirrors that revealed nothing. "Do you?" I repeated, voice rising.

He bent his head, one hand toying with the crease in his trousers. "Don't do this, Ash."

He wouldn't look at me. Why wouldn't he look at me? Fear clawed my stomach, redoubled the burning fingers gripping my throat. "What else am I supposed to do?" I said. "My aunt is missing, I'm sitting here, going crazy and I can't do anything. It's not like you need an accountant right now."

I was useless. Useless and Bug was missing because of me.

"No," Dan said, almost as if he could read my mind. His head lifted and his eyes sharpened. "There is something you can do."

"Anything," I pounced on the chance to have anything to take my mind off the endless circles of horror it was manufacturing.

"I need you to make a list of any place you can think of Bug might go. Check around for any appointments she may have written down."

"She puts everything in her phone. Did you find that?"

Dan shook his head. "The cops found her purse but no phone. Do you know if she syncs her phone calendar with her computer at all?"

I shrugged helplessly. Bug knew her way around a computer but I didn't know if she was likely to have linked her phone to the PC. "I don't know."

"Why don't you take a look? Her laptop has a password. You've got a better chance of getting into it than anyone else here."

True. Okay. I could do this. I took a deep breath. "All right. But I'd like to get some air first."

"Good idea." He pushed off the bed and held out a hand. I could still smell his scent, wild and oh so good, all around me. I wanted to pull him down to the bed and make him hold me again. Which was madness. I couldn't risk weakening when I was fighting so hard to stay strong. I stood without his help, looking away so I couldn't see his expression when I avoided his hand.

Dan followed me down the stairs but Kenny waylaid him when we got to the bottom. I took the chance to slip away, heading for the backyard. I hoped it would be quieter than the front.

My phone rang just as I opened the screen door and I jumped. I hadn't even known I had it with me; Jase must've slipped it into my pocket. I was tempted to ignore the call, after all it was probably just one of my clients bitching about something but then again, a distraction would be welcome. Anything to take my mind off the churning of my stomach, and the fear trying to take me over.

"Ashley Keenan," I said, walking into the yard a little, away from the noise of the house. I stopped by one of Bug's roses, breathing in the perfume floating on the warm evening air. It helped. A little.

"Hello, Ashley."

The voice was low and smooth and cold. I didn't recognize it.

"Who is this?" I pulled the phone away from my ear quickly to check caller id. The number was blocked.

"You don't know me."

I wasn't in the mood for prank calls. Especially not ones made by men with voices that made something stir uneasily in the pit of my stomach. "Well then, you'll have to excuse me but I'm kind of busy at the moment."

"Ah, yes. Your Aunt."

I froze. How the hell did he know about Bug? "Who is this?"

"Call me an interested party."

"If you know anything about Bug—" I looked around, wishing one of the officers would suddenly appear. I needed to tell someone what was going on. How far was it to the door? Fifteen feet, maybe. I turned toward the house.

"I wouldn't do that," the voice warned.

Oh God. Could he see me? Fear that had nothing to do with Bug spiked down my spine. "Do what?" I said, trying to sound casual as I scanned the garden. There was still a little light but not enough to see clearly. Shadows clustered around the branches of the trees and the sides of the garage. Anyone could be hiding in the depths.

I shivered. Nothing buzzed in the air to let me know a were was nearby but the man on the phone might be human, or a vamp.

"Just stay put. We're going to have a little talk, you and I."

I gripped the phone tighter. "I don't talk to strangers." Great. Apparently I was three years old when I got scared.

"Ah, but Ashley, I'm not a stranger."

Shit. That was even scarier. I swallowed hard then asked the question I had to ask. "Tate?" I closed my eyes for a second, praying I was wrong.

"If I was, do you think I'd answer?"

"No but I—"

"Ms. Keenan?"

One of Kenny's men—a tall wiry guy with a Caldwell PD cap pulled down low on his head—loomed up in the darkness. I didn't know him but I'd never been so happy to see someone in my life. Then I heard the dial tone in my ear. My mystery caller had hung up. I didn't know whether to be relieved or frustrated that I hadn't gotten any information out of him. I looked at the officer. "Yes?"

"Agent Gibson asked me to bring you this." He held out a blue spotted mug. I took it automatically, holding it tight so my hands wouldn't shake. The smell of hot, sweet coffee rose in the air and I took a mouthful, trying to calm my nerves. I was safe. There was an officer right beside me. The house was half full of vampires and weres and police. No psycho caller could grab me.

But the fact that there *was* a psycho caller was something Dan needed to know. "Thank you," I said to the officer. "Is Agent Gibson in the house?" I drank again, feeling the caffeine and sugar clear my head a little.

"Yes, ma'am. Was there something you wanted?" He was watching me intently and I suddenly realized my skin was tingling like he was a were. But as far as I knew, the Caldwell PD was one hundred percent human. Had been since Tate's attack.

I paused mid-swallow. Who was this guy?

Or was I just being jumpy? Maybe Caldwell had decided to join the 21st century. Only I was pretty sure Bug would've mentioned it. I swallowed and studied the man over the rim of my mug. There was nothing that screamed werewolf about him. Of course, there wasn't anything that screamed werewolf about Dan either, if you didn't know. Except for the tell-tale sensation that flowed over my skin around him. The same one giving me goose bumps now.

This guy was *definitely* non-human. And if he wasn't a Caldwell cop, I was in trouble.

"Nothing important," I lied. I didn't want to tip whoever this was off that I was onto him. My instincts screamed "run!" but that was pointless against a were. I had to try and bluff, hope that someone else would come out.

Jase, if you can hear me, help.

I didn't know whether Jase's talents extended to telepathy or whether he could hear a human like me but I was desperate.

But there was no movement from the house, no vampire running out the back door to my rescue.

I turned slightly, so I was more clearly visible from the house and drank more coffee while my brain raced. "Could you ask Agent Gibson to c-co-" I stumbled over the word, wondering why my tongue suddenly felt thick. "Come out here?"

My voice sounded weird and echoey. I tried to move and couldn't. The were's pale eyes seemed to flare then blur in the dying light. I shook my head, trying to remove the fog stealing over my brain. *The coffee*, I realized belatedly. There was something in the coffee. I opened my mouth to scream for help but nothing came out.

"Sorry ma'am," the were said, his voice falling and rising in a wave of distortion. "But we've got other plans for you."

The world went dark.

CHAPTER EIGHT

SOMETHING THUMPED IN MY ears. Or maybe thumped wasn't the right word. Pounded, perhaps. The sound was rhythmic. Regular. It should've been comforting, but something about it disturbed me. I rolled to one side then stilled as dizziness swept over me. The pounding grew louder and I finally worked out it was the sound of my pulse, throbbing in my head.

Something was wrong.

Why did I feel so strange? My eyes felt dry and crusted, resisting my efforts to open them. Even after rubbing them, I wasn't sure I'd succeeded. Wherever I was, it was dark. Pitch black. Hot. And moving. I levered my arms underneath me, tried to sit up. My head hit something with a thump.

Pain flared and I slumped back down, cursing. The new ache didn't make it any easier to remember something—anything—that would explain where I was. I searched my memories but it was like grasping at snow. Images flitted before my eyes then melted away. A man with dark hair, another with eyes that flared ice blue, and a pale rose tilting sideways in a darkened garden. None of it made sense.

Only one thing was clear. Wherever I was, it wasn't good.

My pulse pounded harder at that realization, racing as panic swept through me. I grasped for calm, schooling myself to breathe slowly. The air smelled like dirt and oil and something less pleasant like rot or mold. Not comforting.

Nausea rose as the scent and the continuous motion made my stomach churn. I swallowed hard. Throwing up wasn't going to help anything.

Abruptly the motion ceased and I lurched sideways, banging my head again. Light blazed as the surface above me suddenly vanished.

Hands grabbed me. I screamed and kicked out at them, blinking back the tears the burning light brought to my eyes.

"None of that, you shouldn't even be awake," a male voice snarled.

I kicked harder, connecting with something warm and solid.

"Ow. Bitch." Fingers twined in my hair, grasping hard, bringing a gasp of pain to my lips. "Not so fun now? Good." The grip tightened, raising my head then slamming it backwards. Sparks flashed behind my eyes then darkness took me again.

When I woke for the second time I wasn't moving. Or, at least, whatever I lay on wasn't moving. My head, however, was spinning and it took me three tries just to roll over. A move my muscles protested vigorously, adding a chorus of aches and throbs to the sharp twinges in my skull.

Keeping my eyes closed so as not to make the spinning any worse, I ran my hands cautiously over the bits of me I could reach. Nothing felt broken or bleeding, though there was a lump on my forehead and another one at the back of my head that made me see stars behind my eyelids when I touched it. I was still wearing my suit trousers and my shirt but my feet were bare. And the cross around my neck had vanished.

Good news. I wasn't naked and I didn't seem to be tied up.

Bad news. I felt like someone had driven a tractor over me and then left the remains out to be trampled by elephants. Even my fingers hurt. What I really wanted was to go back to sleep and hope that this was all a nightmare. But I knew it was real. The fear quickening my pulse told me that.

I had to face my situation.

The surface beneath me was soft. A bed? I cracked my eyes open cautiously. The pain in my head stayed at the same level so I risked opening them further, desperate to find out where I was. My vision was blurry at first but soon the details came clear. A single bed in a room of about ten feet square. Dim light came from recessed bulbs in the ceiling, a sort of diffuse glow that gave no indication what time of day it might be. From my position I could see a door the same pale maybe-white, maybe-cream color as the walls and nothing else. I stared at the door—something about it was off. Then it hit me. No handle.

Locked in.

Fear flared stronger. Where the hell was I?

I drew a shuddery breath and steeled myself for the pain of rolling to my left. It took an effort. I panted through my mouth until the worst of the sensations subsided. I shouldn't have bothered. My new view revealed nothing. No windows, no pictures, no other furniture. Just a few slits high in the roof that had to be some sort of ventilation system and more of the lights in the ceiling. The air was cool and smelled kind of stale, the way rooms get when they haven't been used for a while.

Four bare walls and a bed and me. That was it.

I shivered and dug my hands into the blanket covering the bed, rolling again so I wrapped myself in it. The wool was scratchy and uncomfortable but it was warm. Not that warmth helped my shivering as my situation sunk home.

I was alone. Trapped. God knows where.

The shivers turned to shudders and I curled into a ball, huddling into the blanket. As I lay, my head eased a little and I suddenly remembered. Bug. The garden. The coffee. The not-cop.

Kidnapped.

Most likely by whoever had Bug. Call me wimpy but on top of everything else the thought was enough to push me over the edge. Sobs racked me, deep, heavy, gasping noises, the kind you can't stop even if you try. The kind you just have to cry out.

Eventually I did and then I just lay there, eyes and throat burning, trying to make some sense of what had happened. Trying not to succumb to the terror lurking in the back of my mind.

I had no idea how long I'd been unconscious. My left wrist, usually occupied by my mother's watch, was as bare as my feet but I was desperately thirsty and despite the residual sick feeling in my stomach, starting to feel hungry as well. So hours, not days. Surely I'd feel worse if I'd been out for days?

Though whatever they'd drugged me with could be affecting me. I'd had some screwy reactions to anesthesia in the past.

So really, I knew nothing. I lay still, trying to calm myself, and listened for clues to my location. Nothing. No road noise, no outside world noises, nothing at all to indicate anything lay beyond the four walls of the room. There was a soft background sound that made me think air conditioning but that was it. Wherever I was, it was well sound-proofed.

I reconstructed events in my head. I'd been in some sort of vehicle when I'd woken the first time. The details were sketchy but I was sure I'd been in a trunk. Which wasn't entirely useful. After all, I had no idea which way we'd gone or how long we'd traveled.

But arriving in a vehicle meant there might be one around if I managed to get free.

Big if.

But I was alive, so whoever had taken me didn't want me dead—not immediately anyway.

Hello not-so-comforting thought.

I burrowed deeper still into the wool blanket as another set of shivers wracked me. I breathed deep, hoping its stale scent could drive all the scary thoughts from my head.

Focus on the positive, Keenan. One bout of hysterics was all I was allowed. All I could give into if I was going to survive.

Okay, so I was alive. That might mean Bug was too. And, if I had anything to do with it, we were both going to stay that way until Dan—because if I knew anything, I knew Dan would leave no stone unturned to find me—rode to the rescue.

Summoning more courage than I knew I possessed, I forced myself to sit up. They might as well know I was awake, if they didn't already. Just because I couldn't see any cameras in the room didn't mean they weren't there. And there was no sense playing dead. A vamp or were could hear my heart beat several feet away.

Mr. Not-cop had been a were, so it seemed reasonable to assume that there could be more of them around. I might as well find out what I was up against.

I sat clutching the edge of the bed and waited. And waited. I have no idea how long I sat there but it felt like hours. And with each beat of my heart my nerves grew tauter and tauter.

Just when I was starting to think no one would come, that maybe they were just going to leave me here to rot, the door slid open with a faint hum.

And the face of the man who walked through the door was enough to make me wish that rotting *was* my fate.

Tate.

His face had haunted my nightmares for twelve years.

I knew every line of his features. I'd studied the pictures in the paper obsessively, wanting to be ready if I ever came across him. Ready to do what, I'd never been entirely sure but it involved pain and death. His.

But the papers couldn't convey the reality of the monster.

He looked normal enough. About six foot, average build, sandy brown hair in a nondescript spiky cut. The sort of guy you'd pass in the street without a second glance.

As long as you didn't look in his eyes.

That was the part the pictures didn't reveal.

Whatever was behind those eyes had nothing human about it. It wasn't just vampire but something far more primitive. Soulless. Something that screamed predator. Evil. Run. Hide. Die.

The sort of terror in the night that men had discovered fire to protect themselves against.

I pushed myself back on the bed instinctively.

"Ms. Keenan," Tate said. "How nice to see you."

He might have been greeting someone at a garden party. The sheer detachment in his tone was creepier than any threat or menace could be. Despite myself I inched further back until I felt my butt hit the edge of the mattress. Any further and I'd fall.

"Pity I can't say the same," I managed to say with a mouth suddenly dry as dust.

"Now, now, be polite." He leaned against the door, a slight smile on his face as if he were admonishing a naughty child.

I bit back the retort that rose to my lips. I didn't want to bait him. Not when I had no idea how he might react.

No taunting the serial killer.

Instead, I studied him, avoiding his eyes.

He submitted to my examination, the smile still playing around his lips. It looked fake somehow. Like expressions and emotions were something he practiced in front of the mirror rather than something he had any real experience with.

Whatever it was that lurked inside him, it felt nothing.

"See anything you like?"

I dropped my gaze, tried to grow smaller. I didn't look away completely though. Number one rule in every self-defense class I'd ever taken is don't take your eyes off the attacker.

I had no idea what Tate might do.

"I'll take that as a no." He flowed into the room, put a hand—inhumanly cool—under my chin, and forced my head up. I didn't resist but made sure we didn't make eye contact.

"You've grown up quite nicely, haven't you? One of the lucky ones."

Lucky ones? I jerked away. His grip tightened, stopping me.

"You have an interesting definition of lucky," I said.

"You're alive. That's pretty lucky."

Alive and held captive by the monster who killed my family, oh yeah, I was rushing right out to buy a lottery ticket. "My family isn't."

"Ah yes. Caldwell. That was fun. So much pain in one night. Do you like pain, Ms. Keenan?"

I shook my head, suppressing a shiver.

Tate laughed delightedly. "Excellent, I knew I picked the right one."

I jerked my head up. "What does that mean?"

"You didn't think I left you alive accidentally? Oh no. I chose my survivors."

"Ch-chose?"

"Yes," he sat on the bed beside me.

He smelled almost human. Normal scents of cotton and soap and aftershave surrounded him. But underneath it was something I couldn't describe. Couldn't name. But the smell set my teeth on edge, made me want to run.

"You see, it's not very interesting just to kill everyone." He ran a hand across my hair and my stomach turned over. If there'd been anything in it, I might have thrown up.

"I would've thought that was plenty of entertainment for someone like you."

"Yes. You would. No one understands." He sounded scornful. "No one has the vision to realize it's better with survivors."

"Better?" I didn't want to hear this but somehow I couldn't stay silent. Not if he was going to tell me something about that night. Or offer some justification—however twisted—for what he'd done.

"Someone left behind to feel the pain." He pushed off the bed, faced me. "Someone to suffer. To hate being left alive. I picked the ones I felt would survive best. The ones who would hurt most even though they'd lived. You looked strong. You saw me...do you remember?"

I shook my head, swallowing against the pain and regret tightening my throat. I didn't remember anything about that night between the time I'd gone to sleep and the time I'd been woken by the sound of sirens to find my sister dead on the floor beside me.

"What a shame. We had a moment, you and I. You saw me. Standing over your bed. But you didn't scream. No. You reached for your phone. So I had to put you under. But I knew then you were a survivor. A strong one. I wonder, if you'd screamed, would you have warned them? Would they have lived?"

No! I almost screamed it. *No.* There was nothing I could've done.

But part of me doubted.

Part of me wondered if he might be right.

Part of me died a little, thinking if I'd screamed, maybe I'd be dead, yes. But maybe they'd be alive.

"Think about it," Tate continued, "If you'd screamed, perhaps your father might have heard you. Saved you all." His hand stroked my hair again and I fought not to leap away. Stay still. Don't attract attention. Don't draw the gaze of the big bad predator.

"Then again, he didn't hear me come into their room. At least, not until your mother started screaming."

I clapped my hands over my ears, bile rising in my throat. I couldn't listen to any more of this or I'd go crazy. But despite the desperate press of my palms, I could hear Tate laughing.

A rolling, cutting, low sound that twisted humor into something much darker.

You know, I suddenly heard him, clear as a bell despite the fact he was still laughing. *If you don't take your hands down, I'll just talk to you this way. But you might not like it. This way I can do more than talk. I can* show *you. Show you their faces.*

I dropped my hands like my ears had caught fire. Only to be greeted by even louder laughter.

"Good," he said. "This will all be dreadfully boring if we get to that part too quickly."

This time I almost retched as I struggled to breathe.

Fear flooded my body, paralyzing me.

I knew I was meant to stay calm in this situation. To think. To help myself. But all I wanted to do was curl up and hide. Somehow I forced myself to stay still, to suck in air and continue trying to function. "What do you mean?"

"Ah." He cocked his head, regarding me with an expression you might see on a small boy deciding whether or not to squish a bug. "I didn't finish explaining."

"Explaining what?" I didn't want to know the answer but I could almost hear Dan in my head, the old rules he'd drilled into me when he'd been a cop. Self-defense if you're attacked. Keep them talking. Buy time. Don't antagonize but be strong.

Tate just smiled at me with those dead eyes.

"Explain what?" I repeated. "What do you want with me? Where's my aunt?" Get information, that was the other rule. Though I'd learned that one from overdosing on cop shows rather than anything Dan had told me.

"I was explaining about survivors. All that lovely pain. And you know what the best part is?"

I stared up at him, unable to think of any sort of reply. He'd avoided my question about Bug. Was she even alive? He leaned in closer so his face was only inches from mine. His breath stank like something had rotted in his mouth. "The best part is that survivors start to forget. They think it's over. They *relax*."

"I haven't forgotten anything," I spat.

He smiled, baring his fangs. "No? Maybe not. But you did relax, didn't you, Ashley? You thought one bad thing was all that you were going to get."

Not really. Not after Dan. Did he not know about Dan? Somehow I doubted it. If he'd been watching me all these years then he had to know about the most serious relationship of my life. But maybe to Tate, anything short of death and mutilation didn't qualify as bad. "I'm not a child. I know bad things happen."

Tate, just for a moment, looked almost pitying. "But you're all children. You never learn, you humans. Never learn it's best to not to hope."

Right now, the only thing I was hoping for was Tate's death.

"All that hope for the future," he said softly. "Shiny bright hope." His finger ran across my cheek, making me flinch as he dragged his fingernail just under my eye. "Too bad. You shouldn't have gone poking around in my accounts." His hand grabbed my chin, fingers digging hard. "Silly girl. You reminded me."

"Reminded?" I was sure my heart was going to explode as it raced, every instinct shrieking for me to run. I couldn't think.

"That it's time for the next step." He released me and then, almost too fast for me to follow, rose to his feet and grabbed both my wrists in one hand, hauling me to my feet as easily as a man lifting a kitten by the scruff of its neck.

He held my wrists above my head, leaving me almost dangling, toes just on the floor. My shoulders shrieked with pain and my heart hammered loud enough for me to hear each beat.

"Time for round two," he said and ripped my shirt from my body.

CHAPTER NINE

I SCREAMED THEN, TERROR welling out of my throat and into the air before I could choke back the sound. Tate let me scream, holding me motionless while he ripped my clothes off with his free hand. Wool and silk and elastic all parted under his touch like tissue.

For a long moment he held me there, looking at me with a dispassionate expression then he released my hands so quickly my knees buckled and I collapsed to the floor biting my lips until I tasted blood to keep from screaming again.

Tate crouched in front of me, yanked my head back by my hair, eliciting another shriek. I dropped my eyes, determined not to let him capture my mind.

"Oh, be quiet," he said, sounding bored. "I don't fuck humans."

I curled my knees up as far as possible, trying to expose less of myself to him.

"Of course, I can't say the same for my compatriots but they're fairly obedient. When I tell them to behave. Do you want me to tell them to behave? Look at me when you answer."

I dragged my eyes to his and nodded, fighting not to throw up for real this time. I swallowed hard, tasting bile.

"Hear that?" Tate said, turning his head towards the doorway. "You're to play nice. Ashley here is going to be a good girl." He tightened his grip on my hair and tears trickled from my eyes. "Aren't you, Ashley?"

I nodded again, watching as a man and a woman, both dressed in black, stepped into the room. The woman was a vampire. At least, that's what I assumed from the blood stains she hadn't bothered to wipe from below her lips.

Like Tate, she looked fairly ordinary. Dark brown hair pulled back from her face, pale skin. Her eyes were brown and she smiled in delight as she saw me huddling on the floor. "Pretty," she said, turning to the man beside her.

"Boss said, behave," he replied but he too watched me with enough predatory interest to make my skin crawl. His eyes were pale blue. A familiar blue. *God.* He was the were who'd snatched me.

Out of the uniform, he didn't look ordinary at all. He had the sort of pretty boy blondness that would make Jase sigh in delight. His body was taut under the black t-shirt and pants and he'd completed his look with long knives strapped to each thigh. They shone dully in the dim light, making it hard to look away from them. A lovely shiner bloomed around one of his eyes.

I wondered who had hit him, hoped maybe it'd been Bug. Or me.

It was just as likely to have been Tate. Or maybe pretty boy liked things rough. His vamp friend looked like she definitely did.

I had no time to continue speculating. Tate hauled me up again and pushed me towards the duo with enough force to almost make me cannon into them.

The vamp caught me. "Easy, Pretty," she muttered as I squirmed away from her. Her grip tightened. Nails painted the same color as the bloodstains on her face dug into me.

"Take her to the doc," Tate said. "Tell him I want the works."

"Doc's no fun," the man said with a grin.

"Doc first, fun later," Tate said.

I didn't have much of a chance to take in my surroundings as they half-marched, half-pulled me down a long corridor. The walls were dark brown paneled wood and well-worn dingy linoleum covered the floor. I stumbled when one of my toes caught in a hole in the surface.

The vamp let go of my arm, would've let me crash to the ground but the man caught me. His hands were warm, and my skin tingled as he touched me. Definitely a were.

"Stupid humans," he said, righting me. "Boss spends too much time on them."

"You going to tell him that?" the vamp drawled.

"Bite me," he replied good-naturedly.

"You wish."

"I'd rather bite Pretty here," he replied. The hand that gripped my arm wandered briefly, squeezing viciously at my breast. I tried to pull away, only to have the pain worsen. I planted my feet, unwilling to give into their games. These two were scary, and I didn't doubt they could hurt me, but they were normal everyday supernatural scary. Not like Tate. Being with them was an improvement.

The man squeezed again then his hand moved back to my elbow. "Now, now Pretty. Boss told you to be good."

"He told you to be good, too, Rio," the vamp pointed out, hands on hips. Rio shoved me in her direction, smacking my ass as I lurched forward.

"Go with Elvira here, Pretty."

"Don't call me that," the vamp snapped. She grabbed my wrist and starting walking again, pulling me along. I followed as quickly as I could, trying not to mind that I could feel Rio's gaze. It made my spine crawl but not as much as the cool grip of the vampire's hand.

Of the two of them, Rio struck me as less dangerous. Sure, he probably wanted to rape me but the vamp would hurt me, possibly kill me, if she started playing. Werewolves weren't known for killing in human form. Of course, these guys worked for Tate so they were probably not exactly high on the sanity scale.

We turned left when the corridor forked. I tucked the directions away in my head. With each step away from Tate, the terror he'd inspired eased a little and I could think again. Getting the lay of the land might be useful later on. I looked for any landmarks as I mentally counted steps. But the walls were all the same unbroken paneling. If there were other rooms behind them, the doors were well-disguised.

The only distinguishing feature at all was the fact the air in the corridors smelled vaguely like mud, making me wonder if we were underground. Certainly we'd passed no windows. Obviously interior decoration wasn't high on the list of priorities for your psycho vamp these days. Then again, maybe Tate wasn't as crazy as I thought. Wherever I was, it was organized. And he had people working for him. Surely you had to be functional at some level to manage henchmen? Somehow the thought wasn't comforting. Crazy was one thing, but if Tate was sane, then his actions were even more terrifying. I refocused on counting steps, needing the distraction to keep the fear away.

I'd reached four hundred steps, with another left turn and a right before we came to a halt. The vamp hovered her palm over a spot in the wall and a door slid back.

"In you go, pretty." She planted a hand on my back and shoved. I stumbled forwards, blinking in the glaring white light while I regained my balance. It was some sort of laboratory, the walls lined with glass cabinets and various pieces of medical equipment. An examination table stood in the center of the space. It was fitted with restraints.

Fear bloomed in my stomach again, cold spikes racing along my nerves, weakening my knees. The air smelled like antiseptic. Which was better than mud; but the strong smell combined with apprehension to make my stomach heave. I clamped my teeth shut, sucked air in through my nose as the room whirled around me for a moment. Gradually I regained control.

Across the room, a gray-haired man wearing a black lab coat was perched on a stool drawn up to a metal counter, looking at something through a microscope. He lifted his head as the vamp cleared her throat. His rimless glasses glinted under the lights, his gaze dispassionate as it met mine. I might as well have been the specimen he'd been studying. He looked past me to the two standing behind me. "What's this?"

"Boss's new toy," Rio said. "He said to give her the works."

"Already?" The man sighed, pushing his glasses up further up his nose. "Fine. Leave her with me."

I didn't hear any movement behind me.

"I said leave her."

"Pretty might try and run," the vamp said.

"Then I suggest you lock the door behind you, Kyra. It's not like she can get far from here." He frowned at her, sounding impatient, like a man explaining something to a dense child.

Kyra made a hissing sort of noise that raised the hairs on the back of my neck.

"You can't make me leave," she spat.

Interesting. Obviously the doctor—if that was what he was—and my two escorts weren't exactly sharing the love. But I wasn't stupid enough to assume that meant he was on my side. After all, he was working for Tate. What I needed to do was figure out how not to become the ground meat in the sandwich.

"Really?" The man's stare grew colder. Kyra snarled but she didn't move. The doctor shrugged. "You know you just interfere with my work, Kyra. Go find someone else to play with."

That earned him another hiss but footsteps retreated behind me then a sliding hum suggested the door had closed. The doctor came out from behind the counter, went to a drawer and drew out a package, tossing it to me. "Here."

I examined the package. Some sort of hospital gown wrapped in plastic. Clothes. Anything was better than standing around naked. I ripped open the package and shook out the papery fabric trying to figure out how to put it on.

As I tied ties and tried to get the gown to cover my butt, I watched the doctor. Just because he'd kicked Rio and Kyra out didn't mean he'd turn out to be an improvement over them. I'd already spotted a tray of nasty looking medical instruments near the examination table.

He ignored me for a minute or so, while he pulled things out of cupboards and lined up stuff on trays covered with those green cloths you see on the hospital shows. Including a bunch of vials like the ones they use when they draw blood. Except that there were about fifteen of them, far more than I'd ever had taken from me by any real doctor. All of this made no sense. Why did a psychopathic killer vampire need henchmen for, let alone a medical staff?

"What's all that for?" I was proud my voice didn't shake when I spoke.

"You wouldn't understand." He walked over to the examination table. "Come here."

I stayed where I was.

He looked at me and sighed. "I suggest you do what I say. After all, I can always call Kyra and Rio back. They enjoy making people cooperate, even if their methods get a little *excessive*."

His tone told me I wasn't likely to enjoy their ministrations. Obeying him seemed like the lesser of two evils at this point. I walked over to the table but didn't climb up on it.

Up close the doctor had mild blue eyes and a face that might have seemed kind if he hadn't been holding one of the biggest syringes I'd ever seen.

I eyed the needle reluctantly. "What's your name?"

"You can call me Doctor Smith."

Smith? Yeah, right. Hello, fake name. *But maybe it is his real name*, a little voice inside my head whispered. He didn't need to lie if they didn't intend me to get out of this place alive.

I shook my head, squashing down the doubts. There was enough going on without me screwing with my own mind.

Dr. Smith pulled a stethoscope out of his pocket, hooked it around his neck and moved closer. He smelled like antiseptic and some old-fashioned cologne—like the one Bug's friend Stanley wore. A weird combination of pine trees and sharp spices. "How do you feel?" he asked.

"Like I've been kidnapped, drugged, stripped and beaten up," I said.

He didn't smile. Okay, no sense of humor. But I had to try and make some sort of connection with the guy. My skin didn't tingle around him, so he wasn't a were. He didn't move like a vamp and I'd never seen a vamp his age—most people chose to turn young.

So maybe he was human. And if he was, then maybe I could get him to help me.

He put the syringe down on the table. "Can you be more specific?"

"You're the doctor."

His hand swung out and backhanded me, hard. It hurt. A lot. Like the side of my face had just been pushed into hot oil or something. Tears ran down my face as my cheek burned with a deep aching throb and I struggled to breathe. The shock of realizing that, human or not, the doctor was firmly on the side of the bad guys sent my stomach into freefall. How was I going to get out of this?

"Answer the question, young lady. Or I will let Kyra and Rio back in." He strapped a blood pressure cuff round my arm and started pumping it up as if he hadn't done anything out of the ordinary.

"My face hurts." It was all I could think of.

He raised an eyebrow and I stepped back instinctively, hitting the edge of the table.

"Stay still," he said. "And sit."

I sat and tried to obey. It was hard. I'd started shivering again. I didn't know whether it was shock or fright or the after effects of whatever they'd used to knock me out.

The doctor didn't seem to notice, just kept pumping the cuff until it reached that almost painful point, and then he did the weird stethoscope thing doctors do to take blood pressure. "What else?"

"I feel sick. My shoulders hurt. I'm cold."

He nodded absently then removed the cuff. Then he started interrogating me about my medical history. One question after another about my diet, my health, my parents' health. On and on until my head started to hurt even worse than it did already.

"Why do you need to know all this?"

"Research."

"What sort of research?"

He frowned at me. "You don't need to know. Lie down."

Despite my better instincts, I did. I should've listened to my gut. Quick as a snake he had one of my hands clamped in the restraints, snapping the heavy leather cuff closed.

I tugged at it. "What are you doing?"

He'd moved around the table. "I said, lie still." He grabbed my other arm, twisting it so white fire lanced up my elbow and bicep. I stopped struggling and bit my lip, trying not to cry out as he released the pressure then secured that arm as well.

Another strap went across my waist, pinning me to the table.

Dan, I thought desperately. *Jase. Anyone.*

"Good." He walked to my feet, grabbed an ankle and pulled my leg down before tying it in place. He repeated the action, leaving me helpless.

"You're not pregnant?"

I shook my head, not trusting my voice.

"You're sure?"

Another nod.

He pushed the gown up out of the way and I closed my eyes. Whatever was about to happen, I didn't want to see it. Something cold was sprayed on my abdomen then I felt the prick of a needle, a big needle. It slid through my skin like iced acid.

"Please," I said. "Don't." I didn't know what I was asking for. "Please," I repeated and my voice cracked. The pain of the needle ceased and the sudden relief made me dizzy. Maybe the worst was over.

Or maybe not. I heard the doctor move and opened my eyes to see where he'd gone, wanting to know where the next hurt was coming from. He had moved a few feet away, put the empty syringe neatly into a disposal unit on a nearby bench. A tidy maniac. Just what I needed. Turning back to me, he wheeled a metal trolley back over to the table and pulled up a stool.

"I'm going to take some blood now," he said. Another needle stung my arm, adding to the pain in my abdomen and face. I turned my face away.

"Squeamish are you?"

"No." I'd just had enough. Sweat trickled down my forehead, mingling with the tears and only the thought of choking on vomit was keeping me from throwing up. I grew dizzier and dizzier as he clicked vial after vial into place until eventually everything went black again.

I woke to feel a hand on my breast, teasing the nipple. I murmured a protest and the grip turned hard and painful and someone laughed.

"Like that do you, Pretty?"

My eyes flew open. Kyra was leaning over me, watching me curiously. She'd cleaned the bloodstains off her face but her breath, hot in my face, smelled like Tate's, like rotting meat. I gagged and she smiled as I tried to move, tightening her fingers until I felt nails pressing into my flesh. I was still tied to the table in the lab. I turned my head but I couldn't see the doctor. Just Kyra.

"Doc said you fainted, Pretty. Said you needed sleep. But I can think of better things to do than sleep, can't you?" Her other hand came to rest on my abdomen then drifted lower. I screamed when she touched me. It hurt my throat.

"Boss said to leave her alone, Elvira."

Rio. I never thought I'd be thankful to see him but at this point, I'd take whatever rescue I could get.

Kyra hissed at him but withdrew her hand and I almost started to cry again in sheer relief.

Rio came into my field of vision, standing at the foot of the table. "Are you going to behave if I untie you?" he asked, staring at me. "Or will I leave you with Elvira here?"

I licked my lips, swallowed to ease the burn in my throat. "I'll behave."

"Don't think he's any better than I am," Kyra said softly. "Rio likes to play too."

I shuddered. "Tate doesn't want me hurt."

Both of them laughed.

"Is that what you think?" Rio said. He'd undone both restraints around my ankles and I slid my legs closed but didn't make any other movement. I wasn't free yet and even if I had been, I doubted my legs would hold me up.

I felt terrible, worse than before if that was possible. My stomach throbbed where Smith had done whatever he'd done with the needle, my face ached and even though I was lying down, the table seemed to sway beneath me. It was an effort to follow the conversation. "That's what he said," I managed.

Rio laughed—not a nice sound. "He told us not to play with you. Doesn't mean *he* won't."

Fear snaked through me again but I was getting used to feeling scared and tried to push it away. Two more rapid movements and my hands were free. Rio unbuckled the strap around my waist. I sat up cautiously, pushing the gown down to cover my thighs and he let me.

My head spun as I straightened and I took deep breaths.

"Don't faint, Pretty. You never know what might happen when you're asleep." Kyra said nastily. She moved away, wandering around the lab, rattling things out of sight while I tried to obey her instructions.

I could feel Rio watching me from the end of the bed but I didn't look at him. Instead I tried to see anything in the lab that might give me a clue as to where I was or even the time of day.

The tray the doc had been using was still beside the bed, another discarded pair of gloves crumpled on it beside a tourniquet band and two syringes.

Two syringes?

I frowned. One of them was small, normal sized, unlike the other, which still held a little blood. My right arm, where he'd taken the blood ached and I knew I'd be bruised but had he given me something else? Shit. I looked down at my arm but I couldn't see any other marks.

"Doc said you have to drink this," Kyra said.

I jumped, I hadn't heard her come back. She was holding a paper cup filled with yellowish liquid. "What is it?" I asked suspiciously.

"Relax, Pretty. It's just Gatorade."

I took the cup and sipped. It tasted like Gatorade and suddenly I was ridiculously thirsty. I gulped half the cup down.

"You'll make yourself sick," Rio said. "And I don't want to clean up any messes." He came around to stand in front of me, tipping my chin up with one finger. "Got that?"

I nodded and sipped more slowly. If there was anything else in the cup, there was nothing I could do about it and the sugar might clear some of the fog from my head.

Rio kept watching me, then took the cup, crumpling it in one hand and tossing it to Kyra. Then he leaned forward, so his face was only inches from mine.

"You stink, Pretty," he said. "You stink of fear." He breathed in deeply and his hands closed over my knees. I froze as I looked down. He wore a watch—one of those big complicated things with multiple dials men like. One of the dials said 'Wed'. Wednesday? Shit. We'd gone to Bug's on Monday night. If I'd been gone over a day already and Dan hadn't found me...I tried to see what the time was but Rio distracted me.

"Fear. I *like* that smell, Pretty."

He leaned closer still and nuzzled my face. I shivered, wanting to pull away but scared of what he would do. I felt something warm and wet touch my cheek. His tongue. I almost gagged. He licked his way down my cheek and neck until his tongue was tracing the pulse at my neck, currently going at about four thousand beats a minute. When I felt him rest his whole mouth there, I couldn't help it. I reached down, grabbed one of the knives strapped to his leg, yanked it free and slashed it at him.

He jerked back, yelping in surprise. Then he grabbed my arm, squeezing my wrist until I felt the bones grind. I opened my hand so the knife fell.

"Bitch," he bellowed.

I had a second to register the anger on his face and the pain in my wrist before his hand connected with my face, hitting me on the same side as the doctor had and making stars of light ignite behind my eyes as I flew off the table and crashed to the floor.

I lay there, braced for the next blow. It didn't come. Instead Kyra snarled. "Can it, Rio."

"Bitch sliced me."

"Pretty has teeth." I couldn't see her but she sounded amused. I opened an eye a fraction. Rio's shoes were only a foot or so away from my head and I tried to stay still. Play dead. Maybe he'd leave me alone.

"Not for long if I have anything to do with it." Fury snaked through his tone. I prayed the threat of whatever Tate would do to them if they really hurt me would stop him from doing anything else. Apparently it did because Rio's feet retreated then something went flying with a crash of metal as he took his temper out on something else.

Kyra crouched beside my head, tapped my face none too gently. "Open your eyes, Pretty."

I did as she said, biting back the groan of pain as the light hit my eyes.

"Don't play with Rio, Pretty. It's dumb."

I could only agree with her as she lifted me over her shoulder and carried me out of the room.

CHAPTER TEN

WHEN WE GOT BACK TO the room I'd woken up in, Doctor Smith was there. He still wore the black lab coat. Kyra deposited me on the bed with a thud that jarred every aching muscle in my body. I groaned and wondered whether I was about to barf the Gatorade up all over myself.

"What happened?" Smith asked. "She should be feeling better."

"Pretty decided to hit Rio," Kyra said cheerfully. "Rio hit back."

That was an understatement. The nausea lessened as I lay without moving but my cheek was still on fire, burning with an intensity that made me wonder if maybe Rio had fractured something.

"She better not be really hurt. We want to start tomorrow," Smith growled.

Start? Start what? I didn't have time to wonder. Smith moved over to me and touched my face, probing at my cheek. I winced at each touch, starting to feel dizzy again as the pain flared.

"Nothing broken," he said eventually and stepped back. "You need to eat."

My stomach roiled at the thought of food. "I feel sick."

"I took a lot of blood. You need to replace it."

When you're being held captive by a vampire, that phrase has more than one potential meaning. And contemplating all the possibilities didn't help my stomach settle.

"Kyra, go to the kitchen. There's soup there."

The door hummed open and shut, leaving me alone with Smith. I stayed curled up on the bed, watching him warily.

"You'll feel better once you've eaten."

Right. Because nothing cheers you up after a beating better than soup. I didn't answer him; just lay there, in a semi-daze, trying to ignore the pain in my face.

Eventually the door hummed again. I opened my eyes to see Kyra wheeling in one of those little room-service-type trolleys like. There was a huge bowl of soup of some sort steaming on the trolley and several packets of crackers. The sight was weird enough to almost make me smile. I wondered idly whether I should tip her then bit down on the thought. I didn't need to fall into hysterics just now and I could tell from the rising whirl of my thoughts I was heading in that direction. I'd had it happen to me a few times after my parents' death and couldn't risk it now.

Smith helped me sit up and then made me try the soup. Chicken noodle. I thought I'd gag but the first mouthful tasted wonderful, salty and warm and I swallowed greedily.

"Eat slowly," Smith warned and I nodded. I polished off the soup, another bottle of Gatorade and nibbled the crackers at a cautious pace.

When I finished, Smith pulled a vial and a syringe out of his lab coat pocket. I shrank back on the bed. "What's that?"

"Vitamins." He grabbed my right arm and plunged the needle in without ceremony.

I winced, biting my lip. Vitamins. Yeah right. The bottle disappeared back into his pocket but I'd caught a glimpse of the label. There was a logo on it that seemed familiar. I wracked my brains, trying to remember where I'd seen it before. But I was too tired and the memory stayed stubbornly out of reach.

Smith let go of me and I cradled my arm against my body. My stomach rumbled. I needed a bathroom. Desperately. "I have to pee."

Smith made an irritated noise but walked over to the far wall and swiped his hand over a spot that didn't look any different than anywhere else to me. But sure enough, a door swung inwards, revealing a small bathroom with a toilet, sink and shower. "Don't be long. But shower." He wrinkled his nose. "You stink."

He was right. I reeked of sweat and another acrid smell I couldn't identify. There was soap in the shower stall and a towel on the rail. So I took advantage of the facilities then climbed into a warm, steamy shower, scrubbing myself with the soap until I felt a little more human. The water stung my face and the sore spots on my arms and stomach but it still felt better than anything else I'd felt all day.

I stayed under the water as long as I dared then dried off. The room held nothing I could see that offered any chance of escape: there was an exhaust fan that an anorexic baby might fit through and no windows. Apart from toilet paper, the soap and a tube of toothpaste, the room was as bare as the bedroom.

I squirted toothpaste onto my finger and scrubbed it over my teeth several times until they felt clean. I swished water, gargled and spit. The back of my throat had stopped tasting of soup and the sour aftertaste of bile. Then I picked the hospital gown up from where I'd dropped it on the floor. It was splashed in a few spots, it smelled and it was a bit soggy from the steam but I wasn't going back out there naked. I pulled it back on and then walked to the door and banged on it.

The door slid open. Smith pointed to the bed. Another paper gown lay on top of the blanket. "You should sleep," he said.

The idea was tempting and I didn't hesitate to switch gowns as soon as he'd left the room. They'd left another bottle of Gatorade on the floor by the bed. I was still thirsty but reluctant to drink too much when I didn't know if I could access the bathroom.

Instead I prowled round the room, trying to figure out what made the outer door open. The bathroom one—to my relief after several long minutes of futilely waving my hand at the wall at approximately the spot I thought Smith had—opened at my command but the outer door remained shut no matter what I did. I figured the bathroom door had to be motion sensitive and the outer one worked some other way. Some sort of recognition system. And I wasn't recognized.

Defeated, I sat on the bed then lay back as fatigue washed over me. I tried to sleep but my mind kept circling endlessly. How was I going to get out of this? Where was Bug? Where was Dan? The police? The FBI? And why the hell were they taking my blood. My thoughts circled and swooped but I had no good answers to any of my questions. Only fear.

Gradually I realized the lights in the room had gone off, leaving me in darkness. Without sight, I felt disoriented, vulnerable. All alone. I huddled under my blanket and tried not to let the fear take over. But it did. Sweeping over me in waves of terror. I was going to die here. No one would find me. No rescue was headed my way. Tate would hurt me then kill me. I had no illusions there would be any merciful death offered.

I fought the fear with something I hadn't done in a long time. Not since I'd lost my family. Lying in the darkness, I prayed. To anyone or anything that would hear me. Hoping against hope, someone would answer. Prayed like a child, repeating any snatch of hymn or bible reading I could remember, begging for rescue. Until eventually, as the room remained dark and no one answered me, I knew Tate had been right. There was no point hoping.

"How are you today?" Tate appeared as the door slid back for the second time the next morning.

The first time had been Smith bearing a huge breakfast which I had devoured before he'd given me yet another shot. I hadn't been able to see the symbol on the vial this time but the more I thought about it, the more I thought the one I'd seen looked like the same company that made the vamp and were vaccines. But that made no sense...why would Smith be giving me more vaccine?

"I've felt better," I said, skirting the line between submission and defiance. Somewhere in the long night that had just passed, I'd decided that survival was up to me. I couldn't rely on hoping for rescue, so I had to watch and wait, bide my time then take a chance when I could.

Which meant surviving Tate. I had the feeling surviving Tate meant keeping him interested. If I bored him, I'd be discarded like a broken toy. If I annoyed him he'd break me himself. So I had to walk a very thin line somewhere in between the two.

Tate studied me. I could feel the path of his gaze as he took in my battered looking face—which had come up in a brilliant shiner overnight—and my other bumps and bruises. "Rio shouldn't have hit you."

"I did try to stab him."

He laughed. "He shouldn't have been so careless. He knows better than to let a weapon get within range of a..." he paused, as if searching for a diplomatic term, "...guest."

"Is that what I am?"

"It is a somewhat fluid term. But you don't want to be a prisoner. Prisoners receive less friendly treatment."

Hell, no. If my treatment had been what he considered to be friendly then no, I definitely didn't want to be a prisoner.

"So, as my guest, if you would be as good as to come with me?"

Reluctantly I walked across the room, adjusting the gown so it covered as much of me as possible. It had mostly survived my restless night but it was somewhat crumpled and torn in a couple of places and I was horribly aware of just how flimsy it was. Tate had torn normal clothes in seconds. If things turned ugly, how long would it take for him to dispatch a paper gown?

I followed Tate down the corridor in the opposite direction to the previous day. Rio and Kyra had been waiting outside my room. They trailed along behind us. Rio had greeted me with a smile that hinted at all sorts of unpleasant things he might do to me if Tate hadn't been there. I did my best to ignore him and the crawling sensation his expression caused.

nodded at Kyra and Rio. "And we have other employees who are even less civilized. Do you understand?"

I wrapped my hands around the arms of the chair, digging my fingers into the fabric in an effort to maintain control. "Yes. May I ask a question?"

Tate nodded. "Go on."

"You obviously have more in mind for me than just killing me. I'd be dead now if that was all you wanted."

"Is that a question?"

I didn't know where my courage was coming from but I literally had nothing to lose. There were only three possible outcomes to this situation. Both Bug and I would both die here, or one of us would or we'd both survive. I wanted to slant those odds in Bug's favor. "It's not exactly a question. More a request."

He arched an eyebrow, looking amused. Except for his eyes. They stayed blank and empty. "You think you're in a position to request a favor from me?"

"I think I've earned that much. After all, you've taken a lot from me already."

"True."

I held my breath as he pressed his hands together and stared at me. "All right, make your request. But be aware, I may choose not to grant it. And, if I choose not to do so, there may be consequences for asking." As if to emphasize his point, the monitor flared back into life with a close-up of Bug's face, looking old and drawn.

My throat dried. Was this worth the risk? My stomach twisted but it felt like now or never. I gulped. "I understand. This is my request. If I go along with what you want, if I don't fight you, then whatever happens to me, I want my aunt to go free."

Something that might have been surprise flickered in those dead eyes. "You would do anything I ask?"

I licked my lips, nodded. "Yes."

"But you have no guarantee I would keep any agreement we might make."

"I'm willing to take that chance."

"Interesting." He looked back at the monitor. "Humans never cease to surprise me."

I wondered if he ever remembered that he'd been human once. Then again, given he'd been a psychopath or a sociopath back before he was turned, if the rumors were right, maybe he never had been. "Do we have an agreement?"

"Anything I want?" He smiled broadly, revealing his fangs, reminding me I was making a deal with the devil. "All right, Ms. Keenan, we have a deal. If you see this through to the end, your aunt will be freed."

"Alive."

He waved a hand as if that were a given.

"And not turned," I added.

He frowned then nodded again. "Do not try my patience any further. Free. Alive. Still human. That is all."

"Then we have an agreement." I wondered if I was insane to speak the words but it was done. Bug would live. I had to believe in that. It might just help me survive too.

"Good. Take her back to her room. Then to the doctor." Tate said.

Kyra hauled me to my feet and started hustling me out of the room. As we reached the door, Tate said, "Wait. I forgot something."

All three of us turned back to him. He stalked across the room, stopping in front of me. He reached down and took my hand then raised it to his lips. His mouth was slightly open as he kissed my skin and I felt the brush of fangs and had to fight not to snatch my hand back.

"I will see you tonight, Ashley," he said softly as he straightened.

My stomach flipped over and I was glad that Kyra's hand was still tight around my arm. Otherwise I might just have crumpled to the floor again. What the hell had I gotten myself into?

CHAPTER ELEVEN

THERE'S NOTHING LIKE AN imminent date with a homicidal vampire to focus your mind on impending doom and make a day drag by. Turns out you can't be terrified all the time. It comes and goes in waves. I alternated wildly between wanting to curl up and wait to die and thinking maybe I could get through it. Which was exhausting on top of the fear.

They left me alone, mostly. I was fed and taken briefly to the lab for more prodding by Smith, this time confined to taking measurements, peeing in a cup and only one more tube of blood. And another 'vitamin' injection. I tried to get a better look at the vial he used for the injection but his hand was in the way. Then it was back to my cell. More food only distracted me briefly.

So I had plenty of time to spend thinking I'd go crazy if I had to wait much longer, staring at the walls and trying not to think about what might be happening to Bug and what might be about to happen to me.

Then Kyra arrived with a garment bag and a scowl. She dumped the bag beside me on the bed and ordered me to be ready in half an hour.

Suddenly, the walls seemed fascinating.

Kyra left and I stared at the bag, wondering what exactly might be inside. "No time like the present," I muttered and undid the zipper.

What lay inside was long, black and made of velvet. I rolled my eyes a little as I drew it out. Talk about your goth maiden's delight dress.

But I wasn't going to argue with Tate's taste. If he wanted me to wear black velvet, I'd wear black velvet. I showered hastily then wriggled into the dress. Its shoulder straps were barely threads and the neckline just skimmed the tops of my breasts, leaving me all too aware my shoulders and neck were horribly bare. I felt like a piece of meat lying on display in a butcher's window.

Prettily wrapped food.

Where was the chain mail collar when I needed it?

There was lipstick and eye make-up in the bag. I applied both, wincing a little at the bright red color against my bruised face. Red lipstick isn't really my thing. And it didn't go with the lovely purple bruising surrounding my right eye.

Apart from combing my hair there was nothing else I could do but wait and try to remember how to breathe each time fear tried to close my throat and crush my chest. Luckily it didn't take long for Kyra to reappear.

Unfortunately Rio was with her.

His eyes lit up at the sight of me. "You clean up good, Pretty," he said, prowling around me. "I'm looking forward to the boss being done with you." His hand skimmed my butt and then snaked round my waist, pressing me back against him.

His erection pushed against me and I fought not to flinch away. I wasn't going to let them see me freaking out. "What makes you think he'd give me to you?" I said coolly.

He growled softly in my ear, a grumbling, pure animal snarl. "Believe me, Pretty, by the time he's done with you, you'll be happy to come to me."

Hopefully before anyone had time to be done with me, the cavalry would arrive. If they had to kill Rio and everyone else in the place in the process of rescuing Bug and me I wouldn't be sorry.

"Don't count on it." I looked to where Kyra was leaning against the door watching us with a smile playing around her lips. "I don't want to keep Tate waiting."

"If you knew what was waiting for you, you wouldn't be so eager," Rio said but he let me go. "And remember, Pretty," he added as I reached the relative safety of the corridor. "I owe you one." His hand drifted over his stomach and down to the knife at his thigh. I hid my smile of satisfaction. Sure, being a were, he'd healed the damage I'd done but I'd managed to hurt the son of the bitch and, if he came near me again, I'd do my best to do even worse. Somehow.

"You like doing things the hard way, don't you, Pretty?" Kyra commented as she shepherded me out of the room and into the seemingly never ending corridor. This time we went right at the junction, instead of left towards the lab. "Just remember, tonight, if he offers you an easy way then it would be smart to take it."

I pretended not to hear her, schooling my face not to reveal the fear blurring my senses. I don't know why I bothered. She could hear my heart thumping and no doubt could smell my panic as well. But not letting her see it made me feel better.

My small act of bravado lasted until we reached Tate's room. I stepped over the threshold and stopped dead instinctively.

Everything about the room screamed danger.

Trap.

Flee.

The walls were painted a deep, dangerous red, which made the silver chains decorating one of them gleam starkly in the muted lights. There was a huge bed covered in some black fur against another wall. A rack of whips and various things I couldn't name hung above it. And in the middle of the room was the most disturbing item at all.

I didn't even know what you'd call it. A whipping post was the closest thing that came to mind but this was shaped more like a cross with upwards-slanted arms so it didn't form a true crucifix. It dominated the room, looming like a malevolent black insect.

A man, or maybe a boy—I couldn't see his face, just pale blond hair and a slender frame—hung from chains attached to the slanted arms, his feet not quite touching the ground. The muscles in his shoulders bulged unnaturally and bruises blossomed like rotten flowers all over his bare arms and legs. His back was a mass of raw bloody welts.

Tate stood behind him licking blood from those wounds. Naked. Blood spattered. A long whip dangling from his left hand. And, I saw as he turned at my indrawn breath, he was aroused. His erection rose long and thick between his legs and I backed up a step automatically. Only to bump against Rio and freeze again.

A dead smile, stained with blood, spread across Tate's face. It turned me to ice, frozen in place like a mouse who senses a hawk high above ready to plummet, rend, and tear. Not breaking our gaze, Tate ran his forearm across his face, wiping most of the blood away.

"Ashley," he said as if we were standing somewhere perfectly normal instead of a chamber of horrors, "How nice to see you."

Rio shoved me and I stumbled further into the room, almost tripping on the long skirt of the dress. Every nerve screamed at me to turn and run. Run for my life.

Tate stayed still, watching me intently. Then he reached out slowly and ran his fingers down the man's back, drawing a pained moan from him. Then he licked his fingers clean of the blood. Slowly. Delicately.

Like a cat cleaning its claws. "I thought you might like to see what happens to guests who aren't co-operative."

Not really, I thought wildly. I wanted to close my eyes but I didn't think Tate would like it.

"Pavel, here—" he reached out and yanked the man's head back so I could see his face—"tried to escape." He ran the whip up Pavel's thigh.

I shuddered and Tate's smile grew wider.

"He won't try again. Will you, Pavel?"

"No, Master," Pavel slurred through bruised looking lips. His eyes—I couldn't tell what color they were in the dim light— fastened on Tate's face like a dog watching its owner. Adoring. Mindless. Determined to please.

I shivered with revulsion. Tate had taken his mind. Pavel had probably enjoyed what Tate had done to him and might just willingly step up to the post again if Tate asked him to. He would probably even let Tate beat him to death.

I turned away. Only to be met by Kyra's and Rio's vicious grins.

"Not so pretty, is he?" Rio purred.

I wanted to faint. To black it all out.

Help me, I screamed inside my head.

"I want you to remember Pavel," Tate said, crossing the room to where a black marble vanity almost the size of a bathtub loomed against the wall. "Because if you disappoint me, your Aunt could be the next one I play with."

He washed his hands and face, and then pulled on a shirt and, I was relieved to see, trousers. "Take him away."

Kyra and Rio obeyed silently, unlocking Pavel from his chains and dragging him out of the room. His eyes stayed on Tate the entire time, looking hurt.

I remained standing where I was, trying to control the tremors running through me. I wasn't terribly successful.

"You look scared," Tate said as he walked towards me.

"I am scared."

"Don't worry. I didn't bring you here to teach you the same sort of lesson."

I didn't want to ask him what he had brought me here for. I no longer wanted to know.

"It's fascinating to me," Tate said. "What humans will do for love. I can hear your heart beating, do you know that?"

I nodded.

"It's racing. I can hear how scared you are. And yet you stand there waiting. You don't run. All because you don't want me to hurt your aunt. Because of love." He cocked his head to one side. "It's really quite stupid of you."

"You wouldn't understand."

"Wouldn't I? Maybe you're right. But it makes me wonder."

I felt my pulse leap and catch. His purring tone did bad things to my nerve endings, grating like steel fingernails down a blackboard. But I stayed silent.

"I wonder exactly what you would do to save her from me."

"I already said I'd do what you wanted."

He walked back to the whipping post, eyes still fixed on mine. "Yes, but did you mean it? When faced with reality. With pain. Will you still be willing? Would you step up to the post and let me do to you what I did to Pavel? Without me thralling you?"

I had to swallow several times before I could speak. "Is that what you want?"

His eyes narrowed. "I'm still deciding what I want. But I want to know what you'd do. You interest me, Ashley. Most women would be begging by now."

"Will begging do me any good?"

"Are you good at it?"

"I don't know. I don't usually beg."

That made him smile again. I preferred the frowns.

"Something to remember. But we were discussing what you'd be willing to do to save your aunt. What would you do, Ashley? If I told you to take off your clothes, if I said lie down on the bed and spread your legs, would you let me fuck you?"

"I think the term you want is rape me." As horrifying as the image was, I didn't think Tate had brought me here for sex. Not when he'd made it so clear he didn't fuck humans.

"Not if you consent."

"Consent obtained under threat of torture and murder doesn't count."

"Brave words." He picked up the whip from where it had fallen, moved closer. "You're thinking I don't sleep with humans, so you're safe."

Shit, was he reading my mind? Sometimes I thought Jase could. If Tate could I was really and truly screwed. "I don't think safe applies in this situation."

"Smart girl." He ran the tip of the whip up my arm.

It felt damp and sticky and left a reddish smear. Pavel's blood. Dizziness swept over me.

"I could just as easily tell you to strip and then let Rio fuck you. I know he's keen to have some fun. You really shouldn't have annoyed him."

The thought of Rio raping me was slightly better than Tate. Somehow I managed to stay standing while Tate stroked the whip over my shoulder.

"Or I could ask Kyra to do the honors. She has all sorts of interesting proclivities. But she breaks her toys so easily."

The whip brushed my face. It smelled like leather and sweat and something heavier. Blood maybe. I didn't really know what blood smelled like. I didn't want to find out. I jerked my head back. "If you wanted me raped, I'd be raped already. Why am I here?"

"Patience." He tossed the whip to one side, then walked over to the bed. "You know, I used to fuck humans. When I was one. Even when I first turned. I'd go to the clubs. The S&M clubs. The dark clubs. There were always people there who wanted to be hurt. Who wanted the pain. Probably not as much as I gave them, but still. I met the vampire who turned me at a club."

"Oh?" It wasn't exactly a story I wanted to hear but every second I kept him talking was one more second I delayed whatever Tate was planning.

"Yes. She liked pain. Pity she didn't warn me she liked inflicting it as well. It felt so good when she bit me. But then I turned and I realized she'd used her mind on me. I killed her, you know."

"I'd heard rumors."

He smiled smugly. "You should believe the rumors you hear about me."

Oh, I believed them. I was just trying my best not to remember any of them.

"Anyway, I stopped going to the clubs when I finally understood the truth."

"The truth?"

"That it's no fun giving pain to those who want it. The fun part is giving it to those who hate it."

My stomach rolled. Part of me wanted to put my hands over my ears but I knew I needed to keep him talking. "So you started killing people instead?"

"Oh, I killed people before I was a vampire. I just got better at it."

"Practice makes perfect."

"Something like that."

"It must be boring for you."

He smiled again and this time the expression really made me shudder. "You have no idea. But we were talking about you. You don't like pain, do you?" He patted the bed beside him.

I stayed where I was. "No."

"That's a pity...for you." His eyes held mine for a few seconds before I had to look away. "Come here, Ashley."

His tone demanded obedience so I moved. My path brought me closer to the whipping post. My legs trembled as I walked, every instinct telling me to turn and run, but I couldn't. If I did, then the next person Tate had in this room would probably be Bug. I could almost see her chained there. Hurt and bleeding. Dying.

It didn't matter what Tate did to me if I could keep Bug safe. Surely I could survive if I just held onto the thought of Bug alive?

My stomach didn't seem to agree. It churned with each step. I wanted to do something to wipe the superior expression off Tate's face but I knew who would suffer if I tried.

Was I a coward? Should I choose death before dishonor? Face to face with both possibilities, I knew I wanted to live. Which meant giving myself over to Tate. To doing what the monster wanted instead of trying to kill him like he deserved.

I wanted him dead. And the truth was, unless I was willing to sacrifice Bug and myself, I couldn't see how that was going to happen.

My thoughts still whirled as I reached the end of the bed.

"Such a carefully blank face. What *are* you thinking?" His hand trailed up the velvet from my thigh to my hip, a cool weight through the heavy material.

"That you should've just killed me."

"Careful what you wish for," Tate said and pulled me down onto his lap.

One arm snaked around my waist and I knew I had about as much chance of moving it as a steel band. I was trapped.

Up close he smelled of dirt and rot and blood underneath the cleaner smell of soap. The hairs on the back of my neck rose in response. It was like sitting in a nest of spiders and waiting for them to bite. I wrapped my arms around myself, shivering.

Tate's free hand stroked my throat briefly. "You know, I've worked up quite an appetite with Pavel. What do you think I should do about it?"

I closed my eyes. "If you're going to feed, feed." I could handle this, surely? After all, some people let vampires drink from them voluntarily. Seriously deranged people in my opinion but they survived. Of course, the vamps they let suck on them weren't Tate. Somehow I knew in the depths of my soul that not many of the people Tate fed on survived.

"So eager? That's not the way we play this." His fingers rested on the pulse in my neck, my skin vibrating against his with each beat of my heart. I wondered what it felt like to him. Good? Exciting?

Please, God, let it not be exciting. But I knew it was. I knew from Jase that feeding from live victims was intimately bound with sex for most vampires. Why should Tate be any different? And if he didn't use sex, then the other options for him channeling the energy he derived from blood were unlikely to be things I'd enjoyed.

Still, Tate was in charge of this little scenario. I didn't want to end up on the receiving end of the sort of treatment Pavel had endured by pushing him too far. "What do you want?" I said.

"You've never done this before?" He pressed his thumb to the pulse on the other side of my neck, so his hand circled my throat.

For a moment I thought he was going to choke me then he loosened his grip a little.

"You've never been a vessel?" he asked again.

I shook my head, puzzled by his use of very old-fashioned vampire terminology. Tate was a young vamp, only fifty or so. It was the older ones who spoke of vessels and the dark gift—the ones who remembered the days when draining a victim completely was commonplace. Was that what Tate intended?

I flinched away from him and his arm tightened until the pressure against my ribs and stomach was almost painful.

"You're not going anywhere, Ashley. Cooperation, remember?"

My brain remembered. My body wanted to get the hell out of there. Full points to animal instincts but I had to stay calm if I didn't want to end up like a vessel. I licked my lips. "I remember. I'm just..."

"Scared? I know." His voice grew lower, more pleased sounding.

For some reason it made me mad and I latched onto the anger, using it to fight the terror. "So let's get this over with."

His hand released my neck abruptly. "But I haven't decided what to do with you."

I frowned. "Neck. Fangs. Isn't that how it works?"

Tate laughed, I felt it rumble through his chest.

"Believe me, there are many ways to make the gift." A hand closed over my right breast and his thumb brushed my nipple. "Some women like it here. My teeth piercing their skin. It can be exquisitely painful." His fingers tightened and I gasped in pain. Then he released me, hand dropping to my thigh, sliding under the slit in my skirt so he brushed bare flesh. "Or here, perhaps?" His fingers brushed against me, delicately and I was horrified to feel myself shudder in response.

"Fear is an aphrodisiac...perhaps I should teach you that after all."

"No!" I grabbed his arm, pushing at it. It didn't move an inch and his fingers continued to play, sliding lower and probing into me as he laughed at my dismay.

"What's the matter, Ashley? Has your wolf never introduced you to the rougher pleasures? They like to play too."

No. Not Dan. Dan would never hurt a woman. "I don't have a wolf," I said, still pushing at his arm. "And I'm not interested in learning to play."

He snarled. "Careful. Remember your agreement." He plunged his fingers into me, hard. It hurt and I bit my lip trying not to give him the satisfaction of hearing me scream.

"Please." Tears welled up in my eyes as he pressed deeper. "Don't."

Abruptly he withdrew. "Don't push me," he warned. "You won't like it. I was going to make this easy on you but I've changed my mind. I could thrall you and you'd do anything I want. You'd enjoy anything I did to you."

Fingers twined in my hair, yanking my head back so my throat was exposed. He licked up the skin and I did scream, I couldn't help it. His fingers tightened until it felt like he was going to rip off my entire scalp. He held his mouth near my ear and whispered, "Now we do things the hard way," and plunged his fangs into my neck.

CHAPTER TWELVE

IT FELT LIKE SOMEONE plunging two red-hot ice picks into my neck. Pain seared up my throat and exploded in my brain. I clutched convulsively at Tate's shoulders, dug my fingers in and fought to push him away but he was immovable. Moving made it hurt more.

My heartbeat roared in my ears as he sucked and my vision wavered and darkened.

Pain.

Every time he pressed his lips harder or drew harder, renewed waves of fire flowed through me. I was vaguely aware I was crying, sobbing, but mostly I knew pain.

Pain and a growing realization there was a terrible kind of intimacy to this act. That, as much as my body was shrieking and my head was spinning with every beat of my heart, there was an insidious sort of communion between us. Tate's pulse echoed down his neck, I could feel it thumping in time with mine like we were linked in some weird way.

Like this was right or meant to be.

And that hurt almost as much as the physical act.

As Tate drank on, I fought to keep my eyes open as my head spun and the room whirled around me. How much was he taking? There was a limit to what I could give and survive. What if he crossed that line? Part of me didn't care. Part of me fought to live. And part of me just went away somewhere completely different, taking me to a world of pure sensation, riding the pain like a wave to distract me from reality.

In that place I cried out for help again only to have silence echo around me like waves of despair. *Please. Help me.* Nothing. Except a faint breath of something that might have been...*Ash*? Or might just have been my imagination.

Pain spiked again as Tate moved his head, burying his fangs a second time. I came back to myself in a nauseating rush. I gasped and choked, close to fainting. I beat at Tate's shoulders. "Stop. *Stop.*"

In response he just lifted his head. The pain of his fangs withdrawing was worse than the actual bite. He stared at me, my blood staining his lips, then smiled and struck at my neck again. This time, as his fangs pierced me, the darkness engulfed me completely.

I came half-awake when I heard someone say "Sorry, Robert." Robert. My mind floated. The only Robert I knew was my Dad. I had to be dreaming. Then something brushed my hair and I jerked to full consciousness. I was back in my room, Doctor Smith standing by my bed, staring down at me. Dreaming. I must've been dreaming. Why would Smith use my father's name? I squinted up at him, trying to make my mind work through a fog of pain and confusion

"Don't try to get up," he said. "Tate got a little carried away."

I lifted my head slightly so I could see him better and fire raced up my neck.

Carried away. Right.

My neck felt raw and burnt, like something had been chewing on it. Which, I guess, they had. It throbbed each time I breathed, the bandage around my throat feeling a rough as burlap against the damaged skin. I swallowed and even that hurt. "Can I have something to drink?" My voice rasped.

Smith nodded and handed me a glass filled with the now familiar Gatorade. It was cold and wet and that was all that mattered, even though I was getting heartily sick of Gatorade. I never liked it much in the first place. When I finished the glass, Smith helped me sit up, shoving an extra pillow behind me. Then he peeled back the bandages around my throat, none too gently.

"You're healing fine," he said. "You just need to rest and eat."

"I'm sure that's exactly what Tate has planned for me," I said sarcastically.

"You're alive," he said curtly. "Be thankful."

"I'll put it in my gratitude journal." I figured Smith might hit me again but after last night, that didn't seem so scary a prospect.

Smith glared but luckily he didn't do anything else. "You'd do better to focus on recovering. I'm sure Tate will be asking for you again, this evening."

I cringed. Again? Just thinking about the feeling of teeth in my neck made my skin go cold. I hadn't seen what lay under the bandages but it didn't feel like there'd be much skin left. "Why me? Don't you have any other guests for him to torture?"

And that was a stupid thing to say.

A malicious smile spread across Smith's face. "Well, there's always your aunt."

I sat up—too fast. "No!" My head swam and I was forced to lie back, cursing Tate and Smith and everyone else I could think of in my head.

Smith laughed. "Then you'd better stop complaining. Two more times won't kill you." He paused. "Or maybe it will if you keep up with the attitude."

Two more times? What the hell did that mean? Tate was going to feed from me twice more? Then what? I died? "What do you mean two more times?"

My confusion must have shown on my face because Smith frowned as he reached into his pocket. He didn't look at me as he pulled out one of the now familiar vials and a syringe. "Ask Tate. If you dare." He filled the syringe, flicking it a couple of times with his fingernail.

Ask Tate? I didn't even want to see Tate. So I needed to work out what was going on for myself. I took advantage of Smith's distraction to study the vial.

Yep. The logo was definitely the navy blue horse's head that Synotech used. I was familiar with it. My father worked for them for a few years before he joined Genasys, one of their competitors. Synotech was a major supplier of the vamp vaccines in the US. Color me confused. It made no sense for Tate to be vaccinating me. Not every day. What could that possibly achieve?

Wondering distracted me as Smith jabbed the needle into my bicep. I was beginning to feel like a human pincushion. Not least because of the wounds on my neck.

"Get some rest," Smith said as he walked to the door, leaving me alone to contemplate the thought of going a second round with Tate.

Eventually I slept again, only to wake screaming from a nightmare of blood and pale faces looming at me in the dark. I staggered into the bathroom and splashed water on my face, staring at my haggard reflection in the mirror. I looked almost ghostly, pale even for me with my Irish heritage skin. In addition to the black eye and bruised cheek, I had huge dark circles under my good eye, and a cut in my lip I didn't remember getting.

I wondered whether I'd bitten it while Tate had been feeding. Then of course, there was the bandage around my throat. I touched it gingerly and winced at the answering sting.

The only thing I could come up with was that it had to have something to do with whatever they were shooting me full of. Though I couldn't imagine what that might be.

But I was going to ask before it was too late. Tonight. The third time. I didn't know what happened after that but on the off chance I'd still be alive, I wanted to know what the hell was going on.

Tate was all solicitousness when Kyra delivered me to his room that evening. Two elegant chairs and a table covered in white linen were set up by the end of the bed. He ushered me to a seat then took the other chair.

"What's this?" I surveyed the food arrayed on the table with suspicion. I'd already eaten dinner when Smith had arrived to give me yet another injection.

"I thought you might be hungry."

Yes, because waiting for a vampire to suck my blood was guaranteed to give me an appetite. "I already ate." His expression darkened and I knew I was once again skirting shaky ground. I swallowed, trying to summon a semblance of enthusiasm. "But I would like some wine."

Anything that took the edge off had to be good. But not too much. I needed to be able to think. Tate lifted the decanter of wine and poured. It was some heavy red that that looked almost black in the light of the candles. I sipped it slowly. Despite my meal, the alcohol hit my stomach like a firework exploding, spreading waves of warmth through my body. Okay, so blood loss and alcohol didn't mix well.

I put the glass down. "May I ask a question?"

Tate nodded, looking almost relaxed. Something had put him in a good mood tonight. I didn't want to speculate about what.

"What did you mean last night when you said the third time was the charm?"

He shrugged, playing with his own glass. "You will find out soon enough."

My jaw clenched in frustration. "Then why not tell me now?"

"Because I don't choose to."

Well, that was plain enough. I didn't know how to wheedle a serial killer into telling me what I wanted to know so I just picked up my glass again. "Will you tell me why you've chosen me?"

He blinked. "I told you. Round two."

Which told me nothing. Round one was Caldwell, I got that. But I had no idea why he'd come back. Or why round one had been Caldwell in the first place. "What—"

"Enough questions." His voice was sharp. "Unless," he added, straightening in his chair, "you wish to make another bargain with me?"

My spine prickled. A bargain? In exchange for information? That couldn't be good. But I couldn't just let the offer slide. If I got out of this, any information could be vital. "What sort of bargain?"

He considered this. The white silk of his shirt gleamed as the candles flickered. I hoped the white wasn't significant, he'd worn black almost every time I'd seen him. "There is information you want. The question then becomes what are you prepared to give in exchange?"

The wine suddenly soured on my tongue. "What did you have in mind?"

"Your aunt—"

I jerked in denial and my hand hit the wine glass. The liquid spread across the tablecloth looking very much like blood. "No! You don't *touch* her."

"Then what do you have that I want?"

The question really was, what did I have that I was willing to give him? My eyes flicked to the whipping post. Could I? Bile rose and I turned away, looking down at my lap. No. I couldn't imagine a lash cutting into my flesh, my back looking like Pavel's. *No.*

"There is one other thing," Tate said.

I lifted my head. "Yes?"

"You could let me thrall you. Let me show you what the gift should be like."

My hands clenched as a picture of Pavel's face, battered and worshipful, rose in my mind. To let Tate take my mind, to let him take me over...to force me to *enjoy* what he did to me.

It felt like he was asking for my soul. Maybe he was.

No pain, an insidious part of my mind whispered.

No. It wasn't worth it. Knowing my fate was worth giving up the only real freedom I had left. I straightened my spine. "I—"

"I would release you, once it's over."

"Release me?" Thralled was thralled as far as I knew.

"Take away the bond."

"You can do that?"

"Some of us can, yes."

Huh. That was something the vamps hadn't bandied about. I wondered why. "And you would have no control over me once I was released?" My resolve was weakening. I knew Tate was up to something. But if I could find out any information at all, it might save someone. Bug maybe. Or even me.

No pain, my mind whispered again.

No such thing as a free lunch, another part of me retorted. Why did Tate want to do this? He got off on pain. So offering to make me suffer less made no sense. There had to be something in it for him.

Something I was missing.

But as much as I twisted and turned it in my head, I couldn't see what that might be, not if he was telling the truth about being able to break the thrall.

"If you agree, I will let your aunt go. As soon as we're done."

Careful when you're dealing with the devil. Now I was really suspicious. If something looked too good to be true, it probably was. A terrible thought occurred to me. "How do I know she's still alive?"

Tate pushed his chair back then walked across to the wall that wasn't decorated with chains. He made a gesture and a panel slid back, revealing three screens.

"Surveillance," he said briskly. "Room seven."

I watched the bank of screens carefully as the center one brightened. Bug sat on the bed in another identical room. Maybe the same one as before, I couldn't tell. She was frowning. In fact, she looked royally pissed. But she was alive. And unhurt as far as I could tell.

Of course, it could be a recording but it was as close to proof as I was going to get. I drank in the sight of her, thought about her walking free out of this nightmare.

And knew I had no choice.

"Do we have a deal?" Tate asked as he darkened the picture with another gesture.

I nodded, wondering if I was about to make the biggest mistake of my life—a potentially fatal mistake. "Yes."

A strange expression crossed his face. Something not quite greed, not quite lust. Something closer to fulfillment, perhaps. He walked back to me and held out a hand. I took it, holding onto those cold fingers as he drew me over to the bed.

"Now," Tate said when we were finally standing face to face, so close I could see the pulse in his throat. "Give me your eyes."

CHAPTER THIRTEEN

IT WAS LIKE FALLING. Like diving into a deep dark chasm.

Weightless. Seductive.

Tate took me over, took me into his control and it was intoxicating. Better than any wine. Better than any drug.

"Ashley?" he said softly.

It was the most beautiful sound I'd ever heard. If I could've crawled inside that voice and curled up there for the rest of my life, I would have.

"Yes?" I swayed towards him, breathing in his scent. It didn't smell like death any more, it smelled like a promise, like an invitation. More alluring than Dan even...I felt my forehead crinkle in a small frown. Better than Dan? That couldn't be right. For a moment I hesitated but then Tate spoke again and I didn't have any desire to worry about the wrongness.

"Ashley, come lie down."

I obeyed silently. Doing what he asked felt oh so right and I smiled with the pleasure of it.

Tate coaxed me out of my clothes. I was happy to oblige. Anything he wanted. *Anything.* Drunk on the nearness of him, I put my hand down between his legs to find him hard and aroused.

I wanted that hardness. Wanted *him.*

He grasped my wrist. "Not that way."

I pouted. "Why not?"

"There's something better." He flicked a thumb over my nipple as he pressed his face into my neck. "Don't you want me to show you?"

Better than what I was already feeling? It was hard to conceive. Just his brief touch had ignited my skin, bringing me so close to the brink of orgasm that small tremors throbbed between my legs. I arched my hips, impatient. "Show me."

He laughed softly then moved himself closer beside me, rubbed a finger over my lower lip. "Do you make the gift freely?"

I nodded, eagerness surging through me.

"Do you give yourself to me?" he asked.

I nodded again.

"Then I claim you," he said hoarsely and he bit me. Not my throat but my breast, mouth closing around my nipple, teeth piercing my skin above and below.

I came, screaming with pleasure stronger than anything I'd ever felt before. Mind blowing waves of sensation, almost too strong to bear. I felt myself slide towards the edge of unconsciousness as he suckled me then buried his fangs deeper.

My mind cleared a little as he moved and I learned the truth about thrall.

That it didn't take you over completely, at least not when what was being done to you was something you'd never do willingly.

There was a small part of me that was free of Tate. Not enough to move or protest but enough to be aware of what he was doing, of how I was responding to the touch of the thing who had killed my family. That part of me was screaming.

That part of me still felt the pain of his bite.

That part of me hated.

That part of me pleaded for help. And again as I begged, just faintly, I thought I heard someone speak my name.

Tate withdrew his fangs and moved over me. I registered that somehow he was naked. The free part of me redoubled its efforts to escape. To be raped on top of everything, to *enjoy* the rape. I wasn't sure I'd survive it. But my body didn't respond to my mind. It only responded to Tate.

He didn't enter me, just lay on top of me and plunged his fangs into my neck. Just the feel of him, thick and heavy against me was enough to send me into another orgasm.

I clamped my legs and arms around him, drew him closer to me, pressed into his bite, whispering words of need to him.

Wanting to die every second.

I didn't know how long we lay there, how many times he made me come. When he finally pulled free and lifted away from me I was only semi-conscious. But I still felt the loss of him like a knife sliding through me and rolled towards him.

He climbed off the bed and stood above me, looking golden tinged in the candlelight, licking blood—my blood—from his fangs and all I wanted was for him to bite me again.

He smiled as I lifted my arms towards him. "Sorry, my dear, but we're done here."

Tears rose in my eyes and his smile grew wider. "You're very tempting. I'd like to play some more but I will keep to our agreement. We're done."

Tears welled up in my eyes and I reached toward him again.

"Don't move," he said. "See that her aunt is freed, dump her somewhere out of the way. Make sure she's well restrained. Maybe she'll die before they find her," he added to someone over his shoulder.

The tears streamed down my face as my heart broke. I didn't care about Bug. I only cared that Tate had left me.

"Oh, and Ashley?"

I stared up at him as his voice sent a final shiver of pleasure through me. "Yes?"

"I release you," he said and walked out of sight.

It took less than a second for the words to take effect. One moment I was lying sated but bereft and the next my mind was free and the reality of what had just happened hit home with a surge of horror that sent nausea spinning uncontrollably through me.

I rolled off the bed, somehow lurched to my feet, only to throw up in the ice bucket—a sour spill of wine and the steak I'd eaten for dinner—before collapsing again.

What had I done?

Oh God. What had I done?

"Take her away," I heard Tate say—triumph clear in his tone. I closed my eyes as hands lifted me and didn't open them again until I was dumped on the floor of my cell.

I spent the night alternating between throwing up and curling on the floor of the bathroom, shivering as my mind replayed what Tate had done to me. Even when I was left dry-retching, I couldn't stop the spasms.

I'd let him *touch* me. I'd *come* because he touched me.

I'd wanted the monster.

I'd found pleasure in the thing that killed my family.

And it felt like I'd killed them all over again.

Part of me tried to argue that it wasn't me, that I'd been thralled, but I couldn't bring myself to believe it. Somewhere, deep inside, there had to be something in me that liked what he did for me to react to him.

That was something I couldn't face. The only thing I could cling to was that Bug was free. I had to believe Dan would find her. That she'd be okay.

One of us had to be.

Because if I'd let Tate do that to me for nothing then— I retched again. Then collapsed back into an exhausted heap, teeth chattering.

Which was how Kyra and Rio found me the next morning.

"Hello, Pretty." Kyra nudged me with her boot, not so gently.

"Not so cocky now, are you, Pretty?" Rio added.

I ignored them. I didn't really care what happened to me anymore. I just wanted it all to be over.

"She stinks," Kyra said and the next thing I knew I was on the shower floor with water blasting over me. Cold water. I flinched and curled tighter.

They laughed at me but eventually turned off the tap, hauled me out, dried me off and dressed me in black pants and a shirt much like they wore. Clothes didn't make me feel any better. I just kept shivering, only staying upright because Rio held me up.

"Bet you liked what he did to you," he whispered in my ear. "Liked his fangs in you. Did he fuck you, Pretty? Or did you just want him too? Bet it made you come, didn't it, Pretty?"

I shuddered as the memory of how good it had felt swept over me. And retched again, although my stomach was beyond empty.

Rio laughed, holding me at arm's length as I writhed. "Remembering, Pretty? Maybe if you're extra nice he'll give you another go. Maybe this time he'll let us watch."

"Or join in," Kyra added.

Vamp hearing, I thought vaguely. Rio scowled at Kyra. "I get first dibs at Pretty. I owe her a scar or two." He touched my neck. "Though she's acquired a few over the last couple of days. Want to show me the rest, Pretty? I saw your tits. Did he bite you anywhere else?"

I shook my head frantically, wishing I was back in the shower with hot water and soap. A lot of soap. Maybe if I scrubbed myself for a few days I might feel clean. Pity there was no way to scrub my mind out.

"I guess I'll know soon enough." He sounded smug but I didn't care.

"C'mon. Boss's waiting," Kyra said.

I walked obediently between them, not wondering where I was going. I was more focused on what I should do next. It would be easiest just to provoke them. Let them hurt me. I deserved it. If I made them mad enough, they might even kill me. The thought made me smile.

"What's so funny, Pretty?" Kyra asked as she opened the door to the lab.

I shrugged.

She scowled. "Don't think you'll find this so amusing."

She pushed me through the door and I went. To my surprise, Tate was sitting on the examination table and Doctor Smith was drawing blood from his arm. A lot of blood. Tate was hooked up to the sort of bag they use at the blood bank.

"Good morning, Ashley." Tate said.

I looked down at my bare feet. Anywhere but at him. I wasn't going to risk him being able to thrall me again.

"Feeling shy? After what we did last night? Silly girl. Are you done?"

I assumed the last was directed at Smith.

"A little more, to be sure." Smith said. Silence reigned for a minute or so then. "That's enough."

"Bring her over here," Tate said and I was bundled forward. I still didn't look up.

"Losing your nerve now? How disappointing. Because now is when all we've done pays off. Then we will begin the real game, you and I."

That finally drew my attention. I raised my head. Tate stood by the table, rolling down his sleeve. "What do you mean?"

"You've forgotten our agreement? Your unfortunate reaction to last night has clouded your memory?"

I frowned. Our agreement? Then it came to me. I'd wanted to know why he'd kidnapped me. The detached feeling receded a little as my brain kicked in. Tate had fed from me. And now Smith had drawn *his* blood.

God, *no*. I looked from Smith standing there with the bag of blood back to Tate. "No!" I shoved at Tate and tried to duck around him.

"Kyra." Tate sounded bored. Within seconds Kyra was in front of me, one hand around my throat, almost choking me. I fought her until she squeezed harder and I started seeing spots in front of my eyes.

"Where do you want her, boss?"

"Strap her down."

I yelled and started struggling again, not caring when Kyra's grip tightened. Let her choke me to death. If what I thought was about to happen was my alternative then death was merciful. But it didn't help. Rio and Kyra dragged me to the table in about five seconds.

"Don't. It won't work. I'm vaccinated," I said desperately as they locked me back down onto the table as easily as if I hadn't been fighting them at all. I bucked against the restraints but that only earned me extra straps across my chest and hips. I could barely move. "You *can't* turn me."

"Ah, but we can," Tate said, coming round beside me. "We've got something new." He looked at Smith and grinned. "The doc here has been working hard."

The *injections*. The fight drained out of me. There was something in the injections. God. Tate was going to turn me. I had to stall for time. "What?"

Tate leaned in closer, looking at me with puzzlement. "Do you really care?"

"We had an agreement," I reminded him. "You said you'd tell me. What was in those injections?"

His eyebrows shot up. "Quick, aren't you? But I did agree." He nodded at Smith, who started wrapping a tourniquet around my arm. "Doctor Smith has found a way around the vaccines. Almost an improvement, you could say. We've been trying for years now and we think we've got it right. We thought we had it right last year but they caught on to us."

Who? I tried to think. What did he mean? What had happened last year...then I remembered. There'd been what the CDC had claimed was a batch of bad vaccines. Almost twenty people had turned as a result of vaccinations.

There'd almost been a panic and the government had spent a fortune trying to convince people to continue to be vaccinated.

"The bad vaccines. That was you?"

Tate nodded, then glanced at Smith. "Now we've come up with something better. Kind of a supercharged version of the mutation. It will overcome your immunity and, even better, once you're turned, it will overcome the immunity of anyone you bite."

It was a horrifying picture. "Anyone bitten by a vampire who has this mutation would turn automatically? They wouldn't have to drink the blood of the vamp who bit them?"

"No. A much more efficient system."

One that would result in a vampire population boom. A plague. I wanted to scream. "You won't get away with it. They'll stop you."

"Not for quite some time. Time enough for our work to spread. By then it will be too late."

"But why? What's wrong with vaccinations?"

Tate scowled. "Humans are getting the upper hand. And humans are boring. No challenge."

"You want to make more vampires so you can kill them?" Even for a lunatic that was twisted logic. There had to be another reason, surely? One they weren't telling me.

"Supernaturals are worthy prey."

"You're crazy." I looked from Tate to Smith, who was watching the vampire with a strange look on his face...almost impatience. "You're *both* crazy." Smith didn't react and I focused on Tate.

"Maybe," he shrugged. "Let's find out." He nodded at Smith and there was a prick at my arm. Smith slid a funny looking needle into the crook of my elbow then attached the bag of Tate's blood.

"What are you doing?" I tried to move my arm and dislodge the needle but the restraints held me motionless.

Tate smiled at me. "Transfusion works better than you drinking my blood. More of the mutation survives without the stomach acids. Plus, there's none of that tedious throwing up."

"No!" But even as I watched Smith did something that sent a stream of dark red blood down the tube connecting the bag to my arm. "*Stop.*"

"Don't worry, Ashley." Tate said. "This won't hurt much. Apart from the bit where you die. That bit hurts." He sounded vaguely nostalgic. "But it won't happen for another twelve hours or so. Once you are reborn, I'm sure you'll see things differently."

No, I wouldn't. I'd still want to die. If I turned the first thing I would do would be walk out into a sunrise and let it take me. "They'll stop you," I said to Tate.

"Who?" He paused then turned towards the door. I didn't know what had interrupted him then I heard a distant rumbling noise.

"What was that?" Smith said with a frown.

Tate snarled. "The wolf. Alert security." Smith hurried over and lifted a phone in the wall.

Dan? Dan was here? For a moment hope swept over me then I realized the truth. It was too late. No one could save me now. Tate had already killed me. I stared up at the bag of blood, already partially empty, already setting a chain reaction off in my bloodstream.

I couldn't become a vampire.

"Security says the place is surrounded. I've initiated the computer wipe. Everything's backed up at the other site." Smith said.

The look of fury on Tate's face was terrifying and the metal tray beside the table became airborne as he smashed his hand into it. "Stupid humans."

"We need to leave," Kyra said. "The tunnels..."

"No!" Tate roared.

"Don't be stupid," Smith said. "She's not worth it. We'll lose everything."

Tate took a deep breath and his face cleared, even as a second louder rumble shook the walls. An explosion? "All right."

"What about her?" Rio asked. I heard a snicking sound I recognized. The sound of a safety on a gun being released. "Want me to take care of her?" He came into my line of sight at the end of the bed, a revolver aimed at me.

Please, God. I begged. *Let him kill me.*

Tate stared down at me for a long moment. "No," he said eventually and Rio made a protesting sound and looked at Smith. Almost as if he was asking for a second opinion. Like Smith was in charge. That didn't make sense. But I was too busy trying to will Rio to shoot me to care. Smith shook his head. Just a little. "They're too late anyway. They can't save her. And they won't be able to stop the mutatio." He looked at the line in my arm with satisfaction.

Panic made my head swim. "Kill me," I said to Rio.

Tate shook his head. "No. That would be a waste." He nodded at Rio who lowered his gun—and Kyra. "Let's go."

"Until Round Three," he said to me then flowed away with a vamp burst of speed. I couldn't see which way they went. Just caught a last glimpse of Kyra's dark hair as they ran through the door, leaving it open behind them.

The walls shook again with another rattle of sound. Then I heard gunfire. Short staccato bursts. I hoped it was Tate. Hoped they'd killed him. Like he'd killed me.

I looked back at the bag of blood. It was almost a third empty. Tears ran down my face as terror caught me. I couldn't be a vampire. I *wouldn't* be a vampire. A monster.

"Ashley!"

Dan's voice. Just like I'd dreamed of hearing over the last few days. I wanted to call out to him but there was no point. Tate was right. It was too late.

"Ash? Are you here?"

Booted footsteps—running footsteps—thudded down the corridor then I heard him again call my name again. Closer this time.

"God. Ashley." He sounded relieved and terrified.

I turned my head. Dan stood in the doorway, face smudged by smoke, wearing dark fatigues and carrying some sort of automatic weapon. The sight should've made me happy but it just made me realize exactly how much I'd lost.

He stared at me then sprinted across the room, coming to a halt by the table. He tore at the restraints at my legs and the leather popped like rubber.

"Ashley? Are you okay? Are you hurt?" I saw his gaze go to the bag of blood.

"It's Tate's blood," I said wearily.

His gaze went to my throat. I knew the moment when he spotted the fang marks. His , eyes flew back to the bag and he made the same connection I had made. "Christ, Ashley."

"You're too late," I said. "Kill me."

Horror rushed over his face. "What?" He eased the needle out of my arm and hurled the bag across the room.

"Kill me. You're too late, Dan. He's turned me."

"No!" Dan's voice was rough. "No, I won't let him."

"Sir?" Behind Dan several more men in fatigues appeared in the doorway. "Sir, did you find her?"

"Leave us alone," Dan roared. The men looked at each other but retreated.

"Ashley, listen to me," he said, taking my hand. "You're vaccinated, aren't you? You're okay."

"No. I mean, yes, I am vaccinated but they've done something to me. You have to kill me." My voice broke. "If you ever loved me, just do it. Don't let me become like him."

Pain flooded Dan's face. He shook his head. "I can't do it, Ash. I can't lose you again."

"You already have," I said.

"No!" He dropped my hand, rubbed the back of his across his forehead. Then he stilled. "There's another way."

I closed my eyes, wanting him to just do it. I couldn't fight any longer. "There's no other way. If you don't do this, I will."

"Lycanthropy is more contagious," Dan said slowly. "If I bite you—"

"No!" That option wasn't any more acceptable to me. I'd seen what the monsters were really like up way-too close. And it had made me even more convinced I couldn't live like that.

"We could be together." His voice was deeper, rumbling almost.

I opened my eyes and the expression of hope on his face felt like he'd stabbed me. "Daniel, no. Listen to me. They said what they did would affect my immunity to vampirism. They didn't say anything about lycanthropy. It won't work."

"It might." His voice was rough. "I love you, Ash. You love me."

God, it hurt. Why did everything in my life always hurt? It was too much. "If you love me, you'll kill me. Please." I was crying now. "Please, Dan, let me go. I can't be a vampire."

His face twisted. "I'm sorry," he said, backing away from me, shaking his head. "I can't. Not when I can save you."

"Don't do this," I screamed at him. "Kill me."

"I love you. Forgive me." Dan blurred and suddenly a huge black wolf stood in his place.

"No." I twisted against the remaining restraints, as the wolf paced towards me, whining softly. "Daniel, don't!"

The wolf put his front paws up on the table, pressed his nose into my hair and whined again. His eyes were silver, still, I noticed through my tears. And Dan's wild scent rose from his fur.

"Please, don't," I begged one last time.

He nuzzled my hair again then dropped back down off the table and took my forearm in his mouth ever so gently, warmth surrounding my skin.

He looked up at me. I shrieked at him to let me go, to change back. To *stop*. Then there was a searing pain in my arm as he bit me.

CHAPTER FOURTEEN

I WOKE IN AN AMBULANCE with Jase sitting beside me as a female paramedic worked on me. Tears streamed down his face. I opened my mouth to ask what was wrong but all that came out was a croak. But even that was enough to alert him.

He leaned forward with a smile. "Hey, you're awake. You scared the crap out of us. Don't do that again." He patted my right hand and the motion sent a searing pain up my arm.

My bandaged from wrist to elbow arm.

Horror filled me as the memory came flooding back. "Dan bit me," I croaked.

Jase nodded, his expression carefully neutral. "Yes."

The paramedic shook her head. "You shouldn't talk too much, Ms. Keenan."

There wasn't really that much to say. I was either going to be a vampire or a werewolf. I swallowed, trying not to think about either option. My throat hurt. "Thirsty," I managed.

She looked apologetic. "Sorry. They might have to give you an anesthetic at the hospital. It's better if your stomach's empty."

I swallowed again then looked back to Jase. I needed a distraction. Or else I was going to lose it right here in the ambulance. "Where?"

"Where were you?"

I nodded carefully.

"Way the hell in the country. Up near Sutton. Big old house. Tate had built this whole complex underneath. They're still checking it all out. What's left of it." His expression turned savage for a moment and

I suddenly noticed he was dressed like Dan had been, in black fatigues. He looked pretty grubby and tired.

Had he been *looking* for me too? Was that how they found me? Sutton was miles from Caldwell. Why would they even look there? "How?" I whispered.

"We've been looking for you ever since we realized you were gone. Five days almost. Dan's been a mad man."

Mad was right. Insane, I thought as pain flared again in my arm. He *bit* me. Worse, he didn't kill me.

And I didn't even want to think about the bit where he turned into a wolf first. My arm throbbed again and I bit back a moan. I wanted to ask Jase for more information but it didn't seem to really matter. Vampire or werewolf, I could only see one path left to me.

"He wouldn't kill me," I said, so softly I didn't think Jase would hear.

"Who? Tate?"

Damn vamp hearing. "No. Dan."

Alarm flared in Jase's eyes. "Why would Dan kill you?" He turned to the paramedic. "She seems a bit confused, what did you give her?"

I shook my head. "Not confused. Don't want to change." Tears started leaking from my eyes again and it brushed them away with my good hand. I was getting tired of tears. Tired of fear. Tired of hurting.

Jase stroked my hair and I flinched, reminded of Tate.

He froze and then took his hand away, putting it back on top of mine. "Sweetie, it will be okay. You'll see."

I didn't see at all but I knew as soon as he said the words that Jase wouldn't help me either. He didn't understand wanting to die. He'd chosen to turn when faced with a death sentence. He thought *any* life was worth living.

Maybe I was just going to have to help myself.

It should be easy enough once I was free of the hospital.

"I'm tired," I said and closed my eyes. Jase just held my hand while I pretended to sleep. The ambulance rushed towards the hospital, sirens wailing. It seemed to take forever and the whole time I thought about dying.

As they wheeled me into the ER, another thought occurred to me and shame heated my face. "Bug? Where is she?"

Jase grinned even as nurses and doctors began to swarm around me. "She's okay. The FBI had the place surrounded when a car drove out with Bug and two weres. The Taskforce let 'em get about ten miles down the road then stopped them. She's fine. Better than you."

Bug was okay. Peace swept over me. So I'd achieved that much. Even if I died, she was okay. That was enough for now.

"Ashley!"

I turned my head and saw Dan striding through the doors. "I don't want to see him," I said to the room in general.

"Whatever you want," one of the nurses said and the last thing I saw before they pumped me full of something very pleasant that took all the pain away was Dan looking shocked as they pulled the cubicle curtain across in his face.

"Are you awake?"

I didn't know the voice. Female, though it was unusually low and husky. A nurse? I opened my eyes slowly, not wanting to jar anything. "Kind of."

My voice cracked and I winced. But at least this time I remembered where I was.

I'd woken screaming during the night thinking the darkness of the hospital room meant I was back at Tate's. It had taken three nurses, a sedative and Jase to calm me down. They'd left the light on after that. But I'd still tossed and turned for the rest of the night, despite the drugs.

The woman standing at the foot of my bed was tiny. Five foot if she was lucky and built along elfin lines. She wore a deep green tee-shirt and black skinny jeans and her head was covered in the sort of dark red curls Little Orphan Annie might have had if she grew up and was having a very good hair day. Not a nurse. I reached for the call button.

"It's okay, I'm a friend," she said.

I pressed the button anyway. Being around a stranger had the fear streaming through me again. My pulse raced and I wished desperately I had a gun. "You'll excuse me if I don't take your word for it."

She nodded. "I'd do the same in your place."

The door opened and a nurse stuck his head in. "Is everything okay?" He looked toward my visitor.

"I don't know who this woman is," I said.

He looked surprised then shrugged. "The agents let her in, it's okay. Do you want me to get one of them for you."

I shook my head, feeling foolish. I should have realized my room was guarded. And I didn't want to risk it being Dan who came to answer my question if I asked for an agent. I wasn't ready to deal with Dan. The nurse nodded and withdrew.

I turned my attention back to my visitor."

Do you want some water?" she asked.

I ignored her question. "Who are you?" I vaguely remembered something about guards on my door so presumably anyone in my room was allowed to be there. Then again, Tate had snatched me from a house full of police the first time.

"My name's Anastasia Rogan, but most people call me Ani."

She *was* Annie! For some reason that struck me as hilarious. I half-laughed then choked it back. I didn't want to explain the joke. She waited, watching my with her head tilted on one side. It was almost as if she thought I should know who she was.

I didn't. "Is that supposed to mean something?"

She frowned. "Dan's never mentioned me?"

Dan? Nerves started to bubble in my stomach. "Until last week, I hadn't spoken to Daniel in years."

"Ah."

There was a world of meaning in that small sound. "Why should Dan have mentioned you?" I coughed as I finished speaking, my throat still felt like I'd been drinking battery acid or something.

She poured some water from the jug on the tray table at the foot of the bed then brought it to me. "You must be thirsty. The doctors said you were dehydrated."

"Having someone drink half your blood does that," I quipped but I took the water and drank. "Why are my doctors talking to you? Who are you?"

"Your tests came back."

It took me a second to remember. Tests. Right. Vampire or werewolf. Feeling sick, I put the glass down. "Are you some sort of counselor?"

"Kind of." Ani perched on the end of the bed. "I'm the pack's Alpha."

"Excuse me?" *She* was a werewolf? *The* werewolf, kind of? She didn't look big enough to boss anyone around.

She grinned as if used to my kind of reaction. "Well, one of them. But we thought you'd be more comfortable with me than Sam, given what you've just been through."

I wondered who Sam was but then the meaning of what she'd been saying sunk in. "Does this mean I'm a werewolf?"

"It looks that way. The Stoker variation hasn't taken hold. But you are carrying lycanthropy. Of course—" she put a hand on my leg "—we won't know for sure until the full moon."

"But I was vaccinated." It was all I could think of. Tate hadn't said anything about their anti-vaccine or whatever the hell you'd call it affecting the were vaccine. "Was it what Tate did to me?"

Ani shook her head, looking sympathetic. "The doctors can't tell. The lycanthropy is already affecting your antibodies."

Shit. I should've figured that out. Weres don't get human bugs 'cos of their hyped-up immune systems. It's part of what helps them heal so fast. And apparently it was going to help Tate get away with this by wiping the evidence of whatever he'd done to me out of my bloodstream "So maybe I'm just fucking unlucky and my vaccination didn't work?"

Ani frowned a little and I realized that I'd just insulted the Alpha by telling her turning into a werewolf was a bad thing.

A werewolf. *God.* I closed my eyes, leaned my head back on the pillow, not knowing what to say as Ani's news started to sink in. Grief welled up inside me. I'd lost. Tate had won. I was going to be one of the monsters.

Even worse, I was going to be a werewolf. At least as a vampire, one good dose of sunlight would solve the problem for me. As a wolf—

"Ashley? Are you okay?

I blinked back tears. "No. I'm going to be a fucking werewolf."

"You should be happy. Dan saved you from becoming a vampire."

"Is that any better? He should've just killed me." I believed what I said. I'd never wanted this. After Tate and everything else I didn't want to have lost my humanity. I was never going to forgive Dan.

I heard a rustle then a hand closed over my mine. "It's going to be okay, Ashley."

I didn't believe her any more than I had Jase but her hand was warm and it felt good knowing someone else was in the room. Her perfume was fresh smelling with an undertone that reminded me of...something elusive. A forest maybe. Green growing things and earth and air. It was strangely comforting.

"Who's Sam?" I asked absently, feeling calmer as I breathed in the smell.

"Sam's my husband. The other Alpha."

"I thought there was only one?"

"Wolves mate for life. So Alphas are usually pairs." She chuckled. "And before you ask, yes, I'm big enough. Size isn't everything you know. And I'm normal sized in wolf form."

"How does that work?"

"Let's talk about that later, when you're feeling better. You need to rest. Once the doctors give the all clear, you'll come and stay with us."

What? I opened my eyes and sat up. "I want to go home with Aunt Bug."

Ani sighed. "You can't. The full moon is a week away. You need to learn some things before you change and you need to be controlled when you do. The first time is...unpredictable."

Unpredictable. That was a nice way of saying 'sometimes people die'. I shivered, shaking my head. "I don't want to change."

"You have no choice. Not if the tests are right. You have seven days to get used to the idea. And you'll be spending them with us."

I wasn't sure whether us meant her and Sam or the whole pack. I wasn't comfortable with either idea. Or with being ordered about by an elf. So I changed the subject. "When do they think I'll be out?"

"Apart from your arm, you're in pretty good shape, considering."

I was glad she'd added the last bit or I'd have to wonder what she considered to be *bad* shape. Then again, she was a werewolf.

"Wolves heal faster than humans, even ones that haven't changed yet," she added. "I'd say tomorrow unless there are any complications. The doctors will talk to you about options for therapy. But you don't need to be in here for that."

One more day. One more day and I might get a chance to be alone. To do what Dan should've done. But there was something else I needed to do first. "I want to see my aunt."

Ani didn't blink at the second switch of subject. "Of course, I'll get someone to arrange that. The police and FBI are all keen to ask you some questions and," she paused in the doorway. "Daniel wants to see you."

"I don't want to see him," I snapped. He'd fucking bitten me. Made me a monster. Why would I want to see him?

"He is the agent in charge of the investigation."

"Anyone but him," I said firmly. I didn't care if Ani was the Alpha or queen of the freaking universe. Daniel Gibson was not going to come anywhere near me.

Ani left without saying anything else. As her scent faded, I found myself growing anxious again, sadder. Tears pricked at my eyes. I sipped water and tried to ignore the pain in my arm. After ten minutes or so the door opened and I almost leapt out of bed before I saw it was just a nurse. She took my temperature, my pulse and gave me still more pills to swallow.

"What are these?" I asked. I'd had enough of mystery drugs. From now on, there'd be full disclosure or I wasn't taking them.

"Antibiotics and painkillers."

"Isn't it a bit late? I'm already infected."

"With lycanthropy, yes. But we want to make sure everything else is taken care of, just in case."

In case Tate and his cronies had dosed me with anything nasty. If my blood was changing the doctors wouldn't be able to tell. But I didn't think he would have. He wanted me to turn, not die. But I guessed the doctors were just being thorough. From what I understood of werewolf physiology, the first time I changed any bugs in my system would be zapped. And most injuries healed. Pity it wouldn't do any good for the place I'd been hurt the most.

It was a moot point, anyway. I didn't intend to make it to my first change.

The nurse left and a minute or so later, the door opened again and Ani appeared, wheeling Bug in a wheelchair.

I flew out of bed before I could stop myself, tumbled to my knees in front of Bug, buried my face against her lap and started sobbing. "I'm so sorry, Aunty."

"I think I'll take it from here, thank you, dear."

Aunt Bug's gravely tones just made me sob harder. The door opened and closed quietly and her hands came down on my head. "Go ahead and cry, I'm here."

So I did. Sobbed like a baby, breathing in the strange yet familiar smell of Bug's perfume mixed with hospital, while Bug made soft shushing noises and rubbed my back.

When I finally stopped and lifted my head, Bug pulled a precisely folded white linen handkerchief from the pocket of her robe—her very much non-hospital robe. The gesture was so Bug that it made me laugh and cry all over again.

"Feeling better now?" she asked.

I nodded as I blew my nose. "I'm so sorry," I repeated.

"Sorry for what?"

"They took you. Because of *me*."

"From what I hear, they also let me go because of you. And treated me fairly well in between."

Relief flooded me. She really wasn't hurt. I'd managed that much.

"You, on the other hand," she reached out and put a hand under my chin. Her eagle eyes inspected my face. I could only imagine what my bruises looked like. "What did they do to you, child?"

I swallowed and looked down, as fear rose. I wasn't ready to talk about Tate. Not to Bug. She wouldn't understand. No one could.

Bug sighed and let go of my face. "You'll tell me when you're ready, I expect."

No, I wouldn't. I'd take it to the grave with me.

"Why don't you get back into bed and we can talk?"

I didn't argue, feeling more exhausted than ever after my crying fit. I just hauled myself to my feet, trying not to wince as all my bumps and bruises protested. Bug wheeled herself across the room before I could offer to push her.

"Damn fool chair," she said as it bumped into the tray table. She got the chair arranged to her satisfaction then poured herself a glass of water, refilled my glass at the same time and passed it to me when I'd gotten the covers settled around me.

"So. Daniel tells me you don't want to see him."

I choked on water, coughed hard. "Did he tell you why?"

Her blue eyes showed sympathy for a second then turned no-nonsense. "Yes. He said he bit you."

I nodded.

"And you'll be a werewolf now? Not whatever that bastard wanted?"

I assumed she meant Tate. "Yes. But that doesn't excuse what Dan did."

Bug drank some water and frowned. "A werewolf is better than a vampire. You can still have a relatively normal life as a werewolf. You could even have one with Daniel."

I ignored the Daniel part. "I don't care. I don't want to be either."

"Doesn't seem to me that you have a choice."

"Yes, I do." Just not one I was going to discuss with Bug.

"Right." Bug looked me straight in the eyes with a hard stare. "He told me about that too. About what you asked him to do. I thought I raised you better than that."

Crap. Apparently she knew me better than I thought. I burrowed deeper into the covers. "You don't understand."

Her gaze didn't falter. "I understand all right. You've had a bad time. You're hurt. But I didn't raise you to just give up."

"I don't want to be a monster."

"Then don't be. Be who you are. No matter *what* you are."

If only it were that easy. "I don't know if I can."

"You have to try."

"Why?"

"Because you're alive and they aren't."

I knew who 'they' were. My family. Tears started again and I blinked them away. "They wouldn't want me to live as a werewolf."

"Why not? They'd want you alive. Just like you'd like them to still be. Don't give up without trying, Ashley. That's what he wants you to do."

I stiffened. "What do you mean?"

"That Tate. He'd like for you to just crumble, I'm sure."

I looked away, staring out the window at the brilliantly sunny day outside, as my throat tightened. She was right. But that didn't make hearing it any easier.

"You're alive. And Daniel loves you. He's been crazy in love with you for years. And I think you still love him. That's something to live for."

I kept watching the clouds drift across the blue sky, wishing I could drift away with them. "I don't know if I can."

Bug sighed. "You try. You get help to deal with whatever was done to you and you try. Give it a year."

"And if I can't do it after a year?" I looked back into her eyes.

They never left mine. "If you really can't. After one year. I'll help you. But if you give up before then, if you do something stupid, then I will hunt you down in whatever place you end up in after I die and whup you senseless."

I didn't know whether to laugh or cry. Bug was deadly serious and her offer floored me. I was, for all intents and purposes, her only child and she was offering to help me die. On my terms.

I watched her as she waited calmly for a response and, for the first time, noticed how tired she looked. And old. The circles under her eyes rivaled mine. But the expression in her eyes was fierce. Maybe she hadn't gone through what I had with Tate but she'd come out of her own experience spitting and kicking. She hadn't curled into a ball and given up.

The least I could do for her was try not to either.

"Okay," I said at last. "I'll try." I pressed my lips together, trying not to think about what I'd just agreed to. Living. As a werewolf. God.

She smiled. The joy and relief in her expression let me know I'd made the right choice.

"I'm glad," she said.

"This doesn't mean I forgive Daniel though." I wanted to nip that train of thought in the bud before she got carried away with trying to patch things up between Dan and I.

Her smile widened. "Of course not."

Yeah, she wasn't plotting anything. I could almost see the wedding she was planning in her head. I wondered whether she'd be including raw meaty bones on the menu.

CHAPTER FIFTEEN

THE NEXT MORNING I WAS arguing with Ani and my doctor about whether or not I was ready to go home when Jase walked through the door.

"Sorry, Ash," he said. "They wouldn't let me in before now."

I glared at the doctor. "Why not?" Then I remembered the endless hours I'd spent after my talk with Bug being interrogated by various law enforcement agencies and grimaced. There'd been no time for visitors and I'd fallen asleep almost as soon as the doctors put their feet down and declared me off limits to the FBI for twelve hours.

Jase came over and kissed my cheek. "How are you?"

"I'm fine, as I was just telling Doctor Blair." It was true, mostly. My bruises had faded and the majority of the aches had faded back to dull twinges when I moved. Even my arm had stopped hurting much. Guess it was true what Ani had said about werewolves healing fast.

"She's coming home with me as soon as the doctor discharges her," Ani added.

"And you are?" Jase asked, wearing his over-protective big brother vamp look. It was kind of cute. The thought of any other vampire made me want to run and hide but not Jase. And that was a relief. I needed a friend.

"My name's Anastasia Rogan."

Jase's expression flipped to respectful so quickly I almost laughed. "Oh. Sorry, pack business." He actually stepped backwards a little. Obviously he knew who Ani was even if I hadn't.

"Yes," Ani said.

"I want Jase to come with me," I said suddenly. If I was going to be forced to live amongst a bunch of strange werewolves for weeks then I didn't want Dan to be the only familiar face.

"What?" Jase and Ani said simultaneously. Their tones of shock were identical.

"I want Jase," I repeated.

"Vampires don't usually come to pack houses," Ani said. "We're not really set up for vampires."

"Jase is my assistant. So you'll have to come up with something. You can cart me off for weeks but I have a business to run. And I need him." Needed him as a big old vampire security blanket. Not to actually do any work, although, now that I thought about it, that made good sense too. Jase could be my go between with the outside world.

"I'll ask Sam," Ani said. "He won't like it."

Jase looked kind of worried.

I crossed my arms. I didn't intend to be bossed around by a red haired midget and her as yet unseen husband. I was doing the werewolf thing on my terms. "I don't care if he doesn't like it. I'm not going anywhere without Jase."

Ani pulled out a cell phone and the doctor shooed her into the corridor. Given that I wasn't hooked up to any machines I wasn't sure why.

"I'll just go check on your final test results," Doctor Blair said. "If they're normal, then you can go."

What was normal for an incipient werewolf? But I was more interested in Ani. As soon the doctor left, I turned to Jase. "What's she saying?"

Jase's mouth dropped open. "I can't eavesdrop on your Alpha." He looked horrified at the thought.

I was horrified that I had an Alpha. "Sure you can. You hear her anyway, right? It's not like you're trying."

He sighed. "Ashley, you're going to get us both into trouble."

I snorted. "You think shorty out there is scarier than Tate?"

"No," Jase said. "But only because she's not a psychopath. Don't underestimate her. The Old Ones respect Anastasia and Samuel."

Hmmm. The boss vamps rated the boss werewolves. Something to think about another time. Right now I wanted to know what was being said about me. "Good. She's tough, I get it. Now what's she saying? Remember who signs your pay check."

Jase frowned then sighed again, directing his attention towards the door. "She's talking to a man but I can't really hear what he's saying. Something about pack and stubborn—I guess that's you." He grinned. "And now she's saying okay and—"

"And she's coming back in," Ani said, opening the door. She glared at Jase who shrank back a little. "Wolves have good hearing too," she said, turning the glare on me.

I remained right where I was. "Sue me, but I'm kind of sick of people bossing me around." I'd told Aunt B that I'd give her a year. I hadn't agreed to do it cheerfully. Mad was better than scared so I was going with mad.

"Oh yeah, you're going to fit in great in a wolf pack," Jase muttered softly. It earned him glares from both of us.

Ani turned back to me. "Sam has agreed to the vampire coming to our house. The Retreat, however, is for wolves only."

"The vampire's name is Jason Trent." I said, lifting my chin. "What's the Retreat?"

"Where we go for full moon. It's private."

She obviously wasn't going to say anything else in front of Jase and I'd probably pushed her far enough for one conversation. "Okay, then I accept."

Ani smiled tightly. "Good."

"There's one more thing," Jase said just as the door banged open.

"What?" I asked before Dan stormed through the door. He headed straight for me.

"Ash," he said, almost a breath and before I could do anything he hauled me against me and kissed me.

Pleasure roared through me.

Without thinking I opened my mouth and Dan took me over, kissing me hard and hungry like he'd never thought he'd kiss me again.

Which was, the rational part of my mine pointed out, exactly what he *should* have been thinking. Holding tight to the last shreds of my common sense, I ignored exactly how good his mouth felt on mine, the instinct to wrap myself around him and the ripples of pleasure spreading through my body, put both hands against his chest and *shoved*.

To my shock, he actually moved back a few steps.

"What the hell was that?" I demanded, folding my arms across my chest and trying to focus as the aftershocks of his kiss still hummed through me.

"Hello?" he said, rubbing his chest as if I'd actually made an impression.

Okay, I was stronger. Something else to file away. I contemplated socking him again, just to see how strong but decided Ani and Jase would probably try and stop me. Plus hitting him would mean touching him and if one kiss could scramble my brain then touching him in any way was *not* a good idea. It didn't matter how good his kisses felt. He'd *bitten* me. "I told you I didn't want to see him," I said to Ani. "You're his Alpha. Leash him."

Ani made a 'what can I do' gesture. "I can't stop him seeing you in his official capacity."

Official? He was here for the Taskforce? I doubted it. I narrowed my eyes at Ani, then turned my attention to Dan. "You kiss everyone in your *official* capacity, Special Agent Gibson?"

His mouth twisted. "Christ, Ashley, give me a break."

"No." I said bluntly. "Get out."

He ignored me. "Did you tell her yet?" he said to Jase.

God. Not Jase as well. I couldn't cope with him being on the Ashley and Dan bandwagon on top of everything else. I fixed Jase with a laser beam stare. "He sent you in?"

"No, I wanted to see you." But there was a guilty flash in his eyes and I knew Daniel had suborned him in some way.

"Remind me to bite you if I do change," I snapped then I turned back to Daniel. "Why are you still here?"

"There's something else you need to do before you go with Ani," Daniel said.

"What?"

He nodded at Jase. "You explain."

Jase looked reluctant but came over to me. "It's about Tate."

I ignored the cold that swept over me but did sit back down on the bed. "I already told them all about Tate."

"Yeah, you did. And you said he thralled you."

Jase's voice was gentle but I couldn't look at him or anyone else in the room. Suddenly my anger died leaving room for the shame of exactly what I'd let Tate do to me. And how I'd enjoyed it. "Yes. But he released me." I wrapped my arms around myself. I'd won. I'd *survived*. That's what I had to remember.

"He *said* he released you," Jase said.

My head snapped up. "What do you mean? He released me. I felt it."

"Yeah but he could've done something while you were thralled, left some subconscious command."

Oh God. Another charming vampire power I knew nothing about. "You mean like hypnotism? I'm going to start clucking like a chicken if someone says carrot or something?"

"More like brainwashing," Dan said. "And it's unlikely to be something as innocent as chicken dancing."

Shit. *Tate* could be lurking in my mind. I had the sudden urge to scrub my brain out with Clorox. But that wasn't possible. "How do we know if he did? Can your guys take care of it?"

Dan shook his head. "None of the Taskforce vamps are strong enough."

"Then what?" My voice rose a few notes. If Tate had done something to my mind, I wanted it fixed. *NOW*.

"Lord Marco could do it," Jase said.

My stomach rolled and I stopped breathing for a moment. Lord Marco Sebastiani was an Old One. They wanted me to see an Old One. Not just any vampire but the oldest one in Seattle, the head of the largest lineage. Jase's lineage. Effectively the ruler of the vampires in this city *No. No. No.*

"No." I managed to gasp when I got my breath back.

"Ashley, you have to." Dan crossed his arms. "Tell her, Ani."

"Lord Marco is okay," Jase added.

Okay was not the word I would use to describe an ancient vampire. The thought of any vampire was bad enough but the Old Ones got to be Old Ones because they were the most powerful. Marco could take me as easily as Tate had. Probably even faster. And, even if he did seem to be one of the more civilized Old Ones, based on what I'd seen of him on TV and read about him, he'd spent plenty of years living the more traditional vamp lifestyle.

"No," I said again as a shiver crawled across my skin.

"Daniel is right, Ashley," Ani said softly. "You can't be trusted if Tate has planted something in your mind. We'd have to lock you up."

"But we don't know if he has," I argued, heart beating furiously. "He said he released me."

"You're trusting Tate now?" Dan asked sarcastically.

"He kept to our agreement," I retorted.

"He beat you up and tried to turn you," Dan roared. I could smell him, clearer than ever and just as clearly I could smell the anger rising within him, rousing the wolf.

I just didn't care.

"And you bit me. You're the one who actually changed me," I yelled back. "So why should I listen to you?"

Dan's eyes went that silver glass shade and I knew I'd hurt him. I couldn't really bring myself to care all that much but it hurt me too, just a little.

"Because I'm trying to save your life," he said in a flat no-arguments tone. "I don't care if I have to tie you up and drag you there, but you are going to see Marco."

"You and whose army?" I snarled.

"That would be mine," Ani said and we both snapped our heads round to face her. Suddenly her scent seemed much stronger. "Daniel is right. I won't let you endanger the pack. You will see Marco."

"I didn't ask to join your stupid pack," I said even as my determination not to see Marco faded a little.

"I know you're upset, Ashley," Ani said evenly. "So you get a few breaks. But you're acting like a child. Why would you want to carry the touch of a vampire inside your head? The fact you are arguing about this only suggests that Tate has indeed left his mark. You cannot come amongst the pack until it is gone. And believe me, you need to be with pack right now." Her tone held a rumbling edge that drained the protests out of me. It made me want to sit up straighter and do as I was told.

Not my favorite feeling. It was bad enough when Bug did it but she, at least, had earned the right. Ani the elf hadn't. Not yet. "I—"

"Silence," Ani snapped. "You will go with Daniel and Jason to see Marco. Then they will bring you to our house. If you refuse then I have plenty of wolves who will assist Daniel in enforcing my will."

Go willingly or be carried kicking and screaming. That message was coming through loud and clear. Nobody was going to tie me up again, that was for sure. "Fine," I said. "We'll go see Marco. Once the doctor clears me."

"Excellent," Ani said with a smile that had a distinct feral edge. She turned to the boys. "Perhaps you two should wait outside while I help Ashley get ready to leave."

Jase and Dan both made a beeline for the door and Ani turned her smile on me. "Let's get you ready. And then we can have a little chat about pack rules."

Oh great. A pissed off alpha and an Old One. This was going to be a fun, fun day.

Ani's lecture on pack etiquette was still ringing in my ears when I climbed into the back of Dan's Jeep an hour later. The woman could give Bug lessons on how to make you feel like an idiot. I crossed my arms over my chest as we pulled out of the hospital parking lot and refused to look at either Jase or Dan.

Neither of them seemed very interested in starting a conversation so a chilly silence reigned in the car as we negotiated our way into Magnolia.

Just when it was becoming unbearable, Dan turned into a driveway and stopped the car. The way forward was blocked by tall iron gates and he lowered the window to speak into the intercom.

"Lord Marco's done well for himself, then," I said sarcastically to Jase as we drove slowly down a long graveled drive lined with giant oaks.

"He's an Old One," Jase said, as if that were enough.

"What's he like?" I asked, trying to prepare myself for whatever lay ahead.

"He's okay for an Old One," Jase said. "But he won't put up with the sort of stuff you pulled on Ani."

I'd already figured that much out. Ani had barely put up with what I'd pulled on Ani, and I got the impression the main reason she hadn't kicked my butt was because I hadn't changed yet. A vampire wouldn't care about that. I intended to be scrupulously polite and get the hell out of there as fast as I could. I might want to die but I'd promised Bug I'd wait a year. So no doing anything suicidal like offending an Old One.

Daniel pulled the car up in front of the house when we reached the end of the drive. It wasn't as big as I'd imagined from the grounds. Don't get me wrong, it was big but it wasn't the sort of huge Queen Anne style mansion I'd expected. Instead it was a sprawling white house with arched windows and a red-tiled roof. Dark green vines with tiny white blooms twined up columns and over the archways and red geraniums flourished in tubs leading up the stairs to the front door. It all looked vaguely Spanish or Italian or something.

Out of place in rainy old Seattle, that was for sure.

If there hadn't been an Old One inside waiting to meet me, I would've liked it a lot better. I gripped the handle of the car door, not wanting to move another inch. Unless it was to run back down the drive and the hell away from here. I tried to breathe. It didn't help. "How about I just stay here and you two can go inside?"

"Don't joke around, Ashley," Dan said impatiently.

I wasn't exactly joking, I was starting to feel hot and vaguely sick at the thought of walking into a vampire's house.

Shade sails made of UV proof fabric guarded half the drive and the path up to the house, making it safe for vampires to walk during the day. Which only emphasized that there *were* vampires inside. Sweat started to trickle down my back.

Dan and Jase climbed out of the car and headed towards the stairs, then stopped and turned back as one when they realized I wasn't following.

Jase came back over to the Jeep. "What's the matter?"

"Maybe this is too soon," I said through clenched teeth, still clinging to the door handle.

"You don't really have a choice," Jase said. "C'mon, boss. Out of the car."

I tried to open the door, I really did, but my body wouldn't obey my mind. It knew exactly what was inside that pretty white house and it didn't want any part of it.

"Ashley, stop kidding around." Dan grabbed the door and pulled it open, almost yanking my arms off in the process. Only my seatbelt kept me from tumbling out onto the drive.

"I'm not," I said honestly.

He looked from my hands to my face. "What's going on?" "Oh, you know, just having a disagreement between my feet and my brain." I tried again to breathe deeply but my heart pounded like I was running a marathon and I couldn't quite catch my breath.

"About what?" His voice had dropped to a low, soothing tone.

"About whether I'll die if I go into that house."

"Who's winning?" He moved a step closer and put his hands over mine, stroking the knuckles.

"At this point, it's kind of fifty-fifty." I closed my eyes and sucked in another breath, focusing on his skin sliding over mine. Dan's hands were warm and my grip loosened a little as he kept rubbing mine. For a moment I forgot how angry I was with him as the fear started to ease.

"Anything I can do?" Dan said, fingers still moving in slow waves that felt just a little too good.

"Distract me."

"I could sing," Jase offered. "You know..." and he burst into the opening lines of *Climb Every Mountain*.

The incongruity of a vampire singing *The Sound of Music* made me giggle and Dan managed to unlock my fingers from the handle and slide them free. They closed around his arm instead and I didn't try and let go.

"Listen to me," he said softly. "I'm not going to let anything bad happen to you."

"Neither am I," Jase said, breaking off his song. "We have safe passage here."

Whatever that meant. But I felt better. I wasn't alone here. I wasn't trapped. So I was just going to walk the hell in there under my own steam and let Marco kick Tate out of my head once and for all.

CHAPTER SIXTEEN

JASE HAD PICKED THE WRONG song. *A Few of My Favorite Things* would've been more appropriate. Wasn't that the one they sang to distract themselves from fear?

Somehow I didn't think imagining raindrops and kittens was going to work in this situation. I stood behind Dan and Jase as Dan rang the doorbell and tried to convince myself I was safe.

I wasn't buying it. My heartbeat sounded loud in my ears. I wondered why Dan and Jase weren't deafened by it.

The door swung open and a very human servant with, from what I could see, a bite-free neck, ushered us inside.

I looked around to distract myself. The foyer of the house was almost as big as my entire office suite. The white walls were hung with huge and colorful landscapes. A intricate mosaic of various creatures cavorting amongst flowers covered the floor. Not at all what I'd pictured. Weren't vamp dens meant to be all dark walls and red velvet?

Or was that just Tate?

I shivered and gave myself a mental shake. Lord Marco was *not* Tate. And I had a werewolf and a vampire protecting me. I moved closer to Dan.

Another servant—a woman with cropped blonde hair—joined the first. "Lord Marco is expecting you," she said with a slight bow. She led us away from the foyer, along a passageway lined with a series of doors. I focused on trying to slow my breathing, rather than thinking about what happened next. It worked, a little. My heart was only racing a little rather than pounding by the time the servant paused at one of the doors before knocking twice and opening it.

The room she showed us into was somewhere in the middle of the house. It had no windows but looked fairly normal apart from that.

If your idea of normal was very expensive furniture, extravagant floral arrangements, and an Old One, that is.

Not that Lord Marco looked like I expected either.

He rose from a chair pulled up to an elegant antique desk as we entered. He looked about my age.

That was the first surprise. For some reason my mind equated Old Ones with pictures of Nosferatu-ish monsters.

But this man was no monster. He was anything but. In fact, he was flat out gorgeous. Olive skin, dark hair cut close to his head that looked like it would curl if he let it grow longer and eyes a curious clear shade of green.

He wore a beautifully cut pair of pale linen pants and a white shirt and pretty much looked like he'd just stepped out of the pages of GQ. Or maybe Italian Vogue. I wondered exactly what European country he was from originally and what period of time. Despite his young appearance, there a sense of age surrounded him. Age and power. My heart sped up again.

Dan and I stopped, letting Jase going forward. To my surprise, Jase bowed. "My lord, this is Special Agent Daniel Gibson and—"

"Signorina Keenan," Marco interrupted. "Ashley, is it not?"

His voice was deep, lightly accented and musical. Kind of sexy, in fact. Which only made me more nervous.

"Yes, my lord," I said, following Jason's lead on how to address him. I wanted to be polite and not upset him. But I didn't bow and I kept my gaze away from his.

Marco came towards us and sweat started to break out on my back again. It didn't matter that he looked like a model, my gut knew what he really was. I took an involuntary step backwards and he paused.

"You are afraid of me?"

How did I answer that and not sound rude? I decided honesty was the best policy. "I seem to have a problem with vampires at the moment."

He looked from me to Jason. "But you are not afraid of Jason?"

"No, my lord. I've known Jason a long time."

"And me you do not know. Ah."

I hoped I hadn't offended him, tried to smile. He stayed where he was, looking at me curiously.

"I will not hurt you, Ashley. I do not take from the unwilling."

I couldn't help wondering how easily he turned someone from unwilling to willing with the power of that face and voice alone.

"It's not you, exactly." I managed.

"*Si.* I understand. It is Tate. He has done this to you. Allow me to apologize, Ashley. McCallister Tate is a problem I thought would no longer trouble us. It seems I was mistaken. He is no credit to my house."

Nice to know that Tate had managed to fool everybody. And wait a minute, Marco's house? Did that mean… "Tate's from your lineage?"

He sighed, looking apologetic. "*Si.* Yes. Sired by a wayward child."

"Tate's of your lineage?" I said, this time to Jase. "You never told me that." It made me feel kind of weird.

"I didn't know," Jase said, holding up his hands.

"It is not something I advertise," Marco added. "It is difficult enough managing our relationship with the public as it is. And after all, every family has its…what do you call them…bad seeds?"

"I think Tate is a bit more than a bad seed," I said, only just managing to keep the sting out of my tone.

Marco nodded. "He should've been taken care of long ago, but he has evaded us. Believe me, now that I know he has survived, I am seeking to rectify the situation."

That made me smile. I wouldn't want to have the Old Ones after me. I hoped if they caught Tate, it would be a painful end.

"And of course, you will turn him over to the authorities if you find him," Dan said.

Marco arched an eyebrow, looking almost amused by the concept. I found myself siding with him. The only thing to do with Tate was put him down like the rabid dog he was. No trial required. We all knew what he'd done.

"We have our own justice," Marco said.

"And you're trying to convince the public you're just good citizens," Dan retorted.

"You think Tate should be spared, Agent Gibson?"

I was kind of interested in the answer to that myself. What did Dan want to do to the man who had kidnapped and almost killed me?

Dan straightened his shoulders, "No. But I think there's a system to follow."

For some reason his answer annoyed me and I found myself feeling a little more sympathetic towards Marco.

"You are young," Marco said. "Idealistic." He made a dismissive gesture. "But you did not bring Ashley here to discuss legal ideologies."

Jase nodded. "My lord, Tate—"

"He thralled her," Marco said with another flick of his hand. "So I was informed. May I come closer?" he added, turning to me.

I nodded but couldn't stop myself taking another step backwards as soon as he moved. Marco stopped again with a frown. He took a deep breath, almost if he was smelling the air and his face cleared. Then he looked at Dan. "Perhaps if we do this on the couch. If you hold her, your touch, it will comfort her."

"We're not bonded," Dan said.

Marco looked surprised. What did it take to surprise an Old One? I had no idea what the hell they were talking about but decided to add it to the long list of things I needed to discuss with Ani.

"My mistake," Marco said. "Still, you care for her, yes?"

"I can do it," Jase said.

"I do not think adding another vampire to the situation will relax Signorina Keenan." Marco retreated to one of two long sofas in the middle of the room. "If you would bring her over here, Agent Gibson."

Dan held out his hand and I took it, allowing him to lead me over to the sofa. Under Marco's instructions, Dan settled into the corner against the arms and I sat with him, my back resting on his chest, his arms locked around my waist.

The feeling of Dan at my back was almost as unsettling as having Marco only a few feet away. He was warm and solid and smelled better than ever. And the shifter buzz I'd normally feel was different somehow...warmer. More appealing. I moved away slightly but he tightened his grip, drawing me back.

"Relax, Ashley," Marco said. "Your wolf will protect you."

"He's not my wolf," I muttered, ignoring the warmth spreading through me wherever Dan was touching me.

Marco smiled. "As you say. Now, may I approach you?"

I nodded and with Dan holding me, managed to stay still as Marco came nearer. Thankfully his scent was nothing like Tate's. He smelled earthy and strange but not unpleasant. I relaxed a little.

Marco reached out and touched my forehead. Then I flinched, shivered and started sweating again. Marco lifted his fingers.

"Peace, *cara*," he murmured. "This will not take long." His fingers descended onto my skin again

I leaned back against Dan and closed my eyes, fighting the panic the touch of cool skin had awakened. Then the touch was gone.

"Well?" Dan asked.

"There is something there," Marco said. "I am not entirely sure..."

My eyes flew open. That didn't sound good. "What do you mean, not sure?"

"I can take care of this, Ashley," the vampire said, "but I fear you will not like my method."

I shrank back against Dan, heard him murmur something soothing in my ear. It didn't help. "What does that mean?"

"I need deeper contact to determine exactly what Tate has done and to remove it. I will need to thrall you myself."

"No *way.*" It was an automatic response. Dan's arms tightened around me.

"Ashley, you have to let him do this," Jase said from the opposite sofa.

I cringed. "I don't want to."

"You will be free of him after this," Marco said.

"Yeah but will I be free of you?" I snapped and saw Jase wince. I took a deep breath, trying to calm myself. I couldn't piss off an Old One.

Marco pursed his lips. "I give you my word.

"That's what Tate said."

"My word carries more weight than his. My word on my line."

Jase made a choking noise.

More vampire games. "What does that mean?" I demanded.

"It means, Signorina Keenan, that if I play you false in this you are owed a debt by my lineage. An unlimited debt. You may call on us at any time."

That won't help me if I'm dead because you're lying. I managed to bite my lip before I spoke the thought out loud then glanced guiltily at Marco, realizing he might just be able to hear me anyway.

"You would almost own us," Marco continued.

My own private vampire army. Just what every girl needs.

So, Tate in my head or Marco? Marco, whose blood had spawned Tate. But it had also spawned Jase and I knew there was no evil in Jase. I wasn't so sure about Marco but his eyes didn't carry the same inhuman expression as Tate's.

Maybe he was just better at hiding what he was but I was going to have to take that risk.

"All right," I said with another shuddering breath. "Do it."

"All will be well," Marco said. He knelt by the sofa, reached up and put his hands either side of my face. "Now, *cara.* Look at me."

I had to fight to obey him but finally I managed to meet his gaze.

This time it didn't feel like falling, more like a cool green breeze blowing through me. I floated, surrounded by warmth and that pleasant sense of green, like lying in sunshine in a forest. It was even more seductive than Tate had been. Panic flared.

"*Tutto bene, cara,*" Marco's voice whispered in my mind. "I will be done here soon." He paused and I floated again, more relaxed.

"Hold a moment," the voice came again. He made a satisfied sound. "I have it. Now, *cara,* listen to me. I can ease these memories for you...take them away."

To not remember. It was an enticing offer. But I needed to remember. It was important. For me and for the case. "No," I said. "No, I don't want to forget."

"Brave," he said. "Then I leave you with this, Ashley. You are free. Of Tate and any other. You are safe."

The greenness surrounded me, flooded through me and I sighed happily, nestled in warmth and the teasing scent of Dan.

"I release you," Marco said, and this time it was my ears that heard him, not my mind. The green warmth washed away slowly. I blinked, feeling not quite awake.

"Ash? Are you okay?" Dan's voice sounded loud in my ear, sending a pleased shiver down my spine.

I blinked again. For the first time in days I felt truly relaxed. Boneless almost. I wanted to melt into the man holding me. Which made me realize that perhaps I felt a little too good.

And, even though I couldn't see Dan, I somehow knew that he didn't want to let go of me. That he was turned on too. I straightened, pushing at Dan's hands. He loosened his grip slowly and I wriggled free. "Yes. Yes, I'm fine. Thank you, my lord."

Marco rose to his feet and held out a hand to help me up.

"The pleasure was mine, Signorina Keenan." He looked at me strangely for a moment and grinned, a wicked dimple flashing in his cheek. "And should you ever decide you are willing..."

I couldn't help smiling at him, even as I shook my head. Behind me Dan made a rumbling noise and Marco looked over my shoulder.

"Perhaps not. Your wolf does not seem to wish to share."

"He's not my wolf," I repeated and Marco laughed as Dan rumbled again.

"Well, that was fun," I said as we drove out of Marco's gates. I stretched my arms above my head, as far as the ceiling of the Jeep would allow, feeling loose and relaxed. "What's next?"

Jase peered at me curiously. "Are you okay? You sound a little buzzed."

I bounced on the seat. "I'm fine."

"You're not fine," Jase said. He peered at me closely, a wrinkle appearing between his eyebrows.

"Relax," Dan said. "Her metabolism is doing some weird things right now. It can have some odd effects. And the full moon is only six days away."

That sobered me for a moment but then I started humming *Blue Moon* under my breath, swaying softly. Dan was wrong. The buzz I was riding wasn't the moon or lycanthropy. It was a combination of

CHAPTER SEVENTEEN

TURNS OUT IT WAS FUN, kind of. Apart from those moments when I seriously freaked out about becoming a werewolf. But the counselor the Taskforce set me up with helped with that a little, even if I had a long way to go.

But I liked Ani a lot and Samuel was nice too, once I got over the fact he was tall and blond like Rio. I guess the fact that he favored jeans and faded basketball team tee's rather than black and knives helped.

And their three children were normal, healthy, well-adjusted kids, as far as I could tell—not having been an entirely normal kid myself once my family had gone. None of them seemed perturbed by the fact they'd be werewolves one day. And all three of them had an innate talent for mayhem.

The first morning, I woke thinking a riot had broken out downstairs but it was only the kids screaming in delight over some game. And my increasingly sensitive hearing as it turned out.

The lycanthropy virus was having its way with me and I spent the first few days wincing at noises or smells I would never have noticed before. Jase and I scrambled to catch up on work after the impromptu week off and Ani and Sam tried to prepare me by stuffing me full of werewolf lore. There were a lot of rules to being a werewolf. Lots. And I was only getting the Cliff Notes crash course version.

The smell thing made it hard to be in the same room with Dan. He smelled better than ever and he didn't even have to be agitated or mad for me to notice the wild wolf scent now. I avoided him as much as possible, which wasn't as much as I would've liked. He lived only a few blocks from Ani and Sam and they insisted on letting him into the house. And he was still Agent in Charge on the Tate investigation. It helped that most of the time I still wanted to knock him on his ass for putting me in this situation in the first place.

Scary thing was I'd probably be able to once I'd changed.

Two days before the full moon, I walked into the kitchen, picked up a mug to pour myself a coffee and it shattered in my grip. Ani was at the sink, washing dishes. She jumped at the noise then looked at the mess and then over at me, her expression strange. I had the sudden urge to flee. There was a sort of wild triumph in her eyes.

"I think it's time to go to the Retreat," she said and turned back to her dishes as if nothing momentous had happened.

The Retreat.

It had assumed almost mythical proportions in my mind. The place where the pack celebrated and hunted under the full moon. Where they guarded and guided werewolves going through their first changes. Where they buried those who didn't survive.

The reality of my situation suddenly sank through me like a stone. In less than forty-eight hours I'd be a werewolf or I'd be dead.

If you'd asked me in the hospital, I would've chosen the latter. But now I wasn't so sure.

The Retreat made Marco's house look like a shack. The main building was built along hotel lines and there were ten or so smaller guest houses scattered about the grounds. The grounds themselves were several hundred acres of forest and woodland, stocked, though I didn't want to think about that bit, with deer and other animals.

Plenty of room to run.

Plenty of room to die.

Ani, Sam and I stayed in the Alpha's house, which wasn't part of the main building. Apparently I would be easier to control if I wasn't surrounded by too many wolves just now.

Up to a hundred were expected to arrive for the full moon. There were more than that in the pack, but those who had been wolves for a long enough time were trusted to keep control and they didn't have to attend if they chose not to. Younger wolves came unless there was some reason for them to be away. And in those situations, arrangements were usually made with whichever pack whose territory they were in to provide a guide.

Not-quite-yet wolves like me were kept under close surveillance.

Which didn't sit well with the increasing edginess I had about the whole thing. I felt like ants were crawling under my skin when I thought about changing. And I was filled with a restless energy that made it impossible for me to relax.

Ani took me for long walks through the grounds and I spent time working out in the gym, and running with Jase—I'd nearly had a panic attack at the thought of Jase not being there so Ani had relented—but it didn't help much.

I wanted space and distance and freedom.

I wanted to howl at the moon, I realized with some shock as I sat staring out my window on the night before full moon.

The moon hung low in the sky. Not quite full but I could feel the silvery light gliding over my skin like a caress, calling me out to play. I wanted to tear off my clothes and feel that light on my naked skin.

And that wasn't all I wanted. Desire snaked through my veins under the cool light, burning deep in my belly. Ani had explained this to me too, that the energy of the moon awakens other energies. But her explanations hadn't quite prepared me for the overwhelming force of my hunger for skin on skin.

I didn't know whether it was because this was my first time, or because I had been single for a while or because I was surrounded by the scents of male wolves but I hadn't felt like this in a long time…maybe never.

I wanted the weight and feel of a man. Salt and heat and touch. I wanted someone to fuck me senseless.

I couldn't have anyone.

Ani had forbidden Dan to come anywhere near the house and she was keeping the other unmated male wolves away. Intellectually, I knew she was right to do so, that I wasn't in any shape to be dealing with sex right now, let alone sex that was driven by desire not entirely of my own making.

It was too soon after Tate.

But my body didn't understand that fact. My body burned.

My body made me open the window and sniff the night air deeply, seeking something I didn't quite understand. And the air in my room was heavy with my scent, touched with an unfamiliar edge. A hint of the same wildness Dan carried.

The wildness growing within me.

It was a long night.

I only managed to fall asleep when the moon sank below the horizon, easing the longing. The rest of the night I'd paced, taken a cold shower, even taken matters into my own hands. None of which helped particularly.

I slept until noon, only to wake feeling gritty-eyed, muddle-headed and more on edge than ever.

The underlying fear of what I was about to go through only worsened my temper.

I snarled at Jase, snapped at Ani and broke another mug before I'd made it through my breakfast or lunch or whatever it was. At which point I burst into tears.

Ani shooed Jase and Sam out of the kitchen then made me more tea as I dripped tears into my scrambled eggs.

"It will be better after tonight," she said soothingly.

At this point I was willing to concede that almost anything had to be better than how I felt right now. "I can't see how it could be worse." I scratched at my bare forearm. I was wearing a tank and shorts, the lightest clothing I had. Anything else made me feel too hot. And even the thin cotton made me itch today.

"Think of it as going through puberty in a few days," Ani said sympathetically as she gently batted my hand away from my arm. "Your body chemistry is changing radically. There's bound to be a few side effects. You'll find an equilibrium again."

Puberty, huh? At least I wasn't covered in zits but I had to agree with Ani. The bored, restless, weepy feeling did remind me of being a rebellious teenager. I wanted to pick a fight. I wanted to run.

I wanted chocolate.

Or sex.

"This isn't fair," I said, sounding whiny even to my own ears. "I didn't ask for this."

"Many of us don't. But we adjust. Does my life seem so terrible to you?"

I shook my head. Ani and Sam had a good marriage. And great kids when they weren't wreaking havoc. But my head still couldn't reconcile 'happy' with 'werewolf'.

"Daniel is worried about you," Ani said, changing the subject before I could get any broodier.

"So? He should be. This is all his fault."

Ani sighed. We'd been through several iterations of this conversation already. "You'll have to forgive him eventually."

"No, actually I don't. I never have to forgive him."

"Never say never."

I pushed away my mug and empty plate. I was already starting to feel hungry again, even though I'd just eaten three times what I normally had for breakfast. "I'm going to call my aunt."

At sunset I stood in a small clearing near the edge of the forest. Only just standing. Shivers rippled through my body despite the fact I was burning up. Little twinges of pain kept spiking at me in different places. The knob of my right wrist. Halfway up my left thigh. The nape of my neck.

"Just keep breathing, Ashley," Ani said. She stood maybe six feet away from me. "Just a little longer."

I snarled at her, I couldn't help it. A real snarl, low and rumbling that hurt my throat. Humans aren't supposed to make that sort of sound.

"Breathe," she said. "In and out."

I wanted to run. Wanted to move but I managed to stay still and do as I was told. My brain felt foggy, like I was trying to remember something half-forgotten. Why was I here? Why couldn't I move? *Changing*. Right.

"Breathe."

I growled again and Ani moved a little closer. I didn't see her but her scent flowed over me, cool and calming, making me want to do as she said.

Beyond the clearing, I was aware of others moving through the trees as the skies darkened. I heard the tiny cracks of twigs, the pad of bare feet on leaves and grass. Just like I could hear the breathing of the five who stood around the outskirts of the clearing, ready to help Ani if she needed it.

Samuel. And four other female wolves I'd met over the last couple of days. Their scents mingled with the smells of the forest and the night as they stood. Waiting to see me change.

Another shudder ripped through me, pain following immediately in its tracks, driving me to my knees. "This hurts," I panted.

"Only this time," Ani said. "Don't fight."

"How much longer?" I dug my fingers into the dirt.

Somewhere off to my left a howl split the night air. The liquid call of it raised the hairs on the back of my neck. I wanted to answer, wanted to join in the dance it seemed to be inviting me to.

"Not long," Ani said. She sounded annoyed. I got the feeling the howler was in trouble.

"Hang on." She moved a little closer.

It was nearly dark now and I couldn't see her face clearly. She was a pale blur surrounded by dark curls of hair. Like me she wore a white cotton shift. Something that would tear easily. I hadn't wanted to be naked. Not with near strangers watching.

The air grew still around us and I started to feel the energy boil over my skin again. Looking up I saw the moon hit the top of the trees then a cloud shifted and the light fell on me.

The world exploded. Heat bubbled through me and the sound of my heartbeat thundered in my ears. Things moved and shifted beneath my skin with a speed and fury that brought a pained scream to my lips.

A scream that ended as a howl.

The sound was answered by what sounded like an army of wolves, their voices rising eerily from the darkened trees around us.

My howl choked off in surprise and I lay on the ground breathing hard, eyes closed while the pain ebbed away. I felt different but I wasn't ready to look, not just yet. But as the pain faded, the energy rose again and with it, the urge to move.

I opened my eyes.

Everything looked sharper. Details I hadn't been able to make out with human eyes were crystal clear. Twigs on branches. Different shapes of grass. A bird fluttered onto a branch in the nearest tree and the movement riveted my attention, my head tracking it.

"Ashley?"

I turned my head. Ani stood in front of me, still in human form.

She smiled. "Are you okay?"

I considered the question. I no longer hurt but the rush of sounds and smells was confusing. I rolled to what would've been lying flat on my stomach in human form only to find that wolf legs kind of get in the way so I ended up half-lying, half-sitting, trying to get used to the sight of paws where hands should be.

Ani came closer, stretched out a hand toward my nose. I sniffed it quickly, almost sneezing at the scent of the hand cream she used. But under the human scents was an undeniable scent of familiarity, of belonging.

Ani smiled again, then ran her hand down my back.

"You're black, like Dan," she said.

I'd been wondering about that. I could see my fur was dark but in the silvery light I couldn't tell what color it might be. Colors were different with wolf eyes. Or maybe that was the moonlight.

"Try to stand up," she said. "Brace with your front legs, it will feel weird at first."

With her help I manage to stand, trying to adjust to an eye-level several feet lower than I was used to and to the weight of my tail hanging weirdly behind me.

It didn't feel wrong exactly, just odd.

"Hang on," Ani said then she did the blurring thing Dan had done and a wolf stood in her place.

I yipped in surprise and backed up a pace, almost getting my legs tangled up in my tail.

The wolf—Ani—was paler than me in color, a dark red like her hair maybe, and closer to normal wolf size than Dan had been. But something about her made me wary.

She approached me slowly then stood nose to nose.

She was actually smaller than me but I found myself crouching. In wolf form, it was perfectly clear that Ani was the Alpha. Command flowed through her posture and her scent.

She nuzzled my neck briefly then *"Get up."*

It sounded in my head, not my ears and I whined.

"Ashley? Can you hear me?"

"I don't know how to do this," I thought.

"Yes, you do," Ani said with a mental chuckle. Her mouth stretched in a doggy grin. *"I can hear you just fine."*

"So can I."

I spun.

From the trees, another wolf, lighter again than Annie approached. He was big, much bigger than either of us. Sam.

The other four female wolves who'd been watching us ranged around him.

Sam came closer to me and I had the same reaction to him as I had to Ani, crouching low. He nuzzled my neck too then stepped away, letting me stand full height again. When the first of the females approached I bristled, the fur on the back of my neck and spine lifting. Ani and Sam commanded my respect. Anyone else was going to have to earn it.

"Ladies," Sam said looking from me to the wolf with his tail waving slowly from side to side.

Ani made a rumbling noise at the other wolves and they came no closer. *"We don't need to decide any of this tonight. Ashley, let's run."*

CHAPTER EIGHTEEN

ANI THREW BACK HER HEAD and howled. The sound sent a shiver down my spine. It didn't have an exact human translation, something close to *chase*run*free*power* but it spoke directly to the wolf, tapping into the energy burning through me.

I answered the call, howling to the moonlight like I'd wanted to the night before.

Then there was a quick *"Come on,"* from Ani and she took off, running headlong into the trees.

I bounded after her, trying not to think, trying to let this new body do what it was meant to do.

Running in wolf form was a revelation. I skimmed over the ground, the movement an effort, yes, but also pure joy. I felt as though I could run for days as I followed Ani's twists and turns half by sight, half by the scent trail she left and the sounds of her paws hitting the earth.

The smells of the forest flowed over my nose like perfume. Damp earth, ripe leaves, bark, cool water somewhere in the distance. And the smell of other wolves. Not close but identifiable. There was an underlying common note to the scents, something that spoke of home, of belonging.

Pack.

I heard them moving through the forest with me, heard a song of yips and howls begin to build. *Faster* it seemed to say. *Wilder*

Ani disappeared between the trees as she rounded a bend in the rough track we were following and I sped up, only to come to a sliding halt as I recognized the smell of the wolf blocking the path.

Dan.

In the night air, the wildness of him flowed through me like electricity, until I wanted to rub myself along his fur and cover myself in the deliciousness of that scent. I dug my claws into the dirt to stay right where I was, growling in the back of my throat.

"*Ashley.*"

There was longing in the tone of his thought and I dropped my eyes. I didn't want to see how magnificent he looked with the moonlight reflecting off his fur and turning his eyes almost pure silver.

He padded closer, circling me so his fur almost brushed mine. I shivered as his scent tugged at me, wanting to lean into the warmth. He stopped when he was facing me again, our noses maybe an inch apart.

I growled again. "*Get out of my way.*"

I could hear that Ani had stopped a hundred feet or so down the path but she wasn't coming back to find me.

Dan cocked his head to one side. "*Listen to the song. They're starting to hunt. Are you joining them?*"

I could hear what he meant. The howls had grown fiercer. More purposeful. Predatory.

I didn't know if I was ready for the hunt. But I knew I wasn't ready to stay here and find out just how strong an effect Dan might have on me under the moon. And the howls were calling to me almost as strongly as he did.

"*I said, get out of my way.*" I snarled then sprang into a run, ducking around him, sprinting towards Ani and the howls. I expected him to follow me but didn't hear any sounds of pursuit.

I didn't want to think about Dan. Didn't want to think period. So I just ran, overtaking Ani and chasing the chorus of howls growing around me, pounding through my head and my blood.

Gradually I became aware of more and more strange wolves surrounding me and another enticing smell ahead on the path. Something warm and rich that made me salivate.

The howls grew more and more intense. I found myself running with three other wolves behind two deer whose frantic hoof beats pounded on the dirt, inflaming me even further.

Instinct spurred me after them, made me stretch and twist and fly as they twisted and turned, their fear scenting the air.

One of the wolves arrowed ahead of me and leapt. The deer tumbled abruptly, a sudden crack and stillness telling me it had broken its neck.

The wolf sat for a second panting in the moonlight, then lowered its head and tore the deer's throat out.

Blood spilled onto the path. The smell swam around me, blurring my vision as hunger flared to life inside me. Blood. Thick and warm and salty-sweet.

It called to me and I crept closer to the deer, fighting the urge to join the wolves tearing at the skin of its belly, my human mind warring with the wolf. Steam rose from the blood exposed to the cool air, making the smell even stronger. Even more tempting.

"*Feed, Ashley. Join us.*"

Ani appeared at my side and the other wolves melted back from the deer. I hesitated and she walked delicately to the deer and tore free a chunk of meat, gulping it down. Then she came back to me. The blood smell rose from her fur, mixing with the alpha smell.

"*Feed,*" she said again and nuzzled my face, transferring the blood from her fur to mine. Instinctively my tongue flicked out to lick it clean and the salty taste seemed to snap any control the human had over the wolf. Snarling at the others, I leapt for the deer and buried my teeth deep into the wound Ani had created.

Blood and meat. Power. It flowed through me like a drug as I fed and fed until I didn't feel like Ashley anymore at all.

In the morning I felt like Ashley again. An Ashley who was stiff and sore, but a good kind of stiff and sore. My bruises were gone. My nausea at the thought of eating raw deer wasn't.

The smell of the plate of bacon Ani put in front of me made my stomach quiver uneasily.

"I think I'll just have toast."

"It's weird at first," Sam said sympathetically. "But at least you're not vegetarian. It's just meat in a different form. You eat meat."

Not raw meat. I sipped juice and tried not to think about it.

"Just think of it as carpaccio," Jase added helpfully.

I shot him a 'not helping' look. "It's not the same thing."

"How do you think I felt drinking blood the first time?"

"I never thought about it." I looked down at the bacon and my stomach heaved again. I pushed the plate away.

Jase pulled a face. "It was kind of gross. But you acquire a taste for it."

I had no intention of acquiring a taste for eating raw bloody deer. Or anything else. "I don't have to hunt, do I?"

Ani shrugged, forking up bacon and eggs. "Not every time but the less you give into the urge, the stronger it will be. It's easier for young wolves if they change and hunt regularly. Your control will be better."

Looked like I'd be taking the hard way then. Being a wolf was just too weird. Once a month would do me just fine.

"Pack meeting tonight," Sam said as he rose and carried his dishes to the sink.

"M-meeting?" I wasn't sure I was ready to face that many people. Not when I'd seen some of them last night with blood dripping from their jaws.

"Mostly your First Change party," Ani said. "People are staying on because the full moon was Friday night."

A werewolves' weekend away. Lucky me. "I'm not really in the partying mood."

"You need to meet your pack," Ani said. Her tone suggested there was no point arguing. And it was harder than before not to just do what she wanted.

A side-effect of changing I hadn't expected. "Why?"

"It will make it easier on you. You need to see that we're just people."

People who turned into giant wolves and killed deer under the full moon. People who might eat even darker things if they gave full rein to their instincts. I'd known what I'd felt last night. The urge to hunt, to kill and feast. If a human had wandered into those woods I wasn't so sure that I'd have differentiated them from a deer as prey. So how was I different from Tate?

I didn't know the answer any more.

The pack meeting was held in a function room in the main house. It could've been any big party almost anywhere. Men, women, and some teenagers standing around talking and laughing. Eating chips and dip and drinking beers or coffees or sodas. Music played softly under the buzz of conversation, something vaguely jazzy.

I still had the urge to turn right around and leave, especially when I saw Dan across the room, laughing with a short blonde and a tall brunette.

Only the fact Ani and Sam were right behind me kept me from fleeing back to Jase, who hadn't been invited, immediately.

The conversation died down as people turned to look at us. The expressions ranged from curiosity to appraisal to something approaching hostility from the bottle blonde with Dan. I wondered if he was sleeping with her then squelched the thought. Why should I care who he screwed?

Ani moved to stand in front of me. "This is Ashley Keenan," she said when the room was completely silent. "She knows the moon."

The crowd erupted into cheers and applause. The sound hurt my ears and I backed up a step. Sam caught my arm.

"Easy," he said for my ears only.

"The pack increases," Ani said when the noise died down.

"The blood is strong," they answered back.

I stayed where I was, not sure at all what my role in this little ritual was.

"Okay," Ani said. "I call the circle."

Her words sent the crowd into motion, pulling chairs from the stacks around the walls to form a rough circle. Ani and Sam sat in chairs at the end closest to the door. I was ushered into a seat nearby, by a dark haired woman who looked about my age. She gave me a friendly smile but that was it. I wished again that Jase had been allowed to come with me. This many strangers made me nervous. I folded my hands in my lap, trying to look casual.

"Who has business?" Sam asked.

"I do."

Dan's voice. My stomach flipped uneasily, hoping this wasn't about me.

Dan strode into the center of the circle. He wore jeans and a greenish-gray shirt that did very nice things to his eyes. Not that I cared about his eyes.

"Speak, Daniel." Sam's tone was very formal.

"I call claim."

The woman next to me sucked in a breath, shooting a sideways glance at me that only redoubled my nerves.

"On whom?"

"On Ashley Keenan. I call claim until the next moon."

Muttered sounds of surprise came from the assembled wolves.

I leapt to my feet without thinking. "What the hell?"

"Ashley, sit down," Ani said.

"Not until someone explains to me what the hell is going on."

Ani's head snapped back to Dan. "You didn't tell her?"

His expression turned stubborn. "No."

Sam frowned. "This changes things."

"It changes nothing," Dan said. "I still have the right. I call claim."

"Will somebody please tell me what the heck is going on?" I stalked into the circle next to Dan. "Claim what?"

"Ashley, let's talk about this outside." Ani said.

"Hell, no. He's started this in here; he can finish it in here. What exactly do you think you're claiming, Agent Gibson?"

Dan winced slightly but held his ground. Sam rose from his chair, hands spread. "He claims the right to court you. No other male can approach you until the next full moon."

"Excuse me?" My voice squeaked but I was too mad to care.

"It is our custom," Ani said. "When a wolf is in love—"

"The only thing Agent Gibson is in love with is his own ego," I snarled. "I'm not property to be handed over to him." Or anyone else for that matter.

Ani stood. "No one said you were. But we have rules here."

I shrugged. "Fine. I'll leave."

Someone in the crowd actually gasped. Puhleeze. They were all behaving like this was some sort of bad soap opera.

I spun on my heel and started for the door. Ani got there before me. "Get out of my way," I said.

"Stay." It had the unmistakable ring of command. If I'd been in wolf form, it might have worked better. But human and pissed off, it barely made me hesitate.

"Nope."

"Then we'll talk outside," Ani said.

"Whatever." I pushed the double doors open and barged through. Behind me the room exploded into excited conversation. Seemed as though I'd livened up the party.

I didn't stop until I reached the front door and stood gulping in fresh air, trying to beat down the anger burning inside me. Ani stood silently next to me.

"Okay," I said when I felt like I'd regained a little control. "Talk. Explain to me why you were just about to hand me over to Dan all wrapped up in a pretty little bow."

"We weren't," Ani said.

My jaw dropped. Who did she think she was kidding? "Well, that's what it felt like to me. Dan has no claim over me. And you have no right to give him one."

No one had the right to control me. No one *claimed* me. Claim. I hated the very word. It's what Tate had said before he'd bitten me.

I was never going to let anyone else think they had possession of me.

"When it comes to the pack, I have the right to do anything I damn well please," Ani snapped. She gripped the iron rail fronting the porch with enough force I was glad it wasn't wood.

Then again, if it had been wood, I could've ripped a piece off and gone back inside to whack Dan over the head with it. "What, you're running some sort of white slavery ring now? Get a new wolf, hand them over to the first bidder?"

"Oh grow up, Ashley," Ani said. "You have no idea what you're talking about."

"And whose fault is that exactly?"

She made a frustrated noise but she didn't really have a comeback. She'd spent the last week teaching me about pack etiquette but hadn't mentioned anything about claims or courting. Talk about a set-up.

"I didn't think Dan would bring this up so soon. Any idiot can see you need some time."

"Dan's not just any idiot. He's in a class of his own." She sighed. "When it comes to you, that appears to be true. He loves you, Ashley, and sooner or later you're going to have to deal with that."

I leaned my head against one of the iron railings, wondering how to make her understand I was serious. "He sure has a strange way of showing it. And I have dealt with it. I told him to leave me the hell alone. And then he turns around and tries to put his brand on me or something."

"He was just asking for the right to court you."

"I don't *want* to be courted."

"Then you can tell him that and at the end of the month, you can do whatever you want. But the claim has been called."

I looked up at the night sky, at the moon, still looking almost full, shining silver against the ribbons of clouds. The moon that seemed to be causing me nothing but grief. "Explain this claim thing to me. In short words."

"Wolves mate for life," Ani said, boosting herself up onto the railing, legs dangling.

I nodded. "Got that bit."

"And the males can get very territorial. People have been killed fighting over this sort of thing. So we came up with the claim. If someone calls claim, everyone else has to back off for however long. It saves a lot of hassle."

"It won't save me a lot of hassle. I have no intention of getting back together with Dan—"I tried not to think too hard about the way he'd kissed me or about the pull of his scent—"he freaking turned me into a werewolf."

"To save your life."

I shrugged. We were going around in circles again. "So what happens if I don't agree to this claim?"

"Potentially a lot of jostling for your attention. We have quite a few single males at the moment. Do you really want to be besieged by men right now? Wouldn't it be easier to agree? It's not like Dan can make you date him."

She kind of had a point. The thought of dealing with men and sex—particularly strange men and sex, let alone werewolves and sex—was about as appealing as letting Tate kidnap me again. Dan, I could handle, kind of. I had a lot of practice at keeping him at arm's length.

"For one month? And I don't have to actually date him?"

"No dating. Nothing you don't *want* to do." She grinned at me.

"Don't look at me like that. I don't want to do anything with Dan." Except kick his butt all over the Retreat. Perhaps I should find out exactly how much stronger I was now I'd changed. Pounding on Dan might be more satisfying than abusing Ani and Sam's gym equipment.

Ani took a deep breath. "It's your life."

"Nice of you to notice."

"So, we can go back inside and have a good time?"

A good time? I didn't know if that was what I'd call it. But I didn't want to spoil the party. So I followed her back inside.

CHAPTER NINETEEN

DAN STILL STOOD IN THE middle of the circle of wolves, looking like he wanted to do some butt kicking of his own. Well, tough.

Sam stood beside him, talking quietly. The rest of the wolves chatted casually, trying to look like they weren't all waiting to see what I'd do.

As Ani and I approached the circle, the chatter died.

Dan looked relieved to see me. I sent him an 'I'll deal with you later' look and stopped about three feet away from him. Even that was too close. His wildness teased my nose and the fast rush of his pulse, telling me he was nervous or excited or horny or maybe all three, sounded like a crazed metronome in my ears.

Ani whispered something in Sam's ear and they made their way back to their chairs. An expectant hush fell over the room and Dan's heartbeat sped up another notch.

"Claim is called and heard," Ani said. "Daniel Gibson, you have until the next moon."

Dan grinned with relief. I curled my hand into a fist but managed not to sock him. "Don't get too cocky," I hissed at him. "I haven't agreed to cooperate with your stupid plans."

"I'll just have to work on that, won't I?" he replied, not bothering to hide his satisfaction.

"Good luck with that." I hightailed it back to my seat and watched, arms folded, as the pack discussed other business that meant very little to me, pretending not to notice all the curious stares I was receiving.

"Well, you didn't exactly jump for joy," Ben pointed out. "She's a persistent little thing. She probably figures she's still got a chance after the month is up."

Oh, did she? Maybe I didn't want Dan for myself but that didn't mean I wanted him taking up with some miniature Barbie who wore pink heels and too much make-up. I looked at her again with narrowed eyes, something about her grated on my nerves.

"Well, this has been...educational," I said to Ben and Natalie. "But you'll have to excuse me."

They nodded and smiled. "Maybe we can have dinner sometime, once you've adjusted to all this," Natalie said, making a gesture that took in the whole room.

I nodded. It actually sounded nice. Between my weird hours at work and Bug and all, I didn't actually get a lot of girlfriend time. My best friend from college lived in California and the close friends I'd made at my old firm all worked stupid hours like me.

Maybe the pack wasn't such a terrible thing, I thought, as I worked my way through the crowd, pausing to say hello and be introduced when people stopped me. The noise level in the room continued to increase, someone had cranked up the music and put on an old Springsteen CD. Couples and singles started dancing in the middle of the circle.

I had to say one thing for the pack, they knew how to have a good time.

I thought of Jase, waiting back at the Alpha's house and felt a twinge of guilt. He'd love all this.

"A penny for your thoughts?" A too familiar voice asked behind me.

It seemed Dan hadn't waited for me to find him, he'd found me. "I was just thinking that it would be a shame to spoil this nice party by beating you up," I said, turning to smile sweetly at him.

"You're mad."

I batted my eyelashes. "Why, Dan, you're so perceptive."

He grimaced and I couldn't help breathing in his scent, trying to see if I did smell like him. Problem was I couldn't smell myself over all the wolves in the room. But his scent did seem more familiar to me.

Damn. I wrinkled my nose. Was the scent more familiar because it was like mine? Was Ben right?

Bonded?

Shit.

I didn't want to think about the possibility. I wasn't going to let stupid werewolf physiology run my life. I'd just buy stronger perfume and hope for the best.

"What's that face for?" Dan asked as I frowned harder.

"Gee, Dan. What do you think I might be mad about?"

He looked vaguely guilty for a moment. Then jerked his head towards the door. "Can we go somewhere and talk about it?"

"Was that a request?" I arched an eyebrow at him. "You're not just going to swing me up over your shoulder and carry me off like a caveman?"

He rubbed his forehead for a moment then sighed. "I can if you want me too. But for now I'm just asking nicely."

He wasn't getting away with it that easily. "Maybe you should've thought about that before you pulled caveman act number one."

His eyes narrowed, darker gray than silver for once. Stormy gray. "I didn't plan it like this, it was just that—"

"That?" I prompted.

He blew out a breath. "Some of the guys were talking before you arrived. You know, guy talk. They said some things I didn't like. I didn't want them hassling you."

"So you decided to hassle me yourself. Why, Daniel, I'm touched." I noticed Petra standing a few feet from us, looking annoyed. "Though, I'm not sure your friend there feels the same way." I nodded in her direction, saw Dan follow my gesture with his eyes.

He looked back at me, confusion on his face. "Petra? There's nothing between Petra and me."

Sure, and I was happy being a werewolf. For a smart guy, he was batting for the moron major league tonight. "Sometimes I have to wonder about the Taskforce. I thought they only recruited the bright ones."

He shoved his hands in his pockets. "Look, can we just go and talk somewhere?"

I considered him. We did need to talk—or rather, I needed to yell. But between the beer and the lingering energy from the moon and the fact that, despite my wishes and my determination to prove Ben wrong, Dan still smelled—and, if I was completely honest, looked—way too good, I wasn't sure I trusted myself to be alone with him. "I don't think that's a good idea."

"Ash—"

The fact that the pleading tone in his voice made me hesitate told me I definitely needed to leave before I did something stupid. "Tomorrow," I said. "I'm tired, Dan. We can talk tomorrow."

One good thing. Apparently werewolves don't get hangovers. In an attempt to fall asleep and not deal with everything happening to me, I'd made good friends with the contents of my Cuervo bottle after the pack meeting. It had helped a little—I'd slept eventually. And I didn't have my normal post-tequila splitting headache.

I did have Dan knocking on my bedroom door just as I wandered out of the bathroom in my robe. I didn't have to ask who it was. His scent announced him.

"Just a minute," I yelled, scrabbling for clothes. I needed more than thin silk between me and Dan. I shucked the robe, pulling on panties and a bra.

Dan opened the door and walked straight in as I grabbed frantically for my robe...a little too slowly. His eyes flickered over my body, his dimple blinking to life for a second then his expression turned serious. I couldn't help a perverse sense of irritation that he hadn't looked longer.

"What are you doing? I said just a minute," I snapped.

He shook his head. Just once. "We don't have time. Get packed."

"What?" I was meant to stay at the retreat for a few more days until everyone was happy I wasn't going to turn into a ravening beast or something. "What's happened?"

"Holiday's over," Dan said, face serious. "There's been some murders."

My knees buckled and my robe slipped from suddenly numb fingers. "Who?"

"No one you know."

Things swam around me for a moment then my vision cleared. As my panic receded, I fought the urge to pick up the vase on my dresser and fling it at Dan's head. "You couldn't start with that info?"

He looked at me, puzzled. "What?"

"You scared the *crap* out of me."

"Oh. Sorry." His eyes were kind of glazed looking and I realized I was still in my underwear. And that the bra I'd grabbed was one of my skimpy lace ones.

So maybe he wasn't so indifferent.

And maybe I didn't want to think about that.

"Turn around," I squawked.

"Huh? Right. Sorry." He didn't sound sorry. And his one-eighty didn't exactly set land speed records.

I started wriggling into the nearest clothes, trying not to blush. "Why the rush back if the murder's no one we know?"

Dan's back stiffened. "Because they think it's Tate that did it."

I sat back down on the bed with a squishy sort of thud. "Why?"

"His MO. Three dead vampires. Drained."

I didn't want to think what that meant exactly. "Why do you need me?"

"You're still the best forensic accountant in town, aren't you? Now that we know Tate is around and manufacturing dodgy vaccines, we've got a better chance of tracking him down. Plus I have to go and Ani doesn't want you going anywhere without another wolf so she's assigned you to me."

"Assigned?" Man, werewolf matchmaking sucked. Subtlety apparently wasn't big in their arrangements. I yanked up my zip given I had nothing else to take out my frustration on.

"To look after you." Dan said as if I should know that.

"Won't babysitting me be tricky if you're chasing a murderer?"

"I'll be multi-tasking," he said, deadpan.

I smiled despite myself. He always could make me smile. And I didn't like that he was starting to do it again. It was bad enough finding him physically tempting without falling for his mind as well. I pulled my case out from under the bed and unzipped it. "Men don't multi-task."

"We drink beer and watch sports at the same time."

This time I laughed out loud. Then I got serious. "Tate's not a baseball game."

"I know. Are you decent?"

"Uh-huh."

Dan turned around. He looked disappointed when he saw me fully dressed. For a moment I felt pleased then I got a grip and started packing.

"I know you're mad about the claim thing but this hasn't got anything to do with that," Dan said. "I need your help tracking Tate and I also need to make sure that nothing happens to you. You and I are going to be spending lots of time together. Okay?"

I didn't really have a choice. I wanted to bring Tate down as much as Dan did. "How much time?"

"24/7."

Not a good idea. "I am *not* sleeping in the same room as you," I said.

He shrugged, face carefully blank. "That's fine. But you will be sleeping under the same roof. So, your place or mine?"

"Mine." I wanted the home-field advantage. Plus my spare bedroom was way down the other end of the house from mine. Plenty of distance between Dan and me.

"Fine." He headed for the door. "You've got about twenty minutes to finish packing. Meet me at the car."

"What about breakfast?" I yelled after him.

"Jase is taking care of it," floated back to me.

Great. Breakfast was under control. So how come I felt like nothing else was?

"Have you remembered anything else about the stuff they injected you with?" Dan asked when we'd been driving for about half an hour and I'd eaten all the bagels Jase had prepared. I hadn't touched the coffee though. I was wired enough without caffeine.

I shook my head, exasperated. I'd been asked this question over and over. "It's not like they were discussing the chemical formula with me. I've already told your Taskforce guys everything I remember. All I know is the label looked like Synotech's logo."

His mouth twisted. "I just thought something might have jogged your memory."

"Like what? Changing? You think becoming a werewolf makes me smarter or something?" I frowned, wondering if that were even possible.

"Or something would be right," Jase muttered from the back seat.

I twisted around to give him my best 'not helping' look. He grinned at me and slurped up the last of the blood he was drinking out a travel mug. The smell made my stomach rumble despite the fact it was stuffed with bagels, cream cheese and lox. Gross. I turned back to Dan.

He changed lanes and hit the accelerator, scowling at the oncoming traffic. "Changing does give people different abilities."

"Well I'm sorry, but it hasn't given me a photographic memory." Mostly it seemed to have given me a raging case of hormones. Not really helpful in defeating Tate. I reached for one of the coffees. Even if I didn't drink it all, maybe the smell of French roast would keep me from noticing Dan so much.

"The details are still kind of fuzzy." I didn't really want them to become any clearer. Not if it meant remembering all of what Tate had done to me.

"Marco could help you remember," Jase said.

I jerked, almost spilling my coffee. Not in a million years. "No way. There will be no more vampires rummaging around in my head. Tate didn't tell me much. Just that the vaccine would overcome my immunizations and that if I turned, people I bit would turn without having to drink my blood."

"Just what we need, a vampire population explosion," Dan said. He slurped his own coffee and I suddenly noticed he looked kind of tired.

Then told myself how Dan felt was *not* my problem. "We don't even know if he's got the vaccine in circulation," I pointed out.

"No, but that's what you're going to help me find out."

"Can I tell Lord Marco about the vaccines?" Jase said.

Dan looked at him in the rear view mirror. "Why would you want to do that?"

"He might know something useful." Jase said

"Like what?" Dan asked.

Jase shrugged. "Who knows with Old Ones? But I keep thinking that there's a reason vampires are turned the way they are. If Tate is messing with that, then the results could be unpleasant. Lord Marco's network is pretty good."

I twisted to look at Jase. "You 'keep thinking' or you've got a 'feeling'." I did the air quotes thing and Dan's gaze flicked to me, puzzled. I still hadn't had a chance to ask Jase about the voice I'd heard in my head at Tate's but I was going to do it real soon. If my PA was psychic, I wanted to know about it.

"Does it matter?" Jase asked, looking down at his lap. His reluctance didn't make me feel any better about any of this. "Maybe. So which is it?"

"A feeling," he admitted. "It just feels wrong."

Wrong, huh? Great. Just great. My stomach twisted and I turned back to face the windshield, wishing I hadn't eaten quite so much breakfast. "I think you should let him tell Marco," I said to Dan. "We need all the help we can get."

He nodded but didn't look at me. Which was just as well. I didn't want him to see that I was freaked out. I wanted to find out the truth about Jase's abilities before I filled Dan in completely.

"I agree. I'll have to get permission. But I'll see what I can do."

"Good. So, tell us more about these murders."

CHAPTER TWENTY

BY THE TIME WE REACHED my house two hours later, I regretted both breakfast and my curiosity. Turns out I'm better suited to being an accountant than listening to Dan describe a crime scene and why the injuries the victims sustained made them think that Tate was involved. Even vampires didn't deserve to be drained of blood and mutilated. What sort of vampire drank another vampire's blood, anyway? They couldn't survive on it, so it could only for kicks.

Jase looked pale too. The garage door came down behind us, blocking out the sun so he could get out of the Jeep and he got out of the car without a word.

"Has there been anything else like this going on?" I asked him quietly as we unloaded my luggage.

"Rumors," Jase said. "A few vamps go missing every so often. They pick the wrong victim, or something goes wrong in the dark clubs."

"But more lately?"

He looked uneasy, flicking at the luggage tag on my suitcase. "Maybe. I don't really hang out with that sort of crowd."

Thank *God*. That was one of the reasons Jase and I were still friends. "Can you see what you can find out?"

"Sure. But Lord Marco's the one you need to speak to." He picked up one of the bags and I realized he was humming.

Damn. He was *really* nervous. Which made my palms start to sweat. I tightened my grip on the bag I held, telling myself not to overreact. "What about the other lineages?"

"Lord Marco's the oldest. They'll tell him what he needs to know."

Double damn. I didn't want to say what I was about to say but I did anyway. "In that case, I think we should pay him another visit." Jase's eyebrows shot up and he glanced back over his shoulder at Dan, still in the car on his cell. "What about waiting for permission?"

"Oh, I'm willing to wait. For a little while. But the Taskforce isn't paying our salaries, remember?"

"They're paying us a pretty good hourly rate. And didn't you sign some sort of confidentiality agreement? You could go to jail." He was almost whispering.

"Better jail than dead." I hoped I sounded more confident than I felt.

Apparently not because Jase still looked unconvinced. "You know, Lord Marco's a good guy, for an Old One. But you shouldn't be so quick to trust everything he says. The Old Ones have their own agendas."

"You're telling me this *after* you talked me into letting him thrall me?" I punched his arm. "Thanks a lot."

Jase winced slightly which made me smile even though my hand hurt. Before I'd changed, my punching him would've made about the same impression as a fly landing on his arm. Go me.

"You needed to talk to him. He's better than Tate, that's for sure."

I hoped he was right.

"So now what?" I asked Dan after I'd shown him the guest room. Jase's nerves were catching, twenty minutes of lugging bags, throwing laundry into my machine and general busy-making hadn't made me feel any better. The thought of sitting around doing nothing made me even edgier.

"Now I go to work and you go to your office." He drained the coffee I'd made and took his mug to the sink.

Office? "I thought you wanted my help." I stirred my own coffee with more force than necessary.

Dan came back over to me, rubbing his jaw. He hadn't shaved and stubble darkened the lines of his face. Which only made him look more appealing. I curled my hands around my coffee.

"I do. But I'm going to the crime scene. You don't really want to see that, do you?"

I pressed my lips together as my stomach flipped. "No, not really." Not if you paid me, actually.

"Good. Then you go to your office and do what you do. You'll be safe there. I'll send Esme and another agent over."

Safe? What was I? The good little girl who needed to be protected? *Exactly*, the little voice inside my head said. I sighed. I knew Dan was right but I didn't have to like it.

"I hardly think hanging out with Esme is safe. She hates me."

"She doesn't hate you."

I stared at him, wondering if he was really that oblivious. But I wasn't going to say 'she hates me because you like me' because that would require talking about the sorts of things Dan and I were *not* going to talk about.

"What about this whole you're meant to keep an eye on me for Ani thing?"

"The other agent's a werewolf. A married werewolf. He'll know what to do. You don't have any weird urges, do you?" He smiled at me and moved closer. There was a twinkle in his eye that boded no good.

I looked away. *Weird* urges, no. Downright suicidal lascivious urges, well, I had plenty of those.

Dan flirting with me wasn't helping me pretend I didn't.

Time for a change of subject. "Does that mean Esme's not a wolf?"

Dan grinned. "You'll have to ask her that yourself."

Yeah, right. Me and Esme and a cozy little girl chat about shape-shifting, I could just see it now.

"So, you're a werewolf now?" Esme asked as soon as Agent Stevens—the wolf Dan had sent with her—left with Jase to get food.

I almost choked on my water. I wasn't surprised she knew. The whole Taskforce knew what had happened to me. But I *was* surprised she'd asked.

I studied her face but her dark blue eyes gave nothing away. "Yes. I'm a wolf." Was it my imagination or did she look a little disappointed?

Esme crossed her long legs, sitting even straighter—if that were possible—in the chair she'd pulled round to my side of the desk. So she could watch the door apparently. Personally, I figured it was to drive me nuts.

"Dan must be happy," she said, looking at me without blinking.

"Yes, he's thrilled," I deadpanned. "What do you want to know, Esme?"

She swallowed but her eyes didn't leave mine. I knew this game, whoever looked away first was weaker. It was a dominance thing as I'd started to learn from the pack. And I'd go to hell before I'd let Esme think she was higher up the food chain than me. So I just stared back, not blinking.

My eyes were just about to start watering when she looked away. Thank God.

"Does this mean that you and he..." she trailed off, looking closer to flustered than I'd ever seen her.

Did I want to wind her up or should I tell her the truth? I considered the issue. Annoying Esme was a fringe benefit but whatever I told her was sure to spread around the Taskforce pretty quickly—I had no illusions she'd keep her mouth shut. So did I want them thinking I was going along with the whole claim thing—if only to buy myself some peace and quiet—or did I confess?

And if I confessed, would I become an object of interest for any single male werewolves in the Taskforce?

Regardless of what Ben and Natalie had told me about bonding and smelling like Dan, there'd been a few men at the Retreat who'd not so subtly let me know they were looking forward to the end of the month already. I didn't know if there were single agents in the Taskforce but the law of averages said there had to be. I wanted to focus on Tate, not letting werewolves down gently. Of course, there might be one or two who I didn't want to let down.

Oh, who was I kidding? Until I got my yen for Dan safely locked away again, another man was about as likely to raise my interest as Jase was.

I leaned back in my chair, trying to look casual. "Dan called claim on me." I said.

For once Esme's expression was uncontrolled. She looked shocked. "And you agreed?" She *sounded* shocked.

Was it petty that her reaction was somehow satisfying? I slouched further into my chair, put my hands behind my head. "What can I say? He's pretty persuasive."

"I wouldn't know," she said. Her voice seemed a touch...sad, maybe?

Guilt twinged and I dropped my hands. The ice princess had feelings after all. It was nice to know but I still didn't know if she'd had genuine hopes. She'd need to be a wolf to have those. Because long term, Dan wouldn't be settling down with any who wasn't.

"Can I ask you something?"

She nodded.

"Are you a werewolf?"

"No." She uncrossed her legs and slumped just a little.

Ah. Then she might be upset with me but she couldn't really hold Dan against me. It was the perfect opportunity to satisfy my curiosity about her. "Do you mind if I ask what you are?"

"Can't you tell?"

"How would I do that?"

"My scent?"

I frowned. Then took a deep breath through my nose, trying to break down her scent. She wore perfume—something precisely floral with a sharp green undertone. But underneath the perfume there was the tang I was beginning to associate with shifters.

But Esme didn't smell like the wolves. No. She smelled exotic. Less like earth and woods and more like lush green things that needed heat and sun. I closed my eyes took another breath, trying to *see* the smell.

Gold. And heat. And... no, I couldn't get it.

"I can tell you're not a wolf, now that I think about it." I opened my eyes. "But I haven't smelled any other species since I changed. So I don't know what you are."

"Do you want to take a guess?"

She looked kind of smug. I figured that meant she was something a little out of the ordinary. If I had to go by her appearance, I'd guess something Nordic but my knowledge of Scandinavian wildlife wasn't exactly great. And she hadn't smelled like ice and snow.

She sat still while I looked at her. Something in the way she held herself seemed vaguely feline. So maybe a lion? Or a tiger? Those were the two most common cat breeds. But I doubted Esme was common. "I give up. Bobcat?"

It wasn't a serious guess. I didn't even know whether there *were* bobcat shifters. But I didn't want her thinking I thought she was the Queen of the Jungle type.

Esme practically bristled, mouth pursing. "*No*. Do I really look like a bobcat to you?"

I hid a smile. I wouldn't know a bobcat if one bit my ass. "Leopard?"

She looked slightly mollified. "No. But closer. I'm a jaguar."

Ms. Tall and Blond was a jaguar? Weren't they black? Or was that something else? Then again, maybe cat's coloring didn't reflect their human form like wolves' did.

"Interesting. Are there many jaguars in Seattle?"

She shook her head. "Just me. We're not pack animals."

I shrugged. Not pack animals sure, but being one of a kind had to be kind of lonely. Maybe that explained the terminal snottiness.

But lonely or not, Esme wasn't really my problem. My problem was Tate. So I really needed to turn on my computer and get to work. But I hadn't touched it since the day Tate had snatched Bug and now I found myself highly reluctant to do so.

"Is something wrong?" Esme asked after I'd spent five minutes shuffling files around my desk.

"No. What could be wrong?" Hopefully she didn't know what a forensic accountant did and wouldn't catch on I was stalling.

"You haven't turned on your computer."

So much for stalling. "I'm thinking."

"Thinking isn't going to catch Tate."

"Thinking is the only thing that's going to catch Tate," I retorted. "He's smart. And he's about fifty steps ahead of us already."

"All the more reason for you to turn on your computer and get to work."

Snotty yet accurate. That was annoying.

I gritted my teeth. "It's hard to concentrate with you sitting there."

"Dazzled by my beauty?"

I blinked. Was that a joke? What? We'd bonded now because I knew she was a jaguar?

Great. A big, black, cat as my new best girlfriend. Some people would take that as a sign of bad luck. Mostly I just wished I could chase her out of the room. "Sorry, you're not my type."

"Then quit stalling and get to work. I have to watch you, Dan made it an order."

Fabulous. Perhaps the black cat thing *was* bad luck. I certainly hadn't been catching any breaks since the Taskforce had come back into my life.

Out of excuses, I reached out and hit the power button on my computer. It took its time warming up but eventually my familiar island beach wallpaper filled the screen.

For a moment I wished I could escape to an island and laze around sipping mai-tais but that wasn't going to happen as long as Tate was on the loose. Which was going to be quite some time if I didn't start looking for him again.

But first things first. I checked my email—lots of increasingly demanding messages from clients frustrated with my sudden absence—then went to open my Tate files. Only to come up with a big fat zero.

The folders had disappeared.

I swore softly under my breath.

"What's wrong?" Esme asked, looking up from her PDA.

"Nothing." I tilted the monitor towards me so she couldn't see. I wasn't ready to confess the disaster just yet. After all, everything on my computer was backed up daily. So there might not even be a disaster.

I heard Jase and Agent Stevens come through the front door. "Jase, get your butt in here," I yelled.

He appeared in roughly a second. "What's up?"

I motioned him round to my side of the desk and pointed to my screen. "Take a look."

His eyes widened as he took in the blank space on my screen where the Tate files should be. "Oh crap. Don't worry, I'll check the backups."

Esme reached out and straightened the monitor. "What's going on?"

"Small computer glitch. Don't worry, Jase will restore my files."

"Um, no he won't," Jase said, coming back into the room. "The server's bare too."

My stomach plummeted, "Everything?"

"Only the Tate files. But to get those, they would've had access to everything. Assuming it's not just a glitch." The look on his face made it obvious he didn't think it was.

"Someone's hacked your system?" Esme said in a dangerously quiet voice. "How?"

My turn to bristle. This wasn't my fault. I'd been busy turning into a werewolf. I hadn't even *been* in my office for a week. "You tell me, your Taskforce geeks were meant to secure it."

"Don't touch anything," she ordered, pulling out her cell phone. "I'll get a team here."

Wonderful. More feds swarming my office. Why couldn't I just have a nice normal day chasing debits and credits?

An hour after Esme called in the nerd squad, we were still no wiser about what had happened to my data and then, to complete my wonderful day, Dan stormed in. Closely followed by Bug.

"Aunt Bug!" I sprinted into her arms. I hadn't seen her since the hospital. I'd talked to her but the wolves hadn't wanted her around for my change. "How are you?" I pulled back so I could take a good look. She looked good. Far less tired.

She fixed me with those eagle eyes. "I'm fine. You're the one we should be talking about."

"I'm okay," I said, hugging her again just so I could breathe in her perfume and feel safe for a second. "What are you doing here?" I didn't want to go into all the details of the last week with an audience of agents. Or Dan. Who stood just next to Bug, looking furious.

"What?" I said to him.

"Esme said your system's been hacked," he rumbled.

I nodded. "It's not my fault."

"I didn't say it was. But you're working at the Taskforce from now on."

Looking at his face, I knew there'd be no point arguing. He looked ready to bite someone's head off. And for a werewolf, that might just be literally. I liked my head where it was. Plus he *smelled* mad. All kind of electric and smoky. It was almost arousing in a weird kind of way. I threw up my hands. "Fine. But not today." Any more drama and I was going to have to hurt someone.

"Why not?"

"Because I want to spend time with Bug," I said defiantly. "And besides, your team's taken my stuff hostage."

Bug's head was swiveling between the two of us, amusement unmistakable in her eyes. Which didn't improve my mood.

"Everything here is replicated at the Taskforce, you know that."

He meant the data, not my office itself. The Taskforce didn't have my favorite chair, or my music or my very expensive Italian espresso machine. And it had Dan. That was four strikes you're out as far as I was concerned.

I folded my arms across my chest. "How am I supposed to see my clients at the Taskforce?"

"You're not."

My jaw dropped. "Excuse me?"

"We don't know who's safe and who's not. It's too risky."

"Me going bankrupt because all my clients dump me is risky," I protested. "I've known a lot of my clients for years."

"Some, not all. And I wouldn't put it past Tate to set something up years in advance, would you?"

My next protest died on my lips. Planting some sleeper crazy in my client list was exactly the sort of thing Tate would find amusing. "What am I supposed to do? I have commitments. I have bills to pay."

"*We're* paying you." Dan didn't look sympathetic.

"Yes, but I'll need other clients once this is over." I didn't want to think about how long that might be. My clients would cut me some slack for a few weeks, maybe a month but after that, they'd go hunting for a new bean counter.

"Tell them there's been a death in the family."

Bad choice of words. I winced, glancing at Bug reflexively. Her expression said 'let it go' and I sighed. "I give up, c'mon Aunty."

"Esme and Agent Stevens have to go with you."

Across the room, Esme looked up and my heart sank. I didn't want to hang out with weres, I wanted a nice peaceful lunch with my Aunt. But then, where could I go that was safe? "Oh, bite me," I snapped at Dan.

"Been there, done that," he snarled back. My jaw dropped over. Whatever the Taskforce had hired him for, it really hadn't been tact and diplomacy. And possibly not for brains either. "You really want to remind me of that right now?" I glared at him, ignoring the fact that everyone in the room had given up any pretense of working and were just listening to us fight. Jase was smiling.

Dan just stared down at me and I knew I had to leave before I slugged him. I stalked over to Jase.

"You're coming with me. Put all our current files on a hard drive and grab the hard copies."

"Where will you be?" Dan asked loudly.

"Home."

He looked almost relieved. "I'll be here for a while with all this."

"Good," I said. "I wasn't planning on making you dinner anyway."

He took a step towards me then seemed to change his mind. He straightened then walked back out into reception. I headed into the back room to help Jase with the files. "Tonight," I said to him as soon as we were alone. "We talk to Lord Marco *tonight*."

CHAPTER TWENTY ONE

LORD MARCO'S HOUSE DIDN'T look nearly so appealing by moonlight. In fact, it looked downright creepy. The vines threw nasty snaky shadows everywhere and I was all too aware that once I walked through the front door I'd be surrounded by vampires.

"Are you absolutely sure about this?" Jase asked as we walked towards the front door.

I summoned a very fake smile, ignoring the fact my thundering heartbeat made it perfectly plain how scared I was. "Absolutely. If anyone knows anything about Tate then I want to know."

"And if Marco doesn't want to tell you?"

I hadn't thought that far ahead. I was counting on the fact Marco seemed to like me and had offered to help. I didn't know what I'd do if he'd changed his mind.

The door swung open as we approached and I jumped backwards. Jase put his hand on my back. "Easy."

"You take it easy," I muttered back. "That was spooky."

"I prefer to think of it as efficient, Signorina Keenan." Marco appeared in the doorway.

Heat flooded my cheeks. Way to go, Ashley. Insult the vampire before you ask him for a favor.

I decided to ignore my gaffe altogether as he ushered us into the entryway. "Lord Marco, thank you for seeing me."

"I am always happy for beautiful women to come and see me," he said with a grin that revealed his fangs. In the warm yellow light of the hall, his eyes looked a much darker shade of green than I remembered. "Regardless of whether they find me *spooky*."

Was he teasing me or making a point? His face revealed nothing. Note to self. Never play poker with an Old One. I decided to play things safe and stick close to Jase. Marco led us to the same room where he had removed Tate's thrall from me. I didn't particularly want to remember the last time I'd been here but it was unavoidable once Marco gestured for me to sit on the same sofa as I had before.

I was grateful when he took the opposite sofa rather than sitting beside me. Jase waited until Marco was seated before taking the empty space on my sofa. Our backs were to the door which made my spine tingle uneasily.

I tried to ignore the feeling, focusing on Jase instead. It didn't help, Jase looked nervous. Not for the first time, I wondered whether I should've brought more back-up. Jase and I had given Esme and Agent Stevens the slip but it would've been nice to have more firepower on our side. But I could hardly have asked Dan.

I jumped when someone knocked on the door and opened it. Torn between playing it cool and staying alive, I chose staying alive, and twisted around to see who'd walked in.

A woman—vampire I assumed—stood by the door, holding a tray with glasses. Four glasses. Deep red liquid shimmered inside them and I frowned, wondering what exactly we were being offered. Then saw Marco watching me and smoothed my expression out. "I didn't realize anyone would be joining us."

"You don't care for refreshments?" he asked with another easy smile.

One I didn't trust. We were playing a game and this time I was the one asking for a favor. The hairs on the back of my neck lifted as the woman approached. Whoever she was, my instincts didn't like her.

Plus I wasn't sure what was in the glasses and I didn't want to offend by refusing if it was only wine. "She's not a servant." I nodded towards the strange vamp. She wore a simply cut black dress but I didn't make the mistake of assuming that meant it was cheap. She had long dark curly hair, much as I imagined Marco's might be if he let it grow long, and her lips were painted a deep red. I hoped it was lipstick. Marco raised a dark eyebrow as he leaned back against the sofa, adjusting his brilliant white cuffs. "No? What makes you so sure?"

Dark green stones the size of quail's eggs gleamed in his cufflinks. Emeralds? If they were, he was wearing a small fortune on his wrists. Then again, he'd had centuries to pay them off.

"There are four glasses on the tray."

He laughed and the woman shot me a startled glance, bent and placed a glass before each of us. She took one for herself and knelt at the edge of the low table separating the sofas.

"You did not tell me she was clever, Lord Marco," she said. Her voice sounded American but something felt odd about it.

"Many humans are, *bella*," Marco replied, eyes twinkling. "Ashley, this is Leah."

I nodded then waited, assuming there was more of the explanation coming. The name wasn't one I recognized.

"Leah works for Esteban."

"Lord Esteban," Leah said softly. There was just a hint of an edge to the tone. Like she wanted to be nastier but didn't want to upset Marco. I knew the feeling.

Marco inclined his head, acknowledging the correction. From what I understood of vamp politics, as the ruling Old One in the city, he didn't have to give anyone the courtesy of a title. That he chose to do so meant he was playing nice.

With Esteban; of all people. I certainly recognized *that* name. Esteban was famous. Or infamous. He owned many of Seattle's dark clubs and didn't necessarily keep those who enjoyed them on a tight leash. He wasn't as enthusiastic about sticking to human rules as some of the other Old Ones.

Though the courts had yet to find that he was implicated in any of the more extravagant excesses that occurred in his premises from time to time.

Yet being the operative word.

"And what is Lord Esteban's interest in this?" I asked delicately, trying not to scrunch away from Leah. Her long arms could reach me without her even moving. I didn't like the proximity. She smelled of something heady and exotic, the spice and musk almost overpowering. But it didn't completely mask the fact she also smelled of blood. I eyed the liquid in the glasses with renewed distrust.

"Let's just say that all the Old Ones are interested in Tate ceasing to plague us," Marco said.

I glanced from him to Leah. She sat utterly still, watching me with dark brown eyes. I didn't meet her gaze directly but I didn't look away. She bared her fangs at me.

I kept my gaze steady. After all, I was a werewolf now. She probably couldn't do too much damage to me. If I was lucky, that was. I'd been a wolf for less than a week and I guessed she'd had a bit more practice than that at being a bloodsucker.

A bloodsucker who worked for one of the bad guys.

But in terms of the lesser of two evils, when it came to choosing Leah—and therefore Lord Esteban—or Tate, it was a no-brainer. Still, I wouldn't be going down any dark alleys with Leah any time soon.

"Careful, *bella*," Marco said. "Wolves have teeth. And we are here because of mutual interests. Why don't we drink to that?"

I looked down at the glass in front of me. Leah's scent was so strong that I couldn't smell whether it held blood or something more innocent. Jase picked up his glass and sniffed it with evident pleasure. Did that mean it *was* blood? My stomach flipped as I picked up the glass, feeling distinctly queasy.

"Don't look so worried, Ashley," Marco said as he lifted his own glass. "Yours is wine."

Mine was wine? Was that supposed to make me feel better? That I was sitting with three people who drank blood willingly? I was used to Jase and his travel cup, but this was something else altogether. My fingers tightened around the delicate stem of the glass. How the hell had my life gotten so complicated, this fast?

I was meant to be an accountant.

Staid.

Sensible.

Wearer of navy suits.

No drinking of bodily fluids involved.

I waited until everyone had drunk, then took a careful mouthful and put my glass down. The wine was slightly sweet and fruity. Italian maybe? "So, have you heard anything more about Tate?" I asked.

Marco shrugged, a fluid boneless movement. "We are still investigating, like your own Taskforce."

Was that a no? Or an 'I'll tell you when I'm ready'?

"Was there something in particular you wanted to know?" Leah asked. Her voice, like Marco's, was low and musical. There was definitely a faintly odd twist to her accent. Something that told me that English wasn't her only language. I wondered how old she was.

Marco seemed to trust her. Or respect her, at least. Which suggested she might be quite the old. Vampires get more powerful with age. Perfect. I tried to stay casual. "It's just with these murders and—" I cut off, not sure how much I should say about my missing files.

"And?" Marco prompted. He raised his glass and sipped again.

Oh, what the hell. Dan was going to be furious regardless of what I did or didn't tell Marco. So I might as well be honest. "Someone hacked into my system and wiped the information I had on Tate," I admitted. "So you can understand my urgency."

"I understand," Marco said. He leaned forward a little. The light reflecting through the liquid in his glass cast a reddish glow over his hands. "But I do not yet understand what you are willing to give us in exchange for this information?"

"*Give* you? You said before that you would help us."

"I said we would seek out Tate and deal with him. But you are coming to me with another specific request now."

I looked at Jase, seeking guidance. "You didn't say anything about this."

"I didn't know he would ask," Jase said.

Marco chuckled and my head snapped back to him.

His eyes bored into mine. "Young Jason is not a player in our politics. He stays in your world. How should he know?"

Because I paid him very good money to make my life run smoothly, not to lead me into vampire traps. And what about his other abilities? Hadn't he had any inkling that Marco might want something in return? Did he not care…or, another less pleasant thought occurred to me, were those very abilities the reason that Jase didn't want to get involved in the vamp world too deeply?

"What exactly are you asking for?" I said. Might as well find out the worst.

Marco blinked slowly. Perhaps he wasn't used to the direct approach.

"Well, *cara*, there is always the usual…"

"He means a blood offering," Jase whispered.

I stiffened. "Not going to happen." One vampire biting me was enough for this lifetime. And any other lifetimes I might have. I had zero interest in being thralled again and I definitely wasn't going to volunteer for the pain of being bitten.

One corner of Marco's mouth curled up. "I do not often drink wolf blood, anyway."

"Lord Esteban does not share your distaste," Leah offered.

I turned my gaze to hers. "Read my lips. *Not. Going. To. Happen.*"

She bared her fangs again. I smelled blood on her breath and flinched.

"Then what do you offer to us?" she asked.

"Information?"

Marco rubbed a finger round the rim of his glass, making it sing. The sound hurt my ears as I focused on him.

He tilted his head at me with a small smile as he lifted the finger. "I believe we know everything you know already. Your Taskforce has not gotten very far, has it?"

"We're doing okay." I said, stung. Since I'd been rescued, we'd started to close in on a few of the aliases Tate had been using. But we had a long way to go.

"You are like children, hunting for the monster with a flashlight, pretending you are not scared of the dark," Leah said scornfully.

Oh no, I knew I was scared of the dark. "What are you hunting for him with?"

She smiled nastily. "Torches. Many, many torches."

I couldn't help smiling back. It wasn't a nice image. But hey, I didn't want Tate to die easily. I wanted him to *suffer*. A much as inhumanly possible. If the vamps found him first and tore him to pieces then I didn't think I'd be all that upset.

Dan, however, would be.

Jase put down the glass he'd been toying with. "We may have other information."

Startled, I swiveled my head in his direction. "What other information."

"Don't worry," he said and I suddenly knew. He was going to tell Marco about his psychic abilities.

Bad idea. Bad, bad idea. I had no desire for Jase to become a pawn in vampire power games. It tended to be a world of vamp eat vamp where only the strong survived. Darwin would've loved it.

I doubted Jase would.

I put my hand on his arm. "We don't have any other information."

"But—"

"We don't," I repeated, squeezing hard. "So, Lord Marco, where does that leave us?"

The pleasant look had left his face. "With difficulties," he said.

My spine prickled. "Can't you just tell me?"

"It is not our way," Leah hissed.

"But I'm not a vampire."

"No, you're a wolf. And we do not give favors to the wolves. You have to accept our ways."

Their way or the high way. That much was clear.

My head began to throb. I wished I'd brought Dan. He knew more about this stuff than me. Sure, I dealt with vamps a lot at work but that was when they were doing human things like managing their finances. I had no idea how this whole other world they had actually operated.

And I was starting to think I probably didn't know so much about the wolves either. Which I would have to worry about later because right now I had to get Jase and me out of here without offending Marco or Leah—and through her, Esteban.

"I do accept your ways, I'm just not sure what else I can offer."

"There is one other way," Marco said. "An obligation."

I looked at Jase, wanting the translation. His teeth were pressed into his lower lip and I wondered how he kept from pricking himself with his fangs. Then wondered what was making him nervous enough to chew on his lip. "He means a favor?"

Jase shook his head, just a fraction. "Not just a favor. An unlimited right to call on you."

Unlimited? That didn't sound good. Spine prickles turned to a full-blown shiver and I clasped my hands in my lap before anyone could see they were shaking.

"That is not exactly true. We can set some limitations," Marco said.

"Like what?" At least I managed to keep my voice steady.

"Like no blood, nothing that would harm you."

That still left a lot of options. "How exactly does this work?"

"If you agree then, at some point in the future, if I have need of you, I will ask and you will comply with my wishes."

"I could do your taxes," I offered.

He smiled but Leah frowned. "This is not a joking matter, wolf."

Yipes. She was annoyed. "I'm sorry," I said, trying to sound suitably contrite. "I was only trying to give Lord Marco some options."

"Lord Marco will be the one who decides what he wants." Ice dripped from each syllable.

I stiffened. "*If* I agree."

"If you want the information, you *will* agree," Leah said, sounding smug.

She was right to. Because I didn't have any real options other than leaving here empty-handed. Which would get me yelled at by Dan for no good reason.

"All right, I agree. With limitations."

Marco raised his glass to me. "Excellent, then let us negotiate."

Maybe I'd read the vampires wrong but I'd gotten one thing right. Dan was mad that I'd gone to see them. Beyond mad. He flipped out. I hadn't seen him like this since the day he'd lost control after he'd first turned. But this time I wasn't scared of him. I was too busy doing some flipping out of my own.

The resulting screaming match was impressive even though it cost me a very nice vase after I gave into the urge to throw things at his head. When we'd finally yelled at each other enough, Dan backed off to the far side of the room and stood for a minute or so, back against the wall, breathing heavily.

I knew what he was doing. Trying to control the wolf. I felt the same urge to change, the same energy roiling through my skin. My wolf wanted to snarl and rage and run. To bite something. Or someone. I clamped down on the feeling. There'd be no changing. Not until the full moon.

I watched Dan and Jase watched me, looking worried.

"You know, he shouldn't upset you like this. Not when you've only just had your first change."

Dan opened one eye. "I didn't upset *her*," he said in a dangerously calm voice. "She upset *me*."

"She found out some information though," Jase said, folding his arms. Which didn't make Dan look any happier.

But Jase was right. We had information. Marco had found traces of Tate's dealings in Washington that I hadn't uncovered. Even some holdings in Seattle itself. And he'd confirmed that Tate had committed the murders Dan was investigating.

Dan opened his other eyes and pushed away from the wall. "Only by incurring a debt to a vampire. No offence, Jase, but that's stupid."

"Not as stupid as baiting a new werewolf into a rage," Jase retorted. "What would've happened if she'd changed when she was that mad? Could you control her?"

Sudden cool fear swept through me. Jase was right. Ani had warned me about strong emotions during the next few months. I needed to learn how to control my wolf and if my emotions got the better of me, I risked it being the other way round. I could go berserk.

And sometimes new wolves who went berserk didn't come back to human form.

Of course, Ani had thrown me together with the one man guaranteed to drive me around the bend, so I wasn't sure her logic was all that up to scratch.

"Stop talking about me like I'm not here," I said when my heart stopped pounding quite so hard. "I'm fine." In the fucked-up, insecure, neurotic and emotional sense of the word.

"Only 'cos you got lucky," Dan said. "You've got the self-preservation instincts of Bambi."

"Bambi did just fine," I retorted. "He became King of the Forest."

Dan snorted. "It was a Disney movie."

My hand itched for something else to throw at him. I settled for glaring. "What does that mean?"

"In the real world, Bambi would've been toast."

"Like me? You mean? You think I'm toast?" My voice grew louder again.

"I'm saying I'm not going to *let* you be toast," Dan said. "From now on, we stick together. Where you go, I go."

"What? No *way*."

"Sorry, but you gave Esme the slip. So now you're stuck with me. And in case you think you're going to give me the slip, I've tripled the surveillance on your house."

I picked up a glass to throw at him but Jase caught my arm.

"You're supposed to be staying calm, remember?"

"Tell that to him."

"I would but he's right. What we did tonight was dumb. You need protecting."

Crap. Jase was on Dan's side. No way out if Jase wasn't going to help me avoid Dan.

I sighed, rubbing my chest, trying to will the last of the anger away. I knew Dan was right. I wanted to be sensible but everything about this kept rubbing me the wrong way.

And now there would be even more Dan.

Not only in my house but watching me all the time.

Driving me nuts.

Just like it would drive me nuts if I didn't work off some of the excess energy currently making me feel like every nerve ending in my body was firing, full throttle. I couldn't stay around Dan any longer and I didn't want to take my temper out on Jase. So I shot a last glare at Dan and stomped down to my room to change into my gym gear. Maybe I'd just stick a big old photo of Dan's face on my punching bag and go from there.

Five days later my punching bag was a limp shredded heap of leather on my garage floor, I had bruised knuckles, we knew nothing more about Tate's whereabouts, and Dan was still insisted on sticking to me like glue. As an added bonus he seemed to have decided that, just in case he hadn't quite annoyed me enough already, he might as well try charming me into a good mood.

Five days of flirting and teasing and my temper hadn't improved any more than my relentless need to move.

"You know, if you changed you'd feel less frantic," Dan said, looking up from a file as I passed his desk for the tenth time in about twenty minutes.

"Thanks, but I'll stick to pacing," I said. Pacing stopped me doing something stupid like crawling onto Dan's lap like I wanted to every time I got a lungful of his scent.

"It's not like anyone here is going to mind," he said, nodding towards the rows of agent-filled cubicles. "They've all seen weres change before."

I'd mind. I'd decided full moon only and that was what I was sticking to. "My suit would mind," I pointed out. Plus there was the whole issue of what to put back on when I changed back if I shredded my favorite outfit. Being naked in front of Dan was not a good plan at this point.

I bounced on my toes briefly, pivoted then headed back towards the far wall. Dan's office was too small for satisfactory pacing but I couldn't sit still. Couldn't think properly at a desk.

I felt like someone had plugged me into a battery and switched the power to high. I worked for hours, polished my house to within an inch of its life and worked out on the pieces of my home gym still standing. Despite all that, I still lay in bed at night feeling like my blood was fizzing.

"There are other ways of burning off energy," Dan said in a different tone.

I shot him a disgusted look. He kept flirting with me. Pushing my buttons. *Tempting* me. I hated it. Mostly. Except for the bits of me that loved it. "Are you suggesting I take up jogging?"

He grinned and a dimple flickered in his cheek. "I was thinking more of a team sport."

An image of him and me playing the sorts of games he had in mind slid into my head and stuck there front and center. Dan naked. Dan ready for action. Dan all too willing.

I wrenched my mind back to the problem on the table. Tate. That was enough to quell my lycanthropy-fueled libido.

"I never was much of a sports fan," I said, dropping back into my chair.

"That's not how I remember it," Dan said with another one of *those* grins.

The toe-curling, memory inducing, mind fogging ones. I hated those. When I wasn't lapping them up like a woman who'd just found an oasis in the desert. It was ridiculous. I wasn't going to let my hormones and a stupid virus take over my life. Besides which, after what Tate had done to me, I wasn't sure about the whole sex and orgasms thing anyway. What if all I could think about was Tate? If I told Dan that, I knew he'd back off. But I wasn't ready to tell anyone other than the counselor I was seeing what Tate had done when he'd thralled me. She'd said it was up to me when—or if—I ever told anybody else.

"In fact," Dan continued. "I remember you playing very...enthusiastically."

So did I. That was the problem. "Oh, shut up," I said irritably. My mind had doubts but my body apparently was all too keen to relive old times.

He pulled an injured innocent expression. "Hey, I was talking about softball—what were you thinking about, Ash?"

"Your face meeting my fist," I said.

He laughed. My toes curled.

"Changing might improve your temper too."

I twirled my chair from side to side. "No, getting away from you would improve my temper."

Silver eyes narrowed at me. "Not gonna happen."

"Then I guess you'd better get used to my bitchy side."

"Honey, I'm just fine with your bitchy side," he drawled, looking me up and down. "You're the one who's in denial."

"And a lovely part of Egypt it is," I snapped. "Now shut up and let me work."

CHAPTER TWENTY TWO

Denial. I was beginning to wonder if Dan was right about that as I slipped the cross Bug had given me to replace the one Tate had stolen around my neck the next morning. It was platinum. I couldn't wear silver now. Which ruled out most of my jewelry collection.

I stared at my reflection. I still looked like me. Nothing remained of the bruises and injuries from Tate. First change and my new revved up metabolism had taken care of that. My eyes were still greenish hazel, my hair dark brown. I still looked human.

But I was a werewolf. My face could change. My whole body could change. Just thinking about it made my stomach clench.

And changing was the least of my problems—at least I only had to do that once a month. But the super-sensitive hearing and sense of smell? Those were always on. Just like the river of energy that still had me humming.

Or maybe that was Dan who was still taking great delight in torturing me with his smiles. It was driving me crazy. Every time he came into the room my mind went kind of blank and my stomach fluttered.

Hell, he didn't even have to come into the room. It was enough for me to smell him on the furniture in my house. It was worst in the gym, where he'd taken to working out his frustration in the same way as me. The room was layered with his scent and mine, and the combination made me even hornier.

Jase thought I was crazy for resisting. If I'd thought it would be just sex, maybe I wouldn't have. But I wasn't ready for the whole package.

I wasn't ready for life as a werewolf, let alone being bonded to one.

My nose let me know that Dan was outside my room a few seconds before the door opened.

"Ever heard of knock—" My annoyance died as I saw the look on his face. His eyes blazed, standing out like quicksilver against white skin. "What's wrong?"

His face twisted and I put my hand on the dresser for support, fear clutching at me. "Dan? What's happened? Is it Bug?"

He shook his head. "No. Bug's fine. It's Ben." His voice sounded scratchy, almost broken.

"Ben?" It took me a moment then my heart twisted. Ben. Natalie's husband.

"He's missing," Dan said bluntly. "We have to go."

"Of course." I scrabbled for my keys and purse. "Missing since when?" I asked, following Dan at a half-jog out of the house.

"Didn't come home from work yesterday. He phoned Nat from the office, said he was leaving but he never arrived."

My stomach twisted as I climbed into Dan's jeep. Wolves don't stray. It was highly unlikely Ben had disappeared voluntarily. But striking at the Seattle pack was pretty brazen. Or crazy.

Tate kind of crazy.

"Do you think it's Tate?" Anger burned at the thought of someone hurting one of my pack mates. The intensity surprised me. I liked Ben but I'd only met him a few times. Apparently I was bound closer to the pack than I'd understood.

Dan half-growled. "I'm not making assumptions but it's hard to think who else it might be." Rubber squealed as he sent the Jeep flying down my drive and onto the street.

"And there's no way Ben's run off? Have they found his car?" I shielded my eyes from the morning sun. It felt wrong to have bad news on such a beautiful day. Bad news should come at night. Or at least with rain.

"He didn't run." Dan sounded one hundred percent sure of that. "He has one of those satellite security systems on his car but it's been disabled."

Well, that had to be deliberate. Either Ben trying to hide or someone trying to hide him.

My gut told me it was the latter, even though my brain tried to cling to the hope it might be the former. Either way, it wasn't going to be good.

"Where are we going?" I asked as Dan turned in the opposite direction of the city. Away from the Taskforce.

"Ani and Sam's."

Pack. Of course. Where else would we go?

Ani and Sam's kitchen was crowded with wolves, agents and police. But I couldn't take my eyes off Natalie, sitting at the kitchen table, staring at the mug of tea in front of her like she wasn't sure she knew what to do with it. Gone was the happy bubbly woman I'd knew. She looked gray and shell-shocked. Wiped blank.

I recognized the expression. Grief and pain and fear. I was way too familiar with all three.

But I didn't want to intrude, so I hung back while Dan went over to her and enfolded her in a bear-hug. Then stomped down the flare of jealousy that erupted in my chest. He was just comforting a friend. Plus, I had no right to act jealous when I wouldn't let him touch *me*.

As Dan released Natalie and straightened, another woman hurled herself at him, sobbing big dramatic sobs. Petra. This one I was allowed to have a problem with, I decided, narrowing my eyes. I put down the coffee pot and joined Dan. He let go of Petra semi-gently, disengaging her hands from his arms.

"Petra, this isn't helping Nat," he said.

I rolled my eyes as Petra's sobs strengthened.

"But it's so-o-o sad," she gulped.

Dan looked at me pleadingly over her head. I decided to take charge. "Petra, why don't you come with me and I'll make you some tea. Won't that be nice?"

More tears. Wiped carefully away so her mascara wasn't smudged. I shoved my hand in my pocket so I wouldn't smack her.

Big blue eyes blinked up at Dan. "But I want to stay with Nat."

"Dan has to ask Nat some questions," I lied, clamping my hand around Petra's upper arm. Her muscles went rigid in protest but I had the advantage of size and height and all that bashing of gym bags seemed to have paid off. I dragged her out of the kitchen and into the living room.

"Sit there," I said to her, pushing her down into the nearest chair. "Don't move."

She glared at me like I'd just ruined her manicure. I noticed the tears had stopped though. "I don't have to do what you say."

I leaned down so my face was only a few inches from hers. "Listen to me, if you do anything—and I mean anything—to make this harder on Natalie, I will kick your butt into next week."

To her credit, she didn't flinch. "Who made you boss?"

"I work for the Taskforce, and you're acting like a silly child, so I guess I did."

Color stained her cheeks and her eyes sharpened. "I can't believe Dan called claim on a bitch like you," she snapped.

I'd had enough. "Yeah and I can't believe I didn't hose him down with Clorox after you'd been touching him, so I guess we're even. Now stay here and don't make any trouble." Petra's face went pale. I couldn't help feeling vaguely satisfied.

I spun on my heel and headed back for the kitchen, not quite fast enough to miss the snarled "bitch," that floated after me. She was going to cause me trouble; that much was clear.

Which was fine with me. I quite liked the thought of pounding on something other than the heavy bag for a change.

Dan sat at the table with Natalie, talking to her quietly. He smiled and mouthed 'thanks' as I reappeared.

"Is there anything I can get you?" I asked Natalie. I knew it was a dumb question. The only thing that could make her feel any better would be her husband, whole and unhurt. Given that I couldn't produce him, I was stuck with the clichéd things you said and did when people were grieving.

She shook her head, not meeting my eyes, and I moved away again, looking for Ani.

Sometime later I noticed Dan talking quietly to one of the police officers in the den. Everybody had scarfed down all the chocolate chip cookies I'd been handing around so I used my need to replenish my tray as an excuse to head back to the kitchen. Natalie sat at the table, alone. People kind of skirted around her, sending her nervous smiles, as if they were worried bad luck might be contagious.

I figured I'd had my quota of bad luck for the year and sat down across from her. "Are you sure there's nothing I can get you?

For a moment her eyes lifted, met mine. And they were full of so much rage I almost flinched.

"I don't want anything from you."

Who was she mad at? Me? Why me? "What? Natalie, what's wrong?"

Her lip curled. "This is your fault. *You* brought Tate down on us."

I recoiled, denial flooding me. "No, I didn't. He's insane."

Her eyes pierced me. "He would've left us alone if you weren't a werewolf."

"He's been hunting vamps and weres for years," I said quietly, hoping she might see sense if I stayed calm. "And it's hardly my fault I'm a wolf. You can blame Dan for that part."

"Dan saved your *life*," she said loudly enough that several heads swiveled in our direction. "He saved your life and you don't even see him."

"I see him." I was trying to keep my temper under control, trying to remind myself she was hurt and grieving, but she wasn't making it easy. A surge of energy and emotion rolled through me like electricity.

Anger flooded Nat's face. Her cheeks went red and her knuckles whitened around the mug she clutched. "You don't even appreciate what you have. I love Ben and he's gone and you have Dan and you don't even *care*. If he was gone, you'd probably be happy."

A thousand retorts sprang to mind. None of which I could use unless I wanted to prove Petra right and show myself to be a total bitch. But I wasn't staying to get slapped at, no matter how upset she was. I pushed back my chair with a shove. "I'll get Ani for you."

"Yes," she said dully, emotion draining out of her. She dropped her gaze back to the well-loved surface of the table. "Leave. Be alone. You seem to be good at that."

I spent the rest of the day feeling useless and in the way as the wolves rallied round Natalie and Dan did his Taskforce thing. But Dan wouldn't let me leave, not until he was done and could go with me. By the time we made it back to my house the moon had risen and I'd developed a serious case of miserable.

So I headed for the Cuervo. Dan got there ahead of me, swigging straight from the bottle. "Want some?" He held it out to me.

I took it. It wasn't like I could catch anything from him now. "Sure."

Tequila burned down my throat but didn't make me feel any better. I passed the bottle back to Dan.

He swigged then swigged again. "Crappy day." It wasn't a question.

I shrugged my agreement and went to see what ice-cream I had stashed in the freezer. If tequila wasn't going to help, maybe butterfat and sugar might do the job.

"We could make it less crappy," Dan said.

I froze in the act of peeling the lid off my chocolate chip cookie dough, afraid to look at him and see what the low rumbling tone in his voice might mean.

Silence stretched between us until I didn't know whether it would be worse finding out whether he meant what I *thought* he meant, or for him to know exactly what I thought he meant because he'd thrown me.

Playing dumb seemed safest. "You want ice-cream, too?" I pulled open a drawer, pretending to look for an extra spoon. Too bad it was my junk drawer.

"No. I don't want *ice-cream*."

Oh God. His voice. It zinged straight through my ears and connected directly with my groin. I closed my eyes but that made it worse. Because I could smell him more clearly. Mingling with the scent of frozen cookie dough goodness was the tang of Dan.

Calling to me.

I resisted the urge to hold my nose so I couldn't smell him, telling myself I was in control. My hormones didn't believe me. "Well, then, there's plenty of tequila."

Dad made a rumbling noise. "You know what I mean, Ash. Stop fighting me. Help me make all this go away."

Tempting but chasing away one set of problems by sleeping with Dan was only going to leave me with a whole new set in the morning. I felt the ice-cream carton start to buckle as my hand clenched. "Sorry, can't help you."

"Can't or won't?"

I opened my eyes, looked up at him. Tried not to think about how good he looked in the moonlight. "It doesn't really matter, does it? The answer's no." The ice-cream fell to the bench with a thud as his eyes went liquid.

"Is it really?" He moved closer, surrounding me with that damn delicious scent. Beneath the beat of my own heart, I could hear his pounding.

I gripped the edge of the bench. "Yes. C'mon, Dan. You don't really want to do this. It's just the moon talking."

Blatant lie. I knew the moon only affected wolves when it was full. But one of us had to be rational. Reasonable. I was just starting to have trouble trying to remember why that someone had to be me.

Dan groaned. "This has nothing to do with the moon. It has to do with us. Damn it, Ashley. When are you going to stop running away from me?"

"Not tonight," I pushed away from the bench, not liking the way this conversation was going. Or liking the blinding pulses of heat I was getting every time I looked at Dan. "I'm going to bed."

"Alone?"

I pictured my big empty bed. Pictured it not so empty. Then erased the image before I gave in to my stupider self. "How else?"

"No." He moved to intercept me.

"No? Sorry, did I miss the memo where you got made boss of me?" I glared up at him.

"No," he repeated. "You're not running away again."

"I'll do whatever the hell I like."

"If you were doing what you liked you'd be doing this."

Before I knew what he was doing he reached out and pulled me against him. His mouth came down on mine.

Hard.

Deep.

Everything I'd been missing.

Everything I wanted.

Heat roared through me as his lips moved over mine, nibbling and teasing.

I couldn't help it; I leaned into him, opened my mouth and let him kiss me the way he wanted. The way I wanted him to.

To hell with reason and rationality.

Maybe Natalie was right. Maybe Dan was right. Maybe I'd been running away for all the wrong reasons. Fear. Tate. Anger.

Maybe I needed to remember the right ones for letting him catch me. I'd promised Bug I'd try, really try living as a were for a year. So far I'd been trying to keep everything like it had been and that hadn't worked. I was driving myself crazy. So maybe I should *really* try.

Starting with werewolf sex.

Dan growled low in his throat and a shiver ran through me. The good kind. I could feel the need in him, the tension in his shoulders under my hand and the rising call of his scent.

Hunger rose in me too.

I pulled my mouth away. "You really want to do this?"

His hands pulled my hips harder against his. His erection pressed against me through the fabric of his jeans and I shivered again from memory and want. I knew exactly what waited for me under his clothes.

"Does that feel like I'm kidding?" he asked roughly.

"No." I rubbed myself against him. "It feels pretty serious."

He groaned again. "Ash, if you're going to change your mind about this, do it now. Because, in about twenty seconds I won't be answerable for my behavior."

I smiled as certainty flowed through me. I wasn't going to change my mind.

I wanted to burn away all the bad stuff in a blaze of sex. Ben. Tate. Werewolves. All gone.

Nothing left but Dan. "Good. I like you like that." I clenched my hands into the fabric of his shirt and ripped downwards. The fabric tore easily and my smile widened as the shreds fell from his shoulders.

Dan. Almost naked. I licked my lips. It had been so long.

Too long.

The skin bared to my gaze was the same golden color I remembered, the same dark hair dusted his pecs and trailed down to disappear into the waist band of his jeans. His stomach was flat and hard. The only new thing was a set of scars, low on his abdomen. It took a lot to scar a werewolf. Silver. When had Dan tangled with someone using a silver weapon?

I didn't know. But right now I didn't care.

My hands itched to touch him. I wanted to taste that skin, feel it against mine.

"Finished looking?" Dan said when I lifted my eyes.

I laid my hands on his stomach, felt him shiver. Smiled. "No, I'm just getting started."

"I liked that shirt," he said with a grin as he pulled the last few rags from his body.

"I'm not all that fond of mine," I replied.

His grin grew broader, revealing the dimple deep in his left cheek. "Then you won't mind if I do this."

He reached out and did to my shirt what I'd done to his.

For a moment I froze as a memory of Tate doing just that hit me. But I pushed it away. *This* felt good. This was right. And Tate had no place in my mind tonight. "I can see I'm going to need a bigger clothes budget."

"Aren't you getting a little ahead of yourself?"

"Am I?" I shrugged just to see the expression on his face as my breasts moved under the lace of my bra.

"Maybe not," he admitted with a glazed look. "But you still have too many clothes on."

I stepped back, reached up under my skirt and pulled my panties down, tossing them over my shoulder once I'd stepped free of them. "Better?"

"No."

"No?"

"You're too far away." He moved like lightning and picked me up, backing us up against the island bench. I clamped my legs around his waist as he kissed me again, even more furiously than before.

CHAPTER TWENTY THREE

FOR A MOMENT ALL THAT existed was the kiss and the weight of Dan's body on mine. The roughness of denim against my thighs and the heat burning under my skin.
I wanted more. Wanted closer.

I tried to pull him tighter against me, wanted him to just take me then and there so I didn't have to think any more. Didn't have to need any more.

Instead, he pulled away and a growl rumbled low in my throat before I could help it. "Where are you going?"

"Bed's more comfortable than marble," he said.

I growled again as he straightened and tightened my legs around his hips. "But the marble is right *here. Now.*"

He shook his head, laughter glinting in his eyes. "Impatient, are you?"

"Yes." I arched into him for emphasis. I didn't want to move or think or stop for conversation. I wanted raw and fast and hard until there was only sensation and pleasure.

Dan, it seemed, had other ideas.

He scooped his hands under my back and lifted me, backing away from the counter. I growled again as my body came hard against his, flesh to flesh.

He carried me across the room and I knew if I didn't do something to get him back on my track we were going to end up in my bed. Doing nice, polite sex. Or worse. Making *love*.

Not what I needed. Not what I was anywhere near ready for.

I twisted my hand in his hair and nipped at his ear, just a little too hard.

Or maybe not *too* hard, if the lowdown drunken rumble of pleasure that shook him was anything to go by.

I nipped again and he bumped into the sofa as his arms pulled me even closer.

"Ashley." He pressed his face into my neck and held me tight, weaving across the room. His lips skimmed the pulse in my neck, making me shiver.

"No talking." Talking meant thinking. I tugged his head up so we could kiss again, savoring the taste of him—wild and spicy and tinged with tequila—against my tongue.

"Ow," he muttered against my mouth as we half-fell against the door to the hallway, my back coming hard up against the wood.

"Quit whining," I said, wriggling against him. Too much fabric still separated me from him where I most wanted to feel him, so I gripped one hand around his neck and sent the other down between us seeking his buttons. My fingers brushed the tip of him, hard under the fabric and I smiled as he groaned and closed his eyes.

"I want you," I said, tracing circles with my fingers down the length of his erection then back up his zipper. I flicked the button open and made short work of the zip so I could slide my hand against all that lovely hard flesh. "Now." I clamped my mouth over his. "Now," I repeated, more a breath than a word.

Dan groaned. "Oh, fuck it. Whatever you want."

We slid to the floor, tearing at clothes in between kisses. Each touch sent me spinning higher until I was dizzy with the taste and smell and feel of him. I wanted my hands all over him and his all over me.

His mouth closed over a nipple, teasing it to the edge of pain and I whimpered for him to do it again. Lightning bolts shot through me, pure heat from breast to groin as he complied.

God. *Dan.*

He felt so good.

So right.

I pulled his head back up to mine to taste his kisses again. His tongue flickered against mine and his need scented the air like a physical thing, wrapping around me and dragging my senses to some dark, hot place made of nerves and skin and pleasure.

I floated there as our bodies moved, as his mouth traveled down my torso, flicking tiny kisses just where each nerve seemed most sensitive. Drowning in him.

I surfaced briefly with a startled gasp as his fingers slid into me and his mouth sent the burning heat between my legs into flash fire. But then the sheer overwhelming need for him dragged me back down to the darkness so I lay arching and writhing, wanting more with each stroke, each delicate lap of his tongue.

I could feel the orgasm begin to build, tiny tremors running over my skin, making my thighs tremble.

Dan must have felt them too because he stopped, forcing a protest from my throat.

"Not without me," he said fiercely. "Not this time."

He slid up my body until his cock was resting against me, teasing me sweetly, just nudging my entrance. I wanted to move, wanted to take him but I couldn't. I was frozen by the look in Dan's eyes. By the pleasure and satisfaction written across his face.

By the answering emotion that tangled me up as he raised my hands above my head and linked his fingers in mine.

"Not without me," he repeated as he slid inside me so slowly I almost screamed.

My flesh was so sensitized I felt each millimeter of him move into me, felt the hair on his body brush against my skin and his heart beating inside his chest.

I was painfully aware of the heavy thud of my own as I fought not to feel what I wanted to feel, not to let myself be foolish and slip back into love.

When he was finally all the way against me, he stilled as if he was waiting for something. Or as if he couldn't quite believe he was finally with me again. The look on his face was reverent.

Too much.

I shut my eyes. "Please," I said, trying to move against him. "Please, Dan."

His hips were heavy against mine, holding me still. I couldn't do this slow and tender. It would rip me apart.

And, if I was any judge, Dan was riding a knife's edge between control and giving into to instinct.

So I did what I had to do to ease the conflicting needs of head and heart and screaming-for-release skin.

I pulled my hands free, pulled his head down to mine as I tightened my muscles around his cock and whispered, "Fuck me."

He did.

With a cry that sounded like it was torn from his throat he pulled back then plunged into me again. Hard. Fast. Over and over. Everything I'd wanted. Everything I needed to send me speeding back towards pure sensation and overwhelming drive towards release.

It was no longer Dan and me and everything that implied. It was just male and female and the need to claim each other as simply as possible. With flesh and hunger and bodies that spoke things we couldn't say.

I don't know how long it took. But it was glorious and wonderful and I wanted to lie there forever moving with him, rolling and tearing and drinking him in. But my body had other ideas as the slide of flesh quickened and our breathing roughened and the noises and words we spoke grew more frantic.

Dan slid his hands under my hips, angling me up so he could go even deeper, each stroke hitting some point inside me that sent sparks flashing behind closed eyes.

Slick skin against slick skin made me shiver as the sensations built and built. His mouth coming down on mine again finally sent me diving into an orgasm so intense I did scream for him as I just held on, muscles spasming and pleasure I'd never imagined flooding every nerve.

A few seconds later, Dan shouted my name and drove into me again before collapsing against me like he'd forgotten how to breathe.

I wasn't so sure I remembered myself so I just held him and drifted until the aftershocks faded.

Eventually, Dan lifted his head. I opened my eyes to find him grinning down at me. The curve of his mouth did strange things to my stomach. Or somewhere north of that, if I was totally honest. But I wasn't ready to deal with my heart.

"You were right. Beds are overrated," he said in a half-growl.

I laughed though I was starting to become aware that my back didn't necessarily agree with him. "Doesn't mean I would object to one for round two."

"Round two?" He laid his forehead against mine. "Fuck, Ash. You trying to kill me?"

"You got some better way to go?" I moved my hips, felt his cock stir to life.

"Hell, no. Bed it is." He rolled off me then reached out and took my hand.

"Your room," I said as we staggered to our feet and he picked me up again.

He looked confused. "Why?"

I summoned my best just-shut-up-and-do-me smile. "It's closer." And I wasn't ready to wake up with Dan in my bed. Tonight was about now. Not forever. I couldn't cope with forever. If I let Dan into my bed, I was going to have a hell of a time kicking him out again.

Dan frowned a little but then shrugged and headed for his room. Sometime—about four orgasms—later, I left him sleeping the sleep of the righteously laid and snuck back to my own bed. For a long time I just lay under the covers, staring into the dark and wondering what the hell I'd just done.

Especially that last time when I couldn't help it any longer and heat and passion had slowed to something sweeter and deeper, Dan's eyes almost drowning me as he moved softly inside me until we both melted. Just like we used to before any of this had happened. It was enough to bring back all the doubts and fears about what letting him in would mean and send me scurrying back to my own bed as soon as he'd fallen asleep.

Eventually, after the answer had come back as "no fucking idea" about fifty times, I managed to convince my brain to take the Scarlett O'Hara approach and think about it tomorrow.

I fell into sleep like a dead thing and didn't move until my door crashed open around five am and the light blazed into life.

"Get up," Dan snarled, voice like ashes.

I blinked up at him, trying to get my brain to connect. The look on his face worked effectively as a bucket of ice water over my head, clearing the cobwebs with an icy blast that left me chilled.

He looked pissed. More than pissed.

Enraged.

"What's going on?" I sat up, hoping my leaving him alone in bed wasn't responsible for his mood.

"They found Ben," He said, staring at me with eyes like shattered silver ice. "We have to go."

I abandoned all my planned explanations and rationales for why I was in my bed, not his as the words sank in.

Found Ben. Oh God.

It couldn't be good news. Dan wouldn't look like he did if it was good news. I pulled the covers closer around me, suddenly freezing. I didn't want to ask the question. I wasn't sure I could bear the answer. Natalie's face at the pack meeting – happy and laughing as she looked up at her husband – floated before my eyes.

"Found him?" It was as close as I could get to the real question. I prayed in my head, prayed that Dan would say "he's okay" and everything would *be* okay.

But I knew it wasn't, even before Dan opened his mouth.

"In pieces," he said.

The room spun around me. I half-rolled to the side of the bed and threw up.

Dead. Dead. Dead.

Natalie was right. This was my fault. I threw up again. And again and again until I was dry retching.

When I finally lifted my head, Dan still stood by the door. Which didn't make me feel any better. It wasn't just Ben. He was mad about last night. Otherwise he'd be comforting me.

"Finished?" he said icily.

I nodded slowly, not really sure.

"Then get dressed. I'm leaving in ten minutes with or without you."

Then he was gone.

I staggered into the bathroom and ran cold water over my head until the worst of the dizziness and nausea passed. Then I got dressed, hair dripping everywhere and made it downstairs and into the car just before Dan turned on the ignition.

He didn't say anything and I couldn't think of anything to say that could possibly make the situation any better. So I just shut up and hid behind my sunglasses, pretending there were no tears rolling down my cheeks as we sped through Seattle and pictures of body parts filled my head.

Dan took the exit for Sea-Tac and it dawned on me where we were headed. The Retreat.

"Oh God," I said. "Please, not there." The tears came faster. Tate couldn't have come up with a better way to attack the pack than to kill one of its members in the place they were supposed to be safest.

Dan kept his eyes on the road. "Where else?"

His voice was bitter and I knew whatever I was feeling had to be a thousand times worse for him. He'd been a werewolf for four years. A long time. He was friends—family really—with everyone in the pack. With Ben.

And he was the one who'd brought me into their lives. Brought Tate into their lives via me.

Me, who'd just treated him like he meant nothing to me.

Which was pretty much par for the course for how I'd been treating him since he turned. But finally having sex with him and then stealing away in the middle of the night was a whole new level of abominable behavior. Shame mingled with the nausea still riding my stomach. I clutched the armrest by the window, determined not to throw up again.

God. What had I done?

The drive seemed as endless as the chasm that had opened up between us. There were a couple of blue and whites parked at the turn-off to the road that led to the Retreat and an officer flagged us down and made Dan show his badge before the policeman waved us through.

I was tempted to ask Dan to drop me off so I could just stay up here, away from whatever had happened inside the walls. Away from the bunch of angry wolves I'd be facing.

Away from Dan.

As far as I could tell, he'd probably throw me out of the Jeep while it was still moving and not look back.

I wouldn't blame him one bit.

When we got to the main house, Ani and Sam were standing on the front porch, arms around each other. But I couldn't see any of the other wolves. Relief eased the knots in my stomach only to be immediately followed by burning guilt.

Esme stood a little way apart from Ani and Sam. She looked almost relieved when Dan pulled the Jeep to a halt.

She came over as he climbed out and started a rapid-fire report I tried not to listen to.

I didn't want to hear the details.

They walked towards the house and I stayed where I was, unable to move as I watched Ani and Sam.

The last time I'd been here I'd been terrified of what was going to happen to me.

Now I was terrified of what had happened. Because of the pain it caused Natalie and the pack, and because it might take away from me the one thing that looked like it could make being a wolf something I could live with.

The one thing beside Dan, that is.

As I watched, Dan and Esme disappeared into the house with Sam. Ani headed in my direction.

I slouched down in my seat.

Ani rapped on the window. I forced myself to lower it.

"Ashley? Are you okay?"

My guilt intensified. She was asking me if I was okay when she'd just lost one of her family.

"I'm fine," I said quietly. "Don't worry about me."

Brown eyes looked at me curiously. "You're pack. I worry about everyone. Come into the house."

"I don't think Dan wants me in there," I muttered.

Her expression softened. "Dan's upset right now, don't pay any attention to him."

"Is Natalie here?"

Ani shook her head. "She's with her other family."

"Did you have to..." I meant had she been the one to identify the body.

"Sam did." She looked down, swallowed. But then her head came back up, her expression fierce.

"I'm sorry," I said, feeling lower than dirt. "This is my fault."

"This is no one's fault but Tate's. Trust me, he'll be taught to leave the pack alone." Her eyes burned and I knew she believed it. So maybe I could believe we'd beat him too.

And to do that, I had to get out of the car.

When we got into the house, Esme was waiting in the hall. Dan was nowhere to be seen.

"Ashley, come with me please." Esme said.

Ani patted my arm and walked away.

"What?" I said to Esme, "Where's Dan?"

"He's busy," she said shortly. "He wants you to keep working on the financial stuff. We've managed to trace a few more things back to the Sutton place."

I wanted to argue, wanted to go after Dan and the others but I knew I'd only be in the way. So I let Esme lead me upstairs and hid away in a room they'd set up with my computer and a stack of files, trying to think of a new angle. I'd been trying to see if the Synotech connection was real but as far as I, or the Taskforce could tell, they were completely legit with no connection to Tate anywhere. And even though we'd scoured their employee records, none of them, past or present looked like Smith. Without knowing the doctor's real name, there was no way to track him. It was another dead end.

To make matters worse, my mind kept bouncing between memories of being held by Tate—Tate, Smith, Rio—and imagining what they might have done to Ben before they killed him.

After a couple of hours of torturing myself mentally I went back downstairs, looking for Dan, hoping he might have calmed down so that I could apologize. Or grovel. Do whatever it would take to ease the ice out of his eyes. But I couldn't see him. I grabbed the arm of the nearest agent. "Where's Agent Gibson?"

"I think he went outside."

I looked at the crowd of agents, contemplated wading my way through them all to reach the door. Decided I could wait. "Just tell him I was looking for him."

"Sure thing, Ms. Keenan."

I went back upstairs to the computer, glad to throw myself back into the only escape I had. Until we found another way into the Synotech connection, I'd stick to the trails I'd already been following. I'd already tracked the Sutton property back through a trail of seven dummy corporations and had finally hit what seemed to be a real organization. Not one that had Tate's name anywhere on any document associated with it but it was a start...more than we'd had before.

I buried myself in the numbers and the online paper trail until my stomach started to growl a protest, forcing me out of my lair in search of food.

I still couldn't see Dan when I reached the kitchen. I glanced at my watch. Nearly two hours had passed since I'd first looked for him.

Esme was standing by the sink, pouring herself a cup of coffee. She looked immaculate as always, not a hair out of place although I knew she'd been up since before five like the rest of us. I didn't know whether the good grooming was a cat thing or just her, but it didn't make her any more likeable.

She was talking to Agent Stevens as she poured. I joined her. My arm knocked hers as I reached for a mug and coffee splashed everywhere—mostly on Agent Stevens.

"Sorry, Robert," Esme said.

Robert? His name was Robert? I froze as her words made me flash on Smith's face. Why? The memory refused to clear and slid away. I blinked then remembered why I'd come downstairs.

"Where's Dan?" I held up my mug. Caffeine wouldn't stop me feeling scruffy compared to Esme but it would help me think.

She shrugged and poured. "I haven't seen him."

"I thought you two were working pretty closely?" I gulped coffee, rubbing my eyes to try and convince myself I felt better than half-dead.

"We are. But he said he was going to talk to the chief."

"How long ago?"

Another shrug. "I'm not sure. Maybe after lunch?"

It was close to four now. So Dan had been gone a long time. I pulled at my cell and dialed his number. Voicemail.

Voicemail in the middle of an investigation? A distinct uneasy feeling crept down my spine and the coffee turned to acid in my stomach. "Can you ask around, see who saw him last?"

"What's the rush? You two got a hot date tonight?"

I tried to ignore the aggressive tone in her voice. "Esme, we're dealing with a psycho who's been killing vamps and weres. Dan's the Agent in Charge. You don't think he's an attractive target for Tate?"

She had the grace to look a little shame-faced. Just a little. "All right, I'll ask."

"Thank you." I dialed another number on my cell. "Have you seen Dan in the last few hours?" I asked when Jase answered.

"No, he hasn't been by the office at all." He sounded a little confused. "Was he going to come by? He left a message about Ben. I'm sorry, Ash."

"Thanks." I couldn't think about Ben. I had to focus on tracking down Dan. "Have you, uh, felt anything today?" I asked.

"No. Ash, is something wrong?"

Apart from the feeling of dread in my stomach? It took me a second to answer. I didn't trust my voice. "No. I'm just jumpy. Everything's fine. I call you later."

"Okay. I'll let you know if Dan calls."

I hung up the phone before Jase could ask any of the questions that I heard in his tone. It rang again, almost immediately.

"Dan?" I said eagerly.

"Sorry, Pretty, Dan can't come to the phone right now."

CHAPTER TWENTY FOUR

RIO. HIS VOICE MADE MY knees buckle. I'd know it anywhere. I'd heard it often enough in my nightmares. "Where is he?"

"Safe with us, Pretty," Rio said mockingly. "For now."

They had Dan.

Fear beat through me, choking my throat and drying my mouth.

They had Dan.

They'd do to him what they'd just done to Ben. I clenched my jaw to keep my teeth from chattering and forced myself to speak. "What do you want?"

"Boss would like to see you."

Fear turned to blind panic and I slid down the wall white noise roaring in my ears. Put myself back in Tate's hands? How could I?

How could I leave Dan there?

I clutched my cell so hard the plastic cover started to buckle, forcing me to ease up before I destroyed the phone entirely. "Where?"

Rio chuckled. "Ah, Pretty. I can't make it that easy for you. You'll have to find him yourself. Your clever Taskforce friends can help you."

"I'm going to kill you," I snarled. "When I find you, you're dead."

"Ooh, I'm scared."

I could almost see the smirk on his face. A smirk I intended to tear off. He was forgetting I wasn't just a helpless human any more. If I could keep him talking, maybe he'd give me a clue. I strained my ears, trying to hear anything in the background of the call beyond the usual cell phone fuzziness. There. Maybe a faint rumble? And a blast of something almost at the edge of hearing. What was that? *Keep him talking.* "Surely Tate doesn't want to wait. Tell me where to find you."

Rio laughed again. "Sorry, Pretty. Just come alone and don't take too long. We had fun with that other wolf. Pity we couldn't put all the pieces back together. Perhaps this time we'll do better. Offer him all the comforts of home."

"If you hurt him—"

The dial tone buzzed in my ear before I could reply. I tried to think, the urge to scream clawing at the back of my throat. I wanted to hit someone. Hurt someone. But I had to find Dan first. Then there'd be plenty of pain.

Anger bit deep in the pit of my stomach and the need to change grew with it. The wolf wanted out. But the wolf couldn't help me now. I shoved myself to a standing position, took a second to make sure my legs would hold me, and went to find Esme.

Luckily, she wasn't hard to find. She was right in the foyer talking to a bunch of other agents. They all looked tired and stressed, suits wrinkled, ties loosened around necks. Apart from Esme, of course.

"Tate has Dan," I said. No point beating around the bush. I shoved my cell phone into her hands.

Esme gaped at me, blank disbelief on her face breaking through the feline cool. "What are you talking about?"

"Rio called me. He said they had Dan."

Esme snapped back into agent mode. "What did he say, exactly?"

"That they had Dan and I had to come or they'd kill him." Someone in the crowd muttered "Fuck," but I kept looking at Esme.

She looked down at the cell. "This phone?"

I nodded and she handed it to another agent. "See if you can trace the last incoming call. And get the number transferred to a secure phone."

"How long will that take?" I asked.

"Not long. Why?"

Seriously? What the hell did she think I was going to do? Wait around for Tate to kill Dan? Not a chance. Another wild surge of anger flared. "I need to get out of here."

"Ashley, you can't go anywhere. This is a trap."

"I don't care," I said. "We need to find Dan and I can't wait around for the Taskforce to figure out where he is."

Jase. I needed to get to Jase. Maybe he'd be able to work whatever mojo it was that had helped him find me—not that I was even certain that it had been him because I'd never quite gotten around to having that discussion with him.

"You can't go." Esme repeated. "It's not safe."

"Screw safe. This is *Dan.*" My voice was loud enough to carry through the hallway, causing Ani to come running.

"What's going on?" she demanded.

"I got a call. Tate has Dan."

The color drained from Ani's face. "Where?"

I shook my head. "I don't know. But I need to find him and Esme here is being difficult."

Ani frowned then her face cleared. "It's okay," she said to Esme. "I'll calm her down. You do what you need to do."

"Calm me down?" I practically shrieked as Ani took my arm and began frog marching me up the stairs. "What are you talking about?"

"Shut up," Ani hissed low in my ear. "Play along."

Play along? What the hell was going on?

We reached the room I'd been using and Ani hustled me inside and closed the door.

I stood where I was, glaring.

"Stop pouting and tell me what's happening," she snapped as she took a seat on the bed.

"They have Dan."

"I got that bit. What's the bee in Esme's bonnet?"

"I have to go. It'll take the Taskforce forever to track him down. We don't have forever."

Ani winced then straightened her back. "What makes you think you can find Tate any faster?"

I hesitated, not wanting to reveal Jase's secret. "I think Jase can help. Or maybe Lord Marco."

"Marco? Is that a good idea?"

I made a frustrated noise. If one more person tried to stop me doing whatever I needed to do, there was going to be blood. "I don't *care* if it's a good idea. I just want to find Dan." The snarl in my voice surprised me.

Ani blinked then smiled. "At least you've finally come to your senses."

I had no idea what she was talking about. "Excuse me?"

"About Dan. Took you long enough."

"For what?"

She looked at me like I was being dense. "To admit how you feel about him."

Uh-oh. Not ready for this conversation. I didn't have time to try and analyze my feelings. Besides, if we didn't find Dan, there'd be no point. "He's my *friend*."

"Yeah, well, you two don't smell like friends."

I blushed, knowing I'd probably smelled like sex when I first arrived. "So we slept together. That's closure."

"You always go into a panic over closure?"

The question earned her another glare. "I told you, he's my friend. And I'd do the same for anyone Tate had."

She rolled her eyes. "You know, the two of you aren't fooling anyone."

"Ani, I don't have time for this. There won't be any chance of a two of anything if we don't get Dan back."

She rubbed a hand across her forehead and I felt like a jerk for making her feel any worse than she must already.

"You're right," she said. "Sorry. Okay. You need to get back to the city. Without Esme knowing."

"I need my phone back too," I added. "They might call again."

"We can get the phone back. But I'm sure the Taskforce will be listening in to all the calls, so you'd better be careful if you make any plans you don't want them to know about."

I nodded. "I can handle that. Jase can get me another cell. But I need to get to Jase."

"A couple more wolves are arriving soon." Ani pushed off the bed, scrunching her forehead like she was trying to think. "We should be able to sneak you into their car on the way back. If you don't mind riding in the trunk until they're clear of the roadblocks."

I didn't care what I had to do. "That's fine. What about Esme?"

"I'll tell her I put some alpha whammy on you."

"Can you do that?"

Ani smiled smugly. "Sometimes. Esme's some sort of cat, right? So she doesn't really know for sure. In fact, why don't you get into bed, I'll tell her I knocked you out, she can check on you and then once the wolves get here, I'll come get you."

I wasn't sure I could pull off fake-sleeping well enough to fool Esme but I was willing to give it a try. And, to tell the truth, my body thought the idea of lying down was a pretty good one.

So I climbed under the covers and shut my eyes. Ani pulled the blinds down and switched off the computer. As she left I said, "You wouldn't really put a whammy on me, would you?"

She grinned. "Depends how much you'd pissed me off. Now, sleep."

She used her alpha voice and I actually found myself starting to drift off before I managed to snap out of it. Obviously she didn't even need a full whammy when the subject was sleep deprived. But my fear for Dan was too strong to let my mind give in completely, so I lay dozing and turning over a thousand plans in my mind.

Only problem was all of them depended on me knowing where Dan was.

I called Jase as soon as I was safely out of the Retreat and filled him in on what was happening.

"What can I do?" he asked.

"See if you can find anything out." I didn't specify how. Not in front of the wolves.

"Are you coming here?"

"Sure," I lied. "But I'll be awhile. I want to get my car." I wasn't going to the office. I was going to beg yet another favor from Marco. Which Jase would never let me do. So now I was lying to almost everybody I cared about. Something else to worry about.

"Call me when you're closer."

Define closer, I thought as I finally reached Marco's house. My fingers itched to pick up the phone and ask Jase to come with me, but then he'd only try and talk me out of this. He'd be right to do so. I had no idea what I could offer Marco this time. I was already over my head owing him a debt.

This time I wasn't taken to the cozy sofa room. This time, I was led upstairs to an office and left waiting in a highly uncomfortable minimalist chair that poked at my back and tilted my legs at a weird angle.

The whole room made me nervous. Unlike the downstairs, it was all stark white and black and glass. About as cozy as an operating theatre.

"*Signorina* Keenan, what a surprise." Marco walked into the room, holding out his hand. When I rose to shake it, he grasped mine and pressed a kiss to my knuckles. His lips were cool and my skin tingled.

Confused, I pulled my hand away as soon as possible. "Lord Marco, thank you for seeing me again."

He waved a hand at me to sit. "I look forward to your visits."

I doubted it. He was just laying on the charm for practice. And right now I didn't have time for the social niceties. "I'm sorry to be abrupt but Tate has taken Daniel."

Marco's smile disappeared. "Special Agent Gibson? Your wolf?"

I almost said 'not my wolf' automatically but wasn't sure if that would help or hinder my case. "Yes, Agent Gibson. You may have heard that one of the wolves was killed?"

He nodded, eyes somber. "Yes. It is unfortunate."

"I'm pretty sure Tate is behind this."

"He wants you back, cara. You are unfinished business."

More like I was a loose end to be tied up. Tate had obviously found out that he hadn't turned me into one of his super vamps. "Perhaps. I need to find him."

Marco sat on the edge of the glass desk, regarding me with a serious expression. "It would not be wise to put yourself back in his hands, Ashley."

I nodded. "I know that." Knew it down to the bone. The thought of going anywhere near Tate terrified me. "But I can't let him kill Dan."

A dimple twitched in his cheek. "Ah. So perhaps Daniel Gibson is your wolf, after all?"

I hitched a shoulder. "He's someone I don't want dead."

"So you have come to me for another favor? You wish to know if I know where Tate is?"

I nodded again, licking lips gone suddenly dry. "I know there's a price—"

The phone on the glass desk shrilled into life and Marco held up a hand. "Excuse me." He picked up the phone. "*Pronto?*"

I tried to look patient as he spoke rapid fire Italian. My Italian is pretty much limited to Campari and spaghetti so I had no idea what he was discussing but when his eyes suddenly focused on me, I got the feeling I might not like it.

"It seems your friend is here," Marco said as he hung up the phone.

Friend? My heart leapt. "Dan?"

He shook his head. "No. Young Jason." He looked at me, arching an eyebrow.

What the hell? "I have no idea what he's doing here," I said in response to the silent question.

"Then we shall find out together. He is being brought up."

Sure enough, the door opened about a minute later and Jase stormed through. He nodded perfunctorily at Marco. "Lord Marco." Then he turned to me. "You want to explain what you're doing here?" Extreme pissed-off-vampire vibes rolled off him. The hairs on my arms stood on end as I gripped the arms of my chair.

"Speaking to Lord Marco," I said, managing to keep my voice steady. Just. "How about you?"

"Stopping you from doing something idiotic," he snapped. He turned back to Marco, bowed slightly. "I apologize, my lord. But she shouldn't have come to you again."

Marco's eyes went a deeper shade of green. "Ashley and I were just starting to come to an agreement. But perhaps the two of you need to talk first?"

Jase nodded. "Thank you, my lord. I would appreciate that."

"Well, I wouldn't," I said, loosening my grip on the chair as the tension radiating from Jase eased. "This is none of your business."

"I shall leave you," Marco said. He was out the door before I had time to protest any further, leaving Jase and I staring each other down.

Jase broke the deadlock. "Are you *insane?*"

"Unless you mean insanely angry with you, no." I stood so he didn't have quite so much the height advantage as he loomed over me. "But I'd like to know what you think you're doing."

"You can't get into more debt with Marco. You don't know what he might ask you for."

"Do you have a better idea for finding Tate?"

Frustration clouded his eyes. "No."

"So you've got nothing on Dan? I mean—" it was time to stop dancing around the subject—" you can find people sometimes, can't you? You helped them find me, right?"

"You're different."

"You did find me." I stared at him in awe. "How?"

"I just thought I heard you calling. I could tell where from. It's not a big deal."

I didn't know whether to smack him or hug him. "You probably saved my life and it's not a big deal?"

"No. But getting yourself into a bigger obligation with Marco is. Don't do it, Ash. I'll tell him about my...abilities. He'll trade for that."

"Why would you do that? For me, I mean." He looked down at the floor. "Because you never treated me differently. After. You stuck by me. You're the only one who did."

Tears rose in my eyes and I brushed them away. This wasn't the time or place for a Kodak moment. "That doesn't mean you owe me anything. Telling Marco would be—"

"Unnecessary." The accented voice came from the door and we both froze. *Shit.* We'd forgotten about vampire hearing.

Marco was looking at Jase with an expression that was way too smug for my liking.

"Jason was just leaving," I said quickly. "Then you and I can finish our—"

"I'm not going anywhere," Jase retorted.

"In that, you are correct, young one," Marco said. "I believe you and I have things to discuss. However, you cannot make this bargain on Ashley's behalf. She wants the information, she must trade for it."

"Does that mean you have it?" I asked, ignoring the price issue for now.

His eyes fastened on me and I suddenly found the green less intriguing and more disconcerting. "We shall discuss this matter after Jason leaves." He nodded towards the door.

Jase looked wretched. He couldn't disobey a direct order from the head of his lineage. Not if he wanted to keep his head attached to his shoulders. He shot a guilt stricken look at me and then left.

Marco waited until the door was closed and Jase's footsteps had faded.

"You shouldn't be mad at him," I said. "He didn't mean to—"

"That is for me to decide. And you and I have something else to talk about, do we not? Time is of the essence?"

Reluctantly, I bit my tongue on the subject of Jase. I had to focus on one problem at a time. Right now I had to make a deal. "What do you want?"

"You already owe me a debt, *cara*. What else do you have to offer? Information? Has the Taskforce uncovered something fascinating?"

Nothing that I could think of. And if he wouldn't take another debt, that left only one option. I fingered my neck uneasily, feeling the tiny scars that were all the evidence that remained of Tate's bites.

"No. Maybe I'm wasting your time. Perhaps Lord Esteban might know more."

Marco bristled. "I do not think you would want to pay Esteban's price. He does not believe in courtesy like I do."

Bile rose in my throat. Okay, so a threat to go to Esteban was the very definition of empty. Plus, I'd managed to freak myself out into the bargain.

Which kind of left me between a rock and a hard place. And back to the option I didn't want to take.

Quite frankly, the thought of letting another vampire bite me was horrifying. But not as horrifying as the thought of Dan turning up in pieces like Ben. At least, I hoped I could convince myself of that.

I swallowed hard. "Blood. I offer you blood. With limits."

"Limits? Are you in the position to put limits on me?"

His eyes had turned predatory, and I tried to convince myself he wasn't looking at my neck. "You allowed limits before. That should apply again." I had no idea what I was talking about. "You can't kill me or hurt me or thrall me."

"The last two are contradictory, *cara*. I cannot bite you and not hurt you if I do not take your mind."

"I meant hurt me beyond the bite. I won't be thralled."

"Just one bite? You put a high price on yourself."

His eyes hadn't left me and I knew I had him. "You said yourself that drinking from a wolf is rare. So just one." I tilted my head back, closing my eyes. "Go on."

Laughter rang round the room and I jumped.

"Not so quickly. This is something to savor."

I gritted my teeth. I didn't want him to savor me. I wanted him to get things the hell over with.

"Plus, it is not wise for you to go after Tate with blood loss. Let us call this an IOU. After all this is settled, you will come to me and we will do this properly."

I nodded, cursing vampires in my head. He'd want me to dress pretty and smile, just like Tate had. And Dan would hate me for doing what I'd just agreed to.

But at least he'd be alive to hate me. "All right," I said. "We have a deal."

"Good," Marco said. "Now tell me exactly what you know."

I explained what I could. Marco made me go over the phone call several times.

"You're sure he said comforts of home?"

I nodded. "Yes. Why, does that mean something?"

Marco frowned. "Perhaps. We are territorial creatures, vampires. We default to familiar ground."

"I haven't found any new property in Tate's name."

"No, you wouldn't, he's not so careless. But I have been digging into his life. The vampire who created him was wealthy. Her estate was substantial. We've been looking into who controls those assets now."

"And?" I held my breath, wondering if Marco had found a lead, kicking myself for not having thought of this angle previously.

"There are some properties we are yet to trace."

"Anything that they could get to from the Retreat in an hour or two?" Unless Rio had called me from the road, it didn't seem likely that they could have taken Dan further. Esme would already be checking local airstrips to see if anyone had used one but planes didn't seem to be Tate's style. Besides, he wanted me. Which meant he couldn't take Dan too far.

Unless he was just playing another of his sadistic games, and had no intention of me ever finding Dan alive.

I buried that thought deep. I couldn't afford to give up now.

Marco was still frowning. "Give me a little time and I will get that information."

CHAPTER TWENTY FIVE

I DIDN'T WANT TO WAIT while Marco went to work so I drove back to my house, hoping against hope that this was all a horrible dream, or that someone would hand me the keys to a time machine and I could go back to when my life didn't seem full of blood and vampires.

No such luck. It seemed the universe was enjoying kicking me around. Because when I got home, Esme was sitting on my front step. She didn't look happy.

"Don't bother yelling at me," I said, holding up a hand as I walked past her. "I don't care what you think."

"Good," Esme said, lifting her chin. "Then you won't mind when I tell you you're behaving like a stupid, pig-headed, childish, irresponsible bitch."

"Finished?" I unlocked the front door, looking back at her.

"No," she snapped. "What were you thinking? You could've gotten killed."

"Well, I didn't." I stepped into the hall and my heart almost broke. My house smelled like Dan. I almost backpedaled but Esme was right behind me.

I tried to breathe through my mouth as the scent tore at my emotions. The place smelled like sex, too, and stale vomit. I remembered the mess I'd left in my bedroom—God, had it been only that morning?

I felt about a thousand years older.

But no wiser. Though I knew that, now that Esme had found me, I was unlikely to evade her a second time. So I might as well use her. "I may have some possible locations for Tate soon," I said as I moved

"Ashley, don't you dare come after me," Dan's voice sounded rusty, like his throat hurt. "Stay away, do you hear me—"I heard a dull thud like flesh hitting flesh, and then a groan.

"Dan!" I screamed down the phone.

"Me again, Pretty." Kyra said. "Your wolf is being stubborn. He should know better. He won't be such a good wolf if he can't run."

I tried not to let myself think about what the threat meant. "Trust me, I'm coming."

"And I haven't even touched you yet, how flattering." This time, it wasn't Kyra, it was Tate.

My stomach went into free fall. "You're not going to touch me."

"We shall see," Tate said. "If you get here in time."

I was vaguely aware of the agent making 'keep talking' gestures so I didn't hang up. Instead I focused on my anger so I could hold off the fear. "Do you really think you're that hard to find?"

He made a snarling noise. "Finding me might be easy. Getting here could be a cinch. Leaving will be the hard part."

I ignored the automatic shiver that crept down my spine and steeled myself to sound bored. "Well, you know, my social calendar is pretty full these days. So I won't be able to stay too long."

"You're very cocky for someone who's barely a cub. I've killed plenty of wolves, you know."

"Really? How interesting. Why don't you tell me all the details, and then that'll be just one more reason for the state to fry you when we catch you?"

That earned me another wordless snarl and sweat trickled down my spine. Baiting him into a rage before I even got there. Not my smartest strategy. Unless anger made him careless.

I could only hope.

The agent gave me a thumbs-up, which meant they had a trace on the call. Which also meant I could hang up. "Was there something else?" I said, still trying to sound casual. "Because I have another call."

"It's not wise to think you have the upper hand, Ashley." His voice was ice-cold. No trace of emotion at all.

"I guess we'll see when I get there."

"I'm looking forward to it."

I couldn't say the same so I snapped the phone shut with relief. I felt like I needed a shower, like Tate's voice had soiled me somehow.

I tried to shake the feeling off. But truth was, I was terrified. I was an accountant, for Chrissakes. I didn't go waltzing around trying to take down psychopaths. I dealt with numbers and nice safe financial details. No balance sheet had ever tried to kill me.

But numbers wouldn't save Dan. No, that was up to me.

I'd always thought riding in a helicopter would make me throw up. Instead, to my relief, I found it fascinating to be flying through the rapidly darkening sky.

Or at least it was distracting enough to take my mind off where we were going.

Jase, however, spent the flight looking green and clinging to the strap beside his seat.

Somehow that made me feel slightly better.

As cunning plans went, ours was pretty basic. We were flying to Moses Lake, the closest big town to the property we hoped was Tate's hideaway. Esme's team had confirmed a train on the line at the right time for Rio's call. So we'd decided to go with that option. Tate's call had been routed through a web of satellites, so we hadn't been able to confirm our theory from that.

No, we were gambling on the accuracy of train timetables and faint noises that even shifter ears struggled to identify. Perfect.

But it was the best we could do. So Moses Lake it was.

From there, I'd drive to the property where Tate was holed up and walk in.

That was the part I didn't like but we hadn't come up with an alternative. Jase would monitor me, if he could and then the Taskforce cavalry would come rolling in after an hour. So all I really had to do was stay alive for an hour. And keep Dan alive too.

Simple, right?

I had a gun, I was wired and I had several knives—one of them silver. Carrying silver was risky because, while it might give me a chance to hurt Rio, it could also be used against me.

Not that it was likely Tate was lacking in ways to hurt me if that was what he wanted.

I also had Bug's platinum cross wrapped around my forearm, hidden by the sleeve of my top.

As the helicopter came in to land, Esme's voice came across my headset. "You still sure you want to do it this way? It's not too late to change plans."

I swiveled in my seat so I could see her. We both knew Dan was unlikely to survive if we attacked Tate's compound. Tate would kill him at the first hint of an assault.

I had to free him first.

"We stick to the plan," I said firmly.

Esme nodded and I saw her mouth something at Agent Stevens, using his name.

Robert.

I flashed on Smith again. Smith saying "Sorry, Robert." When I'd woken up after Tate. Suddenly I knew I hadn't dreamed it. And if I hadn't then, I thought I knew exactly who Robert was. Robert Keenan. My father. Smith had known my father.

"Esme," I said, mind racing. If Smith knew my father, then we had a whole new lead.

She turned back to me. "What?"

"I've remembered something. I think Smith knew my father."

Her eyebrows rose. "What?"

"Something he said when they had me. I thought I'd dreamed it. But I didn't. If I—" I choked off the words. I was going to be fine. I was coming back. I had to believe it or I'd never get out of the helicopter. "We need to follow that connection. Look at my father."

She looked doubtful but nodded. "Let's get this done first."

I sat back feeling weirdly peaceful. I'd done something useful finally.

The air smelled strange as I climbed out of the chopper. Like oil and hot metal and a damp heaviness—as though a storm was on the way. It was supposed to be a clear night. But maybe the weather had decided not to cooperate.

I shivered as the chopper blades, still slowly circling, whipped my ponytail round in my face. I followed Esme and Jase across the airfield to where the Taskforce team waited.

Away from the chopper, the air smelled cleaner, richer and I breathed deeply. Part of me wondered whether this was the last night I'd smell anything but I squished the doubt away. If I fell to pieces now everything would be lost.

There was really no point putting off the inevitable. I let them do a final check of the tiny wire hidden behind my ear, then hugged Jase and climbed into the waiting rental car.

It had GPS and a navigation system so I followed the instructions until I was well away from the town and headed towards Tate's hide-out. If indeed it was Tate's hide-out.

The Taskforce had done some surveillance. Apparently someone liked Tate rated some satellite time. We had a picture of the property hot off the airwaves, confirming that the buildings were still standing and there were a couple of cars parked near the largest of them. The electricity and water were connected. So someone lived there.

I just had no idea if it might be Tate.

It had to be though. Otherwise, Dan would probably die.

As I drove down the windy road, I really had no idea what to expect. Satellite pictures didn't really show what condition the buildings were in or which ones might be occupied. So I just drove through the darkness battling the fear and rage turning my stomach to water, driving on with no idea what I'd find at my destination. I wracked my brain for any memory of ever meeting a man who could have been a young Smith, back when my father was alive. I came up blank but the more I thought about it, the more certain I became that, if this went back to when my father was alive, then this was bigger than just Tate. Maybe I'd be able to use that against him.

After thirty or so minutes or so the navigation system told me I had about a mile to go. I slowed the car as I pass a small gap in the trees lining the road.

Then I hit reverse and backed up.

If I drove to Tate's then all that would happen was they'd somehow disable the car or take my keys.

So I might as well leave it here where—if by some miracle Dan and I escaped before the Taskforce got to us—we might be able get back to it. My night vision was pretty darn good now that I was a wolf, so I wasn't worried about walking the last mile.

Thankfully the car was black. It didn't show up too much from the road. I hid the keys under a handy rock and set off at a half-jog.

With each step, the tension riding me grew exponentially. I stuck to the shadows at the side of the road, smelling the night air and trying to pretend I wasn't doing what might just be the stupidest thing I'd ever done.

Or the last thing I'd ever do.

By the time I reached an entrance that matched the details on the map (tall wooden gates between brick pillars topped with weird obelisks) I was fighting both my own nerves and the overwhelming desire to change and sneak through the trees.

But changing would mean I lost the weapons, the wire and other minor details such as clothes and hands and of course a voice. Hard to negotiate without that.

Plus I wanted to do this in human form.

Beat the monster without becoming one.

The wolf gave me extra strength and speed in human form. That was all I was going to have to help me. Even that, if I could, I wanted to keep from Tate as long as possible. Let him think his vaccine meant I was weaker than a normal wolf. It might give me some small advantage.

Besides, my emotions were too shaky for me to feel confident about changing and making it back to human form. I didn't really know how to change without the force of the full moon anyway.

I stared up at the obelisks for a long moment. I couldn't see any cameras but that didn't mean they weren't there. So as soon as I touched the gates, I had to assume Tate and his cronies would know someone was coming.

I pressed the tiny switch to light the screen of the heavy watch on my wrist and it read ten p.m. .Pretty much right on schedule. I pressed another button to activate the tracking device in the watch and let the Taskforce know I'd arrived, took a final deep breath and climbed over the gates.

As I dropped onto the gravel on the other side, I crouched and sniffed the air, searching for any trace of Dan.

I couldn't smell him but I could smell cars and grass and, as the wind gusted against my face, the strange smell of blood and dirt I knew as Tate's.

He was here.

"You wanted round three," I muttered to myself as I started up the drive. "Well, here I am."

The gravel path wound almost as much as the road. I couldn't see a house through the dark shadows and the trunks of the oaks lining the path. As I rounded a third curve, the wind shifted, bringing another scent to me.

Wolf. Not Dan. Not pack. A stranger. The hairs on the back of my neck bristled and I felt the wolf snarl within at the thought of an outsider. But this wolf wasn't really a stranger. I knew his scent. Rio.

I slowed my pace, stepping off the gravel and into the trees, keeping to the deeper shadows. He'd probably already heard or smelled me by now, but no point giving him the complete advantage.

I eased my gun from its holster, listening intently. When twigs cracked somewhere off to my right, I whirled and fired.

The gun had a silencer but the soft whine was clearly audible to my wolf hearing. Unfortunately I didn't hear an answering grunt of pain.

"Now, now, Pretty, is that any way to greet an old friend?" Rio's voice came out of the darkness, further to the right than I'd aimed.

I fired off another round. "Depends how badly they pissed me off the last time I saw them." I called, sprinting for the next tree. I didn't think Rio would shoot me—I figured Tate wanted to see *me*, not just my corpse—but I wasn't taking any chances.

"*You* stabbed *me*, as I recall." He sounded closer.

"My aim's improved since then." I didn't fire again. I didn't want to miss again. Until I actually had eyes on him, firing would just be wasting bullets and giving away my location.

Another twig snapped from the direction of his voice. I strained towards the sound, trying to get a better sense of where he was. His scent grew stronger, his animosity towards me as easy to detect as the leafy smell of the grass beneath my feet.

"Pity you haven't learned to guard your rear though, Pretty. And it's such a nice rear." The silky voice came out of the darkness behind me.

I swiveled, just in time to see Kyra dropping out of the sky and her fist swinging towards my head. I ducked but not quite quickly enough. The blow connected with my temple and I stumbled to the ground, pain blooming across my skull. I dropped the gun, heard it land softly somewhere ahead of me, and forced myself to open my eyes to look for it. The moonlight made my head hurt. I winced, eyes snapping shut reflexively. Big mistake.

Four hands grabbed my arms and waist and, even though I struggled, I knew they had me.

"You know, you're making this way too easy," Kyra said as she and Rio hauled me to my feet, laughing as I kicked and spat. The two knives strapped to my waist were tossed into the grass to join my gun, though they didn't search me any further. So I still had the silver dagger strapped to my ankle. But this wasn't the time to go for it, not while they were expecting me to fight.

"Boss's waiting, Pretty," Rio said. Moonlight glinted off his teeth as he smirked at me. I lashed out with my foot, connected solidly with his knee. He howled then his fist ploughed into my stomach. It felt like being hit by a lump of concrete. I bent over, retching and fighting for breath.

"Easy, Rio. Boss wants her in one piece."

"She's in one piece." He grabbed my hair and jerked my head up. "She's just bruised a little."

As the pain receded a bit, I felt the wolf prowling under my skin, fiercer than ever, snarling and wanting to be let free to fight the enemy in front of us.

I fought her back. It was tempting to call on all that power and fury but while I still had some choice, I was going to stick to the plan.

I sucked in deep breaths as Kyra marched me back onto the gravel, having cuffed my hands behind my back. My stomach hurt, as did my head but it wasn't the same level of pain as it had been when I was human. I could wall it off and still function. Could still think. Though I was careful to act more hurt than I was.

We rounded another bend in the path and the house suddenly appeared. It was a big old colonial style farmhouse on a grand scale. It was so not the image I had of Tate that a laugh bubbled up in my throat.

"If I were you, I wouldn't find this particularly amusing," Kyra said.

I turned my head around and bared my teeth at her. "She who laughs last..."

Her grip on my arms tightened painfully and I shut up as we climbed the front steps.

Rio pressed something on the wall near the door and a panel in the wood lifted. He pressed his palm to it and there was a click and hum as the front door swung open.

Okay, so that bit wasn't so much your average country farmhouse.

As the hall light hit my eyes and made them water, I looked around for a clock. Anything to let me know exactly how much time had passed and how much time I had to keep things going until the cavalry arrived.

"Admiring the décor?" Kyra asked sweetly as she shoved me forward.

There wasn't much to admire. The walls were bare and white and there was no furniture. There were, however, security cameras near the roof on either side of the hall way and they moved, tracking us as we passed by.

I shivered. Tate was watching me. I knew it.

CHAPTER TWENTY SIX

THE ROOM THEY TOOK ME to was, at least, furnished. With chairs, a table, and chains that glinted silver in the firelight along the wall. Tate, stood by an open fireplace, warming his hands.

"Ms. Keenan, how nice of you to join me."

Dan was nowhere to be seen. And if he wasn't still alive then my game plan consisted of fight like hell right now and get out if I could. "Where's Agent Gibson?"

Tate smiled slowly. "No hello?"

"Where's Agent Gibson?" I repeated, standing my ground.

"Fetch the wolf," Tate said. Rio's scent retreated behind me.

His ready acquiescence made me nervous. More nervous. If that was possible. I wanted to leap for Tate and tear his flesh with my fingers. Which would be suicide. Instead I curled them into fists, staying where I was with an effort of will that left me shaking.

"Let her go."

Kyra undid the cuffs and I pulled my hands free, rubbing at my wrists. The watch said 10:25. Still thirty five minutes before I had any chance of help.

Jase, I thought desperately. *If you can hear me now, hurry up.*

"Search her," Tate said and I froze.

Shit. If Kyra found the other knife or my cross, I was really screwed. I backed away from her until my back was against the wall with the chains. Metal brushed my hand and it burned like acid. Silver. Fuck.

I leaped away. Kyra watched me like a cat watching a mouse. An amusing mouse who was only providing her with more entertainment.

"Stay still, Pretty," she said.

I quickly pulled off my watch and reached behind my ear for the wire, holding both out to her. "Here. That's all I have."

Except for my cross and the knife, that was.

Kyra tossed them to Tate who threw both into the fire, which spat and sizzled, spewing acrid smelling smoke into the room.

"I'm sure you'd like us to believe that," he said. "Search her."

Kyra stepped closer and I slumped. She patted me down, hands lingering on my breasts and butt. All too soon she found the knife and pulled it free.

"It's not nice to lie, Pretty" she said as she straightened. She pointed the blade towards my face and I flinched backwards. "My guess is silver, boss."

She reversed the knife and flicked it over her shoulder. It stuck in the table top, quivering.

Tate smiled at me and firelight glinted off his fangs. "Interesting. I'm sure we can find some way to use it later on."

"What do you want?" I asked as my mind raced. I needed to keep them talking. I had no good weapons left except my brain. Kyra had missed the cross but while it would hurt the vampires briefly, it wouldn't kill them. Here, in this room with three against one (once Rio returned,) it would be no help at all.

"You and your wolf have made life hard for me," Tate said. He crooked a finger. Kyra grabbed my wrist and dragged me over to the table, pushing me down into a chair. I tried not to look at the knife but the flames reflected in the silver blade, taunting me with how close it was.

"He's not my wolf," I said and Tate frowned slightly. Good. Let him think he'd misjudged what lay between Dan and I.

In fact..."He'd like to be but..." I shrugged. Tate would know I was scared but he had no way of knowing whether that fear was due to Dan or just being here. So he might just buy me lying about Dan. "I'm hardly going to date the person who turned me, am I? So, what do you mean hard?"

Tate bared his fangs at me. "Well, for one thing, you've delayed our plans for the vaccine. And now, I seem to have hostile vampires, police and the Taskforce—" the word was almost a hiss—"wherever I turn. I don't like being bothered."

Our plans. Not mine. Maybe I was right. There were others involved in this. Smith. And whoever was funding this. Research was expensive. And what Tate had said about wanting more vampires to kill didn't seem to warrant spending that sort of cash. Tate's accounts hadn't been accessed until recently so there was other money somewhere. I shrugged again. "Maybe you should take a vacation."

He smiled his dead smile, and then walked closer to me, closing his hand around my throat and squeezing. "Don't push me, Ashley. I have plans for you."

Spots danced in front of my eyes as I fought for breath. Tate let me go as the door swung open and Rio appeared, dragging Dan behind him. Rio wore black gloves and held chains that dangled from the bonds around Dan's wrists. Dan wore only black trousers, torn in several places. Half dried blood stained his neck, drawing attention to several bite marks. Someone had fed from him. He swayed on his feet, but his gaze sharpened when he saw me.

"Ashley! I told you to stay away."

I forced my face to remain blank. Dan sported a huge black eye and bruises bloomed along his bare chest and stomach. My gut twisted. They'd had him less than eight hours. How hard and how had they beaten him to bruise a wolf so badly?

Worst of all were the chains around his wrists. The skin around them looked burned, bubbled and peeling, with dried and not-so-dried blood smeared down his hands and up his forearms.

Silver then. Which explained Rio's gloves. Fuck. I really had to do this myself. Dan couldn't change while bound by silver. And the pain of it would be sapping his strength.

"I take orders from my Alpha, not you," I said coldly. I turned back to Tate before the confused hurt on Dan's face fractured my rapidly slipping control.

"Special Agent Gibson goes free," I said.

Tate looked from me to Dan. "I don't think so."

My heart plunged further. I'd let part of myself hope that Tate wanted me in particular and might be willing to let Dan go. If this had anything to do with my dad then it should definitely be me they wanted—why, I had no idea—but it seemed logical. But we'd planned for the fact that Tate wouldn't be reasonable. "Your argument is with me, not him."

"No, it's with both of you. He saved you. It was his bite that stopped you from turning."

"I think I have the bigger claim on that issue," I said. "I'm the one he turned into a half-crippled werewolf."

Tate's brows rose. "What do you mean?"

"Your stupid vaccine hindered the lycanthropy somehow," I lied, hoping Dan was at least conscious enough to understand what I was doing and not react. "I'm not as strong as the other wolves."

His lips curved. You couldn't really call the expression a smile though. "How unfortunate for you. You'd have been better off if I'd succeeded. I'll have to speak to Smith about the vaccine. We hadn't considered that particular side effect."

You can speak to him in hell, I thought. I clenched my jaw, trying to stop the retort. I had to stay calm. Not easy when the wolf was snarling deep within me.

"My killing you, really will be doing you a favor then," Tate said, sounding almost conversational.

I had to take a few breaths before I could answer as fear flooded me. He really meant to kill me. I heard Dan snarl, felt the wolf snarl again in my head as well. "Maybe it would be. But that doesn't mean I'm going to let you do it."

His hand smashed into the side of my face, knocking me off the chair. Dan's growl—nothing human in it at all—seemed to fill the air as my head and hip hit the floor with painful force. Luckily it was carpeted, which cushioned the fall slightly. Only slightly, though. I lay there, winded, trying to think.

I'd barely seen Tate's movement. My face burned but adrenalin flooded through me blurring the pain into the background. I blinked back the tears in my eyes, saw Dan straining against his chains, fresh blood flowing down his wrists as the silver cut deeper into his flesh.

He could cripple himself with wounds from silver. If he didn't change in a few hours, they might not heal at all. The longer the silver touched him, the harder it would be to change once he was freed.

I had to do something. I pushed myself to a sitting position, watching Tate. When he didn't move, I stood. "I thought you liked a challenge?" I said to Tate, as I fought dizziness. Out of the corner of my eye, I saw Rio force Dan to his knees, using the chains to pull his arms behind him.

"A challenge?" Tate sounded amused.

"You told me you liked to hunt supernaturals rather than humans."

He nodded and I licked my lips. "Maybe you didn't really mean it."

Anger rose in Tate's eyes, turning them to dark pools of malice. "What do you mean?"

"You locking us up here. Killing us here. Three against one. It's hardly a challenge."

"There are two of you."

I looked down at Dan, let my face twist into an expression of disgust. "He's in no position to do anything much. He's braver when he's with his Taskforce cronies anyway."

Tate moved to the chair at the far end of the table and sat, resting his chin on one hand. "Interesting, though, that you still seem to be here, trying to save him."

I raised my own eyebrows. "Like I said, I'm following orders. He's pack, the Alpha wants him saved. God knows why when there are plenty of other males but I need the pack. I wouldn't survive as a lone wolf, not with less strength than the others."

"So you are buying your place in their affections?" Tate seemed almost amused by the thought. "That is very...calculated of you."

"I'm an accountant. I make my living by minimizing risk. I don't like what he did to me," I jerked my head in Dan's direction. "But I have to live with it. The pack is my best option." I watched Tate's face. I had him, I could almost feel it. He was intrigued again.

"What exactly are you proposing?"

I made a vague gesture. "You like to hunt. So hunt us. Outside. Let us free, give us a head start then come after us. There's all that wood out there, we're not going to get away. Anyway you have the advantage."

"How so?"

I nodded at Dan again. "He's wounded. And you know the area." I wanted to appeal to the predator in Tate. Hoping that his sick enjoyment of the game would make my offer irresistible. He could still be confident of catching and killing us; he thought he had us at a disadvantage. And outside, Dan and I had a slightly higher chance of survival. "Two vampires, against two werewolves."

"There are three of us," Tate pointed out.

"Rio stays out of it," I said.

"Why should I even the odds?"

I didn't know if he would and I remembered, all of a sudden, that my silver knife was still stuck in the table.

Closer to me than Tate.

Maybe I could just about even the odds myself. I didn't give myself time to think about it, I lunged for the knife, grabbed it and just had time to send it arcing—putting all my strength into the throw—in Rio's direction before Tate grabbed me from behind.

Almost in slow motion I watched the knife travel through the air. Rio started to dodge but Dan threw himself backwards, tugging the other man off balance and the blade buried itself deep in Rio's ribs. Rio fell backward, clawing at his chest, letting go of Dan's chains.

Dan lunged for him, only to have Kyra bring him up short as she caught the chains and held on. Rio made a few gurgling noises then went silent and I realized I could only hear four heartbeats. Rio was dead. I must have hit his heart. Silver to the heart was enough to kill a wolf if you hit the right spot.

Vicious satisfaction swept through me. I'd only meant to wound him, disable him somehow. I couldn't have hit his heart on purpose if I'd tried. So somebody up there was smiling down on me.

Tate's arm clamped around my throat, tightening. "You killed him."

I laughed, half-hysterical. "Sorry, it was an accident, I swear." More laughter bubbled up. I tried to stop it, without success.

Tate's answering snarl turned my spine to ice water. I bit back the rising hysteria. Had I pushed him too far?

"Tell me why I shouldn't just kill you now." The pressure against my throat grew stronger and I struggled to breathe.

"You wanted worthy prey. I guess I just proved myself worthy."

He snarled again and shoved me away from him. I stumbled into the table but managed to stay upright. Really, adrenalin was a wonderful thing when you were a werewolf.

"Rio was useful." Tate said softly.

"I'm sure you can find other henchmen. So do we have a deal?"

He hesitated.

"What? Do you have to wait for permission? Do you want to go ask Smith? Or your other masters?" The taunt was a long shot but I was gambling on the fact that Tate liked the illusion of control. Would hate anyone he saw as lesser knowing he didn't have it. He was a psycho and everything the Taskforce had told me about his profile told me his pride in his superiority was paramount. Being leashed for years—if indeed he wasn't running things—had to be wearing pretty thin.

Apparently, the profilers were right. Rage flashed over his face. More than rage...something closer to madness.

"I have no masters," he snarled.

I didn't believe him but I didn't care. My ploy was working. He might have been sent to kill me but he wanted to do it his way. Prove he was better. "Prove it," I said, trying hard to make my voice sound scornful, not terrified.

"If I catch you, I will kill you slowly." His voice was flat.

I nodded. "*If* you catch me."

"Kyra, fetch another manacle."

She obeyed and I watched in horror as she approached me with a silver cuff like the ones on Dan's wrists. Tate meant to bind me to human form.

I tried not to panic. It had worked. Tate was going to let us go free. We had a chance. We could do this. The Taskforce would be here soon. Outside we could hide and then they'd arrive and we'd be fine.

I took a deep breath as Kyra locked the manacle around my right wrist, locking her scent in my memory as she slipped the key into her pocket. The silver burned my wrist like I'd dipped my hand into molten metal. I wanted to scream but choked it back, gritting my teeth as I focused on Tate. I nodded toward Dan.

"Take the chains off him. The manacles are enough to hold him to human form." I said, holding my shackled wrist away from my body in case I brushed the silver against any other bare flesh. Tate nodded at Kyra and she obeyed, using the same key, I was happy to see. Dan didn't resist her, which sent renewed fear through me. Just how far gone was he?

Maybe I couldn't count on him at all. So. New plan. Before either of us could fight properly, we needed the manacles off. Once we were free, we had to find Kyra, get the key and then get the hell out of there before Tate found us. I didn't want to try and kill Tate. That was what the Taskforce was there for. Fighting him by myself would be suicidal.

"You will have three minutes once you get outside," Tate said, softly. "Then we will begin."

I nodded. "Agreed." I tried to picture the distance from the house to the trees, wishing I'd paid closer attention. Three minutes should be enough to get to some sort of cover. The place was probably full of cameras but Tate would be outside. So unless he had a Dick Tracy super video watch or something, he couldn't rely on surveillance.

Assuming there weren't others in the house doing the surveillance for him.

Kyra hauled Dan up and I stepped over Rio's body as I followed her out of the room and back down the hallway, fear fuzzing my mind. But I had killed one of them already. I had to believe I could do it again.

Kyra opened the front door. I looked past her to the darkness beyond and knew with certainty that if she and Tate teamed up, Dan and I were going to die. We needed an advantage.

We needed the key.

"Have a nice death, Pretty," she said as she pushed Dan through the door.

I bared my teeth at her. "Right back at you."

She smiled, opened her mouth to say something and I lunged for her, propelling her backwards out the door with all my strength. She fell and I went with her. We landed in a snarling heap on the porch. I screamed as her fangs sank into my left bicep. Luckily my right arm was the one with the manacle. I swung at her head and it connected with a crack that pulled her teeth free of my flesh and made her head hit the wooden floor hard enough to buckle the boards.

She went still and I pushed up my sleeve and tore the cross free, holding it ready as I plunged my hand into her pocket. My fingers closed around something metallic and key shaped. It burned.

Silver. I forced myself to keep hold and pulled it out.

I knew Tate had to be coming for us. The sound of our fight couldn't have escaped him. Kyra was still unconscious but her chest rose and fell. I couldn't leave her alive. But I didn't know if I could kill her in cold blood. Or how to do it.

While I hesitated, Dan knelt beside me and put his hands either side of her head, twisting. Her neck snapped with a hideous crack that made me want to retch.

I didn't know if a broken neck was enough to kill a vampire, but it had to at least seriously slow her down. Leaving only Tate. Tate who would be after us any minute. We needed to get away from the house.

I shoved the cross deep into the pocket in my cargoes. "Run," I yelled at Dan. I staggered to my feet, put my hands around one of his arms and yanked him up. "We have to get to the trees."

We hit the stairs, half-running, half-lurching. It felt as though we were barely crawling as Dan leaned his weight into mine, making my arm throb harder where Kyra had bitten me. Panic and pain and the searing ache of silver against my flesh made my head spin. I ran blindly, conscious only of Dan's breathing beside me, and the deafening thump of my own heartbeat.

I didn't look over my shoulder, didn't know if we were being pursued, just ran on instinct, keeping pace with Dan until we hit the tree line. Once we got deeper into the woods, I forced myself to listen. Even if Tate hadn't heard us with Kyra, it had to be almost three minutes. He would be coming for us.

He'd have a nice blood trail from my arm to follow.

The key still burned my hand. I pushed Dan to our left, the direction of the road. When the trees started to thicken, I slowed. "Stop," I gasped. "We have to stop."

We leaned against the nearest tree, both breathing like racehorses. I pried the key loose from the blisters it had raised on my palm, ignoring the sting against my fingers and tried to unlock the manacle from my wrist. I almost dropped the key once and swore. Dan had his eyes closed, panting. He wasn't going to be able to help. On the second try, the manacle clicked open. I flung it from my wrist into the darkness. The pain burning up my arm eased back from acid fire to mere burning.

I set to work on Dan's manacles, using my sleeves to protect my hands from the silver. I had to pry the cuffs from his flesh and almost fainted from the waves of nausea the sensation of flesh peeling back from the metal under my fingers invoked.

Dan didn't make a sound until I'd finished. Then he opened his eyes. "You should change. Get away from here."

I looked at him. There wasn't a lot of moonlight under the trees and he looked horribly pale. "Can you change?"

He shook his head. "I don't think so, it hurts. I need Ani or Sam." An Alpha could help a wolf change. I knew that much. Problem was neither Ani nor Sam was available.

"Then I can't. I can't help you run in wolf form." Werewolves were big but I didn't think I could carry Dan on my back. He needed help. So I was stuck.

"We need to keep moving," I said, lifting his arm and putting it around my shoulder. "Let's go, Gibson."

"Leave me," he said. "Get free."

He slumped against the nearest tree, breath rasping. But I hadn't come this far for him to give up on me. I grabbed his face and kissed him, willing him to stay with me. He tasted like blood and salt and fear. When his mouth moved under mine, I pulled back.

"I'm not leaving you," I snarled. "Just move." We lurched back into motion, plunging through the forest, no hope of staying silent with Dan so weak. The wind was coming from behind us and, as it strengthened, it carried the stink of old blood and rot. Tate.

"He's coming," I said to Dan. "Run faster."

We stumbled through the next stand of trees and into a small clearing.

I heard Tate laughing behind us, knew he was nearly on us. I shoved at Dan. Maybe I could delay Tate long enough for him to get clear. "Keep going."

He stopped in his tracks. "Not without you."

I looked around frantically, searching for any signs the Taskforce might be anywhere near us.

This way. I didn't know if I was imagining it or if I'd actually heard something but I grabbed Dan's hand and started moving again. I suddenly glimpsed a pair of green eyes in the darkness and smelled heat and the musky smell of cat. Esme. They were here. Tears started running down my face in relief. The Taskforce agents were here.

"Left," I hissed at Dan and we swerved in unison, Dan getting a little ahead of me as my foot tangled in a dead branch. "Keep going," I yelled.

Then something hit me from behind and fangs raked down my neck. Tate had found us.

CHAPTER TWENTY SEVEN

I TWISTED FRANTICALLY, TRYING to dislodge Tate but his fangs went deeper, tearing at my flesh. Wetness gushed over my skin. Blood.

I fought harder, reaching behind me to claw at his face. It worked. He pulled free, swung his fist at my head.

I heard Dan yell "Ashley," and I tried to move but misjudged as Tate twisted with me and the blow connected with my shoulder, rocking me backwards.

"Run," I shrieked at Dan. "*Run!*"

I couldn't protect him and fight Tate. If Dan got free, then all this wouldn't be for nothing.

Tate blurred towards me, hitting me like a truck. We flew backwards and I landed in the dirt, his weight on top of me, fangs slashing at me again.

I remembered my cross, and scrabbled for my pocket. My fingers caught the chain and I pulled it free, pressing my hand into Tate's face as his fangs caught my cheek.

The cross sizzled as it met his flesh. There was a blinding flash of light as he recoiled, snarling and swearing.

"You'll regret that," he said as I scrambled backwards, pushing to my feet.

I lifted my hand, dangling the cross. "Want to try it again?" Over his shoulder I saw black shapes gliding towards Dan, herding him backwards into the trees.

Safe.

He was safe. That was what mattered. I knew the Taskforce couldn't easily take Tate down, not while I was in the way. So it was him and me.

The wolf raged under my skin, the need to change roiling through me, a howl burning in my throat. But I pushed it away. There was too much anger. Too much need and hate and rage. I didn't know how I could possibly control it if I changed. I couldn't risk going berserk.

Tate climbed to his feet as well and stared at me. I wondered what he was doing.

"Stay still," he said in a weird tone of voice.

Suddenly it hit me. He was trying to use whatever he'd left in my head when he'd thralled me. The thing Marco had removed.

He thought he could *control* me.

Well, let him think that.

I stayed where I was, not moving, then, as he lunged for me, I swung the cross again, pressing it into his face near his eyes. There was another flare of light, this time even brighter and heat sizzled up the chain making me drop it.

Tate howled and staggered backwards clutching at his eye. Movement caught my eye in the trees behind him and the shape became a black clad Taskforce agent lifting a gun.

"No!" I yelled.

Certainty flowed through me. Tate was mine.

The gunman hesitated and another shape burst from the woods.

Dan.

He leaped toward Tate and Tate, already alerted by my yell, pivoted almost too fast for me to follow. He met Dan with a snarl, and Dan howled as Tate ripped his fangs into his neck. The smell of blood, fresh and hot filled the air. Too much blood, too quickly. Tate had torn something big. If I didn't do something, Dan would die.

I wasn't going to lose him again.

"Tate," I snarled and the vampire turned back to me. Blood stained the lower half of his face and I froze as Dan fell to his knees behind him, clutching at his neck.

Tate smiled at me, nothing human or sane in the expression and I knew he meant to kill me.

No more games.

No more excuses. If I wanted to live then I had to use everything I had. Every part of me.

Tate started towards me, moving purposefully and I finally let go of the iron control I'd been exerting over my wolf. Triumph surged through me as the world went blurry then Tate was on me and we rolled through the dirt, his fangs against my claws and teeth.

I moved and twisted instinctively, every part of me focused on the need to kill the enemy, to defend the pack, defend what was mine. Tate's teeth slashed through my fur and I howled. An answering howl rose through the night air and I knew some of my pack were there, lending me their strength.

I twisted again and got free of him, leaping backwards to land, my paws planted squarely in the dirt, as I watched his every movement.

I had hurt him. The foul taste coating my tongue was his blood. A growl rumbled low in my throat. I crouched as he stood to face me, every muscle in my body tensed against the pain sizzling along my nerves, each tear and bruise burning like fire.

"At least you have more fight than your family," Tate said into the stillness of the air. "You're still going to die though."

No. I wasn't sure if it was my thought, or Jase's or the packs or something else entirely but I didn't care. Everything seemed to shimmer crystal clear in the moonlight, each leaf of the grass gleaming at me. I could see the hairs on Tate's head moving in the breeze, see the tiny muscle tremors that telegraphed his intentions. Smell his insane urge to kill.

But my anger was stronger and I embraced its power. I leaped for him, arcing through the air with more strength and speed than I thought possible. He moved but I still hit him square in the chest with my front paws, my teeth snapping for his throat.

They closed over flesh and I couldn't control my reactions any more than I could control my need for air. My fangs sank into his throat, tasting warm skin and the rotten taint of his blood, then twisted, tearing through his windpipe and closing around the bones in his neck. I bit harder and as our momentum carried us and we headed for the ground, I twisted savagely then let go and watched Tate's head bounce across the grass as his body thudded to the earth.

Howls and cheers filled the air as I skidded to a halt, rolling over and over in the grass, doing my best to spit Tate's blood out. Wolf mouths aren't designed for spitting. The taste coated my tongue, acid and rotten.

I didn't care. Not with Tate lying dead in front of me. I threw back my head and joined my song to those around me, howling with grief and victory and the sheer joy of being still alive.

They made me stay in hospital overnight in Ellensburg. I didn't think I needed it, most of my wounds healed once I changed back to human form but somewhere along the line I'd fractured most of the bones in my right foot and they would take a few more changes to knit properly. At least the hospital had a never ending supply of mouthwash and toothpaste. I felt like I'd never scrub the taste of Tate out of my mouth.

But apart from a lingering limp and a near obsession with Listerine, I was okay.

Dan wasn't so lucky. They rushed him back to Seattle for surgery on his neck where Tate had damaged the arteries. And on his wrist, where the silver had burned through muscle and started eating its way down to bone.

When Jase picked me up in the morning, I made him take me straight there. Only to be met by Ani in the hallway outside the ICU.

"He doesn't want to see you," she said before I'd even said hello.

Disbelief made my jaw fall open. I'd just saved his *life*. "What are you talking about?"

"I'm sorry, Ashley but he asked you to stay away."
"What sort of male idiocy is this? I want to see him." I went to push past her then remembered how furious I'd been when Dan had charged into my hospital room uninvited after he'd bitten me and flounced over to the bank of plastic chairs in the hallway, planting my ass with a thud. "I saved him, for Chrissakes."

Ani came and sat next to me. "Yes, and currently, he's about as happy about that as you were when he saved you."

My head hurt. And that wasn't the only thing. I rubbed my eyes before I started crying. "That makes no sense. I was mad about the werewolf thing."

"Ash, he's sick and hurt and you probably terrified the life out of him. Plus..." she hesitated and my heart started to beat harder.

"What?"

"They're not sure if his left arm is going to heal properly. The silver did a lot of damage. It took both Sam and I to get him to change. And he's too weak to do it as often as he needs to repair himself."

Dan crippled? I had to close my eyes for a moment as I took it in. Then I opened them. "I don't care about his arm."

"Well, he does. He knows he forced you into the claim and he won't tie you to an injured wolf. He's got a bee in his bonnet about it for some reason."

I frowned. Dan should know I wouldn't care about him being injured. Then I remembered the conversation I'd had with Tate. The one about half-crippled wolves and being useless and needing the strength of the pack to protect me. Had Dan somehow mixed all that up in his head?

A snarl rose in the back of my throat. Idiot male. I wasn't going to let him ruin things now. "Just let me talk to him, we can work this out."

Ani shook her head. "No. I'm going to respect his wishes. You can see him at full moon. If he comes."

Her tone was full blown Alpha. I couldn't disobey. Which didn't mean I had to like it. I pushed up from the chair. "Fine. Tell him he's an idiot, from me."

"You can tell him yourself when you see him. Unless you can think of something else he might like to hear."

I glared at her. I knew what she was doing. Telling me if I told Dan I loved him then maybe I could fix things.

But why would I tell a stubborn wolf who didn't even trust me to stick by him that I loved him? Only someone who was as big an idiot as he was would do that. "I'll see you at full moon."

Two weeks had never passed so slowly in my life. I had plenty to do, between trying to salvage my relationship with the clients I'd left in the lurch and working with the Taskforce to unravel Tate's holdings and try to track down the source of the mutated vaccines. Smith hadn't been found. After what had happened with Tate the first time, no one was making the mistake of assuming the not-so-good doctor was dead. The Taskforce were crawling through my father's papers and records from Genasys. We hadn't found anything yet but we weren't giving up.

Jase helped but he wasn't around as much as normal. He spent a lot of time at Marco's and he wouldn't tell me if it was voluntary or not. In fact, he clammed up every time I tried to raise the subject. Which only made me feel guilty because I was the reason Marco now knew about his powers.

But a girl can't work every minute and I had plenty of time to stew about Dan. I even let Bug lecture me about him when she came to see me.

Stupid man. He had to go and complicate things just when it had started to seem straightforward.

Matters weren't helped by the fact I was getting hornier and hornier as the full moon approached.

By the time I headed for the Retreat the day of full moon, I'd worked up a pretty good head of mad to counteract my nerves about returning to the pack and the place where Ben had died. Still, it wasn't easy turning into the drive and I'd delayed so much that the sun was starting to set as I pulled up in front of Ani and Sam's house.

"Where's Dan?" I asked as Ani opened the door.

She rolled her eyes. "Let's worry about that after you change, okay? You know you shouldn't be cutting it this fine."

I eye-rolled her right back. I was pretty sure I could control my wolf now. "I did okay with my control with Tate."

She smiled wickedly. "Right up until that part where you bit his head off."

My stomach lurched a little. I had tried to avoid thinking too much about killing Tate and Rio. Let alone *how* I'd killed Tate. "Let's not talk about that," I said.

"Okay. Just don't get cocky. This is full moon and you don't get a say. Go change your clothes," Ani said.

It was close to dark by the time I slipped into the woods. Ani was with me again but there was no other circle of back-up. I found myself looking forward to the moon as energy sizzled under my skin. I tilted my head back, smiling up at the sky and waited for the kiss of silver light to fill me with power.

The change was uneventful. I didn't hunt, just ran through the woods, reveling in speed and the sensation of eating up the ground beneath my paws. In reality, I was hunting for Dan but I didn't catch his scent at any point and eventually, I returned to Ani's as the sun rose and crawled into bed, exhausted and even more confused about what I should do.

Ani woke me around midday with a cheerful, "Pack meeting in an hour."

She was way too chirpy and I hid my head under the pillow. Pack meeting. I'd see Dan finally. Question was, what reaction would I get? In all my thinking, I'd known one thing, even if I hadn't really wanted to admit it.

I wasn't ready to let him go. Not again.

Only trouble was, I had no idea how to convince him of that.

The first person I saw as I headed for the main house was Natalie, sitting by herself on one of the garden benches directly in my path. I hesitated, not sure if I should just go around her and avoid the inevitable confrontation. But then she looked up and smiled at me and something lifted in my heart a little.

I walked over to her, sunlight warming my skin. The air smelled like the pink and yellow roses blooming in the garden bed. "Natalie, how are you doing?"

Her smile was a little shaky but she nodded. "I'm hanging on." She ducked her head a little. "I think I owe you an apology."

I shook my head. "No apologies."

"What I said to you—"

"You were upset. Don't think about it."

"Okay." Her smile grew stronger. "Okay, thanks. But if you ever need a favor—"

I felt an answering smile bloom across my own face as something occurred to me, a way of maybe making Dan deal with me. "You know, there might just be something you can do for me."

She looked puzzled. "What?"

I sat down next to her on the bench. "There's something I need to know."

After my conversation with Natalie, I was running late for the pack meeting. She'd answered my questions then gone on ahead. I'd heard her chuckling to herself as she walked across the grass. I was glad someone thought it was funny, because now that I'd had my brilliant idea, I was starting to feel distinctly nauseous.

My foot twinged a little. I wriggled my toes, glad of the distraction. The pain was almost gone after my change but I still limped slightly. It was tempting to use that as an excuse to stay right where I was but Ani would kick my butt for missing the meeting.

So I told myself to stop being a wimp, that facing Dan wasn't as scary as facing Tate, and walked up to the house.

Everyone was already sitting in the circle as I walked into the room, feeling like I might just throw up. Heads turned towards me as I closed the door behind me. Sam was standing in the center of the ring of wolves and I saw Dan sitting near Ani.

My eyes met his and he looked away. I narrowed my eyes. Right. If he thought he could avoid me then he had another thought coming.

Despite the fact he wouldn't look at me, Dan looked good. Not pale and bruised like he had at Tate's. Apart from a bandage around his right wrist, he looked just fine. More than fine, actually, my heart sped up just looking at him and then redoubled as his scent hit my nose.

"So," said Sam, looking at me curiously. "Who has business?"

My throat felt dry but I managed to say "I do." I limped into the center of the circle, ignoring the buzz of voices, looking only at Dan. He, apparently, was fascinated by something in his lap.

"What business?" Sam asked.

I looked at Dan again and wondered if I was crazy. But knew I had to find out. "I call claim," I said loudly. "I call claim on Daniel Gibson. Full claim."

Dan's head flew up as the room exploded into conversation. Full claim meant bonding if we decided. It was a marriage proposal, or close enough to. Or so Natalie had told me in our little chat. If Dan turned me down he turned down any right to pursue me in the future.

"Full claim," I repeated with only a slight quiver in my voice as Dan's eyes finally met mine, all liquid silver that I might just drown in.

The look on his face told me everything I needed to know.